FIRST SPARKS

"I can't believe you've been investigating for all these months and you never pursued this! The one solid clue!"

"The one *solid* clue? That she time traveled? Are you serious, Miss Stone?"

"Absolutely." She positioned herself within inches of him and announced, "I'll tell you something about time, Mr. BlackKnife. It's a fiction."

He could smell her perfume—or was that vanilla? A wave of intoxicating warmth, whether from her anger or her passionate nature or simple body heat, was crossing the slight distance between them and causing his own temperature to rise alarmingly. He wanted to change the subject, or ask for a glass of water, or kiss her full, pouting lips until she moaned . . .

PUT SOME FANTASY IN YOUR LIFE—
FANTASTIC ROMANCES FROM PINNACLE

TIME STORM (728, $4.99)
by Rosalyn Alsobrook

Modern-day Pennsylvanian physician JoAnn Griffin only believed what she could feel with her five senses. But when, during a freak storm, a blinding flash of lightning sent her back in time to 1889, JoAnn realized she had somehow crossed the threshold into another century and was now gazing into the smoldering eyes of a startlingly handsome stranger. JoAnn had stumbled through a rip in time . . . and into a love affair so intense, it carried her to a point of no return!

SEA TREASURE (790, $4.50)
by Johanna Hailey

When Michael, a dashing sea captain, is rescued from drowning by a beautiful sea siren—he does not know yet that she's actually a mermaid. But her breathtaking beauty stirred irresistible yearnings in Michael. And soon fate would drive them across the treacherous Caribbean, tossing them on surging tides of passion that transcended two worlds!

ONCE UPON FOREVER (883, $4.99)
by Becky Lee Weyrich

A moonstone necklace and a mysterious diary written over a century ago were Clair Summerland's only clues to her true identity. Two men loved her—one, a dashing civil war hero . . . the other, a daring jet pilot. Now Clair must risk her past and future for a passion that spans two worlds—and a love that is stronger than time itself.

SHADOWS IN TIME (892, $4.50)
by Cherlyn Jac

Driving through the sultry New Orleans night, one moment Tori's car spins out of control; the next she is in a horse-drawn carriage with the handsomest man she has ever seen—who calls her wife—-but whose eyes blaze with fury. Sent back in time one hundred years, Tori is falling in love with the man she is apparently trying to kill. Now she must race against time to change the tragic past and claim her future with the man she will love through all eternity!

Available wherever paperbacks are sold, or order direct from the Publisher. Send cover price plus 50¢ per copy for mailing and handling to Penguin USA, P.O. Box 999, c/o Dept. 17109, Bergenfield, NJ 07621. Residents of New York and Tennessee must include sales tax. DO NOT SEND CASH.

KATE DONOVAN

TIME WEAVER

PINNACLE BOOKS
WINDSOR PUBLISHING CORP.

To Michael.
*And to everyone
who loved him.*

PINNACLE BOOKS are published by

Windsor Publishing Corp.
850 Third Ave.
New York, NY 10022

The P logo Reg. U.S. Pat. & TM Off. Pinnacle is a trademark of Windsor Publishing Corp.

First Pinnacle Printing: November, 1994

Printed in the United States of America

Prologue

Dear Phil,

So many things have happened! If only you were here, so we could say goodbye and I could tell you how much I love you and what a loving, perfect brother you've been, but that's impossible. You're in Australia and I'm in a cab speeding toward the Susquehannock border. We'll never see each other again but somehow we'll stay close, you and I. Time and distance can't change what was meant to be. I'll always be your loving sister, and I want you to find happiness just the way I've found it at last.

Try to believe what I'm about to tell you, Phil. I know at the hospital they think I'm disoriented and suffering from hysterical amnesia, but that isn't so. Things have never been clearer to me. After I broke off my engagement to Dusty, I went camping, to try to sort things through. I went to the spot where we scattered Dad's ashes years ago. I was feeling cold and started to build a fire—with a little log cabin as a tinder box, just like you showed me when I was a little girl. My campsite turned out to be an old Susquehannock burial ground, and

*lighting fires there was an offense. Anyway, I
passed out, and when I woke up, I was with some
Susquehannock Indians, and one of them was Kahnawakee himself!*

*It took me so long to figure out why I was there,
and at first I was so scared, but once I met John
Cutler, things became clear. You'd love him, Phil.
He's so good to me. Anyway, this is the important
part. Before I went back, the history of North
America was radically different than it is now.
During the eighteenth and nineteenth centuries, the
Native Americans were systematically wiped out
or driven off their lands and forced to relocate,
while the Europeans took over almost completely.
By the nineteenth century there were no Sus-
quehannock Indians anywhere in North America!*

*I know you can't believe that—you see how the
Union of Native American Protectorates is thriving
as a world superpower in your twentieth century, but
that's all because of Kahnawakee, and before I went
back, Kahnawakee was killed before he could form
UNAP. It's not like I saved his life or anything, but
my arrival started a chain reaction that put John and
Kahnawakee in a better position when the danger
came and they survived to form UNAP. The crazy
part is that now everyone takes UNAP for granted,
not realizing things could have been so different and
so tragic—oh, Phil! My cab is at the border and I
have to go. Try to believe me. I love you so much, but
John is waiting and my life is somewhere else now.
Take care and be happy. I'll always adore you.*

Your loving sister,

Shannon

Chapter One

Missing Model Gives Birth to Alien!

Sitting in the driver's seat of his newly restored Mustang convertible, Alexander BlackKnife chuckled as he perused the latest scandal sheet account of the fate of missing blue jeans model Shannon Cleary. While not usually given to reading the tabloids, the dark-haired young attorney had spent the last four months searching for clues to the beautiful blonde's disappearance and couldn't afford to pass up any lead, no matter how laughable. "At least," he murmured to himself, "this doesn't implicate *us* in any way."

The thought immediately sobered him. For weeks following Shannon's disappearance, these tabloids, along with more than a handful of usually responsible newspapers, had pointed an accusing finger at the Susquehannock Indian Nation, and some of the charges had been so fraught with latent racism that they had stunned Alexander BlackKnife and the other "Modernists" among his people. The fact that Shannon Cleary had last been seen crossing the border into the Susquehannock Protectorate had been parlayed into a series of despicable allegations of "marauding war parties," "white slavery," and "clan initiation rituals." This had not only forced the Protectorate to probe the matter and appoint their most promising young council adviser, Alexander BlackKnife, to head a team of four full-time investigators; it had prompted them to reschedule several key elections and conferences usually held in June until either the furor died down or the Cleary woman was found.

Ironically, while the scandal had unjustly tarnished his people's image, it had ignited Alexander Black-Knife's own career, propelling him into a controversial forum wherein his stunning good looks, his poise, and his eloquence could be showcased. Although he was only twenty-eight years old, speculation was now rampant that he would one day be chief, and there were those who even predicted that he would eventually be considered for the coveted role of Sachem for the entire Union of Native American Protectorates. Despite his attempt to retain some vestige of humility, Alex could not completely deny his ambitious nature and felt driven, by personal as well as ethical and national considerations, to discover the truth as to Shannon's fate. If only he could find her, alive and well . . .

As the weeks had passed, that possibility had grown more and more remote. While Alex and his investigators had been tireless, inventive, and meticulous, they hadn't found a decent clue beyond the final sighting of the model at the border, along with the letter she had mailed to her brother on the day she'd disappeared. Still, Alexander BlackKnife wasn't ready to admit defeat. He would continue to reexamine the meager evidence night and day, leaving no stone unturned.

"No stone unturned," he laughed aloud, "including Cassandra Stone, so here I go." Tucking the newspaper into his briefcase, he hopped out of the car and strode confidently down the long gravel driveway that led to the A-frame house where Shannon Cleary's first cousin Cassandra lived and worked.

Alex had studied his investigator's notes and knew he was probably wasting his time with this visit, but she was the only possible lead he hadn't personally investigated; given the simple fact that she and Shannon were close in age and from the same family, he hoped there might be something the others had overlooked. It seemed unlikely, given the fact that Cassandra and Shannon had never met—in fact, if Cassandra's account was true, neither cousin had ever even been aware of the other's existence! It seemed incredible, since the two had grown up in small towns within a hundred miles of one another. Shannon's mother had explained to Alex in painful detail the reasons she had never associated with her husband's family after his death, which had occurred two months before Shannon was born. And there didn't seem to be any reason for either the mother or Cassandra to lie.

There was music emanating from the house, and Alex winced slightly. Christmas songs . . . in August? His investigator's notes had labeled Miss Stone "eccentric"—actually, "eccentric, creative, and very pretty," to be precise—and the description had amused him until now. His eyes were drawn to a thriving garden which, if he wasn't mistaken, seemed to consist of neat, carefully tended rows of weeds. Beyond that point, there was a gazebo with a potter's wheel positioned so as to afford a perfect view of the section of the river for which this tiny town of Little Bend had been named. It was all very peaceful, yet somehow the sun was a bit too bright and hot for *White Christmas* to be filling the air.

She's creative, he reminded himself, as he climbed four steps onto an expansive deck that led to the main exterior door. Even when he caught a glimpse of a fully decorated Christmas tree through the window he refused to panic and with a nervous smile knocked gently on the screen door.

"It's open!" a cheerful voice informed him.

Alex hesitated. The last thing the Susquehannock Nation needed was another scandal, especially one involving Shannon Cleary's 22-year-old cousin. He could just see the headlines: *Eccentric Beauty's Nightmare Ordeal in Bizarre Tribal Sex Ceremony . . .*

"Come on in!" the voice urged. "I'm coated with shortening!"

Bizarre sex ceremony seemed suddenly and uncomfortably appropriate, and so Alex announced loudly, "Miss Stone? My name is Alexander BlackKnife and I'm here as a representative of the Susquehannock Nation. I'd like to ask you a few questions about your cousin, but if this is a bad time, I could come back."

"Wait!"

He heard a crash and a peal of laughter and with a rueful grin pushed open the door and stepped into the room to survey the damage. The eight-foot tree was on its side next to the prostrate, shapely form of a young blond woman dressed in white shorts, a red halter top, a candy-cane striped apron, and a fuzzy red Santa hat. "Never run when you've been greasing pans with shortening all day," she advised with a self-mocking smile.

"Miss Stone?" Alex reached a hand toward her. "Are you okay?" Her hands were slick with grease, so he grasped her above the wrist and pulled her gently to her bare feet.

"Alexander BlackKnife . . ." She seemed to be savoring his name as she studied him. "You sound just like you look, and you *look* just like your name, did you know that?" Wiping her hands on her apron, she added, "I'm Cassie Stone, and *don't* tell me *I* look like *my* name, too."

He accepted her handshake tentatively. She was innocent yet sexy—possibly the most immediately provocative female he had ever seen—and, under ordinary circumstances, he'd have welcomed any opportunity to touch, talk, and perhaps flirt. But the situation with Shannon Cleary—specifically, the outrageous insinuations made by the press in connection with her disappearance—had left him uncomfortable with the political and social ramifications of intercultural relationships. In any event, he was here as an official representative of the Susquehannock Nation, not as a private citizen, and so he quickly relinquished her hand, turning his attention instead to the tree, which he easily righted.

"Thanks." The woman continued to study him openly. "I guess you're wondering about that tree and all this . . ." She gestured to encompass her apron and hat, then moved to the stereo to turn off the music. "There's a perfectly rational explanation. For me, this *is* Christmastime."

"Well, that explains it," he chuckled.

Cassie Stone laughed in return. "I mean, this is the time when I have to start baking all my Christmas ornaments if I'm going to have them ready to deliver to the stores by the end of October. I make about one-third of my income from Christmas-related knick-knacks and whats-its."

"So you do all of this to . . ."

"To get into the mood," she agreed. "I'm even baking some real cookies. They'll be ready in a few minutes, if you'd like to try some with a cup of coffee." Her sapphire-blue eyes sparkled impishly. "I don't know what your detective told you, but it's perfectly safe to eat my cooking."

"Pardon?"

"He thought I was crazy, right?" Cassie stooped to gather a few of the candy canes that had fallen off the tree during the accident. "Did he tell you I tried to buy his shoes?"

Alex shook his head. "He didn't mention that, but he *did* say you were eccentric. I guess that's what he was referring to."

"He was wearing some sort of half-shoe, half-moccasin, and I wanted to figure out how to make them. They looked so comfortable." She glanced at Alex's black boots and then, after her eyes had moved up along his jeans to his white shirt and black leather vest, she added cheerfully, "I think the poor guy thought I was flirting with him, because he made a big point of saying his *wife* made the shoes and his *wife* would be very disappointed if he came home without them."

Alex burst into laughter. "I know his wife and, believe me, she'd be more than disappointed. She's extremely jealous." He caught himself and added more soberly, "I'm sure he didn't take offense. Anyway, if it wouldn't be too much trouble, could we talk about Shannon's disappearance?"

"Sure. Have a seat." She scooped an armload of half-finished Christmas stockings off a rattan loveseat and patted the seat cushion invitingly, then perched herself on a bar stool and insisted, "I have a question for you, too, Mr. BlackKnife. Your detective wouldn't tell me anything."

Alex hesitated, then chose to sit on a barstool himself, drawing it close to Cassie and smiling reassuringly. "My investigators aren't authorized to give out any information—only to collect it. But I can probably answer most of your questions."

"You're in charge?" She nodded, crossing her long, bare legs absent-mindedly. "That's pretty obvious. You have that head-honcho look about you. Anyway, Shannon's brother Philip Tremaine has been here a couple of times and he's given me most of the details, so I really only have one question for you."

"Ask."

"Where do you think my cousin is?"

"That's a good question. Unfortunately, I don't know."

"Come on," Cassie urged. "Your instincts must be telling you something. You've been investigating this for weeks . . . months! Right? What's your gut feeling?"

"What's *yours?*" he countered. "And while we're on the subject, what's Phil Tremaine's current theory?"

"He doesn't think there's a conspiracy, like the papers suggest," Cassie smiled. "He thinks very highly of the way the Susquehannocks have handled this. On the other hand, Shannon disappeared on your turf, so he's understandably confused."

"We all are." Alex took a deep breath. "You say he gave you a lot of details? Did he tell you Shannon was having some strange delusions at the time she left the hospital and took a cab to the border?"

"Hysterical amnesia, right? That's what Phil called it, and since he's a shrink, I guess it's true, although,"

she leaned her headful of shoulder-length blond curls
closer and observed softly, "he was in Australia when
it happened—right?—so he didn't actually make the
diagnosis himself. He got it all second-hand."

"That's true, but he feels . . ." A timer sounded
from the direction of the kitchen and Alex paused.
"The cookies?"

"Give me two minutes." She disappeared into the
hall.

He needed at least two minutes to compose himself.
Her long, bare legs and her soft, flirtatious voice, not
to mention the playful way she had of tousling her
hair with her fingers when she was thinking, were
beginning to get to him. Abandoning the barstool, he
began to pace, reminding himself of the purpose for
this visit. He needed to find Shannon Cleary. Not only
would it remove the cloud of dishonor from his people, but it would secure his political future—a future
that could not include liaisons with sexy blondes.

It was important for him to begin to build a conservative image. While he was still a Modernist at
heart, he was beginning grudgingly to understand
why some of the Conservative old-timers had disapproved of his life-style—the great-great-etcetera-
grandson of Kahnawakee himself, attending Harvard
Law School and adopting other Euro-habits while
simultaneously building a political base among the
young Susquehannocks who believed it was time for
the Native American Protectorates to relax their vigi-
lance against contamination by Euro-culture and values. Alex himself had fervently believed this . . . until
Shannon Cleary disappeared and the world seemed
more than ready to assume that the Protectorates
were teeming with sex-starved malcontents whose ul-

timate fantasy was to indulge themselves at the expense of some yellow-haired goddess captive.

Not that this view had been predominant, of course. Most of the responsible Euro-papers had denounced such blatant xenophobia, but Alex had been stunned by the fact that anyone, in this day and age, could espouse such insulting views. It had forced him to reexamine his Modernist alliances and to court connections with the Conservatives. Most importantly, it had forced him to ask himself, for the first time in a very long while, what Kahnawakee would advise if he were to stand before him now.

Alex's pride in being a direct descendant of the "Visionary" was boundless. Occasionally someone who had seen sketches of the great man commented on the resemblance Alex bore to him—he had the same lean face, high cheekbones, piercing eyes, and raven hair—and the honor inherent in the compliment would warm the young attorney for days thereafter. Now, as he paced Cassie Stone's living room, he remembered the day he had met Shannon Cleary in her hospital room and she had called him "Couteau Noir"—French for "Black Knife"—raving about his looks and the fact that he bore the name of Kahnawakee's firstborn son. It had been a heady moment, and Alex had struggled to maintain his humility.

If only you had talked to her more about her, and less about yourself, he chided himself for the hundredth time. *Maybe she would have told you what she was planning to do, and you could have stopped her . . .*

"Mr. BlackKnife?" Cassie was eyeing him with amused curiosity. "Are you talking to yourself?"

"What?"

"Don't worry." She sat a tray of coffee and cookies on the bar and assured him, "You didn't say anything

I could hear, but you had that look . . . like you were lecturing yourself silently. I do that all the time."

"You do?"

"Sure. I have to remind myself not to offer to buy guys' shoes, for example," she grinned.

"And not to run when you've just been greasing cookie sheets?" he laughed.

"Exactly. So? What were *you* about to do wrong?"

Her expression was playful and challenging, and he had a feeling she knew *exactly* what he'd love to "do wrong" at that moment, but he was determined to dispel that image. "We were talking about Shannon. You were about to tell me your theory about what happened to her."

"I was? Okay, you eat while I talk." She handed him a green-sprinkled Christmas tree cookie. "I never met her, but I've talked to Phil about her so much, I feel like I know her. My mother used to tell me about my Uncle Matt—he was Shannon's father, you know—and Shannon sounds a lot like him. And look what happened to him! He got murdered, right?"

"That's right. Shannon's mother's first husband shot him before Shannon was born," Alex nodded. "You think there's a connection?"

Cassie shrugged. "I think they both tried to help people, and for both of them, it backfired. Uncle Matt got involved with Shannon's mother originally because he was Phil's softball coach and he suspected Phil was being abused by his father. Instead of getting rewarded for being such a nice guy, Uncle Matt got shot. Then Shannon comes along, and models, even though she hates it, so that she can donate all her money to charitable causes. And just like her dad, all the thanks she gets is to be abused by her millionaire fiancé Dusty Cumberland."

"And then?" Alex prodded, impressed by the fact that Cassie's theory was, so far, mirroring his own, "Don't stop now. You sound like you really know what you're talking about. You think Dusty Cumberland was involved in her disappearance?"

"I think she developed this hysterical amnesia because she couldn't escape from him any other way. She got a restraining order against him the week before she disappeared," Cassie emphasized. "But he violated it—he came to the hospital to visit her, knowing his lawyers could keep him out of jail even though he was breaking the law, and . . ."

"You think Shannon's fear of Cumberland caused her to try to hide in the Protectorate, where his influence couldn't be felt?"

"I think she *had* to get away from him. And," Cassie shrugged, "I think there wasn't any way for 'famous model Shannon Cleary' to evade him, even in your Protectorate, so she got some new identity and she's hiding somewhere. She escaped through your country, and maybe she's in New Spain or New France by now. Trying to find a new life for herself."

Alex frowned. Cassie had clearly been deprived of one key piece of information, despite her belief that Shannon's brother Philip had given her "the details." Specifically, Philip obviously hadn't shown her the letter! He had told her about the amnesia diagnosis, but he hadn't dropped the bombshell—that Shannon believed she had traveled back in time! Why hadn't Phil trusted that information to Cassie?

They had all agreed not to release the letter to the media, of course. It wasn't actually relevant, except to establish the fact that Shannon wasn't quite right in the head, which had been obvious from a myriad of sources, most notably a highly publicized quote from her sister, who, luckily, hadn't known much about the time-travel claim other than the fact that Shannon had had vivid dreams involving Kahnawakee and his adviser, John Cutler.

But they were more than dreams. Shannon had sincerely believed she had met those famous seventeenth-century figures, and, at the time she wrote the letter to Phil, she was convinced she could find her way through time back to them, and stated plainly that she would never return to the twentieth century again. It was so sad, and so bizarre, and, ultimately, so private . . .

"You don't agree with me, do you?" Cassie murmured. "I see it in your eyes. Tell me what happened to my cousin, Mr. BlackKnife. Please?"

When his eyes locked with hers, he was touched by what he saw. The impish twinkle was gone, revealing the hurt and disappointment she suffered over the cousin she had never been allowed to know. She was genuinely in need, and he wanted to help her . . . to soothe her . . . to please her, and perhaps to resurrect the sparkle.

Cassie took his hand and whispered, "You think she's dead? You think Dusty Cumberland had her killed?" Her blue eyes were filling with tears. "I can't accept that. It's not fair! She and I . . . we needed each other!" She bit her lip and sighed, "I sound so selfish, don't I? But I hated being an only child, Mr. Black-Knife. And I always loved the stories Mom told me about how she and my Uncle Matt would play, and explore, and hang out together. Shannon and I should have had that chance, too."

"But your mother never told you her brother had a daughter?"

"Isn't it unforgivable?" Cassie murmured. "Just

because Shannon wasn't born until after he died, and her mother wouldn't associate with us. I still should have been told. I would have contacted Shannon somehow, at least by the time we were in secondary school, and we would have—well, double-dated, and done each other's hair . . ." Cassie's chin jutted out defiantly. "She isn't dead. If she were, I'd sense it. I *feel* like she's alive." Her hand reached out again, touching his sleeve. "Tell me, please?"

"I want her to be alive," he confessed softly, "but I think it's probably unrealistic. We would have found something—some clue by now. The whole world knows about her."

"But if she was dead, you'd have found her body. Or some clue of that, right? It doesn't prove anything. Don't you see?" Her voice grew wistful. "Don't you think maybe she's using a fake name, and a wig, and hiding in some remote town, hundreds of miles from here? Either she didn't really have amnesia, but just pretended, or she really has it. Poor Shannon . . ."

"Hey," Alex soothed, "don't torture yourself over this."

"I keep thinking, if she hated her life here, maybe she just needed to escape so much . . . you don't think she did anything crazy, do you? Like, killed herself or something?"

"We'd have found the body," he reminded her gently. "But you're right about one thing. She really hated her life. She hated it so much," he took a deep breath and blurted, "she invented a fantasy for herself, where she fell in love with John Cutler, and met Kahnawakee, and lived in a seventeenth-century world that was more simple and pristine."

Cassie stared at him for a long moment, then glared, "Huh? What's that all about? Kahnawakee?

The guy who united the Native American Protectorates?"

"The Visionary," Alex nodded. "He's a hero to my people, and apparently Shannon knew a little bit about him and chose to . . . integrate it into her fantasy. When I met her, she kept marveling about the resemblance I bear to him. At the time, it seemed a little strange, but it was only after we put all the pieces together that we realized how far gone she was."

"You met Shannon?"

"At the hospital, before she escaped and went to the border. She seemed perfectly sane to me."

"Of course she was sane," Cassie frowned. "Amnesia isn't insanity, Mr. BlackKnife."

"True, but . . ." He paused, wondering how far he should take this. She was no longer misty-eyed and vulnerable, and so he had accomplished his purpose and should probably just stop now. After all, Philip Tremaine hadn't trusted her with this information.

"You can tell me," Cassie insisted, as though she had read his mind. "There's something else, isn't there? I swear I won't breathe a word, Mr. Black-Knife—Alexander. Please? I need to know."

He nodded. "Call me Alex, and definitely don't repeat this to anyone. The fact is, Shannon kept insisting that she had met John Cutler. You know who he is, right?"

"He was a European, but he helped Kahnawakee unite the Protectorates in the 1600s, right?"

"Exactly. John Cutler was a great man. Shannon believed she had married him." He reached for his briefcase and rummaged through some papers, pulling out a photocopy of Shannon's letter to her brother. "Take a look at this."

Cassie grabbed the paper. As she scanned it, her blue eyes widened dramatically. "Shannon says Uncle Matt's ashes are scattered on a Susquehannock burial ground. She says," her tone was hushed, "she went to that burial ground, traveled through time back to the seventeenth century, and prevented some danger to the future of the Protectorates." Cassie raised her eyes to Alex's. "She wrote this on the day she disappeared? She intended to go back to the burial ground again, time-travel again, and join John Cutler forever?"

"Exactly. Do you see how it was?" His smile was gentle. "It wasn't just a simple case of amnesia. It might not have been insanity, but it was a fairly serious delusional state. If you read on a little more, you'll even see she believed history once took a different turn. She believed the Susquehannocks were once completely wiped out before the end of the eighteenth century, and most of the other nations in the Protectorates were either decimated or forced to live in restricted areas under oppressive conditions." Taking a deep breath, he continued, "She apparently thought the Indian nations continued to fight among themselves and never formed a united front against Euro-culture. She believed European powers eventually gained complete dominance in North America during the eighteenth century. It's all very bizarre," he finished, raising his coffee mug to his lips and sipped, pensively, "but poor Shannon believed history once went that way."

"But then, because she went back and warned Kahnawakee, the danger was avoided? And the protectorates survived, and flourished side by side with the French and the Spanish . . ." Cassie nodded. "Have you looked into all this?"

Alex almost choked on his coffee. "Huh? Looked

into?" He felt a sinking feeling in the pit of his stomach. Cassie Stone was now positively glaring at him! "Looked into what?" he demanded finally.

She had jumped to her feet and was gesturing dramatically. "I can't believe this! Everyone probably scoffed at her! I wish I'd been there, at the hospital, to give her moral support."

"You would have humored her?" Alex suggested, hoping she'd agree, but instead she wailed, "I would have believed her! At least," she corrected firmly, "I would have considered the possibility. I can't believe," she added, her voice softening to a subtle reproach, "you've been investigating and digging for all these months and you never pursued this! The one solid clue!"

"The one *solid* clue? That she time traveled? Are you serious, Miss Stone?"

"Absolutely." She positioned herself within inches of him and announced, "I'll tell you something about time, Mr. BlackKnife. It's a fiction. Did you know that?"

He could smell her perfume—or was that vanilla? A wave of intoxicating warmth, whether from her anger or her passionate nature or simple body heat, was crossing the slight distance between them and causing his own temperature to rise alarmingly. He wanted to change the subject, or ask for a glass of ice water, or kiss her full, pouting lips until she moaned, but instead he repeated woodenly, "A fiction?"

"It's a device. Something we use, like . . ." Her eyes flashed with inspiration. "Like boundaries! Take the border between your country and mine. It's a fiction, right? There's no actual physical line. A thousand years ago, it meant nothing. We invented it, to make it easier to understand where the Protectorate's jurisdiction begins and where the Washington Common-wealth's ends. Right?"

"That's true, but—"

"Don't you see? For some reason, we bought into the time fiction. It's practical, of course, and we should use it, but to actually believe it . . ." She shrugged. "It's a fiction."

He couldn't help but smile. " 'Eccentric' is starting to sound like an understatement."

"I can prove it to you," she challenged mischievously. "You believe that once a particular date passes, we can never relive it, right?"

Alex nodded, amused but wary.

"Okay, imagine that all the scientific community got together for a conference and all the astronomers issued a joint statement that, in order to compensate for some cosmic nuances in the Earth's orbit, it was necessary for us to adjust our calendars slightly, and so, on September first, at midnight, we were going to 'make up' a day—an extra twenty-four hours—by having another September first. We'd all do it, right?"

He nodded again, completely fascinated.

"It's group insanity, really," she concluded cheerfully. "We can all blindly accept the concept of living an entire day over again, but the thought of time travel leaves us threatened, I guess. I don't see what all the fuss is about, personally."

"This explains why you feel comfortable having Christmas in August," Alex teased. "You're a fascinating woman."

"Well," she sniffed, "everyone's entitled to his own opinion. You think Shannon was crazy, and I guess you think *I'm* crazy, too."

He glanced around the room. "To tell you the truth, I think you're just creative, and obviously talented. Some of these projects of yours are exceptional. That one over there in particular. Where did you learn to do that beadwork?"

Cassie crossed the room and retrieved the intricately decorated leather wallhanging. "Do you like it? I made dozens of mistakes in it, but I like it, too."

"It's similar to some work done hundreds of years ago by my people."

"I know. I learned it at a crafts fair last year. I'm a hopeless copycat," she admitted without remorse. "My two talents—copying other people's work, and camouflaging my mistakes."

"It looks perfect." He ran his finger over the complicated pattern. "What does it mean?"

"Mean? Does it have to mean something?" She shrugged. "In this case, it means I had lots of blue beads and not many red ones."

Alex laughed and nudged a box of pine cones with his foot. "I guess your next project will revolve around lots of pine cones and not many acorns?"

Cassie grinned. "That's my texture box. Look." She lifted it and pulled out a piece of lava rock. "I feel these different textures for inspiration. In some ways, texture, more than color, guides my work. Speaking of which . . ." Her eyes locked on his hair. "Do you have any idea how gorgeous your hair is?"

The remark caught him completely by surprise, and he flushed slightly. "My hair?"

"It screams texture. May I . . . ?" Her fingers stretched tentatively toward him, pausing inches above his scalp.

She was waiting, innocently, for permission, apparently oblivious to the fact that Alex was fighting an unbridled wave of arousal at the thought of her fingertips caressing him. And of what he might do in return.

Then she pulled back her hand and blushed, "That was so stupid and rude of me—I apologize." Backing away, she added lamely, "Would you like some more coffee? Tea?"

"I wasn't offended, Miss Stone," he assured her, regretting his hesitation. "It just caught me off guard."

"Can we drop it?" she pleaded. "I'm *so* embarrassed. I don't usually manhandle my guests."

"Come here," he insisted calmly. "It's no big deal."

"Let's just talk about Shannon. We haven't even discussed your theory about Dusty Cumberland. Do you think he had her killed or something?"

"Come here," he repeated firmly, beguiled by her panic. "If we don't do this, I'm going to leave here feeling like a real jerk." His tone softened as he added, "I'm flattered. Honestly. You just surprised me."

Again her gaze settled on his hair with innocent adoration. "Are you sure?" Edging closer, she moistened her lips nervously. "It's not some cultural taboo or anything, is it?"

"Hardly," he grinned.

She smiled in return and again her fingers moved, hesitantly, until they were gently stroking, then sifting through, his coarse, shaggy locks. For a moment, Alex allowed himself to imagine how her long, pink fingernails might feel were they to graze his skull, then work their way down to the nape of his neck, then around to his chest . . .

"All done," she blushed. "Thanks."

"What's the verdict?"

"I love it," she admitted sheepishly. "It's *so* thick.

And now that I've thoroughly embarrassed both of us, would you like that second cup of coffee?"

"Some other time, maybe," he began, then reproached himself sternly. There wouldn't be another time, and that was probably for the best. "I have an appointment in Cutlerton in less than an hour."

Her smile was wistful and alluring. "I'm so glad you came here today. It's reassuring to know that . . . well, that Shannon might be living somewhere safe and happy right now, in the arms of the man she loves."

"The man being John Cutler?" Alex groaned. "Back to that?"

"Don't mock me," she sighed. "You're extremely closed minded, did you know that? You're articulate and bright, but you only see what you want to see. You don't have . . . *vision.*"

It stung—hadn't Kahnawakee exhorted his followers and descendants to trust in their vision?—but Alex refused to let her know she had hit a nerve. "If you have any more visions, Miss Stone—of your cousin, or Santa, or anyone else—let me know. Here's my card."

"You should be more open-minded," she repeated, adding impishly, "I could help you."

His pulse raced at the implications. Was she suggesting he should open his mind, and his heart, to the thought of surrendering to the attraction he felt for her? "I should be going," he protested weakly.

"Close your eyes," she instructed, as though she hadn't heard him.

Without allowing himself time to resist, he complied, then waited in anxious silence, uncertain of what he was hoping she might do.

"Don't open them until I tell you," she purred.

"Now, keep your eyes closed, but open your mind. Relax . . ." She moved up close—he could smell the vanilla and feel the heat—and then a whisper-soft sensation teased his mouth, akin to the feel of velvet being stroked across his lips, and he almost allowed himself to kiss her, but didn't dare and so remained rigid and resistant despite the temptation.

"Tell me what you just felt, Alexander Black-Knife," she urged. When he didn't answer, she laughed lightly. "Okay, open your eyes."

Her smile was so alluring he was about to reach for her despite his better judgment when she waved a red velvet Christmas stocking in the air and teased, "You were supposed to take a guess."

Seduced by a crazy woman! he chastised himself. *She almost brought you to your knees!* The most amazing part was, she was clearly unaware of the effect she was having on him! She was playing with fire . . .

Pulling himself together, he frowned. "Would you like some free advice?"

"Sure."

"Don't flirt like that with strange men. Remember what happened to your cousin."

"That's right," she accused immediately. "You never told me *your* theory."

"I think . . ." He caught himself and smiled grimly. "I think someone kidnapped her, on our land, and took her somewhere else, outside the Protectorate. If her body was anywhere on our land, we would have found it by now. We've searched every inch."

"So?" Cassie nodded. "You think Dusty Cumberland had her kidnapped? Do you think he killed her, too, or do you think he's holding her prisoner somewhere?"

Alex scowled, all too aware of how close he was

coming to leaving his nation exposed to liability for defamation of Dusty Cumberland's character. "I didn't say anything about him specifically," he corrected. "I said 'someone.' "

"Who else was rich enough and had the motive?" Cassie shrugged. "If she's still in this time period, I agree with your theory."

If she's still in this time period . . . Alex resisted an urge to argue, knowing that somehow he would enjoy it a bit too much, for all the wrong reasons, and picked up his briefcase instead. "This has been very educational," he drawled. "Thanks for the Christmas cookies."

"Wait!" She caught his arm and smiled reassuringly. "Thanks for telling me about the letter. I really feel much better now."

"Well, that makes one of us," he laughed. "Just promise me you won't tell anyone about the time-travel theory."

"I'll promise that, if you'll promise to give it some thought, with an open mind." Then she shook her head, apparently annoyed by what she saw in his expression. "Never mind, Mr. BlackKnife. I can see you feel threatened by it, so just forget it. I'll keep your secret, though, and . . ." her tone softened to a purr, "thanks for everything."

"Right. Merry Christmas, Cassie." He savored her appreciative smile for a moment, then sighed inwardly and hurried to his car.

Chapter Two

Cassie Stone brushed a mass of curly blond bangs away from her forehead with absent-minded grace as she watched Alexander BlackKnife stride down her driveway toward his fancy black convertible. She was still holding the velvet stocking and now drew it lightly over her own lips, wondering if her visitor suspected the truth—that it hadn't been fabric, but a pair of curious female lips that had brushed across his so longingly.

Pretty typical of your sex life, Cassie, she chided herself. *Ninety-nine-percent fantasy, with a little texture thrown in for realism.* And if texture was her life, as she so often claimed, she could spend a lifetime with a man like Alexander BlackKnife! That thick, coarse hair and those warm, slightly rough hands . . .

And the smells! Just the way a man *should* smell— like he'd lathered up with saddle soap, rinsed himself in a spring downpour, then dried himself with a chamois by a roaring campfire. He was a virtual feast for her senses, from the clear, confident speaking voice that could switch so unexpectedly to a husky murmur, to the piercing black eyes that had memorized every

inch of her body during the moment it had taken for
him to pull her to her feet after her collision with the
tree.

*And you made a fine impression on him, too, I'm
sure,* she derided herself. *Sprawled across the floor,
with grease on your hands, babbling about time travel
and buying people's shoes right off their feet. . . .* She'd
probably never see him again and each of her senses
was screaming for her to do something to remedy
that, so she tossed her pride aside for the moment and
pushed open the door, dashing down the gravel driveway without thought to her shoeless feet.

"Mr. BlackKnife!"

He was sitting in his car but the door was still open
and he seemed to be making notes—she could imagine the word "eccentric" being erased and replaced
with "lunatic"—but he smiled at her arrival and
shrugged back out into the sunlight. She paused for a
moment, impressed by the visual impact of this tall,
handsome man in his simple, rugged clothes.

"Did you forget something, Miss Stone?"

"I forgot to ask you if you'd like to come to dinner
some night this week," she blurted, adding more
lightly, "I promise I won't try to buy your clothing or
touch your hair or anything." The instant the words
left her lips she could see they were a mistake. He was
obviously struggling to turn her down tactfully, and
she felt a sharp stab of disappointment, then her pride
returned and she insisted, "Unless you're involved
with someone, which of course I'm sure you are.
Sorry . . ."

"I'm not involved with anyone," he corrected in the
husky murmur. "But I am involved with my career,
and . . ."

"Your career?" She exhaled gratefully. "I know

you're a busy man, but you still have to eat, right? This would be casual, I promise."

He stepped closer. "Your offer is tempting, Cassie, believe me, but . . . I have certain goals. I want to be a leader among my people and that's a fairly all-encompassing role. Because of that, it makes sense for me to date women who have cultural orientations similar to mine."

"Cultural orientations?"

"When I was in school I dated Euras, but a few months ago I made up my mind to date only women from the Protectorate nations."

"Oh?" She smiled tightly. "I never thought of myself as a Eura. I'm a North American, and so are you. But," she waved her hands in annoyance, "thanks for being honest. I can see how, for a guy like you, it makes sense to be closed-minded about relationships. And believe me," she drawled in conclusion, "it's no big deal to me one way or the other."

"I guess I deserve that," he sighed. "You're an incredibly attractive woman, but even if I hadn't sworn off non-Natives, you're Shannon's cousin, and as long as I'm heading the investigation, I need to stay objective."

"But you're not at all objective. You only pursue leads that you find subjectively comfortable. Your investigations," she added dryly, "are a lot like your dates."

He chuckled. "You say the most interesting things. Are you still implying I should investigate the time-travel angle?"

"Absolutely. When you get back to the Protectorate, go to the burial ground and light a fire. If you don't . . ."

"If I don't, it means I don't have vision?" He

pursed his lips as though honestly considering the challenge. "All right, Cassie, I'll do it as soon as I get back. I'll give you a call and let you know what happened."

"You probably shouldn't call me," she sniffed. "I'm a Eura, remember? But if you see Shannon, tell her I said 'Hi.' " She enjoyed spinning on her heels and striding away, imagining that Alexander Black-Knife was staring at her back with a certain amount of longing. After all, he'd admitted he was attracted to her . . .

But if he's not comfortable with you, because of culture or whatever, why give him a hard time? she chastised herself when she'd reached the deck, and so she turned in time to see him folding his long, lean body back into the driver's seat. When she waved, he grinned in sheepish appreciation, nodded, and drove away in a gravelly cloud.

Cassie watched the Mustang disappear, then shook the pebbles from the soles of her feet and scampered back into the house. She had a sink filled with cookie cutters and rolling pins to wash, and a lot of thinking to do. On the kitchen counter was a framed picture of Shannon Cleary, and Cassie eyed it with fond amusement. She had cut it from a fashion magazine, wistful at not having a real photograph to frame, but somehow grateful that she had a cousin who was hopefully alive and would one day be found and reunited with the family she didn't even know she had.

"But if you're with John Cutler and the quote-unquote Visionary, I guess you don't need a cousin," she reproached the missing model, as she scrubbed and rinsed her favorite gingerbread mold. "I hope that's what happened, Shannon. The alternatives are too grizzly. Alex BlackKnife seriously believes Dusty

Cumberland has you stashed somewhere, and that's just unthinkable for me."

She glanced at the wall clock, wondering when Alex would arrive at the Protectorate and light the fire. She had no doubt that he'd follow through with his promise—the man was almost *too* dedicated and responsible. She also entertained no real hope that fate would whisk the handsome attorney back through time to where he could verify Shannon's "happily-ever-after" status, but it was a pleasant fantasy.

Despite her exhortations to the contrary, she wasn't actually convinced that time travel was possible, especially at the flick of a lighter, but Alexander Black-Knife's complete dismissal of the possibility had bothered her, and so she had, with characteristic impulsiveness, proceeded to champion the theory. Now, as she cleared away the traces of Christmas from her kitchen, her thoughts turned to Philip Tremaine, and her tender heart went out to him. To have received a note like that from his beloved baby sister . . . he must have felt so helpless, especially considering that he was a psychologist!

If she saw Philip again, she wouldn't mention time travel at all. It was one thing to speculate and debate with Alexander BlackKnife—after all, only his career and his sanity were at stake!—but Philip's poor heart was broken over Shannon, and unless there was some proof . . .

She froze, staggered by the question she hadn't thought to ask Alex. He claimed they'd gone over every inch of territory, and so . . . had they found a miniature burned log cabin at the site of the ancient burial ground? Not that that would prove anything, of course, but Shannon had claimed in the letter that it was part of her ritual; it would be a sort of verification, at least. The thought sent a shiver down Cassie's spine and she wished she hadn't told Alex not to call. She simply *had* to know.

"Cassie! Come on in."

"Hi, Phil. I hope I'm not disturbing you."

"Are you kidding? When my receptionist said you were here, it made my day. Come on in." The slight, fair-haired man ushered her into his office and studied her fondly. "What are you doing in Cutlerton?"

"Visiting you," she admitted. "I needed to ask you something. Oh!" She stared in amazement at a replica of a cabin, built out of twigs, on a shelf behind Philip's massive desk. With a shaky smile she added, "Did you build that?"

"Shannon did." The brother's voice was hoarse with regret. "Whenever we went camping together, we used to start our campfires with a little cabin, stuffed with newspaper for tinder. It was sort of a tradition."

"And she built this one for you?" Cassie couldn't force herself to ask when or where. "It's nice, Phil. I'll have to remember that trick the next time I go camping."

"Oh? Do you like to camp?"

"Only in the finest hotels," she admitted. "Indoor plumbing is one of my all-time favorite inventions. I guess Shannon and I are pretty different that way."

"She loved to rough it," he nodded. "On the other hand," his eyes grew misty, "you remind me so much of her sometimes, it's almost . . . painful. But," he hastened to add, "I wouldn't change that for the world. You have her smile, Cassie. It's a lot like your uncle's was—generous and inspiring. And, if your hair were longer and you wore jeans, I think maybe the resemblance would be fairly strong, even to an outsider."

"I wore my hair long for years," Cassie sighed, "but I wanted curls . . . and as for jeans," she brushed her hands along her soft, billowy skirt, "they just aren't my style. I bought some *Dustees,* though, as soon as you told me Shannon was my cousin. I remembered seeing her in those *Dustees* ads all the time, and wishing I was that tall and svelte."

"She lived in jeans," Philip remembered sadly. "It would be so grotesque to think that her involvement with Dusty Cumberland grew out of such an innocent habit as that, and then Dusty hurt her . . ."

"I don't believe that," Cassie whispered. "I don't think he ever saw her again after that day she broke off her engagement to him."

"Thanks, Cass."

"Philip? I don't mean to sound nosy, but . . . when did Shannon make this little cabin for you?"

"She didn't make it for me," he confessed quietly. "She made it as part of some escapist fantasy. It's actually evidence, but the Susquehannocks were decent enough to release it to me, even though the investigation isn't officially over."

"The Susquehannocks found it on their land?" Cassie was straining to keep her tone even and calm. "And Alexander BlackKnife let you have it because he knew it had sentimental value for you?"

"Right."

"I met him yesterday. He's a nice guy, Phil."

"Yeah, he's the best. I still remember the day I went storming up there, half-incoherent with fear over Shannon's letter and disappearance, and BlackKnife let me rail and insult and threaten to sue them into next year, and the whole time, he just listened. He really listened, and that gave me hope, and I calmed down a little and then we talked for hours. He has three sisters, did he tell you that?"

"No. He didn't give me any personal information except," she confided mischievously, "he doesn't date blondes."

The implication teased Philip Tremaine out of his melancholy mood and he smiled sympathetically. "Too bad. As your stepcousin, I'd like to see you involved with someone stable like him."

"Me, too. By the way," she pretended to study the tiny cabin as she murmured, "Alex let me take a look at that letter Shannon wrote you. I hope you don't mind. I seemed depressed, I guess, and so poor Alex needed to cheer me up. It wasn't his fault, and," she returned her eyes to his tentatively, "I gave him my word I wouldn't tell any outsiders about it, and I meant that."

Philip shook his head. "I can't believe he told you."

"You don't trust me with it?"

"I trust you to keep it to yourself," he corrected, "but I don't trust you to handle it well, internally. And your fascination with that little log cabin pretty much proves my point, right?"

"Pardon?"

"Cassie . . ."

"Okay, okay, stop grilling me!" she laughed, raising her hands in surrender. "I find it fascinating. You can't afford to, and I guess Alex can't either, but we eccentrics get to play around the edges of reality, and that's that."

Philip grinned reluctantly. "I knew you'd go for it. The funny thing is, Shannon was never . . . 'eccentric' . . . in that way at all. I would have sworn the concept of time travel would have been completely inconceivable to her."

"Really?" Cassie's pulse was racing at this tidbit of information. Along with the existence of the cabin, it was making the time-travel theory all the more plausible. "I guess she just had incredibly vivid dreams, right? Because of all the sedatives they gave her in the hospital, and because of the concussion?"

"You don't fool me, Cassie," he laughed, "but you'll notice," his voice grew suddenly weary, "the cabin doesn't have a burn mark, or even a hint of smoke damage, anywhere."

"That's true." Cassie winced at the realization that deep inside, Philip Tremaine had wanted to believe the time-travel theory, too, and had been devastated by this "proof" that Shannon hadn't accomplished her plan.

"I guess she was interrupted," the grieving brother explained. "She built the cabin, and definitely intended to light it, but . . . that's when her . . . assailant . . . moved in."

"Was there any sign of a struggle? Look at the cabin, Phil. It's fragile. If Shannon had tried to fight someone off . . ."

"As you said, she was probably still a little groggy from all the sedatives. She was an easy target for any creep who . . . well, never mind."

Cassie's heart ached and she patted his forearm. "No creep got her, Phil. She lit a match—that's the big taboo, right? No lighting fires on that burial site. All she had to do to leave was light a fire, not burn one, and *poof!* She was gone."

"What?" He was studying her face anxiously. "That's nonsense, Cassie. Don't do that. Don't—"

"Don't get my hopes up? Why not? Shannon would want me to say that to you, so I said it."

"She lit the match . . ." His voice was raspy and he turned to stare at the cabin. "And so why did she bother building this, if it wasn't even necessary?"

"I guess she knew how great it would look on her big brother's shelf." Tears were suddenly stinging Cassie's eyes and she wondered if she had taken this too far, then Philip turned to her and whispered his thanks and she sighed with relief. Even if it was nonsense, it was soothing nonsense, and it had worked for a moment, and she was glad she had been able to give him that.

Her next stop was the Susquehannock border. As she eased her car into a parking slot, she reminded herself to appear confident and casual so as not to attract attention. Her modest almond-colored dress, with its high neckline and long, sweeping skirt, would please even the most conservative resident, and the scarf on her head, along with her sunglasses, would hopefully blur any possible resemblance to Shannon. She needed to be inconspicuous—in contrast to her usual "eccentric" self, she teased herself nervously—and so she vowed not to notice anyone's shoes or beadwork, or the texture of anyone's hair, and to stick to the purpose of her visit, which was . . .

"Research," she muttered, glancing one last time into her purse to verify the presence of a book of matches. If she didn't get this nonsense out of her system, she probably would never be able to concentrate again, and so, ultimately, this was a very rational mission.

When the border guard's face lit up in an all-too-

familiar way, she bit back a grin of relief. He was
going to flirt with her. That would make this so much
easier! She had assumed, after the disaster with Alexander BlackKnife, that none of the resident males
would be susceptible to her usual tactics, and suddenly, this was going to be a breeze!

"Can I help you?"

He was fresh-faced and adorable and Cassie didn't
know whether to kiss him or adopt him, but she chose
to smile coolly. "I'd like to visit the museum, if that's
not too much trouble."

"Do you have a passport?"

"Yes, I do." She handed it to him, grateful for once
that the photograph was atrocious. He studied it, then
studied her, and, at just the right moment, she
removed her sunglasses and cooed, "Isn't it hideous?"

He shook his head vehemently. "It's very pretty."

"Aren't you sweet!" She watched with trepidation
as he entered her name into a computer. What if Alex
had reported her as a known time-travel nut? "Any
problem, sir?"

"No problem," he assured her. "It's just our proce-
dure. We've tightened up security lately. So, are you
here for just the day?"

"Two or three hours, at the most."

"Then we're finished here. And," he smiled adoringly, "welcome, Miss Stone. If you'll have a seat, I'll
arrange for an escort immediately." He lowered his
voice and added, "I'd take you myself, but I don't
have a break for another hour. But maybe I'll see you
then?"

"I don't need an escort, but if you'd like to join me
at the museum on your break," she smiled, "that
would be wonderful. In the meantime, just point me
in the right direction and I'll be fine on my own."

"It's a short walk, but we don't allow unescorted visitors anymore. Everyone needs an escort, whether they're going to the village or just up to the museum." Again he lowered his voice and confided, "Because of that model who disappeared here in April."

"Oh, yes. Alex BlackKnife told me all about that. He and I are *very* close friends," Cassie began, then frowned at the guard's reaction. It was as though she had pulled a gun and demanded his wallet! "Is something wrong?"

He shook his head, but was simultaneously dialing the telephone, and so Cassie grabbed his hand, trying for her sweetest smile. "I didn't mean you should bother Alex. I know how busy he is."

"Can I help you, miss?" a deep voice boomed from behind her, and she turned to face two burly security guards. The larger of the two stepped forward and suggested, "If you'll come with us, this can all be taken care of."

"Wait a minute," she glared. "I just want to visit the museum."

"And your name is . . . ?"

"She's Cassandra Stone," the sweet-faced border guard volunteered nervously from behind her. "She seems okay, but when she started using Alex's name, I just remembered the other one—"

"You did the right thing," the security guard interrupted, adding, for Cassie's benefit, "Mr. BlackKnife will be here in a few minutes, Miss Stone. If you'll come with us, you can make yourself comfortable in my office until he arrives."

"Did I *ask* for him?" she protested, but followed the two men dutifully while trying to calm her racing heart. She wasn't sure whether she was panicking over the confrontation or was simply excited at the prospect of seeing the handsome council adviser again so soon. He'd be annoyed, most likely, but she would simply explain that she hadn't asked for him and she would secretly enjoy the encounter whether he believed her or not.

In the meantime she settled into a comfortable chair and helped herself to a lapful of brochures covering the history of the Susquehannock Nation and its membership in the illustrious Union of Native American Protectorates. A huge map of North America on the office wall showed the boundaries of the Protectorate: to the south, the border with the Washington Commonwealth; to the east, the Six Nations Protectorate, home of the Iroquois League; to the north and northwest, Les États, or New France, as it was more commonly called; to the west, the sprawling Central Protectorate.

All members of UNAP were depicted on the map in vibrant forest green, which seemed appropriate to Cassie, given their fierce commitment to preservation of their habitat. New France, per tradition, was colored a pearly shade of gray. New Spain, the color of gold, stretched lazily along the Aztec Gulf, sharing a meandering, peaceful border with the nine so-called Southern Protectorates, while tiny, powerful New England, shown in royal blue, monopolized the upper Atlantic coast. Its counterpart, the aqua-toned Pacific Commonwealth, dominated the western shores. All in all, the young artist decided proudly, her native North America was a breathtakingly beautiful continent.

The Susquehannock Protectorate, as the brochures smugly proclaimed, was small but held a place of honor in the Council that governed UNAP. The reason was simple and well known to any schoolchild. Kahnawakee, a charismatic Susquehannock, had had

the vision and drive to greet the wave of seventeenth-
and eighteenth-century Euro-culture with a united
front of native distrust and streamlined military resistance. Although the Six Nations Protectorate was
nominally the most powerful, especially in matters of
war, and the tiny Delaware Protectorate was indisputa-
bly the most admired in matters of peace and con-
ciliation, the Susquehannocks were considered un-
equaled in their ability to produce leaders of vision
and unselfishness who could set a course for UNAP
that served the modern needs of all members without
sacrificing the principles for which so many of their
ancestors had given their lives.

Cassie winced at the recurrence of the buzzword
"vision," and she wondered if she had unwittingly
insulted Alex by calling him "closed-minded." In fact,
she saw him as incredibly charismatic and intriguing
and was sure he fit the Susquehannock leadership
profile perfectly, if only because of the sincerity and
obvious dedication with which he approached his du-
ties, and which were so strikingly complemented by
his lean, earthy good looks. Closing her eyes, she
remembered him eagerly—the scent, the feel, the
sound, and thanks to the gentle kiss, even his salty
taste.

"Cassie?"

His voice was just as she remembered—ringing
with confidence—and she opened one eye playfully.
"Am I under arrest?"

He chuckled and turned to the security guard.
"Good job, Mack. This not-so-innocent looking
woman is Shannon Cleary's cousin."

"Is that so?" The guard was suitably impressed.
"I'd better go and compliment Johnny. He's the one
who alerted me so I could alert you."

"Now that everyone's been alerted," Cassie said, smiling when the guard had left her alone with Alex, "can you tell me where I made my big mistake? I didn't use your name to try to get in, Alex, really. I just mentioned it in idle conversation."

"Shannon used my name, the day she disappeared, to con a pass from the guard. All the guys know the story, and they're determined never to be fooled again."

"Oh, I see."

"I had just visited her at the hospital," Alex elaborated, "and I offered to leave a pass at the border station so that she could visit the museum. At that time, of course, I had no inkling she was . . ."

"Nuts?" Cassie shrugged, then drew closer and demanded, "So? Don't keep me in suspense. Did you do it?"

"It?"

"Don't be coy. Did you light the fire last night, like you promised?"

He grinned and nodded. "I felt like an idiot, but I did it. And, I'm still here. Even more amazing," he added, his voice now dropping to the husky murmur she adored, "you're here, too."

She nodded, feeling suddenly shy and uncertain. "I didn't come to bother you. I just wanted to look around."

"I'll give you a personal tour." His eyes traveled over her, admiring her graceful outfit. "You look terrific, by the way. I see you even wore shoes for the occasion." Taking her arm, he led her back outside and toward his convertible.

She wanted to say something casual, or intelligent, or provocative, but his grip on her arm, and the masculine smell of saddlesoap—because of his leather vest, she explained numbly to herself—were keeping coherent speech at bay. In fact, she was using most of her willpower to keep from snuggling closer to him and was relieved when he finally released her so that he could open the passenger door for her.

"Nice car," she managed to contribute once she was seated, adding lamely, "it smells like you."

"Pardon?" He had slipped into the driver's seat and now glared in pretend annoyance. "Do I smell like noxious fumes?"

"You smell like leather." She stroked the rich black upholstery reverently. "This is pretty plush."

"My one luxury," he smiled. "When I bought this, it was in bad shape. I've slowly rebuilt it."

"You're very goal-oriented, just like you said," she nodded. "I'm more impulsive, and usually I live to regret it. For example," she took a deep breath, "I regretted telling you not to call me."

"I almost called you anyway."

She flushed at the possible compliment. "I guess I should tell you, I saw Philip Tremaine today and told him about your visit."

"That's good. I was going to call him about it myself."

"He showed me the little cabin."

Alex's ebony eyes twinkled. "I'll bet you got a lot of mileage out of that, right?"

"I managed to control myself." They had pulled up outside the museum and she prodded, "So? Where's the scene of the crime?"

"First, the tour. Then, if you behave, we'll see about the burial ground."

He had her arm again and her incoherence was threatening to return, but she managed to murmur, "I didn't mean to monopolize your day, Alex. If you want to turn me over to the escort service, that's okay with me."

"The escort service?" he chuckled. "Cute, Cassie. The truth is, most of those guys are fresh out of college. I don't think they could handle you and your games. So," he swung the museum door wide open, "you're stuck with me."

"Oh, Alex, look!" She abandoned him, streaking across the room to a display of beaded tunics and wampum belts. "These are so beautiful!"

"Shall we go to the burial ground now?"

"You're in a teasing mood today," she laughed. "But you'd better just find a chair and relax. I'm going to study these for hours. Especially," she indicated a fragile, faded garment, "this incredible piece. Are those porcupine quills? I've heard that's what women embroidered with before us Euros came and ruined everything."

"Did I insult you yesterday?" he frowned. "That wasn't my intent. I apologize."

"When I look at craftsmanship—or rather, crafts-*woman*ship like this—I agree with you. Glass beads and embroidery floss are beautiful, and practical, and easier to deal with, but shells and quills are so delicate and . . . well, so fragile."

"There's a famous heirloom from Kahnawakee's time I'd like to show you someday," Alex murmured. "It's on display at League headquarters right now, but it's due back soon. You'd appreciate it, I think."

"Couteau?" A warm voice interrupted gently. "There's a call for you."

"Oh?"

Cassie noticed the flush behind Alex's tanned cheeks and groaned inwardly. The tall woman who had spoken to him was non-Eura and strikingly attractive, and it was clear Alex was somehow embarrassed to have been caught by her in an intimate conversation with Cassie.

"Shall I tell them you'll call back?"

"No. I told my office to forward this particular call . . ." He had recovered his equilibrium. "Cassandra Stone, this is my good friend Leah Eagle. I didn't know you were working today, Leah."

"I'm just catching up on some paperwork. You can take your call in my office. If you'd like," she added graciously, "I can continue Miss Stone's tour myself."

"Leah's the docent," Alex smiled toward Cassie. "She can answer your questions better than I can."

I'll just bet she can, Cassie retorted silently, but aloud she murmured, "That's great. Thanks."

When Alex had disappeared, Leah prodded, "You're Shannon Cleary's cousin?"

"Yes. How did you know?"

"Couteau went on and on about you last night," she confided. "I can't remember when I've laughed so much! The whole idea of Christmas, in such warm weather . . ." Her eyes mocked Cassie pointedly. "Couteau sees you as quite the comedienne."

Seething, Cassie retorted, "Did he tell you I asked him for a date, but he turned me down?"

Clearly taken aback, Leah shrugged. "He didn't mention that, but I'm not surprised."

"Well, he told me, even though he wasn't involved with anyone right now," she paused dramatically to allow the insult to take effect, "he was too involved with his career, and with the investigation, to risk involvement with me. I admire that kind of straightforward honesty, don't you?"

"If we're being honest . . ." Leah broke off and shook her long, dark hair impatiently. "If you're finished with this display, perhaps you'd like to see some weapons, or pottery?"

"Alex was going to show me a certain burial ground."

"Oh? The one where Shannon Cleary supposedly was abducted?" Leah's dark eyes were taunting her again, plainly proud to be able to demonstrate the extent of her knowledge of the case.

But I'll bet she doesn't know about the time-travel wrinkle, Cassie congratulated herself grimly. And who cares what she knows? She's perfect for Alex's career! She looks the part, she's got killer instinct, and she obviously adores him, so . . . "Do you think you could take me there right now?"

Leah nodded. "It's less than a hundred yards north of here. We can walk."

"Perfect. The sooner I see it, the sooner I'll be leaving."

"Well then, that *is* perfect, isn't it? Let's go right away."

As they walked together in silence, Cassie forced herself to forget the pointless rivalry and to concentrate instead on Shannon. She had conned her way past the border guard that fateful day—using Alex's name, which pleased Cassie no end!—and then she had walked this same path to the burial site. The trees were old along this trail—some were more than two yards in diameter!—and the sunlight barely reached the path due to the density of the leaves above. There was a timeless quality to these woods and Cassie could imagine how such a peaceful atmosphere must have soothed her cousin's tortured soul. Then the two women stepped into a clearing and Cassie gasped with understanding. This place . . . it was so shadowy, so eternal . . .

Her eyes were misting with tears and, to her surprise, they were for her Uncle Matt rather than for his beautiful daughter. Cassie had heard so many stories of the man, and through them, his gentleness and strength had been communicated to his niece. This was a perfect resting place for him—how wise of Phil and Shannon to have scattered his ashes here!—and Cassie longed to tell him that he lived on in the hearts of his family. Turning to Leah, she sighed, "Could I be alone for just a minute or two? I promise I won't disturb anything. My Uncle Matt is buried here, and . . . well, I'd like to pay my respects."

Leah touched her shoulder gently. "Take all the time you want. And," her proud eyes clouded slightly, "forgive my rudeness. I see now you're here to honor your dead, and I feel foolish for having felt threatened by you."

"Thanks." Cassie shrugged. "Like I said, I gave him my best shot and he turned me down flat."

"Couteau is destined to lead my people like his ancestor Kahnawakee once did."

"Why do you call him Couteau? Does that mean 'Alex' in your language?"

" 'Couteau Noir' means 'black knife' in French. It was the name given to Kahnawakee's firstborn son. Now it's the family name for one branch of Kahnawakee's descendants—the BlackKnife family."

"Couteau Noir," Cassie mused. "It's beautiful."

"It's his destiny. He cannot allow outside distractions to ruin his career. If you're able to respect that, it reflects well on you. And now I'll leave you to your mourning. Take all the time you need."

When Leah had departed, Cassie moved to the center of the clearing and raised her shining eyes to the sky. "I always wanted to meet you, Uncle Matt," she confided reverently. "I never met you and I never met Shannon, but we're all in this together somehow, aren't we? People go through life worrying about petty problems and silly rivalries—like that little run-in with Leah, queen of the *over*-Protectorate—but the truth is, she's irrelevant to my existence. But you! You're crucial to me! My mom told me some pretty funny stories, and some pretty sad ones, but the saddest one of all is this—that we never got to meet each other, and sadder still, you never got to meet your only daughter, Shannon. So," she sank to her knees and emptied the contents of her purse onto the soft forest bed, "if it's possible for me to meet Shannon, let's do it. For my sake, and yours, and maybe hers. And definitely for Philip's. I know he was only your stepson, but I know how close you two were, and he's hurting."

She had brought enough sticks to build a miniature high-rise, but she settled for a model of her own A-frame dwelling, complete with deck and four tiny steps. Then she held the match in her hand and whispered, "Okay, Uncle Matt, help me out with this. Send me back to Shannon, and," her blue eyes sparkled impishly, "send Alexander Couteau Noir back with me as my escort." Then she lit the match and stared hopefully into the flame until it burned down to her fingertips and she was forced to shake it in disgust. "Darn . . ." Gathering her supplies, but leaving the little house for the termites to enjoy, she jumped to her feet, smoothed her rumpled skirt, then stifled a shriek as three braves, in war paint and deerskin leggings, stepped into the clearing.

Chapter Three

Cassie shrank from the intruders, who were looking at her as though *she* were the intruder, and she pleaded, under her breath, "Uncle Matt? Can I change my mind? I don't see Shannon . . ." She thought her heart was going to pound right through the walls of her chest and all she could think of was the poor Cowardly Lion in *The Wizard of Oz,* and how misunderstood he really was, when the sound of raucous laughter from the trees behind the warriors reached her and, to her dismay, the braves themselves succumbed to it, laughing so hard they seemed about to roll onto the ground.

She still couldn't speak, but her fear was being transformed, slowly, into mortification mixed with anger and completely untainted by relief. When Alex moved into view, holding his aching sides and trying to bring his laughter under control, she managed to glare, "You!" then she turned her back on the men and took the long, deep, stabilizing breath she would need before she could scratch their eyes out.

"Cassie!" He was still chuckling when he came up behind her and touched her shoulder; and even when she spun to glare at him, his wide grin didn't falter.

"That was *the* most hilarious thing I've ever seen."
When she tried to push past him, he grabbed her arm
and teased, "You should have seen your face. You
thought you time traveled—"

"I *get* the joke!" she spat. "I'm not a *total* idiot, you
know. Now, excuse me." Wrenching her arm free, she
moved haughtily toward the path.

"Stop her," Alex commanded calmly, and the three
costumed men moved to block her path.

"Get out of my way," Cassie instructed, "or the
little scandal you had over Shannon Cleary's disappearance will look like a walk in the park."

The men didn't budge, but Alex was instantly at her
side, motioning for the men to leave them, then murmuring, in his most seductive tone, "You're really
mad? I thought you'd laugh, Cassie. Honestly."

"You and Leah can laugh all night about it, just
like you did last night, Alex," she sniffed. "Now, will
you take me back to my car?"

"Last night?" He slipped one arm around her waist
while his free hand tipped her chin so that he could
study her expression. "I don't know what Leah said,
but you definitely took it the wrong way. She and I
didn't laugh about you, or anything else, last night."
Then he pulled her closer and grinned, "Come on,
Cassie, lighten up. You weren't really scared of those
guys, were you?"

Cassie tried not to smile, but his gentle teasing
seemed so affectionate and innocent, and the feel and
smell of him was so masculine and enticing, she felt
herself melting in spite of the last vestiges of anger and
embarrassment. "Who were they?" she demanded
weakly.

"They were getting ready for a reenactment, and

when Leah told me she left you out here alone, I knew what you were doing, and so—"

"And so you thought you'd teach me a lesson?" Her eyes narrowed. "Am I supposed to thank you?"

"Think of it this way," he countered mischievously. "What if I had shown up here with those guys and we couldn't find you anywhere. Then the joke would have been on me, right?"

"It would have served you right," she smiled, amused not so much by that thought as by the knowledge that, had she been successful in her time travel attempt, her uncle would have sent Alex back with her! Then she *really* would have been the one who had the last laugh.

"That's better," he soothed. "You're smiling. You've got a great smile, Cass." He loosened his hold on her waist and added, as though to lessen the intimacy of the moment, "You ditched me."

"No, *you* ditched *me.* You left me with Leah, remember?"

"You knew I wanted you to stay at the museum." His grin returned. "You really conned Leah. She came back to the museum completely impressed with how overcome by emotion you were. When I told her it was just an act. . . . Hey! *Now* what?"

Cassie had turned her back on him and was striding angrily toward the museum. He caught her by the waist and spun her, his face incredulous. "What's wrong?"

"My Uncle Matt is buried here, that's what's wrong. You know, Alex, you don't have a monopoly on tradition and respect for the past. I never got to meet him, and he never met Shannon, but they were both members of my family, and I care about what happened to them."

"You were thinking about your uncle when you saw this place?" Alex touched her cheek. "I'm sorry. I didn't even think about that. I thought you were pretending to grieve for Shannon, and since we both know you think she's alive . . ." He broke off and announced solemnly, "You have as much right to be here, on this spot, alone, as I do. Our ancestors are resting here. I really apologize if I offended you."

Cassie shrugged. "Never mind. It was just a moment, and then, just as you suspected, I was trying to time travel, and . . . ," she smiled reluctantly, "if nothing else, you managed to convince me I'm not really ready for that. If those guys had been legitimate seventeenth-century warriors, I'd have been dead meat."

"Not necessarily. For one thing," his eyes darkened with admiration, "you're beautiful. They wouldn't have killed you."

"Well, it doesn't matter," she blushed, stepping backward in an awkward attempt to save him from himself. "I broke the no-fire rule, and nothing happened."

"Probably because there's not a 'no-fire rule' anymore."

"What?"

Alex shrugged. "It hasn't really been a punishable offense in years. Centuries, in fact. There's always been a kind of taboo—a tradition of respect more than an actual prohibition. Once I read Shannon's letter, I realized that if the press ever got hold of that information, every crackpot time traveler—no offense—from miles around would show up here, so we lifted the ban completely. Now, it's strictly permissible, with no negative association at all."

"Well," she grumbled, "no wonder it didn't work.

Honestly, Alex, you should have told me that yester-day."

"Then you wouldn't have come, and," he stepped closer and admitted, "I'm glad you're here."

"I still would have come," she sighed. "I just would have done a little research first to find another law to break." Fingering a button on his black leather vest, she ventured shyly, "You're a lawyer. You must know something I'm forbidden to do here."

"Out of respect for the dead," he moistened his lips and suggested softly, "I imagine you shouldn't kiss anyone here."

"Probably not." Her hand slid up to his neck and then behind his head, pulling slightly as she raised herself on tiptoe and brought her lips to his. She intended to kiss him lightly, enjoying the feel of their breaths mingling on one another's lips while her fin-gers reintroduced themselves to his luxuriant hair. Instead, to her profound amazement, his arms wrapped tightly around her and he pulled her against himself, propelling the humble kiss into a more erotic realm. When she didn't resist, his tongue began to explore her mouth while his fingers kneaded her back, then his hands roamed wilfully toward her buttocks, where they lifted her further against his hungry torso.

Each of her senses was reeling with gratitude as an explosion of taste, sound, and texture assaulted her. His salty, delicious, inquisitive tongue was rough and ravenous, and together with her own hungry mouth was making sounds so raw and primitive that she was sure she was blushing under her flush of arousal. His jeans were grinding against her through her soft, filmy skirt, and she was acutely aware of the throbbing ache that fueled those movements. She wanted to touch and caress him—his chest, his muscular arms, his strong back—but her hands would not leave the shaggy black mane that had fascinated them from the first moment they'd met. Alex's hands, by contrast, could not seem to settle on one target, but were frantically trying to memorize every accessible inch of her backside and torso.

This groping was bringing her perilously close to groaning aloud when a familiar voice behind them froze Alex's hands with a harshly spoken, *"Couteau!"*

Unable to be so cruelly thwarted without a few seconds to catch her breath, Cassie buried her face against his shirt front, inhaling the strong smell of leather and allowing her fingertips a few precious seconds in his thick mane.

Then Alex muttered, "Leah? What's so important?"

"Your great-uncle is on the telephone for you, Mr. BlackKnife," Leah reported in a haughty tone. "Shall I tell our chief you're too busy to speak to him?"

The chief? Cassie winced for Alex and hastily pulled free. "Go ahead," she urged. "I'll just die of embarrassment right here on the old burial ground. Convenient, right?"

Alex's smile was tortured. "Walk back with me, Cassie, and I'll have someone take you back to your car. Leah? Go on ahead and tell my uncle I'll be right there."

"Whatever you say, Mr. BlackKnife." She whirled and disappeared into the forest.

"I want to talk to you, Cassie," Alex began, "but I have to take this call right away. It could take an hour or more."

"No problem. Luckily, we didn't time travel, right, or you would have missed it?"

"Right."

"Come on." She took his hand and led him toward the path, then flushed slightly when she realized he was uncomfortable with the intimacy. Dropping his hand, she walked in silence at his side until they'd almost reached the museum. Then he stopped and turned to face her and she winced at the confusion in his eyes.

"I'll contact you tomorrow, Cassie," he began. "In the meantime—"

"You don't want me to show up here and embarrass you any more? Don't worry, Alex. I'm as uncomfortable about this as you are."

"I doubt it." He raked his fingers through his thick black hair and repeated, "I'll call you soon, I promise."

"Maybe you shouldn't bother."

"Pardon?"

"You heard me. You don't date Euras, remember?" Cassie's pride was making an indignant comeback. "Just do your job and find my cousin. Stop worrying about your image so much. If your uncle's the chief now, and you're descended from the great Kahnawakee, you've probably got it made, right? As long as you don't date Euras, and don't have any visions, your career should be pretty safe."

"You don't know what you're talking about," Alex countered. "It's more complicated than that."

"Couteau?" Leah scolded from the doorway. "Are you coming or not?"

"I can't keep him waiting anymore, Cass. It's too disrespectful. He's an old man."

"So are you."

Alex chuckled. "I guess I am. Here. . . . " He pulled his car keys from his pocket and pressed them into her hand. "Just leave it parked at the border."

"Are you sure you trust me?"

"Yeah, I'm sure." He studied her fondly for a moment, then turned and sprinted toward the museum.

Cassie shook her head, confused and flattered, then strolled over to his car, imagining that Leah was watching her through the window and turning green at the sight of the privilege she had been given. Once again, the strong scent of the rich leather interior pleased her and she stroked the seat and the steering wheel before turning the ignition. As the engine roared to life she closed her eyes, enjoying the rush of excitement and power. Alex's car was like Alex . . . Alex's name was like Alex . . . and Alex's kiss was like no other kiss she had ever experienced. He was the lover she had waited all these years to meet, and now, through this unfair twist of fate, she was going to have to let him get away. Whether he knew it or not, she sympathized with and understood his plight. Leah's words concerning Alex's birthright rang in her ears as she drove toward the border: *If you're able to respect that, it reflects well on you . . ."

It was true. Her Uncle Matt would have wanted her to respect the Susquehannocks' need for Alex, and, if cousin Shannon was truly a Kahnawakee groupie, as she claimed, she'd undoubtedly also want Cassie to back off, and so she would. It was some comfort knowing that if she really wanted to make him fall for her, she could probably do it. That kiss had been a two-way street—with heavy traffic in both directions—and if Leah hadn't interrupted, they'd probably still be locked in a hot, electrifying clinch, right there on the resting ground of both their ancestors.

"Tacky, Cass," she teased herself, as she retrieved her passport from the sheepish border guard and headed for home to put the finishing touches on the

velvet Christmas stockings that would always remind
of her Alexander Couteau Noir and his delicious forbidden kisses.

When she called Philip Tremaine that night and
told him her story, minus the romantic overtones, she
could tell by his voice he was disappointed despite his
professed disbelief in time travel.

"The problem is, it's not illegal anymore to light a
fire there, so it wasn't a true test," she explained sympathetically. "I still think it's possible, Phil. At least
we haven't ruled it out."

"We? Meaning you and Alex?" Philip teased.
"Why do I suspect I haven't heard the whole story of
your visit to the Susquehannock Protectorate?" Then
his voice grew stern and he added, "I don't want to
ever hear you've been wandering around up there
alone, Cassandra Stone. If Alex is with you, that's one
thing. But don't let your guard down for one minute."

"I won't. I'm not exactly at home in the wilderness,
as we discussed this afternoon. I'll tell you something,
though, Phil—I'm really amazed Shannon knew
about that taboo against lighting a fire. It hasn't been
general knowledge for years."

"Apparently she read a book when she went camping, right before she landed in the hospital. It's called
The Forest Primeval and the author is the leading
expert on John Cutler and Kahnawakee. In fact, right
before she disappeared, Shannon talked to him on the
phone."

"Really?"

"He's a fascinating guy. He lives up in the Six Nations Protectorate, but he lectures here in town every

once in a while. If you'd like to go with me next time he's here, I'll try to arrange it."

"I'd like to talk to him right away. Can you arrange that?"

"If you can get up there, I'm sure he'll see you, Cassie, but if you think he's going to support your time-travel theory, you're wrong."

"But you'll make the arrangements?"

Philip laughed. "Sure, why not? Call me back tomorrow and I'll let you know what I've set up. And Cassie?"

"Hmm?"

"Thanks for calling. And caring. Hearing your voice makes all this a little easier."

"Goodnight, Phil," she sighed. She held on to the receiver for a long moment, wondering if Alex might call. He was probably confused, and vacillating, and she wanted to tell him it was over, to spare him any more wrestling with the dilemma. She also wanted to make sure they kept in touch. Something inside her was insisting that news of Shannon would come in the next few days and she didn't want Alex's dual role in her life to keep him from informing her of her cousin's fate as soon as he learned it.

Despite Cassie's show of confidence to Philip, she no longer believed Shannon was in the seventeenth century. If nothing else, Alex's little joke had illustrated just how ludicrous that theory had been—not to mention the fact that she had learned first hand how frightening just a brush with such an experience could be! Her heart had pounded so hard it had literally hurt, and she had no doubt but that if anyone ever honestly experienced such a phenomenon, they'd either faint dead away or, more likely, have a fatal heart attack from the shock. It no longer seemed like a romantic fantasy to be wished on her cousin, and so Cassie decided to put the theory officially to rest.

Which left Dusty Cumberland. Alex clearly believed that the millionaire jeans designer had kidnapped Shannon—either himself or by hired thug—but the motive seemed hazy. Would a man like Dusty Cumberland really abduct and harm his former fiancée just because she refused to see him or reconcile with him? Or was he so madly in love with her that the abduction was more romantic excess—an attempt to seduce Shannon anew, perhaps on a tropical island, where no attorneys or brothers could interfere?

Cassie could almost identify with Dusty if this were the case. After all, she would love a few weeks alone with Alexander BlackKnife on a deserted island where no conservative Susquehannocks could monitor their affair.

Amused by the fantasy, Cassie reluctantly returned to the immediate problem of finding Shannon. Philip Tremaine had hired private investigators to conduct weeks of surveillance on Dusty Cumberland's ranch and other holdings, but Cassie knew the man was rich enough, and reportedly selfish enough, to find a way to keep a captive under wraps indefinitely. As much as she enjoyed being unconventional, she decided it was time to abandon her time-travel scenario and to adopt the majority theory as her own, turning her full attention to Mr. Dusty Cumberland.

The lights were off in Alexander BlackKnife's office, with only a single candle flame to illuminate the man as he sat on the edge of his neatly organized desk and stared at the full moon through a wide open window. The building was nearly deserted and thus almost eerily quiet, with the hum of the ceiling fan the only perceptible sound. These August nights were too warm and too humid to be spent in an office building, but Alex was determined not to leave until he'd come to terms, philosophically and emotionally, with this growing involvement with Cassandra Stone.

Their kiss that afternoon had staggered him, promising a hot, insatiable style of loving that might one day consume them both. Should that day ever arrive, it would be the beginning of a world-class love affair and the end of his political aspirations.

And she was almost worth it! She was softer, warmer, and sweeter in every sense than any woman he had ever known or imagined. He had wanted to kiss her from the instant they'd first met, but he'd been completely unprepared for the giant step that first kiss had proved to be. Cassie had been amazed by it, too, he knew. All modesty aside, it had been clear to him that she had never responded to a man in quite that way. There had been wonder in her wide blue eyes, as though she had never imagined she could be aroused to such a fevered degree so quickly.

Alex didn't know if Cassandra Stone was a virgin and he didn't care. He knew she had never, ever given herself over to sensation the way she had that afternoon, and that was more than enough for him. Too much, in fact.

He wanted to take her dancing, and watch her sleeping, and wake up with her. He wanted to confide in her, and to make outrageous, provocative suggestions during their lovemaking. He wanted to feel her and taste her and satisfy her, over and over and over . . .

"Couteau?"

He turned his gaze to the open door and nodded slightly. "I didn't know anyone was still here."

"Can I come in?"

"Sure."

Leah's smile was tentative. "Are you still angry with me?"

"Not really. Are *you* still angry?"

"Not really." She crossed to him and patted his arm. "You have to forget her, you know."

"Do I?" His dark eyes turned to challenge hers. "I wouldn't be the first Council Adviser to become involved with a Eura, you know. It's not that uncommon."

"True. There are several who have even married them. But those advisers were content to remain advisers forever. Are you?"

He shrugged, then admitted, "No, I'm not."

"You *need* the Conservative vote. The Modernists will back you no matter what, but not the Conservatives. They still look with disfavor on your choice of Harvard."

"Don't remind me." He tried for a confident smile. "This whole conversation is premature, Leah. I just met her."

"If it were any other Eura, I'd agree. But she's Shannon Cleary's cousin, and even a brief affair would attract media attention and encourage insulting speculation about the nature of your interest in her."

"Damn," Alex groaned, "you're right. Here I've been worried about the Conservatives' reaction, but I never considered the publicity in the Commonwealth. Shannon Cleary's gorgeous cousin, seduced by a Susquehannock . . ."

"Cassandra Stone would be embarrassed, and

you'd be ruined. What's worse, you'd bring dishonor on every Susquehannock male. Our enemies will enjoy mischaracterizing it, Couteau. They'll say our men can't keep their hands off these yellow-haired women."

"That's so ridiculous!"

"Our credibility is already strained," she reminded him. "With each passing day, it seems more likely than not that Shannon Cleary met with foul play at the hands of one of our men, or, as the press enjoys insinuating, a *group* of our men."

Alex winced, remembering his anger over the luridly explicit tabloid scenarios. Leah was right—any hint of scandal or suggestion of impropriety could be monumentally harmful. He had been so busy worrying about his own career that he had completely overlooked the danger to his people's image. Such selfishness and lack of vision was unacceptable, whether or not he ever became chief.

Leah's dark eyes had been drawn to the full moon and she sighed with undefined longing. "I didn't tell our chief what I saw this afternoon. If I had told him, he'd have taken you off the investigation."

"I appreciate your loyalty, Leah."

"I share your dream, remember?" Her tone rebuked him with tender affection. "Ever since we were children, we've hoped you'd be chief one day. I've wanted that, not only for your sake, but for the sake of our people. You are Couteau Noir."

"It's just a nickname, Leah."

"It's a destiny. Your grandmother told us so."

He smiled ruefully. "I remember. She was so sure."

"And, until yesterday, *you* were sure." Leah touched his cheek. "I still believe it in my heart."

"Thanks." He shrugged onto his feet. "Come on, I'll walk you home."

They walked in companionable silence until Alex paused before an elegant glass display case. "It's back?"

"It arrived late this afternoon. You were in your office . . . I didn't want to disturb you."

It was only an unfinished seventeenth-century ceremonial belt, but Alex never tired of studying it, knowing that it had been touched by the Visionary's hand and knowing further that it reflected the Visionary's simple, priceless legacy to the native peoples of North America. Depicted were two male figures, standing at opposite ends of a rainbow. Over the head of the first male was a dark circle, haloed in white. Over the head of the second was a blazing sun. Although the second figure's body had not been completed, his face was identical to that of the first man.

The identical faces were simple, and might have been any two Susquehannock males, but everyone knew the truth—that Kahnawakee's grandmother had begun weaving those porcupine quills on the night the Visionary was born under an eclipse. The belt had never been completed. The Susquehannock art of quill and shell embroidery had disappeared during this period of time, and so the assumption was that the old woman had been the last to remember the technique and had passed away before finishing the work. The elders of the nation fervently believed that the first man in the depiction was the Visionary and the second was his spiritual heir.

Kahnawakee's grandmother had designed the belt. Generations of Susquehannocks had preserved it. And then, more than three hundred years later, Alexander BlackKnife's grandmother had whispered to her handsome grandson that *he* was the figure shown with the Visionary.

"That could be you, Couteau."

Alex nodded without taking his eyes from the display.

"If our chief heard you were involved with Cassandra Stone," Leah continued stubbornly, "your chances would be ruined."

"I told my uncle all about it this afternoon."

"What?" Recovering her equilibrium, Leah laughed lightly and demanded, "What did he say, Couteau?"

"He said it sounded like I had a decision to make." Alex's tone was wistful. "He gave me until the end of the week, when he returns from Onondaga." Dragging his gaze from the heirloom, he added quietly, "I guess there was never really any doubt, was there?"

"No, Couteau," Leah sighed. "There was never any doubt at all. And, for whatever it's worth," she linked her arm through his, "I'm proud of you. You've done an amazing job managing all of these stresses and complications. Your grandmother would be proud, and I believe with all my heart that Kahnawakee would be proud of you, too."

"No," Alex murmured, leading her through the doorway and into the muggy August night, "he would not be proud of me today. But one day . . ." *One day,* he vowed silently, *I will be worthy of the name Couteau Noir.*

Cassie chewed her lip nervously as she studied the exterior of the *Dustees* Jeans headquarters in Dallas. It was an atrociously gaudy building, with copper-toned windows and garish exterior murals of cowhands and bison locked in exaggerated battle. "If he's holding poor Shannon here, of all places, that's *really* cruel," she quipped to herself as she summoned the courage to enter and demand an audience with the millionaire owner and chairman of the board.

When she caught a glimpse of herself in one of the windows, she couldn't help but smile, impressed, as she had been that morning, by the resemblance to Shannon she had been able to create. The jeans had been a key feature, of course, but when she had paired them with Shannon's trademark white sleeveless leotard, the effect had been almost eerie. Not that anyone would be fooled for long, of course. Shannon was taller, with a slightly leaner face and straight hair to her waist. Still, when Cassie had positioned herself in front of the full-length mirror in her bedroom, striking the pose from the framed advertisement for Dustees jeans, she had actually gasped aloud.

Now, as she readjusted the long, braided hairpiece she had secured amid her own blond curls, smoothing the whole into an amazingly natural-looking effect— or not so amazing, she reminded herself, considering the hairpiece was actually Cassie's own shorn mane, which she had saved to use in an upcoming weaving project—she tried to imitate Shannon's come-hither smile, then giggled nervously. Shannon had always managed to appear sophisticated yet natural in her photos, whereas her cousin seemed capable of appearing mischievous at best. Mischievousness would have to do, she decided, heading for the main entrance.

She could not have anticipated the reaction of the various employees, who stared and pointed and murmured aloud, clearly stunned by the resemblance to the missing model. To further confuse the situation, giant blown-up photographs of Shannon decorated every interior wall, causing even uninformed visitors to stare at the pretty blonde who was determined to stride with casual confidence through the crowded reception area. By the time she'd reached the bank of elevators, her cheeks were burning from the attention. She counted to ten and breathed deeply and slowly as she studied the directory until she found Dusty Cumberland's office, which, predictably, occupied the entire top floor. As Cassie slipped into the first available elevator, she blushed again to realize that, while people were openly studying her, no one wanted to get close enough to ride with her.

By the time she reached the top, she had collected her thoughts and was ready for any conceivable confrontation. Hopefully, Cumberland would be amazed by the resemblance and would blurt out a confession, along with a detailed description of the place where an unharmed Shannon could be found. At worst, however, this would be a dead end, and so Cassie convinced herself that her nervousness was ridiculous and once again managed a confident demeanor as she exited the elevator and approached the desk of a formidable-appearing woman.

"I'd like to see Mr. Cumberland, please."

The woman's haughty gaze swept over the long jeaned legs, then up to the clear, familiar blue eyes, but she didn't seem the least bit confused. "Do you have an appointment?"

"He'll want to see me." Cassie bit back a smile of pride over this line, which she had composed on the airplane and which sounded like something Leah Eagle might say.

The woman's eyebrow arched. "You're probably right. Have a seat, won't you, Miss . . . ?"

"Stone. I'm Cassandra Stone. I'm Shannon Cleary's cousin."

"Have a seat, Miss Stone. Or you might enjoy the photo gallery while you wait." The woman gestured to a long hall lined with framed black-and-white photographs of Shannon, then she hurried through a solid door, leaving Cassie alone with the bizarre collection of pictures.

Either he really loved Shannon, she thought warily, as she studied the endless series of tributes, *or he's really a psycho-obsessive nut and I should get out of here fast!* Even the receptionist's role seemed eerie— as though the woman knew something Cassie should know before she walked through that door into that obsessed man's office.

"Miss Stone? Mr. Cumberland will see you now."

Thanks for nothing, Cassie wanted to grumble, but instead, she smiled and sailed past the woman and into a huge, opulent office, with windows on three walls and a collection of trophies, awards, and liquor bottles on the fourth. The trophies appeared to revolve around rodeo events, and the man who sat behind the desk, grinning from ear to ear, clearly fancied himself a cowboy, although Cassie suspected most true western heroes removed their hats for office work, at least in the presence of their departed girl-friend's female cousin.

He continued to grin, not bothering to speak, and so Cassie took a deep breath, walked to within a foot of the desk, and extended her hand. "Thanks for seeing me, Mr. Cumberland. I'm Shannon's cousin."

Cumberland pushed his chair back noisily and stood tall and straight, his hands on his hips and the grin still wide across his mouth. He had light brown, short-cropped hair and leathery skin, with pale-blue eyes that twinkled with unmistakable lust, although Cassie wasn't convinced it was lust of the sexual variety. He wanted something insatiably, that much was obvious. But what?

He was shaking his head, ignoring her outstretched hand. "Damn," he announced finally, "you look good."

"Thanks," she blushed. "I came here to talk to you about Shannon."

"I'll just bet you did," he laughed. "You're shorter than she was. About," his eyes ran along her form avidly, "two inches?"

"Two and a half," Cassie admitted. "But . . ."

"Turn around."

"Pardon?"

"Turn around. Let me see those hindquarters."

Which answers my first question, Cassie thought to herself uneasily. *This guy is definitely not in mourning.*

When she didn't comply with his request, he walked around behind her and studied her openly, nodding his approval. "I'll say this for you, Cassandra Stone," he drawled. "You look great in my jeans."

"Well, that's a relief." She was trying not to lose her temper. "Listen, Mr. Cumberland . . ."

"Call me Dusty." His eyes were twinkling again. "Damn, you're sexy. Shannie could have taken a few lessons from you."

"Pardon?"

"This could be the advertising coup of the decade," he continued eagerly. "First, Shannie drops off the face of the earth—that increased our sales by fifteen percent—then you sashay in here with that cute little behind . . ."

"I can't *believe* you're talking like this," Cassie interrupted, her anger flaring through her amazement. "You were engaged to her!"

"That was personal. This is business. Don't you want to be rich, Sunshine?"

"You think I came here for a *job?*"

"Sure. You're technically too short to be a model, but it doesn't really matter. You're Shannon Cleary's cousin, and you're sexy as hell, and you'll sell jeans, and we'll both be rolling in money."

Cassie's eyes flashed. "Is that all you care about? I thought you were obsessed with *her!* Is it only the money?"

"The money?" He shrugged. "I've got more than I need. You know what I like?" He moved closer and growled, "I like to see them shaking their heads and saying everything Dusty Cumberland touches turns to gold. Like they can't figure out how an uneducated cowboy like me can run circles around them and their fancy advertising companies and fussy French designers." He fingered her braid and murmured, "Everything I touch *does* turn to gold, Sunshine. How'd you like to turn gold for Dusty?"

"Is that what happened to Shannon?" Cassie gasped, yanking her hair from his hand. "Did you . . . did you kidnap her as part of some stupid advertising gimmick?" Her stomach was cramping with disgust. "Alex was right! You're despicable, and if you've harmed one hair on her head, I'll . . . I'll . . ."

"Alex?" Cumberland's grin faded. "You're talking about BlackKnife? He told you I kidnapped Shannie?" His face turned a dangerous shade of red and he roared, "That smartass just bought himself a defamation suit!"

Cassie winced. "Defamation?"

"He can't bad-mouth me and get away with it," the angry man retorted. "That Susquehannock smart-ass slandered me and it's gonna cost him. And," his eyes narrowed, "as for you . . ." He edged closer and leered, "You're a wild little thing, I'll say that for you. I could make you rich, but you're a little too feisty for me. If Shannie was here, she'd tell you I like my fillies tame, so . . . go home to your pottery and your fancy leather moccasins." When Cassie's eyes widened, he chuckled. "You're surprised? I know *all about you,* Cassandra Stone. My men checked you out real thoroughly. Would you like to see the surveillance pictures? They made my mouth water."

"You're disgusting!"

"I've got pictures of you in the shower, and in all those pretty little dresses, and your nightie, but," he sighed in mock adoration, "I always wanted to see you in my *Dustees.* You should wear them every day. That behind of yours is too pretty to be lost in all those skirts you wear."

"Did you kidnap Shannon to sell your stupid jeans?" Cassie whispered. "Just tell us where she is— please? You've had your publicity—"

"If I had Shannie," he taunted, "why would I be drooling over you?"

"If you ever loved her . . ." The words died on Cassie's lips. Of course he'd never loved Shannon! He'd used her, and when she was no longer useful . . . Cassie's mind was reeling as she backed slowly toward the door.

"Adios, Sunshine," he called after her. "Tell Black-Knife I'll see him in court. Tell him to bring his checkbook."

It's true, she told herself, as she darted into the

elevator and punched frantically at the lobby button—*you have to warn Alex he's going to get sued because of you,* she wiped angrily at a flood of hot tears, *you have to tell him poor Shannon is dead.*

Chapter Four

She wept for Shannon, whose life had been so unfairly dominated by disrespectful, morally bankrupt bullies. The horror story had begun even before Shannon was born, when her mother's angry ex-husband had returned to his former home with a pistol, taking the life of second husband Matthew Cleary.

Cassie remembered now how shocked she'd been when, soon after Shannon's disappearance, she'd learned that the missing model from the headlines was her first cousin and the daughter of her Uncle Matt, for whom she had developed so intense an affection during childhood despite the fact that Matt Cleary was no longer alive. Cassie's mother had seemed relieved finally to tell the story to her daughter, and she had railed anew at the tragic loss of her wonderful brother.

According to Cassie's mother, Shannon's Grandma Cleary had visited Shannon's mother after the murder, offering condolences and help with the grandchild who was on the way. Lois Tremaine Cleary had rebuffed those overtures, insisting that she never wanted the baby to know that her father had been killed by her half-siblings' father for fear of family disharmony. She had then stated quite categorically that the coming baby was "the lucky one" because she had never met Matt and therefore wouldn't miss him, unlike her other two children, who were now deprived forever of the love of their father, who'd been convicted of murder and imprisoned.

Lois Cleary's defensive, hostile attitude had prevented any real contact with baby Shannon, and while the extended Cleary family had kept a watchful eye, they'd also kept their distance. Gifts were forbidden by Lois; she believed her other children would feel undeserving should Shannon be given such "unfair" advantage. As Shannon grew into a beautiful young woman with positive goals and healthy interests, the Clearys had reluctantly remained banished from her life.

"First that murderer kept her from having a father, or a decent chance at a loving childhood, then Dusty Cumberland took over," Cassie fumed through her tears, "controlling and exploiting her and then, when she wouldn't go along with him anymore, killing her for the publicity! It's so sick! No wonder poor Shannon dreamed herself a hero like John Cutler to fall in love with. If only she really could have met him. Or if only *I* had known! I'd have helped her, and even Alex would've helped her, that day in the hospital, if only he'd realized how serious it all was."

Now it was too late. Shannon had died as part of a macabre publicity stunt, and Cassie could only hope that the end had been swift and painless. Dusty Cumberland would never be punished for his crime, and a cloud of suspicion would hang over the Susquehannock Nation for years to come. The thought that Cassie might inadvertently have destroyed Alexander BlackKnife's chances to lead that nation into renewed glory one day was a painful one. He was a born chief, from his tall, straight stance to his dedicated outlook to his intelligent, articulate manner. And now, amid his other challenges, he had a defamation suit on his hands.

She was glad to have her sunglasses to shield her swollen eyes when she again approached the border station with her passport in hand. This time, Alex had apparently left word that she was to be brought immediately to his office and so she was respectfully hustled into the security guard's pickup truck for the drive across the bridge to the village. According to the driver, Alex had been trying to reach her, checking with the border station all day long. The information saddened her. If there had been the slimmest of chances that a relationship might have evolved from all this chaos, that chance had probably been destroyed by her reckless visit to Dusty Cumberland's office.

Alex was waiting alongside his Mustang in the parking lot on the outskirts of the village when they arrived, and Cassie moistened her lips as she studied his appearance. Apparently he had been exercising. In place of the usual jeans and vest he wore scarlet jogging shorts and a cropped white T-shirt, the muscles of his arms and legs rippling and glistening in the hot August sun. His thick black mane was damp and wavy, and as he watched her alight, he raked his fingers through it as though simultaneously grooming and calming himself in anticipation of their meeting.

Cassie remembered her own altered appearance, à la Shannon's wardrobe, and smiled sheepishly. "Hi, Alex. Were you working out?"

"Why are you dressed like your cousin?" His eyes

were sweeping over her with keen, not necessarily approving, interest.

"It's a long story." She gestured toward a wooded trail. "Maybe we should walk? You look like you need to cool down, and," she tried for a charming smile, "after you hear what I have to say, you may *really* need to cool down."

Alex chuckled. "I almost hate to ask what that means. Come on." He took her elbow and urged her toward the path. "I'm glad you're here, Cassie. I've been trying to reach you on the phone all day. I was going to come over to your place tonight so we could talk."

She sighed, wishing they could just walk and talk like this for hours, with no painful realities to come between them, but it simply could not be. There was Shannon's death, all but confirmed, and the lawsuit, all but filed . . .

"Listen, Alex." She paused in the shade of a giant, black-barked tree and faced him soberly. "Did you study defamation at Harvard?"

"Defamation?"

"Like, slander?"

His eyes darkened. "Someone's already been talking about us?"

"Us?" She was momentarily distracted by the suggestion that they might be thought of as an "us," then she rallied and explained, "No, not us. Dusty Cumberland's going to sue you, and it's my fault. I'm sorry, but," her voice trembled slightly, "I have even worse news. Shannon's really dead. He killed her, just like you suspected."

"Like I . . . ?" Alex shook his head. "What makes you think he killed her? And why would he sue me?"

"I went to his office—"

"What?" He stared, then grabbed her and pulled her against his chest. "Are you crazy?" he murmured, stroking her curls. "That man's dangerous, Cassie. What were you thinking?"

"I was thinking he might be holding Shannon until she agreed to marry him, or something romantically stupid like that," she admitted, relaxing easily against his damp chest. "But the truth is so ugly, Alex." She hesitated, inhaling the masculine scent of honest perspiration, then sighed, "All he ever cared about was selling blue jeans."

"And you went there, dressed like Shannon? He could have grabbed you, too, Cassie." He forced her face up toward his own and scolded lovingly, "First you're ready to time travel back to the seventeenth century, where you wouldn't last five minutes, and then you go to that egomaniac's office alone. I'm afraid to let you out of my sight."

She gazed into the dark depths of his admiring eyes and smiled in relief. "You're not angry? About the lawsuit?"

"Cumberland has the finest lawyers in New Texas working for him. They'll talk him out of that lawsuit. Truth is a defense to a defamation action, Cass, and Cumberland's not exactly a sympathetic character. If it came down to a contest of credibility between you and him on the witness stand, they'd lose their suit and he'd probably be arrested for murder on the spot."

"Thank heavens."

"So?" He stroked her cheek. "Any more crazy theories I should be worrying about?"

"Just one," she admitted.

Alex nodded. "About us? I know. We could be great together, Cassie, but . . ." He urged her toward a fallen log and sat her on it, positioning himself directly in front of her, his arms folded across his chest. "I need to be perfectly honest with you now."

"We don't have to go over all of this again, Alex," she protested, shifting uncomfortably. "I'm a Eura. I'm bad for your career."

"Forget my career. I think," he lowered himself to one knee and took her hand, "I could risk my career for you."

"Alex—"

"I've had more fun with you these last few days . . . more fun and more exhilaration, and definitely more . . . stimulation, shall we say . . .? than I can ever remember. You keep surprising me, and enticing me, and distracting me, and," he flushed slightly, "I want to relax and enjoy you, and this, but I can't. You're Shannon's cousin, and the world thinks she's been abducted by a Susquehannock. Somehow, the papers would see our involvement as confirmation of this . . . this ludicrous concept that we're somehow more primitive, and that we lust after pretty blondes . . ."

"You don't have to explain," Cassie murmured, remembering the offensive media hype that had saturated the commonwealth during the first month or so after Shannon's disappearance. While politicians and editors had decried the irresponsibility and inaccuracies of the coverage, the mere fact that such headlines could grab rather than offend readers had been an uncomfortable revelation to Cassie, and she could only imagine how shocking and repugnant it had been to Alex. They could never, *never* allow their attraction to one another to be exploited in such a manner and with so insulting and degrading a result.

Alex seemed to read the agreement in her eyes. "I meant what I said, Cassie. If it were just my career, I'd deal with it somehow. I honestly think," he added with a rueful smile, "even the Conservatives among my people would eventually find you irresistible, assuming this went that far, and," he stroked her hand, "I think it would. You're the most intriguing, unpredictable woman I've ever known. I'll never forget these last few days." His smile widened to a grin. "I'll especially never forget the look on your face when you thought you'd traveled to the seventeenth century and those warriors were about to pounce on you." He broke off, laughing aloud.

Cassie pulled her hand free and jumped to her feet. "We were having a tender moment. Don't ruin it by mocking me."

"I'd never do that, Cassie." He stood to face her. "I want you to know this wasn't just another flirtation. This was an important and unforgettable part of my life."

"Thanks, Alex." She basked in the bittersweet aura of his position. "What will you do now? Are you going to line up with the Conservatives? I've heard they still don't even drive cars or ride planes."

"They reject all of that as dilution of the spirit. They want to protect our birthright, which is inextricably bound up with the land we live on. That's why we call our nations 'protectorates.' With our privilege comes the responsibility to prevent misuse." Alex's tone was solemn. "Kahnawakee was a true visionary. He preached two concepts—unity of the nations, and resistance to Euro-culture. Both were valid in his day, and certainly unity will always be the key, but these days our ability to operate effectively in the marketplace and the geopolitical theater is hampered by our resistance to certain technological and educational opportunities."

"Like Harvard?" Cassie sympathized. "Were you criticized for that?"

He nodded. "I honestly believe it made me more valuable to my nation and to UNAP, but it was perceived by some as disloyal, even though the Visionary stressed flexibility and intelligence." He smiled apologetically. "It's a big mess. Some of the Pacific Protectorates have threatened to withdraw from UNAP because they think our organization is too clumsy and slow-moving for today's world, and I agree. So do the other Modernists. But recent events—especially the publicity over Shannon—have forced me to rethink all of that."

"Kahnawakee's most trusted adviser was John Cutler, and he was born in Europe, right? So your Visionary must have been flexible, just like you said." Cassie could feel the pain and confusion in his soul and wished she had paid more attention during history and political science classes, when all of these issues had seemed so remote and academic. "Remember Shannon's delusion?" she sighed. "She said history once went wrong and there was genocide and greed that wiped out the Protectorates, right? It seems so ludicrous, but maybe she was just politically astute enough to realize how fragile the balance of power is in the world. If you're too inflexible, you become obsolete. If you're too flexible, you lose your cultural identity. It's a fine line."

"Well put, Cassie. Like I said," his hands moved to her waist and began to knead her gently, "I think even the Conservatives would find you irresistible. You're so intuitive and sincere."

"Am I?" she murmured, drawn to the heat in his hands and his voice.

"Absolutely. You really care about what happens, don't you?"

"Most people do, Alex. Don't forget that." Her own voice was now a purr. "Don't let a few thoughtless headlines make you bitter."

"If I'm bitter," he whispered, leaning his head down to run his rough tongue over her moist, slightly parted lips, "it's because those headlines are keeping me from making love to you, Cassandra Stone, when it's all I really want to do."

"Alex—" She stepped fully into him, heady with the memory of their first kiss, wanting this one to be its exact duplicate in every detail except perhaps the conclusion. Alex clearly had other ideas. His hand moved from her waist up over her breast, cupping it through the thin fabric of her leotard and fondling it until her nipple was hard with appreciative need. Only then did he truly kiss her, and his mouth's hunger made her gasp with delight.

Her own hands had found his hair and they were greedily indulging themselves while she moved against him, struggling to acquaint herself with every smooth, hard surface and every tantalizing bulge. Then she raked her fingernails gently over his scalp and down onto his neck, then down his back, encouraged by the slight groan of pleasure resonating deep in his throat. Slipping her hand under his shirt, she caressed his tightly muscled chest adoringly while her tongue sparred with his in rough, playful competition.

The sounds and sensations were like a drug, and she longed to surrender completely to the effect but dared not. They needed to stop this. It was time to walk away.

"Alex," she pleaded softly. "We have to stop."

"No." His rough hand cupped her chin and he

stared with desperation into her sympathetic eyes. "This can't be wrong, Cassie. It feels too right."

"It feels right now, but what about tomorrow? I won't make this mistake with you, Alex. We've known each other three days. We can say goodbye now, and we can imagine how great things might have been, but there's really nothing between us yet but a few wonderful kisses and some strong undercurrents. This isn't love, Alex, it's just infatuation, right? It's got incredible potential . . ." she blushed at the unintended throaty purr, "but we can still walk away from it. If we don't stop now . . ."

"You're right." He shook his head in rueful appreciation. "My investigator called you eccentric, and you're definitely not conventional, but sometimes you're so connected." He cleared his throat. "Can I ask you something?"

"Sure."

"Why are you growing those neat rows of weeds in your yard?"

Cassie ached with desire for him at that moment, aroused by his determination, touched by his confusion, and acutely conscious of his untapped strength. The charisma that had prompted comparisons with his ancestor Kahnawakee was never more evident than when he was striving for understanding and seeking the truth. It tortured her to realize that the very quality that drew her to him would always keep them apart, yet somehow she would learn to accept that and to be grateful for this momentary brush with so fine and rare a man.

She had just insisted this wasn't love, but somehow, she knew she had been wrong. This feeling was tenuous and fragile, and yes, they could walk away from it, but it was love nevertheless, and she knew that that love was shining in her eyes as she answered his seemingly simple question. "I extract dyes from those weeds, Alex, for my weaving and batiking. There are certain subtle, evocative shades of green and yellow that you can get only from a weed."

"I knew you had a good reason. I kept trying to imagine what it could be."

"You have to trust beyond what you know," she murmured. "You have to believe there's an explanation for things, and you have to relax and wait for the time when the explanation can make sense to you. When I was a little girl, my parents used to try to explain things to me—things like thunder and gravity and bread rising—and sometimes I didn't want to hear it. I just wanted to trust, and enjoy. I think you need to learn to enjoy that kind of . . . childishness."

"Vision," he whispered. "That's what you're really saying, aren't you? You're telling me I can have vision if I just. . . . What?"

"Just trust it to come to you when the time is right. You're going to be phenomenal, Alex. You're going to make such a difference in the world. It takes my breath away just thinking about it." When he simply stared in grateful silence, she added softly, "Thanks for trying to find Shannon. I think she's dead, Alex, and I don't think she'd want you to search forever. Don't be afraid to take care of your career. In your case, it's not a selfish tactic, it's a very generous one. I can see that, and it makes me feel good."

He nodded. "You're amazing, Cassie. I'll never forget you. Now," his tone grew wistful, "I guess I should drive you back to the border."

The thought of riding beside him in silence, or, worse, making small talk with him, saddened her. "Could you go and call one of the escorts?" she suggested carefully. "I'd like a few minutes alone here, and then I'll be ready to go home."

"I understand. Here." Again he pressed his car keys into her palm. "Just leave it at the border like you did before. I have to go and shower and change, then I'll hitch a ride down and pick it up. How's that?" He backed away and studied her solemnly. "It's not just a physical thing, you know, Cassie, although you are incredibly pretty. It's more than that."

She lowered her gaze to the ground, uncomfortable with the strong desire in his eyes. It was so hopeless, and yet if she wanted, she could move into his arms and he would make love to her. The temptation was almost irresistible despite the futility. "You'd better go and shower, Alex. If you ever get any definite information on Shannon . . ." She stopped herself grimly, suspecting herself of having an ulterior motive. "Just tell Philip Tremaine and he'll fill me in."

"So this is goodbye."

"Right."

"There's a present for you in the trunk of my car. Be sure to get it before you leave."

"A present?" She raised her eyes and was intrigued by his uncertain smile. "For me?"

"Enjoy it, and if you ever need anything, call me, okay?"

"Thanks, Alex."

"And stay away from Dusty Cumberland."

"Don't worry." She smiled and countered, "You stay away from him, too. He doesn't like you, and he's mean."

"Don't worry about me," he chuckled, "I think I'd love a good fight right now. I don't handle frustration well." He stepped forward and waited, as though for permission.

Cassie blushed, then raised herself on her tiptoes and brushed her lips gently over his. His eyes widened and he murmured, "The day we met . . . ? That wasn't the stocking you touched me with?"

She smiled at the childlike amazement in his tone. "Are you sure you really want to know?"

"I already do. Thanks, Cassie. Take care." His eyes swept over her one final time and he turned and disappeared down the trail.

Cassie returned to her seat on the fallen log and picked at the rough bark, wondering if Alex would ever contact her again. It would be a mistake, of course, but he was only human, and he was entitled to err occasionally, and so it seemed only fair that he might err with her. If only they could escape together to that deserted tropical island, where they could indulge their love without fear of reporters or rumors.

And then what? she chastised herself. *Then you'd fall deeper and deeper in love, and it would hurt ten times worse when Alex had to come back to be chief and you had to come back to be alone. Just be glad it didn't go any further than this.*

Tucking a strip of the bark into her purse for use in some unknown future project, she jumped to her feet.

Stop feeling sorry for yourself, Cassandra Stone. Be glad you have a chance to meet someone else and fall in love—really in love—again. Remember what happened to Shannon, and just be glad to be alive.

Alex had mentioned a gift, and she couldn't help but wonder what a man in love buys for a woman he's about to dump. Hurrying toward the parking lot, she fought a twinge of disappointment at not catching a glimpse of him in the distance, then unlocked the trunk of the Mustang. Amid books and lacrosse equipment she found a package wrapped in bright-

blue tissue paper and secured by tape that also held a
wilted white rose in place.

When she tore the wrapper away and saw the supple handcrafted moccasins, a stab of longing shot
through her for the man who could have remembered
so small and perfect a detail. Alex had apparently
gone to his detective's jealous wife and charmed these
from her, knowing that they would mean more to
Cassie than flowers or jewels. The workmanship was
intricate and meticulous, with a layer of soft sheep-
skin to cushion the innersole and an outer layer of
rich white buckskin to cradle the foot. Slipping her
tennis shoes from her feet and into her bulging purse,
she laced the moccasins up around her ankles and
cooed with appreciation at the comfortable fit.

"I could walk for miles in these," she sighed aloud,
and it seemed suddenly to be a perfect ending to this
emotion-laden day. She would walk back to the border along the cool, shady trail, allowing her heart time
to grieve for Shannon, and to ache for the aborted
affair with Alex, and to plan for the days and months
ahead that she would appreciate more fully because of
these twin losses.

Alex stepped out of a cold, punishing shower and
dried himself briskly with a thick cotton towel. It was
time to put his feelings for Cassie Stone aside. Perhaps
it was even time to put the search for Shannon Cleary
aside, although in his heart he didn't believe even a
bully like Cumberland could actually have murdered
so sweet and innocent a young woman. It still seemed
most likely that Shannon was being held against her
will, but hadn't he done everything he could legally do
to remedy that, without success?

Pulling on his jeans, and then socks and running shoes, he wondered if there wasn't something he could do, after all. If he followed Cassie's advice and looked beyond the obvious, perhaps he could find Shannon there. Not only would that be personally rewarding, and not only would it clear his people's name; it would bring a beautiful smile of gratitude to Cassie Stone's incredibly unforgettable face.

"Except you're supposed to be forgetting her anyway," he growled aloud. "Just let it go, Couteau." He stood himself before a full-length mirror and studied his image critically. He looked like the Visionary, but he had no vision. In the same sense, he carried the name "Couteau Noir" but had not yet proved himself worthy of it.

In the days of Kahnawakee, a warrior earned his reputation in physical battle as well as in council. Alex wondered if that was what was lacking in his background. Three years at Harvard Law School were all well and good, but had he ever been in a brutal knife fight or even a no-holds-barred wrestling match?

"In the old days, you would have had to be strong enough to run the gauntlet if the need arose," he reminded himself sternly. "Today, just a simple ten-mile run had you drenched in sweat! Lifting weights and running may keep you in courtroom fighting shape, but as a warrior, could you have cut it?"

His eyes traveled over his broad bare chest and tapered hips and he was displeased with what he saw. A hard, well-toned body, yes, but without a blemish or scar to speak of true testing. Reaching into his footlocker, he located a small pouch filled with tubes of ceremonial paint, and, with growing fervor, began to streak his chest and face with white, red, and black until his persona as a physically fit attorney had

receded completely, replaced by a lean-bodied, cold-
eyed, ruthless warrior, ready and eager for battle. It
was a side of himself he had neglected for too long. It
was a part of his reality that would help keep thoughts
of Cassandra Stone from interfering with his destiny.

   The moccasins had proved to be more comfortable
in appearance than in actuality, and forty-five minutes into her hike, Cassie was limping and wincing
and cursing herself for having a little too much "vision" and not enough common sense. Not only was
she blistered and weary, she was lost. Having blithely
assumed the trail would parallel the road, so that she
could abandon her walk should the need arise, she
was now hopelessly thwarted. Retracing her steps
seemed impossible, given the fact that the path had
forked at endless points, which Cassie had found initially charming and eventually confusing. Now she
was downright uneasy. Sunset was less than three
hours away, she had no food in her purse, and her
cousin had met with foul play in these very woods,
wearing suspiciously similar clothing.
   Because Dusty Cumberland kidnapped her, she reminded herself without conviction. *Of course, if he
knew you were here, he'd do it to you, too, for the
publicity coup. Anyway, when Alex finds his car in the
parking lot, he'll come looking for you. Maybe this is a
sign that destiny wants to bring you together again.*
Perching precariously on a low, narrow branch, she
pulled off the moccasins and tried to cram her swollen
feet back into her Shannonesque white canvas tennis
shoes, but it was woefully impossible. Just as she was
about to berate herself for being the kind of woman
to whom men gave shoes instead of jewels, she heard

a slight rustle in the leaves behind her, followed by an unmistakable, blood-chilling rattle, and she froze in disbelief, hoping without hope that it wasn't a snake—which she knew it *was*—or that Alex was nearby with a gun—which she knew he was *not*. She knew she shouldn't budge, much less turn fully around, but could not bear to sit and be attacked without having even faced her attacker. She shifted ever so slightly, and as she did, the angry rattle sounded its final warning. With no wish to feel the fangs sink into her delicate skin or the poison course through her terrified body, Cassandra Stone surrendered herself into a dead faint.

Alexander BlackKnife was surrounded by nothingness. He was still standing, as he had stood before the mirror in his bedroom, but the mirror was gone and his room was gone and all else that he held familiar or permanent was gone, replaced by an all-encompassing sensation of belonging that made no sense, given the fact that there was nothing in this vacuum to which anyone *could* belong. The fact that his footing was sure bewildered him—on what could he possibly be standing?—yet even more bewildering was the fact that he was completely unafraid. His heartbeat was steady, his breathing regular, and his curiosity, while piqued, was hardly running rampant. He was somehow enjoying this warm, gentle void. There was no one there, and yet, in a strange sense, it was alive with comfort and camaraderie, as though spiritually rich with goodwill and awareness. And there was a voice, which was a blend of countless loving voices, and the voice told him simply to endure, despite the evils that might seem to befall him, and to be strong, despite the temptations that might soon choose to lure him.

"Stand tall, Couteau," the voice coaxed.

"I will," he responded silently, and the nothingness receded, and once again he felt the earth beneath his feet. For the briefest of moments he believed he had had a vision—the greatest honor and privilege that could come to a man, and the experience he had so fervently craved—but his eyes told him it was not so. His eyes told him more than he wanted to know and he stared, wishing for a moment that he could refuse this challenge. Then he reminded himself of his vow to "stand tall," and so he straightened to a proud, confident stance that belied his confusion at the sight of nine foreign warriors, armed with knives and dressed in scant breechcloths and fringed leggings over sturdy moccasins.

Chapter Five

From the look in the warriors' widened eyes, Alex knew they had witnessed his materialization out of nothingness and that their hearts were pounding as surely as his own. When their stocky leader stepped forward, however, he managed to follow Alex's lead and to appear unruffled, demanding imperiously, "You are the brother of Kahnawakee? You challenge us without cause or weapons?"

The man had spoken in an outdated Iroquoian dialect which only loosely paralleled modern Susquehannock. Alex's mind raced, searching for a response that would somehow counterbalance the image he knew he was projecting. After all, he had decorated himself in the way of one who is seeking battle with his enemies—the streaks of paint on his face and chest would be perceived as nothing less than raw insults to these warriors—and yet he was unarmed. The fact that these men had noticed his physical resemblance to a fine statesman like Kahnawakee was only vaguely reassuring. Depending upon the time period into which Alex had been cast—and he knew, without pausing to dwell upon the knowledge, that he was not in his own time—his association with

the Visionary could be seen as an asset or, more likely,
a distinct disadvantage. It had taken years for the
various nations to come to terms with the vision, and
in the interim, there had been much testing.

"You are the brother of Kahnawakee?" the leader
repeated, motioning for three of his men to move
behind Alex.

"I am Couteau Noir," he replied, seeking a tone
that, while confident, was hopefully unchallenging.
Despite his usual talents as a negotiator, he had an
instinctive feeling that this man was not in the mood
for a long-winded explanation. This pugnacious
leader wanted answers, he wanted them fast, and he
was prepared to carve them from Alex, if necessary.

"Couteau Noir?" Several warriors grinned uneasily
while another reminded the leader, in a grumbling
tone, that Couteau Noir was an infant, not a man.
The leader nodded. "Couteau Noir has seen one win-
ter. You are not Couteau Noir."

But if I am, Alex answered in silent amusement,
then I am a miracle, and you're in deep trouble, right?
After all, I appeared out of thin air, and I'm almost a
foot taller than you or any of your men. Aloud, he
demanded, "Who are *you?*"

The leader's eyes narrowed. "Orimha," he growled,
pounding his chest with his fist, then his arm swept to
encompass his men and he added, proudly, "Gahniencas."

Gahniencas? Alex forced himself to breathe deeply
and to focus, for a moment, on the timeless beauty of
this woodland clearing, where a cool late afternoon
breeze was dispatching the oppressive August heat,
and where the scent of wild grapes was overpowering
and comfortingly familiar. Alex knew this spot well.
This was the very glade in which he had played as a

child, pretending to be a warrior or hunter. This was, in the oddest of ways, home, and he wouldn't allow himself to be dispirited. These men—these Gahniencas—were on Susquehannock turf, and their rights were second to those of Alexander BlackKnife, even if they were members of the most highly feared nation of this or any other time.

Gahniencas . . . to be their enemy, especially during the seventeenth century, was to make a deadly mistake. They called themselves Gahniencas, but their neighbors called them *Mohawks*—an Algonquian term that meant, quite simply, "they who consume living beings." Alex had heard countless stories of the men who had earned this title for their people. Whether they were called Gahniencas or Mohawks, they could be the most generous and eloquent of hosts or the most rapacious and effective of torturers.

Alex also knew that the Mohawks had been one of the first nations to embrace Kahnawakee's plan. Therefore, assuming that Kahnawakee's son Couteau Noir was in fact only one year old, that put this little drama in 1657, which should have meant Alex was not standing surrounded by enemies, but rather by comrades-in-arms against the Euro-invasions. Unfortunately, this particular Mohawk leader—this Orimha, with his broad face, thin lips, and shaven head—did not wear the expression of a comrade, and whenever he spoke Kahnawakee's name, he did not pronounce it with the slightest hint of respect, much less admiration.

The nine Mohawks had knives and war clubs, while Alex had only the elements of surprise and mystery on his side, both of which were apparently fading quickly. Soon the men would manage to convince themselves that the newcomer hadn't truly appeared out of nowhere and that he was simply a relative of Kahnawakee, whom they plainly did not hold in esteem. Not to mention the fact that Alex was wearing his war paint in outrageously bold slashes, as though daring them to test themselves against him. The situation was precarious at best.

"You are the brother of Kahnawakee?"

Alex had a feeling Orimha's patience was at an end, and so he replied quickly. "I am the brother of Kahnawakee. I am also the brother of Orimha. I am the brother of every Gahnienca. I want to talk to you, my brother. I did not come to fight you or to provoke you."

Orimha's hand reached forward to indicate Alex's decorated face and chest. "You came to fight."

"Without a knife, or musket, or quiver filled with arrows?" Alex countered, his tone even and reasonable.

"You mock Orimha?"

Alex frowned. Apparently this guy wanted a fight, and for some inexplicable reason, Alex was anxious to oblige him. If he was to die on this spot for some unfathomable purpose, wouldn't it be glorious to die fighting an enemy of the Visionary, especially one as fierce of eye and stubborn of stance as this Orimha? "You and me, then, Orimha," he suggested carefully. "Keep your knife, but tell your men not to interfere. I'll fight you with my bare hands."

Orimha didn't seem to hear the challenge. "You will stand the gauntlet and then we will talk."

The man behind Alex moved to grab his hands, but Alex had spun and was eyeing him coolly. "Keep your hands off me, all of you. I don't want trouble."

Orimha's laugh was harsh. "You wish to talk?"

"That's correct."

"You will stand the gauntlet and then we will talk. It is decided."

The expression "run the gauntlet" had always been a misnomer, given the tortuously slow progress one could manage to make while being pummeled and perhaps slashed by two rows of assailants. "Stand" seemed to be both accurate and foreboding, even though it seemed likely that in this particular case any gauntlet would be more ceremonial than actual, given the modest number of men available.

It was nevertheless unacceptable. Alex wouldn't passively endure even a ceremonial pummeling, although he realized that the alternative—a knife fight with nine men—was suicidal despite his superior size. He had challenged himself that very afternoon, while standing in front of the mirror in the safety of his apartment, to be tested in just such a confrontation, but he had envisioned having a weapon for himself in any such test, and hadn't expected these preposterous odds. "We'll talk first, Orimha, and then, if I haven't made sense to you, I'll stand your gauntlet."

Orimha stepped aside, and as he did, the warriors advanced on Alex, their blades eerily reflecting the rays of the late afternoon sun. Alex kicked the weapon from the hand of the closest man, then spun to disarm a second, alert to the position of the knives that had fallen to the ground. He needed to commandeer a weapon immediately if he hoped to gain any true advantage in this hopeless confrontation. At least if Kahnawakee one day heard of the man who had appeared from nowhere and called himself Couteau Noir, he would hear that the man had conducted himself skillfully and with valor despite the futility of such resistance.

Again and again he successfully thwarted the war-

riors' movements while aiming kicks at their knife
hands; then, without warning, the smallest of the
Gahniencas jumped onto him from behind, grabbing
a handful of his hair and wrenching back his head.
With the Mohawk still on his back, Alex lunged toward the closest of the fallen knives. He might have
reached the weapon, and perhaps he could at least
have killed the man on his back, but Orimha had
anticipated his move. Just as Alex's muscles were
stretched to their limit, the leader brought a huge war
club down on his neck, then kicked him full in the
face. Alex felt a searing pain shoot through his shoulder and for a split second the world was filled with hot
white lightning. Before his sight could return, he felt
a cold iron blade against his throat and tensed, prepared for the end, which had come too quickly and
with too little testing.

Then Orimha's voice reached him. "You will stand
the gauntlet, and then we will talk. You will tell me
your name and your lineage. Only then will I decide
if you shall live or you shall die."

Alex raised his eyes slowly, acutely aware of the
blade at his throat, the torn ligament in his neck, and
the wrath of the four men he had managed to disarm
or to injure. His reply was a hoarse, yet eerily defiant
whisper. "I am Couteau Noir, the brother of the Visionary, and I spit on your cowardly gauntlet."

Cassie was drifting in a deep, lovely sleep unlike
any she had ever experienced, and she wondered as
she drifted whether it was the effect of the poison from
the rattlesnake or simply the gentle touch of death
itself that was causing her to feel, simultaneously, so
helpless and so all-important. Her ordinary senses

had abandoned her, but their replacement—a magnificent, omniscient awareness—was introducing her to another kind of existence involving spirit rather than flesh, focus rather than sight, eternity rather than time. There were other beings with her in her ethereal world, and it seemed ludicrous to assume they had all been bitten by rattlers or otherwise rendered unconscious. In fact, it seemed as though they had always been there, waiting for Cassie, and, in a curious way, it seemed *she* had been waiting for *them*. A part of her had yearned for this peace and tranquility.

Then she became aware of more conventional sensations, such as the stinging of the blisters on her feet and the smell of fresh dirt under her cheek, and she groaned in relief, unashamed to admit that, for all that the dream had been remarkable, she preferred the world of texture, odor, and taste. When she opened her eyes, she saw that it was morning and she marveled at the realization that Alex had not found her in so many hours of searching. Had she wandered so far from the predictable path as that?

She knew without checking that there were no stinging fang marks anywhere on her body. In fact, she had never felt so rested or healthy! For some reason, the snake had spared her. Now it was a simple matter of finding the road and hitching a ride across the bridge and back to the border, where a cab could take her to the nearest restaurant so that she could placate her suddenly voracious appetite. Stretching her arms overhead as she shifted into a seated position, she noticed for the first time that she was not quite alone.

"Well, look at you." Cassie's voice was soft—almost a coo—as she greeted the gray-furred wolf-dog. He was a beauty, and obviously tame, and he seemed to be waiting for her to acknowledge him and to give him permission to approach and so she extended her hand, in a loose fist, for him to sniff and perhaps lick. "Go ahead, doggie. I won't bite you."

The animal whimpered and moved closer, then cocked his head to one side as though studying her. His eyes were amber-toned and inquisitive, while his thick coat was a multitude of grays, from smoky to almost pure white.

"You're beautiful," Cassie sighed. "This fur . . ." Her fingers stretched out to him, sifting gently through the soft, clean coat. "You're part wolf, right? But you're tame, so you must have an owner. Can you take me to him? We can't stay here. There's a snake somewhere . . ." She glanced about herself, concerned that the snake might return and attack this gorgeous creature.

The dog seemed to understand, and after licking her arm with reassuring thoroughness, he trotted to the bushes and pulled out a long triangular-headed snake carcass, which he carried to Cassie in his mouth.

"You killed it? Oh, good boy!" She rumpled his coat again, this time more vigorously. "What a great dog you are! You're my hero! In fact, I think I'll call you that." Jumping to her feet, she smiled proudly. "Can you take me to the road, Hero? Or to your owner? And we'll just keep this . . ." she accepted the snakeskin and looped it over her purse, "for a souvenir. And maybe I'll make it into a collar for you. Would you like that, Hero?"

The dog barked enthusiastically, then turned and proceeded a short distance along a side trail. When he turned to Cassie and barked again, she brushed the loose dirt from her jeans, slipped her revitalized feet into her canvas sneakers, and scampered eagerly after him.

"You know, boy, I wanted Alexander BlackKnife to be my hero, but you're really much better," she chatted, as they negotiated a narrow, increasingly steep trail. "You've got great texture, just like he has, and you don't have any political ambitions, right? You're the perfect hero . . . almost. Of course," she laughed lightly, "I guess I'm not exactly your dream heroine, right? I only have two legs . . ." She laughed again, enjoying the one-sided banter almost as much as she enjoyed the clear mountain air. They were near water, she suspected—probably the Cutler Reservoir, or perhaps simply a small stream or creek. The air seemed damp, but while she couldn't see enough of the sky to put her father's meteorological lessons to any use, she could tell in her bones that there was no chance of rain. It was simply a glorious day.

The dog led her to a ridge overlooking a homestead consisting of a shed, a well, an outhouse, and a rustic cabin, with an inviting curl of smoke coming from the chimney. "Is this where you live, Hero?" Her eyes scanned the area, noting the absence of power lines. "Is it some kind of vacation house? Let's hope your owners have a cellular phone or something. Anyway," she knelt beside him and patted his neck, "good job. You've officially saved me. Let's go meet your folks."

As they hurried down toward the cabin, a beagle who had been napping in the sunlight raised her head and howled a greeting, then a man appeared from the shed and stood, his hands on his hips and total amazement in his eyes. He wore buckskin leggings and a long, sleeveless tunic laced loosely over a white, collarless shirt. While his hair was simply light brown, his full, bushy beard was a myriad of shades of russet, gold, and tan.

"Let me guess," Cassie joked under her breath to her canine companion. "He's getting away from it all, right? Pretending to be some kind of macho mountain man? I'll bet in his real life he's a stockbroker in a starched shirt . . . but it must have taken months to grow that beard . . . it's fabulous."

Even from a distance she could tell this man was huge. Still if Hero was his dog, she decided he had to be basically gentle and trustworthy, and so she strode right up to him and extended her hand. "Hi!" When he continued to stare, she grinned. "I guess you don't get many visitors in this little hideaway. I'm Cassandra Stone. Your dog saved my life."

The bearded man's eyes moved from her face to her outstretched hand, then down to her legs, where they lingered a bit too long, and so Cassie warned gently, "If you want me to leave, just say so. Point me toward the border, okay? I was hiking in the Protectorate and I got a little lost."

"The border?"

She liked his voice, which was gravelly and low, and loved his eyes, which were hazel dominated by green, but his beard was the feature that was beginning to torment her. She had never seen that shade of red, which appeared almost otherworldly with the sunlight dancing across it. While she wasn't quite ready to touch it—after all, this man had no credentials, let alone a law degree from Harvard or Alex's reassuring smile—she hoped to persuade him, before she left, to sell her just an inch or two for her texture box. Of course, that was assuming he would allow her to leave . . .

"The Susquehannocks are probably looking for me

right now," she bluffed as a precaution, "and so, like I said, just point me toward the border and I'll be on my way, okay?"

"You are familiar with the Susquehannocks? And," he took a deep breath, "are you also familiar with a woman named Shannon Cleary?"

"You noticed the resemblance?" Cassie sighed. "I saw her ads for years and never made the connection myself until the whole uproar over her disappearance began and . . . oh!" She stared, fighting a rush of panic as the nature of his question began to hit her. Why did he connect her so easily with Shannon? The resemblance was strong but not overpowering, unless . . .

Shannon had been wandering in the woods that fateful day, just like Cassie was now doing. Had Shannon gotten lost . . . just like Cassie? Had she then wandered to this remote cabin, to this bushy-faced man, to this . . . what?

Cassie was suddenly certain that she knew her missing cousin's fate. Poor Shannon hadn't time traveled at all, nor had she been abducted by Dusty Cumberland. She had wandered from the safety of the Protectorate, straight into the clutches of a bushy-faced hermit! So where was Shannon now? Was she alive? What did this man know?

Continuing her bluff, but with renewed importance, she insisted, "The authorities have traced Shannon here. They're on their way now, with a SWAT team. Just turn her over to me and I'll make sure they go easy on you."

A broad grin transformed his face. "You must be her sister. The resemblance, in both appearance and babbling, is remarkable." Extending his hand, he announced, "My name's John Cutler. My wife will be . . . even more delirious than usual to see you."

"Pardon?" Cassie looked from the man to the dog, then back again, studying his shaggy face intently. "A rattlesnake almost got me, but your dog killed it."

"Prince is a good dog." The man smiled reassuringly. "I always knew someone would come after Shannon, although," again, his eyes scanned Cassie's body, "I expected a man. A brother, or her father . . ."

"You think you're *the* John Cutler?" Cassie's stomach was churning. "And you think you're married to Shannon Cleary?"

His broad smile faded. "Are you suggesting she's married to some other man?"

"Huh?" The pain in his eyes was decidedly real and Cassie found herself needing to reassure him without truly knowing why. "She doesn't have any other husband, Mr.—well, Mr. Cutler. It's nothing like that. It's just. . . . Can I see her?"

His grin, now one of relief, had returned. "You can see her right away. Just don't be too upset if she doesn't recognize you. She has an ailment called amnesia."

"Amnesia?"

"She remembers nothing of her past life. She wandered here last year and I took her in. I always assumed she had come from the north, but we never could trace the path, and," he flushed slightly, "she seemed content to remain, and I wanted her to stay. Forever. I suppose we didn't look for her kin as diligently as we might, but . . . here you are."

"Yes," Cassie murmured, "here I am."

"You are her sister?"

"Her cousin. I need to see her right away, and . . ." Cassie's voice grew more steady and authoritative despite the pounding of her heart, "you need to ask her to step out here, into the open. Is that okay?"

Almost as though in response, a figure emerged from the cabin, on to the porch, calling out, "John? Who's that with you?"

"Shannon?" Cassie gasped.

"Shannon Cutler, my wife," John confirmed proudly, then he raised his voice and shouted, "You have a visitor, Shannon."

"Shannon!" Cassie broke into a run, with Prince right on her heels, and she almost crashed into her cousin, who was moving forward as well, but at a slightly more judicious pace, given her condition. Cassie embraced her, gushing, "Shannon? You're alive! Are you okay? Are you . . . pregnant?"

Shannon Cleary Cutler pulled free of the excited newcomer and smiled through her confusion. "Who are you? How on earth did you get here?"

"Do you see?" John explained from behind them. "She doesn't remember you."

"Probably because she never met me," Cassie giggled, giddy with relief. "I'm your cousin. Your father's sister's daughter. We all thought you might be dead, but *look* at you! You're so . . . huge and beautiful!"

Shannon shook her long blond hair in amazement. "You came after me? How?" With a furtive glance toward John, she added, "Did you know this man is John Cutler, and we're married? Everything's fine here, but . . . it's 1657, did you know *that?*"

And your husband doesn't know you're from the twentieth century, Cassie finished for her in silent amazement. Was this possible? Her mind flashed back to the spirit-laden dream that had snatched her from the snake's fangs, depositing her into what she had assumed to be the next morning. Now that assump-

tion was being refuted by her cousin's clear, if un-
spoken, message, and by this man's manner of dress
and outrageous claim to being a famous seventeenth-
century figure. It wasn't the following morning, but
rather a sunny, fragrant August day from an August
she had thought to be long since passed.

"So?" Cassie turned back to the bearded man and
smiled shyly. "You're really John Cutler?"

"And you are Cassandra Stone. You're welcome
here, Cassandra."

"Thanks." She locked eyes with Shannon and
added, "I was walking in the woods in the Susquehannock Protectorate and a snake was about to bite me
and I fainted and then your dog here killed the snake,
and so here I am."

"Wow." Shannon lowered herself carefully to one
knee and petted Prince, allowing him to lick her face.
"Good boy, Prince. What would we do without you?"
When John had assisted her back to her feet, she took
Cassie's hand. "Cassandra Stone. It's such a pretty
name. I never knew I had a cousin on Dad's side."

"Even if you never met one another," John interrupted, "this woman can tell you things that may
assist you in remembering your past."

Shannon sent Cassie another warning glance, to
which she responded sweetly, "I don't really know
that much about Shannon's side of the family, Mr.
Cutler, except there was lots of scandal and trauma
and she probably doesn't want to remember it, so
. . ." she eyed him in mock rebuke, "why don't we just
drop it?"

"I naturally assumed you'd want to reunite Shannon with her kin."

"Not really. As long as we know she's safe, that's
all that matters to us."

"That's nonsense." John's jaw tightened with determination. "Explain yourself."

Cassie faced him squarely, her hands on her hips. "This is why no one from our family ever visits you, John Cutler—you're a lousy host." When his eyes widened, she added sternly, "I'm a guest. Stop grilling me like a trout."

John stared, then burst into laughter. "I can see this is going to be an interesting visit, Cassandra."

"Call me Cassie. And did someone mention trout? I'm really famished. Prince and I walked for miles."

"Cassie's right, John," Shannon smiled. "She's our guest, and we should make her comfortable. Go and catch her some fish while I make some tea."

His eyes shifted from one female to the other, as though attempting to fathom this conspiracy, then he nodded. "It will give you time to become acquainted *and* to perfect the details of this preposterous deception."

"No," Shannon corrected softly, moving to him and slipping her arms around his waist, "not deception, John. Never deception. I love you too much for that."

Cassie watched the man become mesmerized with love and trust for his wife and her heart grew warm with admiration. These two had found true love under circumstances so strange and miraculous that they defied any need for explanation. Shannon Cleary, the victim, seemed suddenly to be the luckiest woman on Earth in this or any time and her cousin's thoughts veered, momentarily, to the love she had not been allowed to savor and explore with Alexander BlackKnife. If it could possibly have grown into this marvelous synchrony of trust and adoration, then the fact she had given up so quickly seemed worse than a mistake. It seemed like a crime against destiny.

But Alex was three hundred years or more away. As the reality of this inconvenient detail began to penetrate Cassie's thoughts she felt a wave of light-headed foreboding—or was that hunger? She had been unconscious for hours, hadn't she? The dream of spirits—one of whom had been her Uncle Matt, she decided with belated wonder—had cradled her gently, moving her here so that she could . . . what? What was her purpose here? To verify Shannon's continued existence? Her happiness?

And Shannon Cleary *was* happy. This man John Cutler was taking fine care of her, and in return, she was filling his life with love and, soon, with offspring. If Cassie needed any confirmation of the fact that Shannon was committed forever to this time and this man, the swollen abdomen and lovestruck voice were providing it.

And I want this too, Cassie realized, as she watched the lovers, *with Alexander BlackKnife. How could he and I have given this up so casually? As soon as I get back, I'm going to convince him, one way or another, that we have to give ourselves this chance . . .*

Then she smiled sheepishly, imagining how the handsome council adviser would scoff and tease when she came to him with this time-travel story. He'd remind her she was the same "eccentric" who celebrated Christmas in August and grew weeds in her garden. And then she'd remind him of their kisses, and she'd tell him of the look in John Cutler's eyes when he gazed on his wife . . .

"Except, Alex will *never* believe a word of this," she admitted aloud.

Shannon pulled away from her husband, as though

she had only just remembered that they had an audience, and blushed. "Alex? Is that your husband?"

"He's a friend." Cassie's eyes twinkled mischievously. "You met him once, Shannon. In your hospital room, remember? The tall, handsome, Harvard-educated Susquehannock?"

"Oh! You mean Alexander Black *oops!*"

"Alexander Blackoops?" John frowned. "That's not a Susquehannock name."

"It's Russian," Cassie deadpanned, and to her delight, her cousin collapsed against her husband in a fit of helpless laughter. *This* was what Cassie had come three centuries to find! As an only child, she had craved a sibling or cousin. An ally, an accomplice, a confidant. And this woman needed one, too. Shannon had a marvelous, unmanageable secret that she must be bursting to share with someone who could understand and identify with her plight and her good fortune.

John seemed to be all too aware of the females' need to talk freely. With a rueful chuckle, he motioned toward the porch. "You two women go inside and visit. I'll find us something to eat. Enjoy your conspiracy with my blessings."

"It's hardly a conspiracy," Shannon sighed, "but Cassie and I *are* hungry, John." Raising herself on her tiptoes, she kissed her husband's bushy cheek. "Hurry back."

After he had disappeared into the woods, the two cousins studied one another with frank admiration. "You're dressed the way I used to dress for *Dustees* layouts. Now, of course . . . ," she smoothed her simple blue dress over her swollen abdomen and sighed. "Are you a model, Cassie?"

"Hardly. It's a long story, but I want to hear *your*

story first." Cassie reached for her cousin's hand and held it tightly. "I was beginning to think I'd never find you."

"Let's go in the house." Shannon kept Cassie's hand in her own and led her onto the porch. "Are you thirsty?"

"I'm not drinking anything while I'm here. I'm not the outhouse type, Shannon. We can visit until I get the call of nature, and then, as they say, I'm outta here."

"It's not so bad, once you get used to it, and," Shannon's blue eyes grew solemn, "you have to stay for a long visit. I didn't realize until this moment how much I needed a girlfriend to talk to. I mean, John's wonderful . . ."

"He's gorgeous," Cassie corrected. "That beard is unbelievable. If I ask him for some of his hair, will it offend him?"

"You want his hair?"

"For an art project. I need a donation from your dog, too." She glanced over her shoulder and added fondly, "Isn't that right, Hero Prince?"

The dog barked his agreement, then moved away to join the beagle while the women entered the cabin.

"He's such a smart dog, Shannon."

"He tried to save my life once, too," Shannon agreed, "but John doesn't know about it yet."

"Yet?"

"I'm waiting for the right moment . . ." The former model grinned sheepishly. "I'm a coward."

"I doubt that. You live out here, so isolated, roughing it. I admire you, Shannon, and I can't wait to tell Philip. He's been beside himself with worry."

"Poor Phil." Shannon sank onto the bed, fluffing a

pillow and positioning it against the small of her back. "He didn't believe my letter?"

"A part of him believes it, and when I go back, I'll take care of the rest." Cassie sat herself in John's rocking chair and looked around the simple cabin and its furnishings: a table with two benches for seats, a sturdy bed with a cornflower-blue coverlet, a sideboard and several trunks, and a row of blue-and-white crockery. "This is nice, Shannon."

"You met Philip when he was searching for me?"

"Right. That's how I met Alex BlackKnife, too. Phil sued the Susquehannocks. The newspapers have been going crazy over your disappearance."

"I didn't want to cause any trouble or sadness, but I had to come back to John right away. The first time," she explained, "was an accident on my part. It's a long story, but I had fallen in love with John . . ."

"I get the picture, believe me. You belong here with him."

"And you belong back with Alexander Black-Knife? He seemed like a wonderful man."

Cassie nodded. "He is. I just hope *my* disappearance isn't causing more trouble for him. The furor was just beginning to die down."

"After more than a year?" Shannon marvelled.

"Five months." Cassie laughed at herself then and studied Shannon's pregnant form. "I guess it's been five months for us and at least . . . eight? for you?"

"I've been here for seventeen months and I'm six months along in my pregnancy," Shannon grimaced. "I'm huge. I keep thinking it might be twins, but the women at the Susquehannock village say it's not." Leaning forward, she added plaintively, "John wants me to move to the village so they can deliver the baby, but I want to have it here. If I had someone here with me to help me, he'd go along with it. Otherwise," she rolled her eyes in mock distress, "he'll talk me into going there. He always manages to get his way with me."

"That's obvious," Cassie grinned. "Unfortunately, I don't know very much about childbirth. I've seen lots of films of whales giving birth, but you're not all that big—at least, not yet."

"Very funny," Shannon laughed. "You studied marine biology?"

"It's my mother's career. And my father's a meteorologist, so I actually have tons of bizarre scientific information stored in my head that won't help one bit when your baby starts to come. You're better off with the women at the village. I could make you a birthing sling, but beyond that, I'm useless."

"A birthing sling?"

"I make them from deerskin, even though canvas would do just fine. Then I personalize them, and people pay a small fortune for them. They plan on saving them from generation to generation—like handing down a wedding dress or ring."

"But what is it?"

"You don't remember?" Cassie stood and approached her cautiously. "Do you really have amnesia, Shannon?"

"There were no 'birthing slings' when I lived in the twentieth century. Then again," she smiled, "a lot of things probably changed, thanks to John and Kahnawakee."

"Your letter was so strange. I can't quite picture how it must have been in your old world. Kahnawakee is pretty much the most famous North

American in recorded history, and according to your letter . . ."

"He didn't survive to institute his vision," Shannon nodded. "The incursions of the British into this territory are still pretty infrequent and small, but some scouts and some troops had come here, and they started drinking, and . . . oh!" She struggled to her feet with Cassie's help and smiled at John, who had opened the door almost silently and was studying them intently. "John? Did you forget something?"

He walked over to the women and took Cassie's arm. "I want you to sit down, Cassandra. I have a question for you."

"I have amnesia, just like Shannon," she protested with a nervous smile as she returned to the rocking chair. "Honest."

"No games." His tone was solemn. "I want to know if you came here alone, or were you traveling with anyone else?"

"Just me. And," she reached down and patted the snakeskin wrapped around her purse, "Fang here, of course. Why?"

He shook his head and turned to Shannon. "There's some trouble with Orimha. He and a band of Gahniencas have captured a Susquehannock brave."

"Oh no!" Shannon gasped. "When did this happen? Is it anyone we know?"

"Kahnawakee sent word to us. I met his runner down by the stream. Apparently, this brave is a newcomer to these parts. Perhaps from the southern village, although . . ." He glanced toward Cassie. "They say the captured man bears a striking resemblance to Kahnawakee, and he wears clothing similar to that worn by *my* wife."

"Clothing?" Shannon glanced down at her simple

cotton dress, then toward Cassie's jeaned legs, and gasped again. "Blue jeans?"

John nodded. "He calls himself Couteau Noir."

Cassie's throat had constricted with fear as they talked, but she managed to whisper, "Alex," to a shaken Shannon, who nodded grimly.

"This would be the Russian, Alexander Blackoops?" John glared, concentrating his full attention on his guest. "You told me you came alone."

"John, don't," Shannon scolded gently. "Can't you see she's in shock? Cassie? Didn't you know Alex came with you?"

"He *didn't* come with me." Cassie stood on shaky legs, moistened her lips, and tried to sound positive. "He *didn't*. He *can't* be here! It doesn't make sense . . ." Her silly request that "Uncle Matt" send Alex as her "escort" taunted her. "Captured?"

John put his arm around her shoulder and soothed, "Perhaps it isn't your Alex. He calls himself Couteau Noir."

"Black knife. Alexander BlackKnife. He's my escort. I didn't know it, but . . ." Cassie's eyes locked with John's. "Is he in danger? You sounded like it was an emergency. Would these people hurt him?"

"The Gahniencas are the Mohawks, Cassie," Shannon explained gently. "Most of them support Kahnawakee, but Orimha opposes him. Since Alex looks like him, and calls himself by Kahnawakee's son's name, it could be dangerous. On the other hand, if Alex didn't provoke them, maybe . . ." She touched John's shoulder. "Maybe they're just curious, right?"

"As the story goes, he challenged them. He burst into their midst, in full war paint, and insulted Orimha."

"Oh, no."

"One of Orimha's men was impressed, I guess you'd say, with the captive, and so he brought the story to Kahnawakee. He claims this Couteau Noir appeared out of nowhere and fought bravely. He ran the gauntlet with great bravery and strength."

"The gauntlet?" Cassie groaned. "I don't believe this. It's barbaric." Grasping John's arms, she insisted, "We have to help him. He's not ready for all of this. He's not a warrior, he's a *lawyer.*"

"He's alive, isn't he, John?" Shannon pressed. "And if Kahnawakee sent a runner to you, he must have sent men to go and help Alex, right?"

"Of course." John managed a reassuring smile. "He's probably at the village right now, being treated for his wounds. But I should go and be there."

"Let's go, then," Cassie nodded. "How far is it?"

"You should stay with Shannon. I can make better time on my own, and I can be of more use to him."

"You're wrong." Cassie felt tears of frustration stinging her eyes. Alex had to be losing his mind over this! Plummeted into another, hostile time with no warning and no explanation! He didn't even know about the rattlesnake! He needed rescuing, yes, but he also needed Cassie and the information and comfort she could give him. And if these Mohawks still had him, then she could help with that, too. She could find something unusual in her purse to trade for Alex's life.

"Take Cassie with you, John," Shannon interceded firmly. "I'll be fine alone, and she'll go crazy here, not knowing."

"Kahnawakee's runner has instructions to stay and protect you," John sighed. "We'll take Prince with us, so that he can follow Orimha's trail if Kahnawakee hasn't had success." He dabbed awkwardly at the

tears that were filling Cassie's eyes. "The gauntlet is a
test, not a method of execution, missy. Your escort is
alive, and he'll survive. We need to leave right away."

"I'm fine, really. I won't slow you down, John. I
need to be with Alex." Again a flood of tears threatened. "I appreciate your help."

"We're family," he reminded her, and Shannon
echoed the sentiment, pulling her cousin into her arms
and murmuring reassurances while John began the
hasty preparations for the journey.

Groggy and exhausted, Alex shifted his raw,
bruised back against the tree trunk to which he had
been lashed and tried to sort his thoughts. Sleep had
been impossible, despite the fact that he had been
essentially unmolested during the long night and the
early morning hours following the gauntlet and the
subsequent brief interrogation by the hated Orimha.
To a large extent the other Gahniencas had ignored
him, and two had disappeared completely, presumably to hunt food for the rest, although Alex had been
offered neither food nor drink since his capture.

His body ached, but there had been no permanent
damage, although the searing pain in his shoulder
sustained during the initial scuffle was constant, flaring with excruciating intensity each time he tried to
turn his head to monitor his captors' movements.

In contrast to the neck injury, the dozens of bruises
and welts on his trunk and torso were nothing more
than nuisances and Alex knew that this was all part of
the game. The gauntlet had not been designed as a
means of killing—it was simply a humbling introduction to the dominance of captor over captive. If the
Mohawks decided to kill him, they undoubtedly

would choose a much more creative and lingering
means. For now they seemed content to watch him
from a distance, occasionally ordering him to recite
his lineage or to sing.

They had stripped him almost immediately and
Orimha had attempted without success to don his
jeans, which were too tight to be pulled over the
bully's stocky thighs, and so he had discarded them.
Likewise, Alex's size eleven running shoes had been
rejected, since they were four full sizes too large for
the leader's feet. Now Alex stood, naked and bruised
and shivering just slightly, but still proud, as he had
promised the spirits during his transition through
time.

Stand tall, he reminded himself, *no matter what evils
or temptations present themselves. They haven't killed
you yet, Couteau. Maybe they'll get bored and let you
go.*

Then he saw Orimha move to the campfire, which
had all but died away. The expressionless man
stooped down as though to warm himself, but instead
withdrew a long stick from amid the coals and blew
lightly on the tip until it glowed with red-hot intensity.
Then he turned to stare at Alex with eyes that echoed
both the intensity and the heat, and Alex knew there
was no immediate hope of either boredom or release.

Chapter Six

Orimha stood before his prisoner, the fiery branch held in plain sight. "You are the brother of Kahnawakee?"

Alex bit back a futile retort—how often was this jerk going to ask the same damned question?—and nodded slightly. "He is my brother."

"He wishes to lead the Gahniencas."

"No," Alex countered. "Not to lead. He wants to unite the Gahniencas with the Susquehannocks and with all others to whom these lands have been entrusted."

"He must submit before he can unite."

"Submit? To whom?"

"To the League."

It was a vaguely familiar sentiment and Alex struggled to recall a footnote in the history of UNAP. Among the many obstacles encountered by the Visionary, hadn't there been some insistence, by fringe elements of the five nations of the famous Iroquois League, that the Susquehannocks as a nation submit unilaterally to the authority of the League before Kahnawakee could be allowed to address the Council? Of course, Kahnawakee had refused, saying he

did not have the right to surrender the Susquehannocks to any sovereign power short of the combined
power of all North American nations, and then only
for intercontinental purposes.

It was unfamiliar territory for Alex and he was
quick to admit it. "I cannot speak for Kahnawakee."

"You are afraid?" Orimha jeered. "You will not
speak for him? Will you die for him?"

"Untie me and I'll even *kill* for him," Alex promised.

Orimha chuckled and raised the point of the stick,
blowing again until the tip was aglow, then touched it
to Alex's bare chest, searing the skin just below the
nipple. The sensation was grotesque—a combination
of pain, heat, and the acrid stench of burning flesh.
Chuckling again, Orimha lifted the tip of the stick and
placed it in front of Alex's face, where both the odor
and sight of charred skin could repulse him.

It took every ounce of pride at Alex's command to
keep from reacting, but he managed to focus on the
atrocious sight without really seeing it, then he moved
his gaze to Orimha and smiled. "You're a coward,
Orimha."

The Gahnienca winced slightly, more annoyed than
challenged, and shuffled back to the embers to reheat
his weapon. When he returned, he drew the red-hot
point across Alex's chest, leaving a furrow of angry,
inflamed tissue. When Alex managed even then not to
cry out or flinch, Orimha grinned a semitoothless grin
and order him to sing.

Alex grimaced inwardly, unwilling to allow his
enemy to sense that these constant demands that he
sing or recite his lineage and his accomplishments had
been more effective as means of torture than any hot
poker could have been. They reminded Alex that he

had neglected his own heritage. Of course, he could easily recite his lineage—he could do that in his sleep—but his accomplishments, by Orimha's standards, were paltry and few. Of what import were debating medals and lacrosse trophies to a man who had undoubtedly taken many scalps and routed many warriors?

And the songs! Alex knew the words to three or four ceremonial songs, but to his shame, he had been too elitist and modern to bother to pay strict attention when their uses were addressed. In fact, when most boys his age had been practicing in the choir, Alex had usually been selected to perform a reading or some other form of oratory and had been excused from practice, despite the fact that his singing voice was more than passable. It was his eloquence and showmanship that had been valued, and thus his heritage, again, had been neglected.

To sing the wrong song at a time like this, knowing that countless brave men of his nation and his clan had sung courageously and proudly through brutal hours of torture, ending more often than not in a fiery death at the stake, was unthinkable. Orimha would know that Alex was bluffing, and would carry the tale one day to the Visionary, mocking him for Alex's faulty education. And so Alex had decided not to sing one of the ceremonial songs, and had chosen instead a mindless, irreverent Euro-inspired song that would, at the very least, confuse Orimha.

Ignoring the stinging of his burns, he concentrated on trying to remember where he had left off, then nodded with false brightness and began, *"Sixty-four bottles of beer on the wall, sixty-four bottles of beer . . ."*

Orimha chuckled, humming to the now-familiar

tune, and shifted his greedy gaze to Alex's right hand, which was bound tightly at his side. When the Gahnienca leader leaned down, a sly grin on his lips, Alex's fist instinctively tightened. Orimha chuckled again, deftly pried the thumb free, then moved his bared teeth down to grip the thumbnail.

Still singing, Alex fought against a wave of nausea and panic. He had tried, off and on all night, to imagine this moment, hoping to disarm the pain by anticipating it. This was one of the most common of minor torture tactics—to rip the thumb- and fingernails from their beds, causing exquisite agony in the process. While it was hardly fatal, it had seemed peculiarly grotesque to Alex as a boy and he had always been sheepishly grateful that such things were no longer a part of his culture under any circumstances. Now as he sang—". . . *sixty-two bottles of beer on the wall . . .*"—he braced himself.

"What will they do to Alex, John?"

"Cassandra," he protested, taking her arm to help her over a tangle of vines, "why upset yourself needlessly? We'll know soon enough."

"I have to know so I can be supportive when I see him. If I'm shocked or speechless, he'll just feel worse."

"Most men appreciate speechlessness in a woman."

"Very funny." She pulled her elbow free and sifted her fingers through her tousled blond curls. She could only imagine how disheveled she appeared, wearing one of John Cutler's huge white collarless shirts in place of her leotard. Even with the sleeves rolled, it was laughably loose-fitting, practically obscuring her jeans from view. "I'm really worried, John. Just level with me, okay? What will the Mohawks do to him?"

"They have a wide range of torturing methods, Cassandra. Some are painful, but not permanent, while others are disfiguring or even fatal."

"Disfiguring?" she gasped. "They won't cut anything off, will they?"

"A finger or a toe, perhaps. Anything more and they'll be intending to kill him eventually. I've never heard of them releasing someone after cutting off a limb or castrating him. That's usually a sign that the captive will never be released."

"Castrating?"

John flushed. "Forgive me, Cassandra. I'm not ordinarily so raw, but I thought you were asking . . . well, never mind." He grasped her shoulders firmly. "We have to assume Orimha would never kill Kahnawakee's kinsman without some weighty provocation. I didn't mean to offend you."

"You didn't offend me. I have to know these things. Please, John? Tell me everything you know about these torture rituals."

"You need to rest, and then we'll talk."

"No! I'm fine." She tugged on his hand. "Keep walking."

John pursed his lips thoughtfully. "I suppose if you understood the reason the Gahniencas—or Susquehannocks or Shawnees or any number of other groups—torture a captive, you might feel less anxious. Many of my former countrymen think it's simply bloodthirstiness or ungodliness, but it has its purposes."

"You're defending it?"

"I'm explaining it."

"Okay. Go on. I *want* to understand."

"The simplest example is the capture of an enemy.

He is subdued and tortured to death, to serve as a warning to other enemies. It's military strategy, expected by both sides. Akin to placing a cannon in full view of an enemy in hopes of discouraging an attack."

Cassie nodded. "That makes sense. But they don't even know Alex. How can they see him as an enemy?"

"The rumor is that he provoked them."

"He absolutely didn't. I *know* that. He's very diplomatic and charming, and not at all hostile or aggressive."

"A lawyer, not a warrior?" John grinned reluctantly. "So you mentioned. Let's hope he's a bit of both."

"Okay, so why else do they torture people?"

"When their numbers have been greatly reduced—either through wars or, more recently, severe pestilence—they need to replenish through adoption of a certain number of captives. In this situation, torture serves two purposes. It tells them which captives are fairly hardy, and it serves as a sort of rebirth, for the captive, into the tribe."

"Rebirth?"

"Imagine being repeatedly humiliated, over a period of days, and deprived of all hope of survival, until you have become almost a shell of a person. Until, in a very real sense, you have died, and have left your old life behind you. You are reduced to your simplest nature, without any thoughts or needs other than subsistence and relief from pain." He paused, allowing her imagination time to react. "Then, with unexpected suddenness, just when all hope was gone, you are cut down from your stake, and enveloped in the loving arms of a stranger or strangers, who wrap you in a warm blanket and feed you soup and give you a new name and a place to rest unmolested."

Cassie's voice was hushed. "It's so odd, but I see what you mean, John. At that point, when a person's just grateful to be alive . . ."

"The strangers become their new family," he finished, "and that gratitude becomes a bond. And the old bond to the old life has been severed, perhaps irrevocably."

"Even if they get a chance to escape one day?"

"For persons such as myself or some of the Jesuit missionaries who have been through all of this, the adoption would not necessarily be effective, because it is so foreign to our culture. But for anyone raised with this ritual—who perhaps witnessed gruesome torture during his own childhood—the effectiveness can be greater. In a sense, someone like that is prepared for such a fate."

"But not Alex. He was raised a Susquehannock, but not with these customs."

John shrugged. "They would not be interested in your Alex in this way. Once a man reaches the age of sixteen or seventeen, he's usually not considered adoptable, unless he's so old that he can take the place of someone's revered grandfather or such."

"Take the place of? You mean, they're adopted to replace specific persons?"

"A child who is lost," John nodded, "or a beloved wife who has died. It's fascinating, isn't it?"

"Yes, I guess so. But it doesn't apply to Alex?"

"I just wanted you to understand that these tortures are not simply ghoulish entertainment, although they have that element under some circumstances. They have a purpose. And a warrior who is being tortured has a purpose, too—to bring honor on his people and his reputation by being brave, by singing his clan's song, despite the pain. And by refusing to allow himself to be humiliated."

"Alex probably knows about that part, at least."

"He will know it instinctively," John assured her. "You say he is a fine and good man. He will be proud and brave for as long as possible. And," he finished quietly, "when it is no longer possible, he will hopefully lose consciousness."

Cassie's eyes met his and she nodded. "I understand, and you're right. Alex will be strong. Now, tell me the truth. Do you think they'll release him without permanent injury?"

"Assuming you're correct, that he didn't menace or challenge them in any way, I believe they will simply test him and then release him. He will serve as a substitute for Kahnawakee, perhaps, and they will test the strength and will of the man who claims to have visions."

"They'll hit him? And . . . ?"

"They will burn him with hot pokers," John recited softly, holding her gaze with his own, "and they will tear his fingernails out with their teeth. They will break his fingers, so that he cannot wield a weapon. Perhaps they will break his wrist as well. And Orimha may stab him, but not in the chest or abdomen. The injuries will be confined to the extremities so that in spite of the pain, death will not result. Even if a wound festers and eventually leads to amputation, Alexander BlackKnife will live. Unless . . ."

"Unless he challenges them?" Cassie tried to smile. "He doesn't wear war paint and he doesn't insult people. He's a diplomat." Her lower lip trembled. "You'd really like him, John. He's witty and intelligent and sincere . . ,"

"Shhh . . ." He pulled her into his arms and patted

her curls. "Don't cry, missy. Kahnawakee's probably found Alex by now. He's quite a diplomat himself, and he'll convince Orimha to release your friend, even if he has to offer himself in his place."

"Oh, no!" Cassie pulled free, horrified. "Alex would die before he'd allow his Visionary to be endangered for his sake. Oh, John, what a mess this is. And it's all my fault. If only I hadn't asked for him to be my escort."

"Sit and rest," John insisted, tugging her to the ground. "We should talk of something else for a while."

Cassie was dumping the contents from her purse, desperate to find something of value to trade for Alex's life. His fingers and his toes were broken, perhaps even amputated, and he was covered with burns, but he was still alive. She was sure of it. All they needed was time, and something valuable to trade.

"What's this?" John demanded, pulling the long blond braid from amidst the jumble of pine cones, sticks, and makeup.

Cassie blushed. "It's my hair. I'll explain about it later. Help me find something to give Orimha in exchange for Alex."

"If your scalp were attached to this braid, Orimha would be very intrigued," John teased gently.

"That's disgusting." Her eyes widened. "They won't take Alex's scalp, will they?"

"I don't know, Cassandra. I can't know. I can only assume they will not." He turned his attention to the sticks. "Why do you carry tinder?"

"I was trying to build a little log cabin." She stacked the sticks mechanically. "See?"

"Shannon does that," he mused. "Is it some strange familial custom?"

"Shannon does this?"

"When we argue. It seems to calm her down. We rarely argued until lately," he added mournfully, "but I want her to move to the village, to have the child, and she refuses."

Cassie smiled, grateful for the hint of amusement in the otherwise gruesome afternoon. "So she builds a little cabin? That's hilarious, John. When she does that, you'd better just back off and let her have her way."

"I want to do what's best for her. She needs a midwife." He smiled reluctantly. "Would you consider assisting her?"

"I can't stay for a long time," Cassie sighed. For the first time she wondered what she'd do if they found out that Alexander BlackKnife was dead. Could she go home knowing that? Could she go on with her life, as though it had never been touched by him?

"How far away is your home?"

"Huh?" She banished her fears and pretended to glare. "I thought we agreed you weren't going to pester me about all that anymore. Once Alex is safe, you and Shannon and I will have a nice long talk."

"You're the stubbornest woman I've ever met."

"Thanks." She sorted through the jumble of texture until she found a strand of pink-tinged freshwater pearls. "Do you think Orimha would like these?"

"Yes. He'd like those." John examined a razor-sharp cardboard cutting knife. "He'd like this too. Is it a weapon?"

"It's a tool. It has a razor blade in it. If you ever feel like shaving that beard, let me know. I want the hair."

"Shannon told me so," he chuckled. "You're a

strange woman, Cassandra. Here." He cut off a handful of wiry rust-colored hair and handed it to her.

"Thanks, John. It's gorgeous." Her lower lip trembled. "Alex has gorgeous hair, too. The first time I touched it, I fell in love with it. I can't bear the thought that some beast might be hurting it . . . hurting him . . ." A sudden burst of anger ignited her and she jumped to her feet, scooping the contents back into her purse. "I'm all rested, John. Let's get moving."

". . . If one of those bottles should happen to fall, twenty-one bottles of beer on the wall . . ."

He shifted against the tree trunk, struggling to maintain consciousness, despite the fact that the thought of passing out was growing more perversely appealing by the moment. Orimha and the others were out of sight for the moment, although, given Alex's extremely limited field of vision due to the near paralysis of his neck and shoulder, that didn't mean they were not close by, eagerly planning their next round of amusement. They had particularly seemed to enjoy pelting him with red-hot sand which they had retrieved from beneath the embers of the fire that had provided so many creative means of causing him anguish. His face and body were rough and red with stinging blisters and angry welts, and every breeze, rather than refreshing him, served to fan the burns back to life to torture him anew.

They had broken his right thumb and index finger, and he could still remember the sickening sound of his own bones snapping. In a macabre twist of fortune he had been sent to Orimha unarmed. Had he been wielding a knife, the Gahniencas would have noticed that he was left-handed and would have visited their mayhem on that hand as well, in order to ensure that, if and when Alex was rescued or released, he would be unable to effectively turn the tables on his torturers by means of blade, bow, or firearm.

Not that there was any chance of rescue. No one knew he was there, and everyone who cared about him was hundreds of years away. By now, they would have found his car at the border where Cassie had left it the afternoon before, and they'd be searching fruitlessly for him. They'd go to Cassie for information, and somehow she would know. She would have the vision, and the creativity, to understand where he had gone, but of course, the investigators wouldn't believe her.

He shuddered to think she might try to follow him, naively imagining him in a backwoods paradise. If Orimha ever saw her . . . Alex stifled a shout of abject frustration. She was so beautiful and sweet and sexy, and he cursed himself for having walked away from her without telling her how profoundly she had affected him and without clinging to the possibility that they could have a future together. At the very least, he should have told her what his heart had murmured to his soul the moment he first saw her—that she was the one he had been waiting a lifetime to meet.

"Don't try to follow me, Cassandra Stone," he proclaimed aloud, in English, hoping that somehow she would hear him.

"What is that?" From behind him, Orimha issued a curt demand in his antiquated Iroquoian dialect. Then he moved into view and scoffed, "You speak with the words of the red shirt? 'Stone'?"

"The red shirt?" Alex almost laughed. The English? "Do you speak English?"

Orimha shook his head, continuing in his own tongue, "You called Orimha by the red shirts' name."

Orimha? Alex groaned aloud. He hadn't made the connection until that very moment, but "orimha" was indeed the Iroquoian word for "stone," as in Cassandra Stone. "I wasn't calling to *you*," he assured him arrogantly. "I was addressing someone honorable and admirable, not a coward like Orimha."

"Who is 'stone'?"

"Never mind. Why don't I just recite my lineage again?"

Orimha laughed. "You have amused me today. I will be sorry to kill you."

Alex shrugged despite the pain it caused to his neck. "You have no reason to kill me, Orimha. It will be a cowardly and stupid act."

"And your brother will avenge you?" Orimha reached up and grabbed a handful of Alex's hair. "Your brother is no longer a warrior. His hair is longer even than yours." He noticed Alex's slight wince and crowed, "You feel pain?"

His neck and shoulder were in fact screaming with agony, but Alex dared not confirm it. "Kahnawakee wears his hair long to show that he no longer wars with his brothers."

"Only a fool wears his hair in this manner," Orimha countered, then motioned to his own head, shaved except for one small patch at the crown. "My enemies cannot yank on my hair, Couteau Noir. You provide them with a means of injuring you. Do you want me to cut it for you?"

"No, thanks." Alex tried to sound casual, but the veiled threat had hit home. If this man scalped him, it would be the ultimate humiliation, and worse, it would break Cassie's heart. Hadn't she loved his hair from the start? Hadn't she touched it first? And then, of course, she had touched his lips with her own . . . a brush of velvet, a promise of love . . .

You're losing it, Alex, he rebuked himself desperately. *Stop thinking about her. Just be glad she's three centuries away, and pray she doesn't build one of her stupid cabins and come after you. Just concentrate on dying with dignity, man. Do you want this guy to mock Kahnawakee? Because of you?*

"Sing," Orimha suggested, then he turned to call out to his men, ordering them to bring dried grass and twigs to pile at Alex's feet. "You will die now," he explained to Alex. "You have been brave, but now you will scream like a woman. Sing while you are able, Couteau Noir." His eyes twinkled with maniacal pleasure as he chanted, *"Boddelsa boddelsa beer onawa."*

"Idiot," Alex grumbled. "You can't even carry a tune." It annoyed him that Orimha's taunts to Kahnawakee might include an off-key rendition of this stupid drinking song—was that how Couteau Noir would be remembered?—and so he summoned his pride and began to sing—at first haltingly, and then with growing fervor—the most stirring and uplifting of the songs of the Susquehannock Wolf Clan. There was no longer any doubt in his mind as to which of the many hymns was the correct one, the *only* one, with which to greet death. It rang through the trees as the tinder was ignited and Alex felt a burst of almost mystical pleasure at the sound. He couldn't die without having it mean *something,* and so, when his song was ended, he exhorted the Gahniencas, "Listen to Kahnawakee! Hear his words! He is a great visionary and can lead you into the future! He will make you strong against the invaders, so that you will flourish for centuries."

Orimha's answer was to draw his knife and to plunge it deep into Alex's bare blistered thigh. Blood spurted from the wound, but Alex had blessedly come too far to feel it. He was on the verge of delirium, yet there was a deep well of strength that seemed to accompany that state and he drew from it greedily, beginning his war song again and with astonishing intensity. The flames were licking at his ankles and he knew Orimha's prediction had been all too true. Soon he would be screaming, but at least they hadn't taken his scalp, and he was grateful, for Cassie's sake . . .

Chapter Seven

"Are you hungry, Cassandra? We could stop for a meal and a rest."

"I'm fine," she murmured. "How much farther is the village?"

"It's another hour and you'll never make it." John's tone was grim. "I'll end up having to carry you, and then we won't be there until sunset."

"I really hate this century," she complained under her breath. "No walkie talkies, no helicopters, no indoor plumbing."

"You're babbling again."

"I know. Sorry, John."

"Do you need some privacy again?" He was clearly trying not to grin. "I could check behind that bush over there, to make sure there are no bears or snakes lurking."

"Very funny. I almost got killed by a snake yesterday, so pardon me if I'm overly cautious." She dropped dramatically onto the ground and pulled off her tennis shoe, pounding it on a rock. "I keep getting pebbles in these darned things. I wish I had some boots with me."

"You should have worn those moccasins of yours."

"Those were worse." She jumped back to her feet. "One hour? Let's get moving. It's beginning to look more and more like rain."

John studied the sky and nodded. "Those clouds are beginning to tower. 'From towers to showers.' "

"Right," she agreed, mollified by the folk wisdom. "In other words, a hot pocket of air is driving those cumulus clouds into thick vertical formations, and the water droplets up there are probably just about large enough by now to start being pulled downward by the earth's gravity."

His eyes had narrowed with suspicion. "More nonsense."

"My father makes his living predicting that kind of nonsense, so show a little respect." She reached over and caught his hand in her own. "You're a good traveling companion, John. I think I'd have gone crazy by now with anyone else." *Except Alex, of course,* she added silently.

"You've been fairly entertaining yourself," he smiled. "Tell me more about your father. He's Shannon's uncle?"

"By marriage, but it's my mother who was a Cleary. Her brother was Shannon's father, but he was killed before Shannon was born."

"Is that so?"

"I don't want to go into now, John, but that's one of the tragedies I was talking about earlier when I said she was better off here, with you. Just take my word for the rest."

"Do I have a choice?" he grumbled. He stopped walking and cocked his head to one side, listening intently to the song of a robin reverberating in the distance. Then he raised his hands to his mouth and sent the same call back.

"Signals!" Cassie grabbed his arm and demanded, "Tell me what it means! Have they found Alex?"

"Settle down."

"It sounded so close!"

"Sounds can be deceiving in these woods. Especially," he grinned slyly, "when there are hot pockets of air driving water droplets downward."

Her pulse was racing as the relief in his expression and tone registered in her heart. "They found him, and he's alive?"

"That was Kahnawakee. He's telling me we don't need to hurry. That's a good sign."

"Well, we *do* need to hurry! Who knows what Kahnawakee considers good or bad? For all we know, poor Alex is still in agony." When John settled down onto a low branch and folded his arms across his chest, she glared. "Now what?"

"Now you will answer a few questions. Where is your home? Where was my wife born? Why haven't any of her kinsmen come to find her? And, most importantly," his eyes flashed, "why has she felt the need to lie to me?"

"You think you can extort the information from me," Cassie grinned, "by refusing to take me to Alex until I blab? Guess again, mountain man. I have my own personal hero with me, remember? Prince!" Her grin widened proudly when the wolf-dog sprang to her side. "Can you take me to Kahnawakee, boy?"

His sharp bark proclaimed his eagerness to please her and she ruffled his fur gratefully. "We'll see you at the village, John. Try not to get lost."

"Prince," John drawled, "stay."

The dog whimpered softly and moved to his master, licking his hand in apology. When John instructed him to lie down, he did so without hesitation.

"You're a bully," Cassie laughed, "but I forgive you because Alexander BlackKnife is alive." She felt a rush of love for Alex, and for the world, and for her bushy-faced escort and his loyal dog, and so she dropped to her knees, stroking Prince as she confided, "The truth is, John, you won't believe me even if I tell you, but . . . you'll hear it soon enough, from Alex, so here goes. Right now, it's 1657, right?"

"That's correct."

"In a little more than three hundred years from now, in the twentieth century, a beautiful little baby girl will be born, except, somehow, that part has already happened. Her name is Shannon Cleary, and she's the daughter of Matthew Cleary, my uncle. Through some strange twist of time, she ended up here, with you. I tried to follow her, but I couldn't, until the snake tried to kill me and my Uncle Matt intervened. And since I asked him to send Alex as my escort, this whole crazy torture mess came along, and . . ." she smiled shyly, "I'm just grateful it's over without anyone dying. And I'm grateful to you, for making my cousin happy, after all she had to go through."

"I see." John stood, brushing loose bark from his leggings and scowling slightly. "More nonsense. I should have known you'd spin some tale, Cassandra. I don't know why I bothered."

"I like it when you call me Cassandra. Can we go and see Alex now?"

John's scowl disappeared. "You're in fine spirits, and I'm pleased to see that, but don't forget he's been through an ordeal. You must remember what we discussed. He may be in some pain, and his appearance may be hard on the eye."

"But he's alive," she insisted softly, "and the pain

will go away, and the injuries will heal, and if he's scarred, or even worse, it won't really matter. He has the most expressive eyes, and the sexiest voice, and the most charming smile. . . . They can't take all of those away from him, so he'll always be the most attractive man on earth." Overcome with emotion, she wrapped her arms around John's barrel chest and began to sob. "I'm just so relieved he's alive. I was so scared, John."

"That's enough," he soothed, stroking her back gently. "I wonder if our Russian friend knows how much you care for him."

"Russian?" She laughed through her tears. "You're funny, John. Will you take me to him now?"

"First, I'd like for you to meet Kahnawakee."

"No offense, John, but that can wait. I want to see Alex first."

"You don't have a choice, missy," John chuckled. "Dry your tears and try to make yourself presentable. Then turn yourself around and meet the chief of the Susquehannocks."

Cassie spun and then gasped, wondering if her eyes were tricking her, showing her the sight she most wanted to see. He could have been Alex's twin were it not for the difference in height and the long mane of hair that hung down below his shoulders. She was literally speechless at the resemblance, although her mouth was wide open and trying to find some words to express her amazement and delight.

His skin was bronzed and leathery from countless hours in the sun, and his hair, although much longer than Alex's, was the exact same deep raven black, thick and lustrous and screaming with finger-tempting texture. His eyes were warm and laughing, in a playful way that reminded her of Alex when his guard was down, or when he was about to kiss her. There

was no way Alexander BlackKnife would look upon
a stranger with so mischievous an expression, but
Kahnawakee's eyes were alive with playful energy.

Kahnawakee's outfit was simple—a vest of deerskin, sturdy buckskin leggings, and an ample breechcloth. Across his chest was slung a strap of leather
which held a pouch, a knife, and curiously crafted
beaded trophies in the nature of medals or emblems.
There was a strip of leather around his left wrist and
another securing his hair back from his forehead, although it was not otherwise restrained.

She had expected him to be older—a distinguished,
statesmanlike figure—but he was close in age to Alex,
or perhaps even a bit younger. There was an overtly
sexy edge to his boyish charm that perplexed her.
Wasn't he supposed to be a hero? A great thinker? A
visionary? To look at him, one would think he had
nothing on his mind beyond having a good time—
perhaps a bit of hunting, or fishing, or cruising the
woods for eligible females . . . where on earth was the
sincere, dedicated, idealistic dignity that Alex exuded
so effortlessly? And where was Alex?

"Cassandra Stone, may I present Kahnawakee,
kinsman to Couteau Noir, who," John winked toward the newcomer, "we are assuming is out of danger and in good hands?"

"He is resting, in the longhouse of the Wolf Clan.
Djisgaga is caring for him, and he will recover."

Cassie almost swooned at the familiar voice. She
had feared she'd never hear it again! "You look and
sound just like him!" she gushed. "Are you sure he's
okay?"

Kahnawakee grinned. "He is a fine-looking man."

John chuckled. "Don't flirt with her, Kahnawakee.

She knows you're married and she's in love with your guest."

"She is beautiful," Kahnawakee smirked.

"She's Shannon's cousin."

"I have noticed the resemblance," the chief nodded. "But her hair . . . ," he reached forward and fingered a blond lock curiously, "has many curls. Couteau Noir must lose his way in them."

Cassie blushed. "I'm standing right here, in case you two have forgotten. And speaking of Couteau Noir, I want to see him. Please?"

"You wish to see my son?"

Cassie turned to John, amused but exasperated. "Can you ask the so-called Visionary to be serious for a minute? Please?"

The two men chuckled, then John spoke rapidly in Susquehannock. A full-blown conversation ensued and Cassie was vaguely impatient, yet she was also fascinated. Beyond that, the friendship between John Cutler and Kahnawakee was so clearly genuine and unique, she found herself drawing comfort from it. These men would take good care of her, for the short time she was here, and they would take fine care of Shannon forever. And they would befriend Alex, while his wounds healed, and that would be a source of inspiration and strength he could take back with him to his destined role as a twentieth-century leader.

"Maybe you guys could talk and walk at the same time?" she suggested finally, elbowing John's ribs for emphasis. "It's going to rain, remember?"

"Kahnawakee was just saying the same thing. He offered to carry you, if you're tired."

"That's obnoxious. Honestly, John, get a grip. What did he say about Alex? I want you to talk in English from now on, please."

"Couteau Noir is asleep," Kahnawakee intervened, his grin softening to a fond smile. "He speaks your name as he sleeps."

"Oh?" She was melting rapidly. "Did they break any bones or anything?"

"What she means is, did they cut anything vital off," John clarified, then laughed when it drew another stab of Cassie's elbow. "Don't worry, Cassandra, he's apparently intact."

"I'm not much for backwoods humor," she sniffed, but a smile tugged at the corners of her mouth. "Did Alex really ask for me?"

"Apparently he's still delirious." John took her hand and abandoned his teasing tone. "There are many burns, Cassandra. It will take weeks before he has healed. Two fingers, at least, were broken."

"Oh, no!"

"He was stabbed several times. One knife wound was serious, and caused great loss of blood. When Kahnawakee found him, he was unconscious."

"Found him?" She turned to the chief. "Tell me what happened."

"Orimha tested him. He was brave. It is said that, even in the face of death, he spoke of the importance of unity of our people. At the last moment, Orimha released him, or it may be Orimha never intended to kill, but only to break my little brother's spirit. That did not happen. Couteau never faltered, and I am proud of him."

"He must have loved meeting you," Cassie sighed. "What did he say?"

"He was not conscious. He has spoken in his sleep and that is all. He left Orimha's camp, walking on two burned feet, and soon his fever was too great. When I found him, he was not able to recognize me."

"I'm so grateful to you for finding him." She touched his arm shyly. "Don't tease me anymore. I really want to see him right away."

Kahnawakee's eyes were soft with admiration. "My little brother is fortunate. I understand now why thoughts of you kept him alive."

"You don't know Alex very well," she blushed. "I'm pretty sure it was thoughts of *you* and *your* vision that kept him alive."

"Or perhaps both?" John Cutler exhaled audibly. "It's time I met this Alexander Couteau Noir. Come along, Cassandra." He took her hand and led her toward the village, adding over his shoulder, "Your little brother's Russian, Kahnawakee. Did you know that?"

"He is too tall to be a Susquehannock," the chief agreed.

"All right, you two, just cut it out, *please.*" She was still giddy with relief and knew that these two strong men were likewise savoring this chance to be light-hearted when so much had hung so recently in the balance. As they followed the well-worn trail, she listened to them converse in Susquehannock and enjoyed this opportunity for her mind to drift toward thoughts of the upcoming reunion.

What would she say to Alex? She wanted to tell him she loved him, but first she wanted to apologize for dragging him into this nightmare. Or maybe the first thing she should tell him was that she had a bottle of aspirin in her purse. She blushed with pride at the thought that, in his delirium, he was thinking of her and speaking her name aloud.

Had he guessed that she had time traveled also? Probably not, and so he would be amazed to see her at the village. And because she knew he needed to maintain a proud, stoic demeanor with these illustrious ancestors of his, he would welcome the upcoming moments alone with Cassie to relax, perhaps even to fall apart a little, and to confide the fears and horrors that had haunted him over the past twenty-four hours.

And she needed him, too. It wasn't just relief and joy over the fact that he was alive. It was the need to reassert her claim to his heart, a claim she had been so foolishly willing to relinquish only one day earlier. Now she had seen John with Shannon—the epitome of true love—and she had experienced the world, fleetingly, without Alex in it, and she knew she was ready to fight for him. They could make love here, where no curious newspaper reporters could misjudge them, and if what she suspected was true—if they were meant to be together forever—they would return to the twentieth century with their commitments and priorities firmly in place, ready to fight any gossip or political opposition they encountered.

And if Alex didn't agree—if he still felt their affair would embarrass his people and destroy his career— that would be a sign that she was wrong. They would still have their affair—that seemed as inevitable as the storm massing above her head—but it would end when they returned home and she would still be grateful for the precious romantic interlude. Hadn't she dreamed of whisking him off to a deserted tropical island?

He's speaking your name in his sleep, she reminded herself happily. *He almost died today, and he's speaking your name, and I don't think he's any more willing than you are to let this second chance pass by. You'll nurse him back to health and fall in love, and then you'll be ready to face the twentieth century side by side.*

* * *

She was the most strikingly beautiful woman Alex had ever seen, from her exotic black eyes, huge in a small, heart-shaped face, to her small, perfect mouth which smiled so serenely down upon him. She was cooing his name, and stroking his forehead, and he wondered if perhaps he wasn't back in the time-transition dream. Wasn't hers the very voice that had instructed him, so lovingly, to stand tall despite the evils and temptations?

"I did my best," he whispered.

"We are so proud, Couteau. Kahnawakee's chest swells with pride at the tales of your bravery."

"Kahnawakee? Is he here?"

"My husband will return soon. He longs to speak to you."

"He's your husband? You're Djisgaga, then? You're beautiful."

She smiled as though she had expected the compliment. "And you are handsome. You must sleep, Couteau. You speak through your fever."

"I know." He closed his eyes, all too aware that he was only barely conscious. He even suspected that once he was fully alert, he'd discover he had dreamed this moment with this regal beauty. If so, he needed to thank her, for her advice and for her care. He needed to assure her that her efforts hadn't been in vain. Somehow, he felt driven to promise that he would continue to stand tall and lead his people, no matter what personal sacrifice he encountered, and no matter what evils and temptations presented themselves.

She seemed to understand, and as she stroked his hair, she murmured, "We are so proud of you. You are a fine man, and you will bring us honor and respect for all of your days. Sleep, Couteau. I have sewn your wound, and bathed your blistered skin, and Kahnawakee himself has placed splints on your fingers. You will be whole, and you will stand tall once more."

"I will stand tall," he murmured, trying to nod despite the widespread numbness in his shoulder. "I promise you that, Djisgaga. I promise . . ."

"Go ahead, Cassie. We'll give you a few moments alone with him." John smiled sympathetically. "Are you suddenly shy?"

"I'm trembling," she whispered, as surprised as John by the fact that she hadn't bolted into the longhouse the moment they arrived at the village. "I guess it's just beginning to hit me. He almost died, and we're here . . . so far from home . . ." Her gaze drifted toward the wall of sharpened stakes that surrounded the village, then back to the huge longhouse with the carving of a wolf's head over its doorway.

Kahnawakee gave her a gentle push. "Go and greet your man."

"He's not exactly my man," she sighed. "He's more like my . . . lawyer." When this brought a chuckle from the two men, she blushed and elbowed John pointedly. "No more teasing."

"Why do you insist upon jabbing me?" He tousled her hair fondly. "Don't keep him waiting any longer, Cassandra. The poor man's been calling your name, hasn't he, Kahnawakee?"

"It is true. Go quickly, Cassandra. Send Djisgaga to me."

"Okay." She took a deep breath in a hopeless attempt to calm her racing pulse. The thought of seeing

Alex safe and sound was almost intoxicating, and she didn't want her own curiosity and affection to overwhelm him in his vulnerable state. There would be plenty of time for that later!

With a feeble grin toward John, she edged closer to the longhouse and stepped across the threshold, where she hesitated, confused by the smoky haze that filled the structure. It made the experience slightly surreal but not altogether unpleasant. She spied Djisgaga immediately, and was relieved to see that while she was an attractive woman, she wasn't breathtaking by any means. Although she knew she was being irrational, she was a bit jealous of Djisgaga's role as official nurse for Alex. On the other hand, she was eternally grateful to the woman for being there when she herself couldn't be, and so her smile was sincere as she motioned for her to come to the doorway.

"You're Djisgaga? I'm Cassie. I'm Alex's friend. How's he doing?"

The dark-haired woman stared in haughty silence.

"Oh, don't you speak English? Sorry." She flushed slightly, confused by the obvious snub, then she squared her shoulders and announced, "Kahnawakee wants to see you outside, and I want to see Alex, so . . ." She paused, and when Djisgaga's unresponsiveness continued, she finished, "Excuse me, won't you?" *It's been a real treat talking to you,* she added in annoyed silence as she brushed past the sentry.

Alex was sound asleep and Cassie noted with fond relief that his handsome face, although slightly marred with a kind of rash, was basically unmolested. He was lying on a wide platform built into the side of the longhouse, and a red blanket loosely covered his body. She knelt by his side and brushed her lips over his, then smiled tearfully when the intimate ritual caused him to stir and to moan her name.

"Alex?" she murmured. It was all she could do to keep from calling him "darling." "Alex? It's me. Cassie."

"Cassie?" he repeated groggily. "You're here?"

"I love you, Alex," she blurted, before her hand could fly to her mouth to stifle the untimely announcement. To her bittersweet relief, he didn't seem to yet be comprehending her words, although he was clearly soothed by the sound of her voice, and so she cooed, "Sleep for a while if you want, Alex. I'll be right here when you wake up."

"Cassie?" He struggled to raise himself onto one elbow and then, in an instant, a horrified expression came over his face and he sat upright, grasping her forearm and insisting, "You have to go home. It isn't safe here! You don't know what you've gotten yourself into."

"Shhh, Alex, I'm fine. I'm safe."

"No!" His eyes were bright with fever. "I knew you'd come after me, Cass. You're so crazy, and impulsive, and I love it, but this place . . . this time . . ."

"I know." She was fighting back hot tears at his concern and delirium. "It's all okay now, Alex. Just lie back, please? We're with John Cutler and Kahnawakee, and they won't let anything happen to me. Do you understand?"

"Kahnawakee," he nodded, sinking back onto the bed. "I met his wife, Cass. She's incredible. Elegant and beautiful, and she has the gentlest touch."

"I met her, too." Cassie smiled. "She reminded me a little of your friend Leah."

"Leah?"

"They both want to protect you from me," she teased gently. "But you're stuck with me. I'm not going anywhere without you."

He smiled ruefully, as though his head had just cleared. "You look great, Cassie. I knew you'd come looking for me."

"How are you feeling? I heard a little bit about your injuries. I have aspirin, Alex."

He chuckled, then winced slightly. "I'm fine now. But these last twenty-four hours have been unbelievable." He raised her hand to his lips and kissed her fingertips. "It's great to see you, but I really want you to go home."

"I can't go without you, and you can't go anywhere for a few days. I'm perfectly safe here, Alex."

"You're stubborn," he groaned, closing his eyes but keeping his grip on her hand. "Stay with me for a while, Cass."

"Sure. Just go to sleep. I'll be here when you wake up." She brushed her lips over his high cheekbones. "I wish I had some ointment for this rash."

"It's nothing serious. They threw hot embers a couple of times, just for kicks."

"Oh, Alex! What if one had gotten in your eye? Ooo, I *hate* them."

"Join the club. But they didn't kill me, so I guess we should be grateful. Anyway, it was my own fault. I wanted to be tested, and I guess I got what I wanted."

"It was my fault," she corrected sadly. "I'm really sorry, Alex. I'm going to make it up to you as soon as you're better."

"Yeah? That sounds good. Give me a week or two, and then . . . ," his voice softened to a groggy whisper, "we'll find out what we almost missed."

"Oh, Alex . . ." She cuddled against his arm,

pleased by his words, which echoed her own thoughts
so closely. His breathing grew deep and regular, and
she allowed her own eyelids to droop, grudgingly admitting that she was exhausted from the quick pace of
the four-and-a-half–hour journey from Shannon's
cabin. If it weren't for Alex's many injuries, she would
have climbed up onto the platform with him—it was
definitely wide enough, and she assumed it had been
designed for at least two occupants. The longhouse
atmosphere was cozy, and she even suspected the
communal aspect—there were at least forty such plat-
forms in all—could be a source of comfort after a
tiring day. For now, they had the huge structure all to
themselves, and she liked that, too, as she shifted
closer to him and allowed herself to doze.

"Cassie?"

"Mmm? Alex, hi . . ."

He grinned. "I thought I was dreaming, but you're
really here."

"I fell asleep." She smiled and kissed his cheek.
"You sound a little more coherent. Are you in a lot of
pain?"

"I'm fine. Just a little stiff." He rubbed his neck
gingerly. "In a couple of days I'll be as good as new."

"What happened to your neck? It's so bruised."
She winced as she examined it. "That looks bad, Alex.
I have some aspirin in my purse. Let me find you some
water and I'll be right back, okay?"

"I don't want aspirin."

"Why not?" She leaned closer and coaxed, "Let me
baby you a little, Alex. You've paid your dues; now
relax and put yourself into my hands."

"That sounds incredible," he admitted, then he stared past her, his dark eyes widening rapidly.

Cassie turned and beamed, "Hi, Kahnawakee. We both had a little nap."

Kahnawakee nodded, his face solemn, and he addressed Alex in Susquehannock. Alex replied in a respectful, almost awestruck tone. Cassie was all too aware of the importance of this moment in Alex's life. To meet his hero face to face when three centuries had separated them for so long was a sobering miracle, and she scooted quickly away, allowing them some measure of privacy.

John Cutler was standing in the shadows and she joined him, taking his hand and squeezing gratefully. "Alex sounds good, doesn't he? I was afraid he might be delirious or withdrawn, after all he went through."

"He is a strong man."

"What's Kahnawakee saying to him?"

"He's saying Alex brought honor to his people by his conduct with the Mohawks."

"And Alex is in seventh heaven? I don't need an interpreter to translate that. He's telling Kahnawakee how honored he is just to meet him, right?"

"Yes."

"He wants to meet you, too, John. Go ahead." She gave him a playful shove. "Go bask in all the glory for a while. It's male-bonding time."

"More nonsense," he chuckled, but moved over to introduce himself to the patient.

Cassie listened carefully, charmed by the conversation in spite of the fact that she couldn't understand one word. The underlying theme of mutual respect and appreciation was powerful enough to cross any language barrier and she felt honored simply to be allowed to observe in silence. Then a fourth man entered the longhouse, hesitating some distance away, and she wandered over to him.

Her best guess, based on the profusion of shell necklaces draped around his neck, was that he was a medicine man. She knew a little about the tradition from her study of herbs, and knew that these men had been the forerunners of modern naturalistic healing, which she favored, despite her appreciation of the more prosaic benefits of a healthy dose of aspirin. Hoping he spoke English and would be willing to divulge his plan for Alex's treatment so that she could veto anything too dangerous or bizarre, she extended her hand and smiled. "I'm Cassandra Stone. Do you speak English?"

"Stone," he repeated, staring at her as though completely fascinated. Then he touched his burly chest and repeated, "Stone."

"No, *I'm* Stone," she laughed gently. "I guess that answers my question. You don't speak English and I'm afraid I don't speak Susquehannock, so we'll have to get John Cutler to translate for us. Or I guess Alex could do it." He was still staring, and so she explained, "Alex? Your patient? I guess you call him Couteau Noir?"

He belatedly reached for her hand and seemed content to hold it indefinitely. Cassie grimaced, noting with displeasure the dirt under his fingernails and wondering how she could tactfully insist he wash before proceeding with the examination. He was an unattractive man by any standards, yet there was a compelling, masculine quality to his gaze and stance that could not be ignored.

Then Alex's voice broke through her thoughts with a strangled, *"Shit!* Take your hands off her!"

She whirled to see that he had jumped from his bed

and was struggling to reach her, although John and Kahnawakee were restraining him while advising him rapidly in both English and Susquehannock.

"Alex!" she gasped. "What's wrong?"

"Come here, Cass! Get away from that bastard! *Now!*"

She backed away quickly and Alex stopped his struggling but seemed unwilling to return to his bed, and so he stood, naked and filled with righteous wrath, his body covered with so many burns, welts, and bruises that Cassie felt almost faint at the sight. When she spied the jagged gash in his thigh, clumsily sutured with two thick strands of sinew, she gasped in dismay.

"Cassie?" John had her elbow and was pulling her further away from the stranger. "This man is Orimha."

"Orimha?" A surge of indignation almost propelled her back to the bully, but John caught her neatly and half-tossed her back toward Alex, advising gruffly, "Settle down, missy."

"You should be ashamed of yourself!" Cassie shrieked. "How could you *do* such evil things? You don't even know us!"

"That's enough," John growled. "Alex, quiet her down and get back into bed."

"Forget it. I want him out of here first." Alex pulled Cassie behind himself and waited.

Orimha seemed unconcerned by the fuss, and now spoke dispassionately toward Kahnawakee, who answered in a calm, resonant tone.

"What are they saying?" Cassie demanded.

"Orimha is praising Alex."

"Like I care what *he* thinks," Alex muttered. "Get

him out of here, Cutler. I don't like seeing him anywhere near Cassie."

"I agree," John whispered, "but this is a sensitive
matter. Kahnawakee has wanted to speak face to face
with Orimha for months. You've accomplished something worthwhile, Alex."

"Get into bed, Alex, please?" Cassie coaxed, but it
was as though he couldn't hear her, so intent was he
upon glaring toward his enemy.

Orimha turned his gaze directly toward Cassie and
he made what seemed to be an announcement, which
sent Alex into another seething rage, anticipated by
John, who grasped him by the arm and shook his
head in warning. Alex scowled and muttered, "Tell
him she's my woman and I'll kill him if he looks at her
again."

John winced. "He didn't ask if she was your
woman. He asked if you two are married."

Then Kahnawakee motioned toward the doorway
and Orimha, with one final covetous glance toward
Cassie, left as silently as he had arrived.

"Will he leave the village peacefully?" Cassie demanded. "I don't want him near Alex."

"Cassie," Alex groaned. "Be quiet." He eased himself down until he was seated on the edge of the platform, pulling the blanket around himself awkwardly.
"Come and sit with me and be quiet." When she had
complied, he raised questioning eyes to Kahnawakee.

"You are concerned for her, but she is safe," the
chief assured him in English. "He came to this place
to praise you, Couteau, and it pleases me to listen to
him. He will eat and rest with us, but he will not
approach this longhouse, or your woman, without my
permission."

"Why doesn't he just go away?" Cassie grumbled. "Don't you hate him, Kahnawakee?"

"He is a man of intelligence. He can learn from his mistakes." Kahnawakee studied her intently. "Do you understand what Orimha said to you? He feels there is a connection between you and him, because you share the same name."

For all the tension in the room, Cassie couldn't help but be amused by the ridiculous thought, and quipped nervously, "You mean his name is Cassie?"

Kahnawakee took her comment seriously and corrected gently, "Orimha means Stone. It is the same name as your surname."

"I know. It was a joke, Kahnawakee. Lighten up." She turned to Alex and sighed, "You, too. Don't worry so much about me. I'm not going within twenty feet of that butcher, believe me." Then she stood up and faced John and Kahnawakee with her hands on her hips. "You two go away. Alex needs to rest."

"Cassie," Alex groaned, but Kahnawakee nodded and departed, with John close on his heels.

"You embarrassed me," Alex chided. "You shouldn't talk to the Visionary that way." He paused, listening intently to a burst of laughter from the area outside the longhouse door, then grinned and slipped his arm around Cassie's shoulder, scolding, "You're crazy, Cass. Weren't you afraid of Orimha?"

"You were here to protect me," she reminded him sweetly. "You already proved you were tougher than him."

"I don't remember that part," he laughed, "but thanks. I'm glad you see me that way, but you've got to be careful around here. Don't go anywhere unless John's with you. In fact," he moistened his lips and suggested cautiously, "I want you to go home with him. He told me Shannon's pregnant—that's amazing, isn't it?—and she's anxious to visit with you."

"Shannon can wait. She understands I want to be with you, Alex. I'm not going anywhere."

"John doesn't want to leave her alone for too long," he argued, his voice growing weary, "and I can't relax and recuperate if I'm worried every second about you."

"I'll be right here, where you can see that I'm safe."

Alex's eyes had been drawn to the doorway, and he whispered, "Here's Djisgaga. Isn't she incredible? Have you met her?"

"I've had the pleasure. And I see she has that Leah-Eagle look in her eye again." Cassie was amused by the woman's possessive frown despite a twinge of foreboding. "Hi, Djisgaga. What's new?"

Ignoring Cassie completely, Djisgaga hurried to Alex and urged him to lie back into the bed, soothing and scolding in lyrical Susquehannock. Alex seemed more than eager to please her and was soon tucked under his blanket. "See?" he smiled. "I'm in good hands." Djisgaga murmured something and Alex nodded, explaining to Cassie, "She says you look very tired, and I agree. You should rest, and then go home with John. In a day or so, I'll come and get you and we'll go home."

"In a day or so?" Cassie shook her curls vehemently. "You need to stay in bed for at least a week. And I need to stitch that awful gash on your thigh."

"Djisgaga already stitched it."

"Alex." She tried for a patient tone. "This is my profession, remember? I'm a seamstress. The way it is now, it'll leave an awful scar."

"I don't want to offend her, and anyway," he

shrugged, "what's wrong with a scar? It'll remind me about real life."

"Real life?" Cassie counted to ten and smiled. "Fine. Have your macho scar. And have your visions and your elegant nurse. But I'm not going anywhere until I'm guaranteed that every drop of water and every rag that touches your wounds is boiled first, for at least five minutes. Translate that, please."

Alex murmured toward Djisgaga, who smiled and replied rapidly. Alex chuckled and explained, "She wants to know if you promise to leave if she promises to boil the water?"

Cassie's eyes narrowed. Djisgaga was beginning to get on her nerves, but there didn't seem to be any point in making a scene, so she reminded herself that she would have Alex to herself soon and forced a smile. "That's a deal. Will you take the aspirin, at least?"

"No." He reached up and patted her cheek. "Go and get some rest. Come and visit me again before you leave."

"Can I kiss you goodbye?"

"Absolutely." His hand slipped behind her neck and she leaned into him gratefully, kissing him with gentle but unhurried thoroughness. She could feel Djisgaga's eyes burning into the back of her head and while the animosity was intimidating, she refused to allow it to ruin this tender moment. "Get some rest, Alex," she sighed. "I'm so glad you're safe."

"Yeah. It's been a hell of a day." His eyes were closing, and so Cassie squeezed his hand and moved away, trying to ignore the disquieting sound of Djisgaga's comforting coos.

Chapter Eight

Cassie slept that night on a comfortable platform in the longhouse where Alex recuperated, although it was John Cutler's bearded face, rather than her would-be lover's, that was inches from her own. Alex had insisted she not be left alone for a minute, and while she had intended on sneaking over to his platform as soon as everyone was asleep, her exhaustion paired with the comforting sound of John's rhythmic snoring had thwarted her. Not that she really minded. Alex was safe, the accommodations were cozy, and the world of the Susquehannocks was peaceful and reassuring. Even with the predicted summer storm battering the longhouse, the inside was dry and warm and secure.

When she opened her eyes and stretched the next morning, John had left her side but she could hear his voice, along with those of Alex and Kahnawakee, engaged in conversation. One peek confirmed the fact that Djisgaga was on duty, sitting in feigned submission at her husband's feet. With a rueful smile, Cassie found her purse and her jeans and slipped out the door, anxious to make herself presentable. Several of the women who had befriended her the previous night now descended upon her, and despite the language barrier, managed to understand and meet her basic requirements, which revolved around water, both for washing and for quenching her parched throat.

She brushed her hair vigorously, pleased that her new permanent was cooperating—a sprinkling of water and it was refreshed and manageable—although her former long, straight hair would have been more suited to the style around her. Cassie had never needed to conform in appearance, however, and so she fluffed her curls, recalling with delight Kahnawakee's comment that Alex could get lost in them. Then she scrubbed her face, smoothed the wrinkles out of her shirt, and stepped into her acid-washed *Dustees.* As she was being led toward a neighboring longhouse for a meal, she noticed Orimha's stocky form in the distance and winced with disgust.

Wasn't he *ever* going to go away? The thought of leaving that morning with John, as they had planned, was unbearable with this bully still hanging around Alex's sickbed. Although Orimha had kept his distance—Kahnawakee had assured them all that his instructions were clear and that Orimha was not the type to abuse hospitality—Cassie didn't trust the Gahnienca. In fact, she despised him, not so much for the way he looked at her, although that was fairly unsettling, but for the fact that, having hurt Alex in so calculated a manner, he now dared demand traditional hospitality, knowing that Kahnawakee's plan for unity would protect him from the righteous wrath of Alex's friends.

"I think John and Kahnawakee should take that creep out behind the longhouse and give him a taste of his own medicine," she grumbled to her new friends.

"You're a bloodthirsty woman, Cassandra."

"John!" She turned eagerly to him. "Good morning. How's Alex?"

"If he knew you were wandering around, he'd be livid. As it is, he thinks you're still asleep, and he's doing well. Djisgaga is a good nurse."

"She's the answer to our prayers," Cassie drawled. "Look over there, John. Orimha's still here."

John grinned. "Orimha? Don't you mean, 'the one whose name means Cassie'?" He was chuckling aloud. "Every time Kahnawakee remembers that, he laughs. It's been a long time since I heard him laugh so heartily, Cassandra, and it's a good sound."

"Well, I'm glad I could help. Now, what about Orimha the torturer? He keeps staring at me."

"He's in love with you."

"Well," she paused to glare dramatically, "that explains it, right? I feel much better already."

John patted her arm. "You don't need to be afraid, Cassandra. He won't hurt you."

"Right, he's gentle as a lamb. I'm sure Alex just imagined that gauntlet and those hot sticks."

"That was different. You're not in danger from Orimha or anyone else."

"I despise him and I always will. Why doesn't Kahnawakee make him go away?"

"I explained that last night. Tradition requires that a guest be allowed to stay until he's well rested and well fed. That shouldn't be more than a couple of days. In the meantime, you and I are going back to the cabin, and you won't have to see him anymore."

"I don't like having him hanging around Alex. What if he decides to quote-unquote 'test' him again?"

"Alex has earned Orimha's respect. There'll be no further testing, I'm certain."

"You've been talking to him a lot." She arched an eyebrow and prodded, "Did he tell you where we came from?"

"I owe you an apology for not believing you yesterday," he admitted. "It's incomprehensible, but I can no longer discount it."

"What does Kahnawakee think?"

"He accepts such ideas more easily than do I."

"It must be gratifying, or at least encouraging, to know that all your work together is so successful. UNAP is a supernation, with a lot of power in my world." She glanced hopefully toward Alex's longhouse. "I guess Kahnawakee's going to talk to him all day?"

"You'll have time alone with Alex before we leave. For now, you should eat a hearty meal. The long walk will tax you again."

"I want to see him now. Please, John? Go and arrange it, and figure out a way to distract Djisgaga for a few minutes."

"Come along. I won't leave you alone out here."

"Prince is right over there." She gestured fondly. "He hasn't taken his eyes off Orimha."

John smiled. "That dog is as devoted to you as he is to Shannon. You twentieth-century females have a way about you." Taking her arm, he propelled her into the longhouse.

Cassie's eyes narrowed slightly when she saw the elegant seventeenth-century "nurse" fussing over the seated Alex in a proprietary, almost intimate, fashion. Not that Cassie was jealous in a romantic sense, of course. This woman was married to Kahnawakee, who was a pretty fair catch by any standard. In the long run, Djisgaga was just a nuisance, and it almost made sense for Cassie to let her have her way for a few days until Alex was more rested.

His reaction, when he caught sight of her, pleased and reassured her. While his expression had been solemn, due to some weighty pronouncement by Kahnawakee, no doubt, he was clearly distracted—almost spellbound—by her arrival.

"John," Cassie whispered, elbowing his ribs sharply, "get rid of Djisgaga."

"Would you kindly find another way of making your point?" he chuckled. "My side is aching." Then in a loud voice he announced, "Cassandra needs a word with Alex."

Kahnawakee turned to greet her, a sly grin on his face. "You slept well, Cassandra?"

She nodded, amazed once again by the resemblance to Alex. It seemed stronger than ever, now that the two had finally met and talked. "Good morning, Kahnawakee. Hi, Djisgaga. Alex?" She felt a blush warm her cheeks. "Are you feeling better?"

"Couteau is amazing us with his tales," Kahnawakee assured her. "Come and sit with him, Cassandra. My wife and I will give you privacy."

Djisgaga's veiled scowl was not lost on Cassie, but she decided to find it amusing and moved eagerly to the platform. True to his word, John was hustling the visitors away, and so Cassie turned her full attention to Alex, sinking to her knees and whispering, "Are you healing, Alex? No infections? No complications?"

He moistened his lips and reached for her, using care not to scratch her with his finger splints. "I missed you," he murmured, smoothing back the curls from her forehead and kissing it lightly. "How did you sleep?"

"John snores." She drew her finger lightly over his lips. "I missed you, too. I was going to sneak over here, but I was more tired than I thought."

"I half-expected you," he grinned. "But I was tired, too. We have to wait a few days, but in the meantime, kiss me."

"Mmm . . ." She moved her mouth to his, enjoying the warmth of his breath before allowing their lips to meet. His tongue teased gently, parting and then playing along her lips before tentatively exploring, while Cassie's hand moved into his hair, her nails skimming along his scalp with cautious appreciation. "Tell me if I hurt you, Alex . . ."

"You feel so good. I dreamed about you all night." His mouth grew more demanding and his left hand slid behind her back, urging her to join him on the platform. As she carefully stretched out beside him, she felt a burst of reckless heat that threatened to transform their cautious embrace into a wild, possibly dangerous clinch and so she pulled away, smiling in sheepish apology. "You're not ready for this. Let's talk."

"Cassie . . ." His frustrated complaint was accompanied by a swift grab for her waist and he pulled her back against himself with a triumphant grin. "Like I said, I dreamed about this."

"Me, too. I just don't want to make your injuries worse."

"Every place you touch me feels instantly better, so start touching."

Cassie's hand slipped under the blanket to confirm the fact that he was still unclothed, and her smile turned impish. "I'm glad you're feeling so much better. I guess it was the aspirin."

"I didn't take any aspirin." His mouth explored her neck as he spoke. "I didn't need it."

"Yes, you did. I put some in that tea John brought you before you went to sleep."

"What?" He raised his head and stared. "Did John know it was doctored?"

"Are you kidding? He'd never play along with anything like that. He's got the same noble streak that makes you so conservative."

"Conservative?" His left hand moved to the placket of her shirt, working the buttons slowly. When Cassie realized his unprotected fingernail beds were a source of pain for him, she hastily took over, unhooking her shirt and allowing it to fall open slightly. Alex moistened his lips as he pushed the fabric aside to reveal a firm, rose-tipped breast. "Cassie . . ."

The heat from his admiring eyes was enough to cause the nipple to tense, and Cassie's heart pounded as he lowered his head and began to nip gently. She had never responded to a man with such quick abandon and wondered if Alex knew how alarmingly sexy he could be, even in his debilitated state. His mouth was moving lower, tasting the taut skin across her ribs and abdomen, and she wondered if he was daring enough to attempt to unbutton her jeans with his revered nurse just outside. If so, then it was time Cassie herself got into the act and she slid down until their faces were opposite one another, then pushed his blanket aside and began to move her aroused nipples against his chest, with care not to contact one particularly angry-looking furrow of blisters.

They kissed hungrily as their bare flesh, from the waists up, became acquainted at long last, and their legs tangled, trying to find the perfect position that would satisfy their skyrocketing need. Then Alex rolled Cassie onto her back and positioned his fully naked body atop her, groaning, "This is better than the dream, Cass. You're driving me crazy."

She moaned her agreement, amazed at how damp they both had so rapidly become, then she tasted blood from his kiss and realized, in startled shame, that the layer of moisture covering his torso and lips had seeped from his many wounds. How could she have abandoned herself to this at his expense?

"Alex," she pleaded, pushing firmly against his good shoulder, "cut it out. You're bleeding."

"Huh?" His voice was groggy again, this time from the erotic haze that had enveloped them. Then he looked down to see the crimson smear across her snow-white breasts and sighed, "Sorry, Cass. I didn't know . . ."

"We have to let you heal." She gathered her shirt quickly about herself and covered him to his neck. "I'll get a rag and bathe you."

"Don't worry about it. Come here. I won't go crazy again, I promise."

She smiled and cuddled gratefully against him, promising, "The next time we go crazy, we won't have to stop."

Alex chuckled. "Good. A man only has so much willpower, Cassie. Mine's just about used up."

While she knew he was referring to their sexual attraction, she couldn't help but think of the enormous strain on his willpower and self-control demanded by the recent episode with Orimha. His body had been beleaguered enough, and despite her frustration, she now knew it was for the best that she was going home with John.

"Tell me how it felt to meet Kahnawakee for the first time, Alex."

"It was incredible," he admitted, shifting so that her head was cradled against his chest. "I would have preferred being able to stand to meet him, but even so, it was an awesome moment."

"I'm glad. It makes me feel less guilty for dragging you back here and almost getting you killed."

"Why would you feel guilty about that?"

"I requested you."

"Pardon?"

"As my escort," she murmured. "When I built the first little cabin, I asked Uncle Matt to send you with me."

"But that didn't work."

"I know, but then, a rattlesnake was about to bite me yesterday, and suddenly—poof! I was with Shannon and you were with Orimha."

"You 'requested' me? As your 'escort'?"

The concept seemed to stun him, and Cassie glanced up to read his expression. "Are you upset?"

"Do I look like someone's escort to you, Cassie? I have a full caseload," his voice was hoarse with frustration, "and monumental responsibilities, and you 'requested' me as your 'escort'?"

She was about to apologize when his reluctant chuckle reassured her and she giggled slightly in return. "It was all worth it, right? You got to meet your Visionary."

"It's *going* to be worth it," he corrected, caressing her cheek. "You're going to see to that once I've recovered, right?"

"John promised to bring me back here next week," she nodded, flushing with excitement. "Then we'll see what I can do."

"Next week?" He closed his eyes and shook his head. "That's too long. We can't be gone from the twentieth century that long, Cass. They're probably looking for us by now, and the headlines are blazing about another disappearance of a beautiful blonde in the Protectorate. I have to get back there for damage control, not that anyone would ever believe where we've been."

"Shannon told me she's been here seventeen months, Alex."

"Huh?"

"See what I'm saying? Five months our time is seventeen months in seventeenth-century time, at least in Shannon's case. I don't think time lines up neatly from here to there. Maybe they don't even know we're gone yet."

"Or maybe it's been months according to them?" His jaw tightened with concern. "What a mess."

"We don't have any choice but to wait until you've healed, Alex. If you go back looking like this, the headlines will be *really* wild, like ***Irate Cleary Cousin Takes Revenge on Susquehannock in Bizarre Bondage Ordeal.***"

"That's pretty close to the truth," he laughed. "Dragging me back through time as your escort. And like a fool," he added darkly, "I thought I was sent here to be tested, to determine if I was tough enough to lead my nation. Pretty egotistical, wasn't it?"

"You *were* tested, and you passed with flying colors. Even Harvard never gave such a thorough exam, right?"

"Speaking of which, did you really tell Kah-nawakee I'm 'a lawyer, not a warrior'?"

She winced. "I said it to John, but I didn't mean it the way it sounds. You're obviously a warrior."

"Just don't talk to Kahnawakee anymore, okay? He doesn't know when you're joking, and it makes me look a little foolish."

"I don't think so. He said yesterday you were lucky to have me," Cassie retorted, adding weakly, "he looks so much like you, I guess I *was* a little too familiar with him. I'll watch it, Alex. I didn't mean to embarrass you."

"You didn't. I didn't mean to criticize, Cass. Your stupid jokes are one of the things I like best about you. The jokes, and . . . ," his hand slipped inside her shirt, "all the rest of you." He laughed ruefully. *"You* request me as *your* escort, but somehow *I* end up in a Mohawk camp and *you* end up in a cozy cabin, visiting your cousin."

"Life's funny, isn't it?" Cassie grinned. "But think of all the things you've learned. And you made a great first impression on Kahnawakee and John."

"That's something," he agreed. "Their opinions are important. You should have heard them talking, last night and this morning. They're brilliant, Cassie. They have such vision and commitment. I'm going to learn as much as I can in the next few days."

"But you're also going to rest," she insisted. "When I come back, I expect to see a big improvement." Brushing her lips across his, she murmured, "I'll miss you, Alex. Will you do one little thing for me?"

"Anything."

"Take the aspirin every four hours until your shoulder's better and your fingers aren't swollen anymore."

"Cassie," he groaned, but accepted the bottle, placing it under the platform. "You stay close to John."

"I *slept* with him last night," she reminded him tartly. "How close, exactly, do you want us to stay?"

Alex grinned, then closed his eyes for a moment, and she knew his body needed sleep. As further confirmation of the fact that it was time for her to leave, Djisgaga moved out of the shadows and into view.

Cassie bit back a sigh. "Alex?"

"Hmm?"

"I'm leaving now. Djisgaga will take good care of you, okay?"

"Yeah." He kissed her, then peeked sheepishly over her head at his nurse, mumbling something in Susquehannock that Cassie could only hope wasn't an apology. Pulling free of his arms, she whispered " 'Bye, Alex," gave Djisgaga a sour smile, and hurried toward the doorway.

The more leisurely pace of the return journey suited Cassie, who took the opportunity to collect grapes and wildflowers and, more importantly, information about Djisgaga. John seemed to share Alex's naive opinion of the dark-haired beauty, referring to her as gentle and dedicated, and reverently recounting the story of Kahnawakee's courtship of a shy maiden who had caught his eye from the moment he had first begun noticing females in that way. Cassie was fairly certain Djisgaga had snared Kahnawakee in a well-orchestrated seduction that only appeared, to gullible men, to be demure resistance, but she had to acknowledge it would be worse if Djisgaga were unattached and so she pretended to believe the story, prodding for more and more details.

"She's been invaluable to him. To us," John explained. "Her only thought is to please him, and she supports every decision he makes, even if those decisions take him away from her for months at a time."

"She's practically a saint," Cassie nodded. "What about their baby?"

"This is the first time I've seen her without little Couteau Noir," John admitted. "I guess taking care of Alex is an unrivaled priority with Kahnawakee. But the other women help so much with the infants and children . . ." He scowled. "Shannon could benefit from their customs. The women would fuss over her, and birth the child, and help raise it."

"She likes being alone with you."

"We won't be alone for long," he grinned. "Shannon says eight more weeks, at least, but . . ."

"I agree," Cassie laughed. "She looks like she's just about ready to have it."

"When she refused to go to the village, I tried to convince her to go to my mother's house. At least there she'd have access to a doctor."

"Where's that?"

"New Amsterdam. It's a long journey, and now it's become impracticable. She might have the child on the way."

"Shannon's tough. Maybe she'd like that."

John grinned and tousled Cassie's curls. "Don't give her that notion, missy. In any case, I have the feeling you're the answer to my dilemma. You'll deliver the baby, won't you?"

"Shannon will deliver it, but if I'm here, I'll gladly catch it and give it a bath for you. How's that?"

"That's fine." He paused, then added gently, "You'll still be here, Cassie. Kahnawakee has plans for Alex. I think you'll be here for months."

"Alex would do anything for Kahnawakee, but . . ." She shrugged. "Never mind all that. This area's starting to look familiar. I think I met Prince right over there."

"My cabin is just over that crest," John confirmed. "We'll hear Duchess howling in a moment." He caught Cassie's arm. "Can I ask a favor of you, missy?"

"Sure. Just name it."

"I know you're anxious to reminisce with Shannon, but once you've had a little time alone with her, could you . . . ?"

"You want time alone with her to talk about her past?" Cassie didn't need to ask him what he was going to say. He was so driven by love for his wife that he would undoubtedly say all the right things and Shannon's world would be even more perfect, if that was indeed possible. "Go on ahead, John. Prince and I want to do some reminiscing of our own along the way. And when we get there, I'll play with him and Duchess until you and Shannon have finished your talk."

John nodded. "You may be the stubbornest female I've ever met, but you're also a pleasure, did you know that?" He turned his eyes in the direction of the cabin and, for the first time since she'd met him, Cassie thought she saw John Cutler's confidence waver.

Cassie had been gone for less than five hours and already Alex was wishing he hadn't allowed her to leave. He was her escort, after all—the irony brought a rueful smile to his lips—and he should be near her at all times. And she was so soft, and sweet, and smelled so incredibly fresh. His brush with death had made him acutely aware of the scents and sounds and sensations that surrounded him, and Cassandra Stone was a veritable feast on every score. She had told him once that texture, rather than color, guided her artwork, and he knew that texture also guided her love-making. The way she buried her hands in his hair, and moved her nipples so erotically across his chest . . .

"Couteau? Are you awake?"

Alex struggled to his feet, impressed as always by Kahnawakee's humble manner. The chief spoke the same Susquehannock dialect that Alex had been taught, and acted as though he were just another villager, rather than the leader of this village and Visionary for all times! "It is good to see you, Visionary," he responded. "I wasn't asleep, just resting."

"Sit down." Kahnawakee motioned toward the platform, then sat himself down on the floor of the longhouse alongside Alex's bed. "Are you strong enough to talk again?"

"Yes, Visionary."

Kahnawakee's face was unreadable, but his tone of voice was affectionate, as always. "There is no need to call me by that title, Couteau. You may call me 'brother.'"

"Brother?" Alex shook his head, uncomfortable with the thought. It seemed presumptuous on his part, and overly generous on Kahnawakee's. Had he earned such a privilege?

"Then call me Kahnawakee," the chief suggested. "We are family, little brother. I have spoken to you for hours, and you have listened with great attention. Now, I have several questions for you."

"I'll do my best."

"You say three hundred years will pass before your time comes. It pleases me to know our struggle is not in vain, and I wish to hear more. I do *not* wish to hear certain facts, such as my personal fate, or that of my wife or son or John Cutler. To ask for such knowledge would be an abuse of this privilege we have been given. You must take care, Couteau, with your answers."

Alex nodded, tongue-tied with awe at the great man's self-discipline. Would he himself be so unselfish were he given the means to anticipate, and perhaps avoid, disaster or heartache?

"Tell me about your government." Kahnawakee's eyes were bright with curiosity. "Tell me what use the Europeans will make of this land. Will they respect it? Will they respect *us?*"

"In my time, about one-half of this continent of North America is owned, in trust, by the Union of Native American Protectorates, which is called UNAP. Much of the rich timberland and most of the main rivers are within our jurisdiction, although we own relatively little of the ocean shores and have no navy to speak of. We are united against abuse of the land, which we hold in trust for our descendants. We have a superior army and air force to accomplish this.

"The rest of North America is divided among the English, the Washington Commonwealth, the French, and the Spanish. The Dutch turned their holdings over to the Iroquois League during the eighteenth century. Our nation—the Susquehannocks— occupies the same lands on which you now live. In UNAP, we are called the Voice. The League Protectorate is called The Fist, and the Delawares are the Heart. There are twenty-eight Protectorates, some of which represent combinations, such as the six nations of the League." He noticed Kahnawakee's perplexed expression and added quickly, "Another nation will join them one day. They are the Tuscaroras."

"Tuscaroras?" Kahnawakee seemed to savor the word. "And there are many others? To the south and to the west?"

"Dozens, Visionary. Their appearances and cultures vary, but they share your respect for this turtle's back we call North America. Some of their ways are strange to us, and there are many disagreements in our Council, but we have endured.

"The Washington Commonwealth is the largest colonized area of the continent. That's where Cassie lives. She's been raised to consider herself as much a native as any Susquehannock, and her people have learned to respect the land, too. Together with UNAP and New France, they have formed an organization called the International Environmental League, which has been vigilant in developing clean fuel sources and protecting endangered areas and animals. They've been so successful, in fact, that many of the western protectorates feel UNAP is not necessary any longer."

"And do you agree?"

Alex chose his words carefully. "Until the last six months, I felt UNAP needed to be reorganized. Our traditional emphasis on unanimity and endless debate has made it difficult for us to make decisions. The twentieth-century world moves very quickly, Visionary. A man can travel from Onondaga to this village in a matter of hours—even faster if he uses a vehicle called an airplane. We can communicate almost instantly, and hesitation can often mean opportunities lost.

"On the other hand, we haven't eliminated greed or bad judgment, and so we still must be vigilant at all times. And just as you foresaw, our great power depends on our unity. Our leaders face a dilemma: shall we change, and perhaps weaken ourselves? Or shall we follow our traditional, successful methods and risk losing many of our members due to their perception of us as outdated?"

"And you once favored change, Couteau, but doubts have grown in your heart?"

"Yes."

"You are not chief in your world?"

"No, Visionary. As time goes on, our life span will grow longer, and we stay in our childhoods for longer times. It has been many years since a chief was named who was younger than thirty years in age, and even that was considered remarkable. I only completed my education three years ago, and since then I've been our Council Adviser, which means I attend the Council with the chief, who is also my mother's uncle."

"Oh?" Kahnawakee smiled. "You advise him? He does not advise you? That is strange, Couteau."

Alex flushed. "I didn't mean to sound disrespectful, Visionary. Our chief is a fine man. Very wise. I'm called the Council Adviser because my job is to study the Council's proposals, so that the chief will be informed . . ." He shook his head. "I'm not making sense, am I? It's like Cassie said. I'm a lawyer. I'm also a diplomat. I handle sensitive issues for the chief. Ordinarily, I'm considered to be articulate, but . . . ," he grinned weakly, "I guess I'm trying to impress you and accomplishing just the opposite."

"Your chief is fortunate to have you for his adviser," Kahnawakee declared. "It is the role that John Cutler has unselfishly accepted, and I am dependant on him for guidance. I was not scolding you, little brother. You have impressed me with your dedication and your bravery. There is no need to be concerned, and if you are to instruct me, you must see me as a student, not as a superior."

"Instruct *you?*" Alex took a deep breath. "I want *you* to teach *me,* Visionary."

"I will give you guidance," Kahnawakee assured him with an amused smile, "but you will give me information. We are equals in this, Couteau, do you understand? And now," he added, rising to his feet, "my wife insists you must rest, and so I will leave you to your healing. Tomorrow, if your feet have improved, we will walk together in the woods and talk in more detail." With a slight bow, he was gone.

Alex stared after his idol, dazed and confused by the honor he had just been paid. He had initially thought he was here to be tested. Thereafter he had half-accepted the dubious role of "escort" for Cassandra Stone. Now this! Was it possible he was here to aid the Visionary? He shook his head and grinned sheepishly. To have Cassie as his lover, Kahnawakee as his adviser, and ethereal Djisgaga as his nurse! He was beginning to think he was the luckiest man who'd ever lived, blisters and broken digits notwithstanding.

John approached the bed quietly, pleased that Duchess hadn't yowled and awakened his bride prematurely. He had always loved to gaze upon her when her cheeks were flushed and warm with sleep, as they were at this moment. She was curled into a ball, surrounding and protecting their unborn child, and he struggled with his pride as her beauty and otherworldliness taunted him with thoughts of her sweet deception over these seventeen love-stricken months.

Then she stirred, and her eyelids opened to reveal the sapphire jewels that could sparkle with love and innocence at the slightest provocation. The sight of him seemed cause enough for such sparkling, and as she brushed her long, golden hair from her face, she almost cooed with delight. "You're home? When . . . ?" Without hesitation she raised her arms toward him for his embrace.

He stood towering above her, then grasped her outstretched hands in his own and murmured, "Have you been well, wife?"

"Well, but lonely, husband." Her smile faded. "Did Cassie come back with you? Is something wrong? Oh!" Struggling to sit, she groaned, "I received a message that Alex was safe! Don't tell me something else has happened! Is Cassie okay? John?"

"I want to talk to you, Shannon."

"Oh?" She winced slightly. "I'm starting to understand. Cassie told you about my . . . past? She promised she wouldn't, but," her smile returned, shaky and uncertain, "you made her tell you? I almost forgot how persuasive you could be, John Cutler. Are you angry with me?"

"I am . . . honored by you," he whispered hoarsely, raising her fingertips to his lips. "You have lived here with me, when the world was literally at your feet. Conveniences and luxuries of endless description, and wealth that could have taken you to the exotic ends of the earth." He sank to his knees and murmured, "Why did you choose me, Shannon? How can I ever hope to deserve you? To keep you here with me when that world is waiting for your return?"

Her eyes were swimming with tears as she draped her arms around his neck and forced him to meet her loving gaze. "Don't you know how wonderful you are? If only you knew what my life was like before I met you! I was lost and alone and confused, and then you held me in your brawny arms and made me feel safe and important."

"Shannon . . ."

"I belong with you, John. That other world was a foreign country to me despite all the wealth and convenience. I never belonged there. I was never happy there, and I think I would have died of loneliness if I had stayed there. You rescued me, don't you see?"

His mouth covered hers, hungrily thanking her for the tribute and reassurance, then he stroked her long hair and insisted, "You knew I wouldn't believe you if you told me all this, and you were correct. You couldn't confide in me—your own husband—for fear I would mock you or label your tale a delusion. Can you forgive me for that?"

"Can you forgive me for keeping secrets?" she sighed. "The truth is, John, it *is* unbelievable. Over these last few months, my memories of that world have faded. Your world has taken over my heart and my soul completely. To me, that place and that time no longer exist." She buried her face against his chest and confessed, "I told you all about that world once, the first time I came, and you didn't believe me. And do you know what? I think it made me feel safer to think that you thought I belonged to this world right from the start. I didn't want you to see me as some foreigner from another time. Don't you see?"

"The first time you came?"

Shannon smiled in relief. "I see Cassie didn't tell you everything."

"She told me almost nothing," he complained. "She's the stubbornest female on earth, Shannon. It was Alex who gave me some details, but . . ." He eyed her intently. "The first time?"

"I'll tell you the whole bizarre story *after* you greet me properly, Mr. Cutler. You've been away from me for two days, but it feels like a month, and . . ." she moistened her lips hopefully, "I missed you. Do I have to beg you to make love to me, John?"

"I'd best first bolt the door," he grinned. "That stubborn cousin of yours is getting acquainted with Duchess, but it would be just like her to interrupt us."

"Cassie's been outside all this time?" Shannon pulled away from him and pretended to scold. "She's right, John, you're not a very good host. You should invite her in! She must be tired from the long walk."

"Lie back now and relax," he grinned, pushing her gently into the pillows and fumbling with the ribbons on her lightweight gown. "She gave me specific instructions to make 'time-shattering' love to you, and as I said, she's the stubbornest female on earth. We dare not cross her."

"Oh? Well," Shannon closed her eyes and murmured blissfully, "I wouldn't want to disappoint my only cousin. By all means bolt the door and then shatter time, Mr. Cutler."

Chapter Nine

"It's such an amazing story, Shannon." Cassie was sighing as she took the final measurements for the birthing sling that would be her handcrafted gift to her new cousin. "I still can't believe history was once so different. I can't picture North America without the protectorates." She chewed her bottom lip, then admitted, "I always believed my forefathers came here to establish a more tolerant world, not to impose their will on the native inhabitants, but the way you tell it makes it sound just the opposite."

Shannon nodded sympathetically. "I guess they rationalized the things they did, saying they wanted to 'civilize' the natives or 'save their souls' or whatever, but the results were shameful." She studied her cousin curiously. "What about the rest of history? Weren't there other atrocities? Was there a Hitler?"

Cassie winced. "Of course, but I always thought we North Americans were above that sort of thing. After all, UNAP and the Washington Commonwealth were the first forces to really strike against Hitler out of moral outrage rather than simple border protection."

"I don't think any culture is immune from evil, Cassie. Give them too much power over another group and they'll abuse it. It's the lesson of history."

Cassie winced again. Shannon's words were harsh—*too* harsh!—given the proof of intercultural cooperation and respect Cassie had seen with her own eyes. The Washington Commonwealth and UNAP were allies in every sense, despite their vast cultural differences. And New France had spearheaded the International Environmental League, which was the ultimate in smoothly functioning multicultural teamwork. Perhaps, in Shannon's old history, a few greedy, unscrupulous men had triggered an outrageous chain of events, but that didn't require an indictment of human nature or society! Cassie believed harmony, not dominance, was each culture's ultimate goal. Although she had to admit there had been abysmal moments of cruelty at specific points in history, she attributed them to the rise of occasional megalomaniacs whose frenzied speeches whipped their followers into temporary insanity. Those were the exception, not the rule.

"I didn't mean to upset you, Cassie." Shannon eased her pregnant form into John's rocking chair and grinned apologetically. "I guess I keep getting carried away, but it's so much fun having someone to talk to. Not that John isn't perfect, of course."

"He's wonderful," Cassie agreed. "He's taking all of this twentieth-century stuff pretty well, don't you think?"

"That's John," she nodded. "He takes everything in stride. He's like a rock."

"You mean, he's as stubborn as a rock."

Shannon laughed. "I don't know which of you is worse. He's always calling *you* stubborn."

"Except *he* always gets his way," Cassie reminded her with an exaggerated pout. "He made me move all of my material out to the smithy, and he makes me sleep in the bed when I know he wants to be there with you."

"He made you move your stuff because it was beginning to look like a crafts fair in here," Shannon remembered fondly. "I still can't believe you came three hundred years through time with a purse full of sticks and pine cones, and a long blond braid. All of the things I already have enough of."

"Sorry. If I'd known I was coming, I would have brought a copy of some childbirth book and a giant bottle of conditioner." She fluffed her curls warily. "I keep expecting tangles."

"When you go to the village, ask the women for some sunflower oil. It works pretty well, but I've run out."

"I'll ask them for some advice on delivering the baby, but," she eyed Shannon's huge belly suspiciously, "I may not be back in time to help."

"You sound like John! I told you, the baby's not due until the middle of November. It was conceived on Valentine's Day." She blushed slightly at the memory. "Take my word for it. I even thought about calling it 'Valentine' if it's a girl."

Cassie grinned. "I'm glad you had a romantic Valentine's Day, Shannon, but get real. Call her Noel if you want to name her after the day she was conceived."

"I guess we'll call her Robin if it's a girl, and Philip if it's a boy. That's what John and I have decided."

"Phil will be so honored. I can't wait to tell him, Shannon. He'll be so relieved to hear you're happy and healthy."

"He's the only person I really miss from my old life.

I love my mother and sister, but there were so many problems there . . ."

"You would have loved our grandmother," Cassie sighed. "She was sweet and loving, and sometimes she seemed so sad, and now I know why. She was thinking about you, and wishing your mother would let her visit you."

Shannon nodded. "It would have been wonderful to have known her. But at least I finally got to know you." Her eyes twinkled. "I think I would have liked your mother, too. My Aunt Jennie."

"She's great," Cassie agreed. "She and my father drove me crazy when I was growing up, but now I appreciate them and I think in their own way they appreciate me, too. It was hard for two scientists to raise an artist, but we all survived."

"I loved all those stories you told John and me at dinner," Shannon smiled. "How they sent you to schools specializing in physics and chemistry, when all you wanted to do was learn about weaving and leatherworking."

"An incredible mismatch," Cassie remembered fondly. "I got the worst grades in the history of the school, but my science projects were always the most eye-appealing. I'll never forget my first volcano. It was practically iridescent."

"Did it erupt?"

"No, but my father did." She laughed, then added with a sigh, "Years later, I found out he had saved it, all that time, out in the rafters of the garage. When I asked him why, he admitted it was 'a work of art, in its own twisted way.' It was a turning point in our relationship. After that, they let me transfer to a boarding school along the Spanish Gold Coast to study art. He and my mother were working on a long-term marine project studying weather patterns on the Aztec Sea and it worked out perfectly."

"It's funny. You went to boarding school all the time, and you were completely different from them, but it sounds like yours was a really loving family." Shannon began to braid her hair wistfully. "That's how it is with me and Phil, I guess. I'm years away from him—I'll never even see him again—but I feel like we're close."

"And you'll name your first son after him. That's neat. Shouldn't you name your first girl after John's sister? Her name's Meredith, right? Why did you choose the name Robin? I like it," she added hastily. "Robin Cutler. It's a good name, but . . ."

"Robin is the English translation of Djisgaga."

"Ugh! Are you serious?"

Shannon giggled. "We owe them one, since Kahnawakee's baby was named after John."

"Couteau Noir? Black knife?"

"Because John gave Kahnawakee a black-hilted knife that more or less symbolizes their friendship."

"So, in a way, Alex is named after John, too?" Cassie marveled. "I love that! I wonder if Alex knows?"

"Alex really impressed me that day in the hospital, Cassie," Shannon smiled. "He was so handsome and confident, but also so kind. And when I told him he looked like Kahnawakee, he seemed so genuinely humble. Those are fine qualities."

"He's also ambitious," Cassie reminded her quietly. "It's really helped me, these last four days, talking to you about him, Shannon. When I heard he was being tortured, everything seemed so urgent, but now I'm realizing I'd better take things slowly with him. I wouldn't want to hurt his career."

"It's all my fault," Shannon sighed. "If it wasn't for all the racist publicity over my disappearance, Alex would never have been reluctant to get involved with you."

"But I'd never have met him if you hadn't disappeared," Cassie laughed, "so you're actually the matchmaker in all this. I just wish I knew how long we were staying here," she added wistfully. "It's tempting to abandon myself to my feelings for him and then just see what happens. There aren't any reporters to make a fuss over it, and maybe we'd find out if our feelings were strong and deep enough to face that kind of publicity when we went home. But if we go back too soon, before we're sure . . ."

"Then stay for a long, long time."

Cassie shook her curls. "All night long, I have steamy thoughts of Alex, but all day long, my steamy thoughts are about a long, hot *shower*. I miss my bathroom, Shannon."

Shannon laughed. "You're hopeless, Cassie. Just stay until the baby's born, then." Her eyes narrowed slightly. "How exactly do you plan to get home?"

"Pardon?" Cassie's own blue eyes now narrowed. "I'm going to light a fire on the burial ground, right? Isn't that how *you* got back the first time?"

"Not exactly." She eased herself out of the chair and moved to the bed. "I promised John I'd tell him the whole story first, remember? I haven't told him that part yet. It's pretty shocking, and believe me, you can't duplicate it. I just assumed you had a plan for returning."

"When I lit a fire in the twentieth century, nothing happened because Alex had made it legal. But right now, it's taboo, right? So if I do it, I'm out of here."

"Maybe," Shannon mused. "I'm not so sure it

works that way, Cassie. I'm not so sure you can control the timing."

"But I *am* going back, right?"

"Probably."

"Probably?" Cassie scowled. "I can't stay here, Shannon. I love you and John, but frankly, I can see how this might get boring for me. I'm very eclectic, artistically speaking—"

"That explains the mess in the smithy," Shannon laughed. "Hair and fur and skins and all of those old dresses John's mother gave me, which you've completely ruined."

"I'm redesigning them. Believe me, you'll like them better my way."

"I need to dress for this period of time, Cassie. I already called too much attention to myself, during the early months, by wearing my jeans and tennis shoes. I've decided never to wear jeans again, even assuming," she added doubtfully, "I can ever fit into them again."

"All the more reason for me to alter those dresses. You like this one I'm wearing, don't you?" She jumped to her feet and twirled, allowing the full red skirts to billow slightly.

"The dress itself is fine, it's the plunging neckline that's not quite authentic," Shannon grinned. "If you wear that in front of Alex, he'll rip his stitches trying to rip your bodice."

Cassie pushed up on her full, generously exposed breasts defiantly. "This style is all the rage in Paris this century, I'm fairly sure. Anyway," her haughty expression disintegrated to a grin, "I always wanted to dress like this. The ones I make for you will be more conservative, I promise, but," her blue eyes twinkled, "you may get more use out of this one than you think. Once I'm gone and you and John are back in bed together . . ."

"I may wear it once or twice," Shannon agreed. "Just for John's sake. Once the baby's sleeping through the night."

"Robin Cutler. It's a pretty name, but . . . Djisgaga? We haven't talked much about her . . ."

"I could tell you didn't like her." Shannon curled up on the bed and closed her eyes. "She's always been aloof with me, too. Now that I'm pregnant, she's a little warmer, but . . ." Her voice grew weary. "I saw another side of her once, months ago, Cassie. She's really a good person, and she loves Kahnawakee a lot. Maybe too much. I think that's why she's cold to you. You must threaten her in some way."

"She disliked me before she ever even met me. I don't think she's going to let me have a relationship with Alex."

"Alex doesn't take orders from her," Shannon soothed.

"But Alex *does* take orders from Kahnawakee, and *he* obviously takes orders from Djisgaga, whether he knows it or not."

"That's true. She has the clout in the village. I've seen lots of proof of that," Shannon mused. "There must be something you can do. She doesn't speak English, and you don't speak Susquehannock. But I know she'd love you if only you could talk for a while. Do you know any French?"

"About a hundred words, maximum. I'm almost fluent in Spanish, though, and of course, Greek and Latin, thanks to my parents the mad scientists."

"Well, pretty soon it'll be time for the corn-husking parties the women have. Djisgaga is the unofficial leader of the women, and you'll have time to get to know her better then. I spent a lot of time at the village during the harvest last year and it helped."

"The other women have been great to me."

"That's good. They're powerful, too, you know. Alex will be pleased to see that you get along with them. Their society is different from ours. The women have a lot of traditional political power. They even choose the candidates for chief."

Cassie nodded. "It's still that way in the twentieth century. In fact, some big elections were coming up when Alex and I left. They had been postponed, because of your disappearance, but they're scheduled for September, I think." She shook her head. "It's so confusing, Shannon. I know Alex wants to be the chief, and I know I can only hurt his chances, not help them." *Maybe Djisgaga and Leah Eagle are right,* she added silently.

"You have to follow your heart, Cassie. That's the lesson I've learned from everything that happened last year. Nothing lasts forever, you know. Even the greatest love affair ends one day. You might have a day, or a month, or a decade, or more, but you have to treat every opportunity for love as though it's fleeting and priceless, and you have to treat every obstacle as though it's surmountable. Seize the moment, as they say."

"Speaking of which, I hear John coming. Do you want me to go for a walk so you can 'seize the moment' with him for a few hours?"

Shannon giggled. "John would say that was a 'raw' suggestion. Anyway, I'm too sleepy to seize anything, so just stay and keep John company. Can you serve him some dinner for me?"

"Sure." She smiled playfully as the big man entered the cabin. "Hi, John. No luck with the fishing?"

"I left them outside to be cleaned. By you. It's time you started to earn your keep." He tousled her curls then approached the bed cautiously. "Shannon? Are you feeling poorly?"

"Just sleepy. Cassie's been entertaining me while I rest."

"I hope you've been discussing the plans for the birthing," he muttered. "It could be any day. You need a midwife, not entertainment."

"We have nine more weeks," Shannon corrected with a yawn.

"And we've decided to let Mother Earth be the midwife," Cassie added mischievously, "with gravity as her assistant."

"More nonsense," John growled.

"She's talking about this birthing sling she's making for me," Shannon explained. "Supposedly they're very popular in Cassie's time, John. They were developed in a protectorate in the western part of the continent."

"The Sierra Protectorate introduced the concept, but it's used worldwide, and has become a status symbol," Cassie insisted. "Rich women overpay me to design and decorate leather slings to be handed down through generations, even though I personally think the canvas ones are more practical. But Shannon gets the deluxe package, complete with beading and fringe. If I knew how to do Susquehannock quill beading, I'd do that, too."

"I've seen examples of that craft," John nodded, "but the women have forgotten the method. It is one of Kahnawakee's favorite examples of the loss of culture that has resulted from conveniences such as silk embroidery threads and glass beads from Venice."

"Well, I'm going to use the freshwater pearls you

saw in my purse, and the results will be gorgeous, I promise."

"I don't want it to be 'gorgeous,' I want it to be safe," he complained. "You mentioned gravity once before, Cassie. You said it pulls the rain from the clouds." He turned to his wife and grimaced. "According to your cousin, rain does not fall. It is pulled by the Earth."

"Cassie," Shannon scolded, "you shouldn't talk science with John. This is the seventeenth century, remember. Don't interfere with the natural order of things."

"Look who's talking," Cassie grinned. "Anyway, John knows all about gravity already. He knows things go down, not up. And we stand here, instead of floating away. What's the big secret?"

"We are pulled by the Earth's gravity?" John murmured.

"Sure. It's always working on us, so let's harness it for the baby, okay? The big question is, where's the little one going to sleep once it's born? This cabin is so small."

"I thought I'd rig a loft over there where the warmth from the hearth collects. The warmth rises," he noted sternly, "in spite of your gravity."

"Only because it's displaced by heavier cold air," Cassie began, but caught Shannon's sharp warning glance and nodded in acquiescence. "Never mind. I got terrible grades in science anyway. But one thing I'm good at is designing, and I've got hundreds of ideas for this place." She crossed to tap on the wall near the hearth. "We could knock out this wall completely, and build a little alcove, with a Dutch door that opens into a vine-covered patio. The baby would get a wonderful breeze, and all those colors and scents from the garden would stimulate her imagination and creativity." With a proud smile she insisted, "What do you think?"

"I think I'll rig up a loft where the warm air collects," John repeated with a shrug.

Shannon chuckled sympathetically. "Once John makes up his mind, there's nothing anyone can do to change it."

"Oh, really?" Cassie glared. "Well, maybe it's time he started being a little more open-minded. Try to have a little vision, John." She waited, but the jab that worked so well on Alexander BlackKnife seemed to leave John Cutler completely unaffected. "You're *so* stubborn! If it weren't for that gorgeous beard, I'd tell Shannon to dump you."

John started to chuckle, but paused when Duchess began howling vigorously. Exchanging surprised glances with Shannon, he murmured, "Sounds like visitors."

"Mohawks?" Cassie felt her skin tingle with fear. John and Shannon were always relaxed, here in this isolated cabin, and she had tried to follow their lead but had secretly nursed terrifying misgivings in light of the horrors that had befallen Alex. Shannon's "paradise" was also a lawless wilderness, and the Susquehannocks were not the only men roaming it.

"I've told you again and again," John soothed, "we have no enemies here. We are at peace. The Gahniencas would never harm us."

"What about Orimha?" she countered. "We know he's a brute. Do you have a gun or a musket or something?"

"Orimha has no quarrel with me," he insisted. "Let's find out who's here."

Cassie's apprehension grew and she shrank back

toward the hearth as John opened the door and
stepped out onto the porch. Only when he called a
hearty greeting in Susquehannock could she begin to
relax. "Kahnawakee?" she whispered toward Shannon, who had shifted to a seated position and was
smoothing her hair quickly.

"I don't know, but I think," her blue eyes twinkled
with excitement, "it may be Alex."

"Alex? He can't walk this far—" She caught herself
and took a deep breath, suddenly certain that Shannon was correct. He had walked this distance, on
burned feet, to see her. As unexpected as it was, it was
also understandable. Hadn't she been dying to see
him, despite her casual comments to Shannon?
Hadn't she pleaded with John to arrange to return to
the village without waiting for the entire week, as
originally planned? Was it so difficult to believe that
Alex might have been as anxious as she?

Perhaps he had used a horse or mule, but one way
or another, he had needed to see her, and she was
flattered and hopeful and more than ready to greet
him. With one quick tug on the low neckline of her
red plaid dress, she moved to the center of the cabin
and waited, taking another deep breath for insurance
against a traitorously overeager voice.

He was taller than she had remembered—undoubtedly the encounters with Kahnawakee had played
tricks with her imagination—and she knew she was
staring with uncensored admiration, scanning his
long, lean form for signs of distress or blood, but
noticing only bronzed skin over finely tuned muscles.
He was wearing lightweight moccasins, an intrigu-
ingly decorated breechcloth, and a fringed, sleeveless
vest. His hair, shaggier than ever, was thick and dark
and finger-tempting. His dark eyes were focused on

the neckline of her dress with such exquisite lust that
she wished, for one long, decadent moment, that John
and Shannon would take their two dogs and time
travel away, leaving their guests free to indulge the
fantasies that were teasing them so openly.

Shannon moved to Cassie's side and nudged her
slightly, then stepped forward and took Alex's hand
in her own. "It's wonderful to see you again, Alex. We
were all so worried about you, but I see you survived."

"No permanent damage done," he admitted, tearing his eyes from Cassie's bosom. "You look great,
Shannon. You can't believe what a relief this is, seeing
you happy and safe."

"Cassie's been telling me about all the trouble I
caused you and your nation," she smiled. "I'm sorry
about that."

"You were instrumental in the survival of the Susquehannocks," he reminded her quietly. "You don't
need to apologize for a little inconvenience. Especially," his gaze shifted back to Cassie, "when that
inconvenience brought your beautiful cousin into my
life."

Cassie moistened her lips, grateful she hadn't
sighed aloud in response to the romantic pronouncement. If there had been any doubt as to the purpose
of this visit, it was gone. Alex was here as her lover,
prepared to court and win her, and she only hoped he
didn't suspect how sinfully easy that would be. For
the moment, she would behave herself, and they
would all chat—she and Shannon and John and this
incredibly handsome warrior, and Kahnawakee or
whichever Susquehannocks had accompanied him on
his journey—and eventually, they would find an op-

portunity to slip away and explore the nuances of the passion that was straining to erupt between them.

"You should sit down, Alex," she managed to whisper in a voice that was unrecognizably low and husky. "You shouldn't have come all this way so soon. Did you have a horse?"

"I walked. It was fine."

She moved closer on the pretext of glancing behind him, then frowned when she saw only John Cutler on the small porch. "Where's Kahnawakee?"

"I came alone," Alex murmured, extending his left hand to tentatively brush his fingers across her cheek. "I missed you, Cassie."

"Alone?" The romantic aura was fading quickly. "You came here all alone? For four hours, in those woods?"

"I know my way through this area, Cass," he smiled. "I grew up here."

"I see." She tried to catch her temper, failed, and glared, "Weren't you supposed to be recuperating? Do you realize it's only been five days since you were beaten and burned and God knows what else?" Her hands were on her hips and she knew her eyes were flashing with frustration. "You have blisters all over your feet, Alexander BlackKnife, and a hole the size of the Grand Canyon in your thigh, and you *walked* for four hours without anyone to protect you?"

"Leave him alone, missy," John interrupted cheerfully, stomping past her and pulling open a cupboard. "Do you want a drink, Alex?"

"No, thanks." Alex turned his amused expression back to Cassie. "I was perfectly safe, and the burns from the bonfire are on the sides of my feet, not the bottoms, but . . ." he drew closer and murmured seductively, "nice of you to be concerned."

"You weren't 'perfectly safe'! What if you had blundered into another Mohawk camp? What if a rattlesnake had bitten you, or the wound on your thigh had opened?" She dropped to her knees and examined the stitching with unmasked disgust. "Look at this scar! I could have taken care of this, Alex BlackKnife, but instead, it's a mess." Realizing suddenly that her face was precariously close to the edge of the provocative breechcloth, she jumped hastily to her feet.

"Blundered?" Alex scoffed. "I never 'blundered' into a Mohawk camp, Cassie. I was summoned there as *your* escort, remember? And that," he added with a sly smile, "is the reason I'm here. I'd like to escort you back to the village, Miss Stone."

"Have a drink, Alex," John advised in mock sympathy. "I've lived with this woman for the last five days, and I guarantee, she'll never stop nagging at you for one thing or another. If she's not trying to change your behavior, she'll be rearranging your furnishings or snipping at your hair. If you plan on being her 'escort,' you'd damned well better learn to drink."

"Very funny." Cassie bit back a smile. "At least you made it here in one piece, I guess. Come and sit down at the table, and I'll fix you something to eat."

"I'm not hungry." Alex caught her by the waist and moved her toward the bench. "Sit with me, Cass. I want to talk to Shannon and John for a while." His arm stayed firmly around her even after they were seated, side by side, at the table, and Cassie melted under his muscled warmth.

"Have some water, at least," Shannon smiled, handing him a pewter mug filled from a matching pitcher.

He took a long, appreciated drink. "Thanks. You look great, Shannon. When's the baby due?"

"Not until the middle of November."

Cassie rolled her eyes. "Or tomorrow, whichever comes first. And I think it might be twins."

"Djisgaga says it's definitely not twins, and she's always an accurate predictor," John contributed, settling into his rocking chair, then pulling a surprised Shannon into his lap.

"Djisgaga's a genius at medical matters," Alex confirmed reverently. "Some of my burns have already healed. She's almost miraculous." Oblivious to the cryptic glances exchanged by the females, he continued cheerfully, "So what have you been doing, Cassie? Have you and Shannon been exchanging life stories?"

"Hers wins," Cassie said. "Wait until you hear some of the things that happened to her! And she hasn't even gotten to the good part yet. She's feeding the details to me and John in installments."

"Yeah?" He studied his host curiously. "I guess it's been quite a shock to you."

"It's comforting to know there's some logic behind all of Shannon's illogical behavior and remarks," John grinned. "Unfortunately, none of it explains Cassandra's babbling. She's slightly demented, I suspect, and very stubborn."

"I'm familiar with all of those qualities," Alex nodded, tightening his grip on her waist as he spoke. "She used to scare me, but now I figure, if I could survive Orimha, maybe I can survive her."

"Very funny." Cassie enjoyed their laughter, suspecting that, while Shannon's life story thus far had indeed been the more amazing, it wouldn't always be so. John Cutler and his lusty love had changed her cousin's life, and Alexander BlackKnife, although distinctly different in appearance and temperament from John, exhibited a similar attitude of confidence and mastery that was manifested in each man's hearty laughter and also in the way they possessively handled their women. And she *was* Alex's woman! He was making that clear with every gesture and remark, and she knew he would make it clearer still, with even more telling gestures and remarks, when they were finally alone together. She was suddenly impatient for that moment and suggested, "Would you like to see my workshop, Alex?"

"Workshop?"

"She's littered my smithy with her infernal collection of rubbish," John explained. "Don't allow him to see it, missy. It'll scare him off."

"I'd ask you two to join us," she sniffed, "but I don't think you're ever going to be able to get out of that rocker." When Shannon began to giggle helplessly at the imagined plight, Cassie turned a shy smile to Alex. "Aren't they an adorable couple?"

"Yeah, adorable. So," his eyes were dark with anticipation, "where's this workshop of yours?"

"I thought we'd never get out of there." Cassie led her warrior by the hand toward John Cutler's humble smithy. "John's such a tease."

Alex chuckled. "I didn't mind waiting to feel the baby kick, or hearing the story of how he met the Visionary, but when he started describing his plans for knocking out that wall and adding an alcove to the cabin, I realized he was trying to stall." With a quick tug he had pulled her into his arms. "So," he murmured, "was he worried I was going to try to take advantage of your innocence?"

"Actually," she sighed, moistening her lips, "I think he was worried *I* might attack *you.*"

"Be my guest."

She nodded, draped her arms around his neck, and waited. When he lowered his mouth, she greeted it with gentle hunger, tasting and then exploring with her tongue while her body shifted against his. The smell and feel of newly crafted leather assaulted her nostrils and her hands responded, leaving his hair and skimming slowly down his back and then under his vest. Her fingernails glided over his skin, tantalizing and being tantalized in long, rhythmic movements.

"I love the way you touch me," he groaned, moving his mouth to her neck. "I love the way you smell, Cassie."

"Really?" She buried her face in his freshly washed hair and moaned audibly. The thick, unruly roughness against her cheeks and lips aroused her for reasons she could only begin to guess, as though confirming her original reaction to this man—that he was going to regale her senses with stimulation and variety until she was completely enslaved and totally satiated.

"Let's go inside the workshop," Alex suggested, his voice raspy with desire. "I don't want to manhandle you out here, in case John's got a problem with it."

"Huh?" Cassie took a deep breath and leaned against him, trying to calm her pounding heart. "Why would John have a problem with this? I mean . . ." she raised her eyes and blushed, "I think we should go inside the workshop before this gets . . . out of hand, so to speak, but," her blush darkened, "John knows how it is with us, Alex."

"This isn't the twentieth century, Cass. We should

be discreet about all this. We're not married, and
John's made it clear to me that he sees himself as the
head of your family, for purposes of this time and
place."

"Really?" It pleased her, despite the possible inconvenience. Would bushy-faced John object to their
lovemaking? Would he demand to know if Alex's
intentions were honorable? She was a bit curious herself, although at this point she doubted whether she
could resist him even if he announced with finality
that they could have no future together in the twentieth century. She was more than willing to "seize the
moment," in accordance with Shannon's advice, and
the thought that John might want her to save herself
for a more devoted suitor was simultaneously sweet,
quaint, and hopelessly irrelevant.

Stepping free of Alex, she gestured toward the
smithy, which was now less than ten yards away.
"Come and see my workshop. John won't bother us
in there. He and Shannon will be enjoying the chance
to be alone, believe me. They probably won't come up
for air for an hour or two."

"Yeah?" Alex grinned. "Isn't she too pregnant for
all that? If I were him, I'd be afraid of starting a chain
reaction and having the baby born right there in the
middle of it all."

"I don't know what they do," Cassie laughed, "but
they definitely do something in there when they're
alone. John's been sleeping on the porch while I'm
here and he wakes up in a grouchy mood, then I go
for a walk, they spend some time together, and *poof!*
He's a pussycat."

"You've been sleeping in the bed with Shannon?"
Alex frowned. "I wanted you to sleep with me tonight." He moved closer and lowered his voice seduc-

tively. "I walked all this way on blistered feet to sleep with you, Cass."

"The blisters are on the sides, not the bottoms," she reminded him weakly. "Anyway, are you sure you're up to sleeping together? Shouldn't you still be resting a lot?"

"It's Saturday night," he countered, pulling her toward the smithy, "and on Saturday night, I like to take my date dancing. Would you like to go dancing with me, Miss Stone?"

She blushed as he opened the four-foot-wide doors and began to pull her inside. She wanted to dance with him, and sleep with him, and touch him everywhere with her fingertips and cheeks and tongue and nipples until she exploded. From the far corner of the workshop a pile of rushes and fabric strips that she had been weaving into a hammock for the baby beckoned to her as a love nest, and only her last vestige of common sense was preventing her from dragging Alex across the room and hurling him to the ground.

"Alex, we have to be careful," she sighed instead. "Won't you rest for a little bit from your long trip before we 'dance'?"

"Look at this place," he marveled, ignoring her suggestion. "It's like a shrine to texture."

John had placed a wide plank across the open furnace for Cassie to use as a workbench, and it was now covered with bunches of fur and hair, bundles of twigs and plants, piles of smooth pebbles and nuts, and assorted grinding tools and scissors. Shannon's matronly gowns—in various stages of alteration—were draped from the tool shelf, and a soft deerskin hide was tacked down and ready to be cut into the basic shape of the birthing sling.

Alex's gaze swept over these items one by one, then

came to rest on the craftswoman's face. "You're really something, Cassie. Do you mind if I shut the door?"

"It would make it too dark," she murmured. "There aren't any windows in here. It's never used without the doors wide open, to let out the smoke and heat. . . ."

"The smoke and heat?" Alex grinned. "I guess this place has seen a lot of that and," he stepped closer and traced the line of her jaw with his fingertip, "it's about to see a lot more."

Chapter Ten

It amazed her that a simple touch of his hand to her face could send her entire nervous system into orbit. She was suddenly breathless and speechless, with her temperature rising so rapidly that she anticipated the predicted smoke would soon be wafting out into the yard to inform John Cutler of his guests' incendiary foreplay. Alex was waiting patiently for a signal that he could proceed and she longed to supply one, by inching closer or speaking his name or simply moistening her lips, but she also needed to find a way to ask him to go slowly, for his own sake and for hers. He had been so recently injured, and she. . . .

She had never made love. She had never *been* in love. She had never imagined love to be this way—so hot and quick and devoid of rules. There had been other men, who had kissed her and held her and tried to make demands upon her, and she had cared for several of them, and had even wanted to surrender to the tender, pleasing, enjoyable styles of one or two of them, but she had held back, and now she knew why.

Foolishly, she had believed she was waiting for a romantic courtship, a lifelong commitment and "tender loving care." It was now abundantly clear that her body had deceived her. Knowing instinctively what could happen one day, it had greedily demanded that she wait for a touch that was more than pleasing, and a kiss that was more than enjoyable, and a caress that was more than tender and comforting. Her body had wanted *this*—white-hot heat and mindless frenzy!— and Alex's body was here, inches away, ready, willing, and able to deliver.

"We have to go slowly," she managed to murmur finally. "Please, Alex?"

"We're just going to dance," he reminded her, his smile gentle and all-knowing as he took her hands and drew her further into the smithy, so that they were no longer within view from the porch of the cabin. Then he pulled the door partially closed, until only a narrow beam of late-afternoon sun illuminated the darkness. "Just relax, Cassie."

The realization that Alex had read her expression and knew she was frightened, vulnerable, and aroused intimidated her further. For the moment, he was being solicitous, but what if he decided to turn up the heat? She wouldn't be able to protest—her body would see to *that,* she was certain—and once she began to experience him, she wouldn't be able to stop. She would be ravenous, and undisciplined, and wanton, and he would be misled into believing that she was experienced in these matters, and then he would escalate his needs until they were insatiable, and . . .

"I have to talk to you," she gasped. "Before we dance."

He grinned mischievously. "You should see your face, Cassie. What am I? The Big Bad Wolf, suddenly? You look like you think I'm going to—" He broke off, apparently distracted by an image, then continued, "Do you think I'm going to devour you?"

She nodded, her eyes wide with confusion. "You need to know something," she blurted. "I've never . . . danced, so to speak . . . with anyone before."

"You've never danced?" He was momentarily perplexed, then his grin returned, this time almost deadly. "You're kidding! Come here." Pulling her hard against his chest, he murmured seductively, "This is incredible."

"I've just been busy with other things!" she wailed against his chest. "It's not like I waited for you specifically."

"Forget it," he ordered. "I'm taking this completely personally, and that's final. Now," his voice returned to the seductive whisper, "dance with me, Cassie. You know you want to, and I'm going crazy just thinking about it—about you—night and day."

"I know," she moaned, sliding her arms around his neck and running her tongue over the bare skin of his shoulder at the rough edge of the vest. "You taste so good, and feel so good, and sound so good . . ."

"Cass . . . ," he moaned, pushing her gently until she was flush against the wall and fumbling at the laces on her low-cut bodice, "I don't want to rush you, but I'm so hot for you I'm losing my mind. I keep imagining how it's going to feel, and I swear," he ripped the last of the laces in frustration and her breasts spilled into his waiting hands, "if it feels half as good as I imagine . . ." With no need or time to finish the thought, he lowered his mouth to an erect nipple and greedily enjoyed it.

She knew it was going to feel even *better* than he imagined, and that thought made her temperature soar as she buried her fingers in his hair and encouraged his mouth to explore while she wrapped one long, eager leg around his hips and tried to calm herself by grinding slowly against his pelvis. When he chuckled at the illogical solution, she almost joined his laughter, but his left hand had moved to the inside of the thigh that graced his hip, with clear intent to follow it up to his final destination, and she froze with anticipation. His caresses were inching along, and soon his fingers would be wet and hot from probing her, and she couldn't bear such enslavement, lest her will and her sanity be lost in the bargain.

"Alex," she pleaded in that husky, foreign voice that belied her message, "Wait a minute. I need to think."

"You need me," he corrected gently. "This is it, Cassie, and you're so ready." His fingers plunged into the thick, hot liquid that proved his claim. "I can do it any way you want, Cass, but I know you're ready and I want to be in you . . ."

"I want that, too," she gasped. "I want that now!"

He nodded, his smile slightly desperate with a mixture of sympathy and lust, and he swept her into his arms, striding quickly to the pile of rushes, where he gently lowered her, positioning his body over hers in the same fluid motion. "This is it," he repeated softly. "Cassie?"

She nodded, then pulled his mouth down to hers, hoping that somehow she could muffle the words of need that were struggling to reach Alex's ears. She wanted to feel him deep inside her, and she wanted him to be harder, and hungrier, and grander than any man had ever been, and if she ever said such things aloud, she would perish on the spot without ever having lost herself to him, and that would be so cruel!

He was fumbling with her skirts and then his hands found what they sought and he was guiding himself

toward her, positioning himself against her and waiting, this one last, desperate time, for some sign from
her that she wasn't going to change her mind and
drive him insane, and so she moved her own hand to
join his on the pulsating shaft, enjoying, for the first
time, this new and arousing texture that would soon
be buried deep within her. Alex groaned at her caress,
then pushed, gently at first, and then with more force,
as her damp folds alternately admitted and resisted,
tensed and resisted. She wanted him, and this, but the
resistance continued, and then, blessedly, it gave way
and he was one with her! His long, passionate, grateful kiss overwhelmed her, and as she wrapped her legs
around him she came slowly alive, tentatively beginning to throb around him.

It ignited Alex, although his movements were still
guarded. Only when Cassie's hips began to undulate
did he surrender himself completely to his madness,
and when he did, she thought the power behind his
thrusts might shake the foundations of the Earth itself! He was insatiable and unstoppable, and then,
suddenly, he was groaning with relief and pumping
with desperation and Cassie held onto him, cap-
tivated completely by the man's absolute ecstasy.

"Damn," he growled, when he could finally speak.
"Do you believe that?"

"It was wonderful," she sighed, stroking his face
lovingly. "You didn't hurt me at all, Alex. It felt so
wonderful."

"Wonderful?" His scowl was murderous. "It
wasn't supposed to be just wonderful. I guess I wasn't
as recuperated as I thought, Cass. I'm sorry, but don't
worry." A determined face replaced the frustrated
one. "This isn't over yet, I promise."

"What?" She smiled a nervous smile. "It's over,

Alex, and you should rest now. It was *more* than wonderful. In fact, it was the most amazing and stimulating experience I've ever had, *including* time travel, which you'll have to admit is saying a lot."

"Don't patronize me," he grinned. "It's my own fault for being greedy. So," he stood and glanced slyly around the smithy, "let's play a game."

"Pardon?"

"We'll call it the texture game."

"*Par*don?" She was trying not to laugh as she struggled to her feet. "The texture game?

"You close your eyes, then I'll touch you with something, like a piece of silk or some fur, and you have to guess what it is. It'll be a lot like the game you played with me, using that velvet Christmas stocking, the first day we met."

"You're really nuts," she accused, but his charming tone and sincere eyes were beginning to have their intended effect. He was seducing her—*again!*—and despite his apparent perversity, she was beginning to warm on cue. "You have to rest, Alex. This is fun, but let's be serious. You walked all the way here, and you need to take it easy for a little while. Maybe later," she added soothingly, "we'll go for a walk in the woods and play your texture game. How's that?"

"You're patronizing me again," he chuckled, "and I don't like it. No woman has ever pitied me, and no woman," he stepped closer and murmured, "has ever had a complaint against me. This is no time to start."

"A complaint?" she sighed. "I told you, I never had more fun, or more *anything,* than I just had with you. You're sensational." Rising onto her tiptoes, she brushed her lips across his.

"It was great, wasn't it?" he nodded. "Like you said, I just gave you the best time of your life, and all

I'm asking in return is five minutes, relaxing over there on that pile of weeds. You can call it afterglow if you want."

Cassie blushed as she watched him gather an assortment of texture from her workbench. For some inexplicable reason, she wanted to play this game with him more than she wanted anything on Earth. "You absolutely promise this won't . . . tax your strength?" she demanded weakly.

"It won't tax *me,*" he assured her solemnly. *"You* may get a little agitated if you start losing the game, but if you're a good sport, we'll both feel great at the end."

Suppressing a giggle, she followed him back to the bed of rushes and sat herself down, cross-legged, to wait for his next preposterous suggestion. When she began to fumble at the laces on her torn bodice, his hand interceded. "Don't tie your dress, Cassie. We need those loose."

"Those?" she retorted. "Are you referring to my breasts?"

"Yeah. Leave them alone. They've got sensitive nerve endings, so we're using them for the game."

"Really?" She was intrigued despite herself. In fact, having assumed he would be using another, more intimate set of nerve endings, she was almost disappointed. "So, do you want me to close my eyes now?"

"Lie down, take a deep breath, relax, and then close your eyes. And don't open them until the game is over."

"How will I know when it's over?"

"You'll know."

"Is there a time limit?" she teased nervously, lying back onto the rushes.

"Don't be a brat. Now close your eyes. Good."

She could feel him stretch out next to her, and the simple nearness of him caused a familiar burst of heat that she was fairly certain he could feel even without actually touching her skin. He was winning already, and he knew it.

"Don't open your eyes," he reminded her. "Can I give you a good-luck kiss?"

She nodded, then moaned inwardly as his mouth covered hers. When his tongue coaxed hers into play, she rolled onto her side, eager to completely embrace him and to forget the pretense of games and resistance, but he was determined, it seemed, to follow the rules and pushed her gently onto her back.

"Ready?" he whispered.

She nodded, then felt a brush of thick, slightly rough hair against the hard peak of her left nipple. Before she could guess, Alex was urging her to take her time, then he brushed the nipple again and again while his free hand pulled her skirts high on her thighs and began to stroke her legs tenderly. "Stay relaxed," he advised softly. "Just concentrate on the sensation. Don't pay attention to anything else, baby."

"Don't call me baby," she murmured, groggy from the feel and the sound of him. "I'm ready to guess, Alex."

"You're not ready yet," he corrected. "You've never played this before, Cass. Just relax and pay attention."

"You've never played this before, either," she reminded him in a dreamy voice. "But you're pretty good at it."

He chuckled. "Okay. Don't open your eyes, but you can guess. What's the texture?"

"Prince's fur."

"Very good. Now for something harder." When

Cassie giggled, he added sternly, "It's not that. Try to concentrate, Cassie. Tell me what you feel."

It was his tongue, teasing at her other nipple, and she arched slightly so that he was encouraged to take it into his mouth and enjoy it more thoroughly. The hand that had been stroking her legs so innocently now moved to her inner thighs, urging them apart and traveling with leisurely interest higher and higher until she arched again, this time with her lower body, and the fingers began to tease. When Cassie's groans became louder and more insistent, the teasing became probing, and soon one finger was penetrating so deeply that she could actually begin to ride it and she did, all the time wishing desperately for more.

"Alex," she pleaded. "I want you again. Like before."

He moved his mouth to her ear and murmured, "I know, Cass. I just don't want to take a chance—"

"Alex, I want you." Her hand fumbled at his breechcloth and began to stroke the hard, throbbing shaft eagerly. "Please?"

"I don't want to hurt you," he began, but Cassie interrupted him, gasping his name and again and again during a wild frenzy of movement that signaled more than simply the end of the game. Without hesitation, Alex eagerly slid his aroused length into her in time to feel the final spasms of ecstasy. He didn't move again until she had come almost to rest herself, then he began to thrust gently, working himself into a rhythm that her hips quickly learned and echoed, and they moved together, elated and triumphant and clearly believing that both had won this particular game. When Alex's passion came to a shuddering climax, Cassie stared with wide, adoring eyes at his transformed face, knowing that he had seen a similar expression of pleasure on her own features only moments earlier.

His strong arms gathered her firmly against himself as he rolled onto his back, and they remained joined thereafter for a long, quiet time. Finally Alex tapped her shoulder and teased gently, "You can say it now."

"Pardon?"

"All that stuff about 'the most amazing experience you've ever had, including time travel.' "

"You're obnoxious."

"Okay," he countered, "just tell me it was mildly satisfying. I'll settle for that."

She propped herself onto her elbow and smiled shyly. "It had its moments."

"The moment when you kept yelling my name?" he suggested with mock sympathy. "I was afraid maybe I was hurting you."

Cassie's smile was sheepish. "I've spent years trying to imagine what this would be like, Alex BlackKnife, and I wasn't even close."

"Is that a compliment?"

She nodded. "Go ahead and be smug. I guess you earned it. Now, will you tell me something truthfully?"

"Sure."

"How do you feel? I mean, physically. This burn," she touched the furrow across his chest gingerly, "looks so angry still. And your thigh wound must be hurting, at least a little."

"Nothing hurts. Every part of me feels fine, and some parts are deliriously happy."

Cassie blushed. "I have to fix my dress now, Alex. You tore the seam a little, and I don't want John or Shannon to notice."

"John and Shannon heard you, Cassie," Alex assured her gently. "If I had known what a screamer you were I would have taken you deep into the woods for this particular game."

"It's time to stop being smug," she warned, hopping to her feet and moving to the workbench to find her needle and thread. "It's time for you to get some sleep, while I go and help with dinner. There are fish to clean."

"I'll help. I can't sleep. I'm wide awake, and," he joined her at the bench and tipped her face toward his own, "we need to talk. I was in a rush, before, and I didn't say the things a man should say to a woman like you."

"That's not necessary," she flushed. "We haven't known each other very long, and this was a mutual decision, so let's just forgo the platitudes, okay? I'm a big girl, and this was at least fifty percent my idea."

"Yeah?" He grinned. "Don't tell me you've been having wild dreams and wilder fantasies, just like I have."

"I'm afraid so." She finished repairing the seam and relaced her bodice. "Why do you think I made this dress?"

"To make me the happiest man on earth?"

"That's right."

"Well, it worked. I'm also the *luckiest* man on earth, Cassie. I almost let you walk away, but we got this second chance with each other, and I value that."

"I agree." She backed away, hoping to appear casual and nondemanding. "I've been thinking about that, too. We couldn't date each other, in the twentieth century, without causing embarrassment to you, and to your Protectorate. But here, without any reporters or detectives around, we can spend a little time together and see how we really feel. And, once we go home, we can cool it, if that's what's best for all concerned, and at least we'll have had this chance to . . ." She faltered, wanting to tell him she was falling in love with him, for better or for worse, and was willing to trade a week in his arms for a lifetime of sanity. But wasn't that unfair? If she really meant what she said—if he could walk away from her in the twentieth century without a pang of guilt—didn't she owe it to him to make it easier, by leaving the emotional boundaries as blurred as possible?

"I've been giving it a lot of thought, too," Alex confessed quietly. "I thought we could get to know each other here, for a while, and see what developed, but—"

"But that still doesn't change the fact that, once we went back, we'd have to face the music or split up, right?"

"Right. So, it made more sense to 'face the music' right now. I needed to decide, from the start, if I was willing to accept the consequences, to myself and to my nation, of being involved with you. And then," he rested his hands on her waist and pulled her gently toward himself, "I realized it really doesn't matter, because I'm never going to find another woman who has this strong an effect on me and I'm never going to settle for less, so unless I'm willing to face a celibate, solitary, childless life—which I'm not—it's gonna have to be you."

Stunned by the commitment behind his words, she tried to find a reply, or even a voice, and failed.

Alex smiled. "We'll spend some time together here, to be sure it's the real thing. Like you said, it's only been a week, even though I feel like I've been waiting for you my whole life."

"Alex," she sighed. "That's so sweet."

"Yeah, I'm a sweet guy," he grinned. "So, what do you say? We give this a little time, just to be sure. And by the time we go home, if you're still as crazy about me as I am about you, we 'face the music,' as you call it? How's that sound?"

There were tears stinging at her eyes from the sheer beauty of his overture and she turned away quickly, afraid he might misunderstand her reaction. He would think she had already decided, and he was now trapped, but it wasn't so. She was loving this moment—*seizing* this moment!—and she could face anything in the future in exchange for this priceless respect and passion.

"Cassie?"

"I want to say something," she insisted. "Just listen and don't make me turn around."

"Sure. Go ahead." His tone softened. "You're not crying, are you?"

"No," she whispered. "I just need to concentrate. I want to make myself clear about this. Whatever you decide at the end of this time here will be fine with me. We weren't going to have any time at all before, and now we have this chance. It's perfect, even if it has to end when we go back."

Alex came up close behind her back and slid his hands around her waist. "When it's time to go, we'll decide about our future together." He hesitated, then murmured, "I keep forgetting to ask you, Cassie. Does Shannon know how to get us back to the twentieth century?"

"Of course. We'll burn the little cabin."

"Great." He turned her briskly toward himself and insisted, "A week isn't usually a long enough relationship to base a lifelong commitment on, so we're going to be sensible, but we're not blind. We both know what's happening here, Cassie. Let's enjoy it, shall we?"

She nodded, moistening her lips to accept his kiss. Shannon's voice from the yard, calling their names, threatened to interrupt, but Alex ignored the summons and lowered his head, kissing her gently and with unhurried thoroughness. Only when Prince barked a sharp rebuke from the doorway did the couple reluctantly separate. "What's with that dog?"

"He's wonderful, and I think maybe a little psychic."

"The beagle was friendlier to me. This one acts like he's your protector."

"He killed the rattlesnake that I ran into in the woods."

"Did he?" Alex whistled, then approached Prince, lowering himself to one knee and praising softly, "Did you save my woman's life, boy? Good job."

Cassie watched as the dog warily accepted Alex's appreciation. Her two heroes, face to face. Could this day become any more perfect? And could Alex be in love? There was no doubt as to his passion and his sincerity, of course, but where was the future chief who selflessly put his people first? Was it possible he now saw a way to reconcile their affair with his responsibilities? If so, there was nothing on earth, in this time or any other, that could stop them. And if not, then she could at least take comfort in the knowledge that, for a brief moment, he loved her enough to struggle, just a bit, with his destiny.

"Come on, Alex," she urged finally. "Let's go back to the cabin."

"Wait." Again he caught her by her waist, detaining her while he instructed Prince to "Get lost." When the dog had obeyed, Alex continued, "I want to tell you something else."

"There's more?"

Brushing a mass of curls from her forehead, he nodded. "Earlier, when I told you I walked four hours on burned feet to sleep with you, I wasn't talking about sex. This was terrific, but," his lips moved along her neck, kissing and tasting, "I walked all this way because I want to hold you in my arms and watch you sleep."

"Alex . . ."

"I want to see you, all peaceful and vulnerable and quiet. Without all those gears turning in your brain. I want to stay awake all night and watch, and protect."

"I want that, too," she breathed. "Alex, you're so romantic. I didn't know you could be like this."

"You're inspiring." His mouth returned to hers, rewarding her tenderly. "I just didn't want you to misunderstand what happened here between us. It was great, but it's not the whole story. There's a lot more I want from you, and there's so much I want to give you . . ." He straightened reluctantly in response to another, more demanding summons from Shannon. "I guess we'd better join our hostess."

Cassie slipped her arms around his chest and rested her cheek on a bed of hard muscle. "I'm so glad you came, Alex. I didn't know how you felt about all of this, and I wanted to be casual and worldly, but every time I think of you, my heart starts pounding and, well, the 'gears in my brain' start grinding." She raised her face and sighed. "Now I can relax and enjoy it, just like you said." To herself, she added gratefully, *This can't be a mistake, no matter what happens when it's time to go back.*

He held her hand as they strolled through the empty yard and up onto the porch, where the odor of freshly grilled trout greeted them. "What a life," Alex grinned, pushing open the door for her. "I may stay here forever."

One glance at their host's face was enough to change anyone's mind, however. John Cutler's scowl was pointedly murderous, and Shannon's tight-lipped smile did nothing to reassure Cassie, who tried nervously, "Dinner smells great. I hope we didn't keep you two waiting."

A derisive snort was John's only answer, prompting a stern warning glance from his wife. "You're just in time," Shannon insisted. "Alex, sit over here and help yourself. You must be tired and hungry after . . . well, after your walk."

"John?" Cassie hurried to her bearded host and took his huge hand in her own. Alex's comment was suddenly ringing in her ears. This big-hearted man saw himself as the head of her family, responsible for her well-being, and only Shannon's interference was keeping him from interrogating Alex, or perhaps even evicting him. The thought that the Cutlers had been arguing while she and Alex were making love—the thought that John had wanted to storm into the smithy and break up the lovemaking—was sobering and endearing.

"We'll discuss this later, missy," John grumbled. "Just sit yourself down and eat."

"I've explained everything to you, John," Shannon sniffed. "There's nothing to discuss. Alex, would you like some cornbread?"

"I'd like to talk to John, alone, on the porch," Alex replied, in an even, self-confident tone.

"No!" the females chorused, with Cassie adding lamely, "If anyone should talk to him, it's me."

John's angry green eyes had locked with Alex's ebony ones. "I can't think of anything you could say that would change the way I feel about this, Alex. My wife tells me times have changed, and I should respect that."

"Some things never change," Alex shrugged. "I have three sisters, John."

"That's enough!" Cassie wailed. Alex's tentative commitment to her had been so sweet, and welcome, and unexpected—and had so greatly surpassed anything he owed her, under the circumstances—that she cringed to think John Cutler might dare to demand more. It was *none* of his business, even if he was the so-called head of her family. Not only was this entire drama vaguely insulting and unbearably chauvinistic, it might also damage the fragile truce that had been declared between Alex's competing needs.

John was ignoring Cassie's declaration while plainly considering Alex's. "Three sisters?"

"That's right."

"So? After dinner, we'll talk?"

"Absolutely not," Cassie muttered. "Who do you think you are, John Cutler?" Her chin rose defiantly. "Just drop it, or you'll be sorry."

"Is that so?" John studied her with a knowing grin. "Are you threatening me in my own home, missy?"

Alex chuckled and patted Cassie's shoulder. "Back off, baby. John and I just need to have a little talk."

"That does it!" Cassie's fist pounded the table. "I'm not *your* 'baby,' and," her voice became a hiss, "I'm definitely not *your* 'missy,' John Cutler. I make my own decisions, is that clear?"

"I just need to know that his intentions toward you are honorable," John soothed.

"Which they are, I swear," Alex promised.

Cassie groaned in disbelief. "Aren't either of you listening to me? Shannon?"

"It's hopeless," Shannon sighed. "I tried to explain it to him, Cassie, but he argued with me the whole time you and Alex were outside. You should see how he gets when his sister Meredith tries to have a life. And," her eyes rebuked her husband playfully, "he's also a hypocrite, considering the way he acted when he first met me. Everyone else has to have honorable intentions, but if I recall correctly—"

"That's enough," John protested. "I'm satisfied, for the moment, with Alex's attitude. We'll eat now, and you," he added to Cassie, "will try to keep a civil tone to your voice, missy."

Cassie sent Shannon a knowing glance. "His sister Meredith? Is she pretty?"

"Men flock around her," Shannon grinned. "And she's as stubborn as John, and twice as willful."

"Females," John chuckled, handing a plate of food to Alex. "Do you see what you're getting yourself involved with?"

"Like I said," Alex grinned, "I survived Orimha, so I might as well live dangerously." He hesitated, then added quietly, "You don't have to worry about Cassie, John. She's safe with me. I'd like to take her back to the village for a few days, if that's okay with you."

"You don't need his permission," Cassie glared. "For heaven's sake, Alex."

"A few days?" John shrugged. "We need her here, for the birthing."

"I'll bring her back in a week or so, after I've had time with the Visionary, and then we'll both stay.

Maybe I can help too. I delivered my sister's baby . . ."

Cassie's eyes widened. "You did?"

"Yeah. There wasn't time to get her to the hospital, and her husband passed out, so I was elected."

"And did you use one of these contraptions Cassandra raves about?" John demanded. "This 'sling'?"

"Luckily, we didn't need one," Alex remembered fondly. "We didn't have any equipment or expertise, but it went well. It was a miracle. But," he added hastily, "birthing slings are supposed to be indispensable."

"I'm making one for Shannon," Cassie informed him. "That's why that piece of leather in the workshop is all marked up."

"Great. We'll be back in time for the baby, John. According to my sister, the first one usually takes twelve or fourteen hours, so even if we're not here when labor starts, just send the wolf-dog for us, and we'll be here in less than four hours. Maybe we could even bring Djisgaga."

"I want Cassie," Shannon corrected with a smile. "And your expertise will reassure John, I'm sure, Alex. The baby's not due for two months at least, so if Cassie wants to go with you, I guess we can't be too selfish. We've had her for four days, and she needs to see all the beautiful craftwork the women at the village can do."

"Then it's decided," Alex nodded. "Thanks."

"It's decided?" Cassie heaved a sigh of exaggerated frustration. "This is getting a little strange, people. Shouldn't I have a say in this?" Then she caught sight of Alex's hopeful, slightly lustful eyes and blushed, knowing that she wouldn't miss those hours alone with him, on the trail to the village, for anything.

Even thoughts of Djisgaga's disapproval and possible interference couldn't dispel her growing faith in the power of love to bind them together forever.

"Djisgaga doesn't disapprove of you, Cassie," Alex was reassuring her the following day, as they made their way from the clearing toward the edge of the woods that separated the Cutler homestead from the Susquehannock village. "She's just a little shy. Give her a chance."

Turning to wave one final time to her cousin, Cassie smiled. "Men are so blind. Didn't you notice that 'Leah Eagle' look in her eye every time I came near you?"

"You're fixated on Leah," Alex chuckled, reaching for her hand and drawing her more quickly toward the cover of trees that would allow him the privacy to touch more than her hand. "Has anyone ever told you you're beautiful when you're jealous?"

"Jealous?" Cassie sniffed. "I'd say it's Leah and Djisgaga who are jealous. Remember," she slipped her arm around his waist, "I've got you and they don't, at least for the moment."

"And I've got you, for six long, hot, sexy hours."

"Six?" Cassie grinned. "Four for walking and two for talking?"

"Yeah, right." They had reached the trees and he backed her playfully against a stately elm. "Start talking."

"Mmm . . ." She opened his vest and drew her tongue avidly across his chest. "Shouldn't we go a little farther before we start all this? John still can't handle the thought of his kinswomen having any fun."

"I just want a little preview," Alex coaxed, "and this shirt is so sexy, it's driving me crazy."

Cassie's eyes danced as his hands worked the buttons on the worn, oversized linen shirt she had appropriated from John Cutler's wardrobe. "I came three hundred years without a bra, just because of that dumb leotard I was wearing when the time zapper got me."

"Great timing," Alex agreed, cupping her breasts in his hands reverently. "You don't need a bra when you're with me, missy."

"Please don't start calling me that." She moaned with appreciation as his hands slid down to her waist. "I missed you last night, Alex. Did John's snoring keep you awake?"

"I slept like a baby," he grinned. "You wore me out in that workshop of yours, but now I'm rested and you feel so great . . ."

"Mmm . . ." She relaxed against the tree, allowing his hands to caress her breasts once more. "Do you know what I'd like to do, Alex?"

"Yeah," he chuckled. "I have a pretty good idea what you want."

"Wait." She straightened and slipped her arms around his neck. "I want to find someplace hidden and private. Not out in the open like this. Please? We can make love," she paused to savor the expression, "and then we can sleep a little, together, like you said you wanted. I've been thinking about that, and you're right. It sounds so blissful."

"Yeah." His left hand abandoned her chest and came to stroke her cheek. "We'll find the perfect spot and we'll stay there for hours."

"Maybe even days," she sighed.

"That sounds great." He pulled her into his arms.

"Here I have the chance to study with one of the greatest men of all times—my lifelong hero—and I'm going to play in the woods with you instead. I think that officially makes you a temptress, Miss Stone."

"I'm willing to share you," she protested shyly. "Eventually. But today is my first day as an experienced woman and I want to make the most of it. I think I always wanted to be a temptress, anyway."

"You've tempted me from the moment we met," he remembered, burying his face in her hair. "That sexy smile and all these curls and those long legs . . . I knew you were trouble, but I couldn't stop thinking about you." He took a deep breath and suggested, his voice low and husky, "There's a place I know, about two miles from here, where the underbrush is always thick. It's off the path, and we'd have complete privacy."

Cassie's heart began to pound. "Just two miles away?"

"I'll bet it hasn't changed in three hundred years. This time of year, the grapevines will be heavy with ripe fruit—so ripe you'll be able to smell them before you see them—and there's a stream nearby. The sunlight filters through the leaves, but it stays pretty cool . . ."

"And you've taken women there before?"

"No. I've never taken anyone there, and now I know why. It's there for us, Cassie. You and me, and no one else. We can sleep together there all afternoon," he whispered seductively.

"After you tire me out all morning?" She pulled free of him, her eyes sparkling with anticipation. "Let's go."

Chapter Eleven

Alex stared down at the serenely exquisite features of Cassandra Stone's face as she slept by his side. Her breath was soft and even, and when she stirred, it was to cuddle closer to him, enjoying the texture of his skin and hair even in her dreams. He had longed for this experience, yet had not even begun to imagine how invincible it would make him feel. To be her lover and protector, to be trusted so completely by her, was an honor he could never hope to deserve.

His investigator had labeled her "eccentric," but Alex had come to understand that she was so much more—a complex blending of warmth and curiosity and vitality, with an almost eerie vulnerability. Her quick wit and quicker blush could confound and frustrate him, requiring him to abandon his usual tactics with women and to trust only his gut instincts, which were all too eager to respond to the challenge that was Cassandra Stone.

She had been rash and unembarrassed during their first lovemaking, despite the fact that she was a virgin, yet here, in the secluded privacy of this thicket, she had been shy and unsure, pretending to be absorbed in studying the grapevines while he had removed her loose shirt and tight jeans. Since then, she had not spoken except to murmur his name, again and again, as though "Alex" were the only word left in her vocabulary. She had whispered it, first in wonder and then in husky appreciation, while he had pleasured himself in her control-shattering loins. They had climaxed together and then he had held her, and soon she had been sound asleep in his arms.

He knew she had stayed up past midnight the night before, finishing the birthing sling for her cousin, but it was more than simple fatigue that allowed her to cuddle against him with such complete tranquility. She loved him. It was apparent in her every sound, her every glance, her every caress, and it was a source of such heady pride to him that he wondered how he had survived without it for so long. She was warm and rosy and soft, and yet her spirit and her commitment were sharp and solid, and the combined effect was so unique and beguiling that he could no longer even pretend to resist it.

He wanted to stay here forever with her, but there were less than three hours until nightfall and he had been away from the village, and Kahnawakee, for too long. His sole purpose in leaving the Visionary so abruptly had been one of practicality. Despite the greatness of the man's words and the honor of being allowed to study with him, Alex had been distracted, to an unbearably frustrating degree, by thoughts of Cassie, and knew he would be unable to concentrate with her so far from his touch. Now he would return, with her by his side, and he would be able to benefit from the Visionary's words by day and this golden-haired vision's kisses by night.

"Hey, Cass," he whispered, brushing a curl from her warm cheek. "Wake up, baby. It's getting late."

"Hmm?" She stirred and opened her eyes. "Hi, Alex."

"Hi."

"Did you sleep?" She snuggled against him, her eyes closing once again. "You feel so good."

"I was watching you," he reminded her, his voice unexpectedly hoarse. "You're beautiful." His fingers traced a path along her shoulder and down her bare arm. "Did you dream?"

"I don't know," she murmured. "I think I just remembered . . ." Shaking her head slightly, she raised herself up on one elbow and smiled an embarrassed smile. "Did I dream it, or did we make incredible love right before I went to sleep?"

"We had a pretty good time," he grinned. "But if you don't remember it, I'd be glad to replay it for you."

"Okay."

Alex chuckled. The shy, uncertain pre-nap mistress had been replaced by the temptress and he was more than ready to welcome her. Lowering his mouth to hers, he allowed her to play with his breath, as she always seemed to do, then his tongue invaded and she sucked gently, then with more insistence. Her hand was sliding down his back and over his buttocks and he knew she was going to touch him, and so he caught her hand and scolded, "Not yet, missy."

"Don't *call* me that." Cassie's blue eyes twinkled with desire. "I'm trying to hurry because *you* said it's getting late."

"Some things shouldn't be hurried." He cupped her soft, full breast in his hand and teased the nipple with his thumb, then moved his lips to the spot and tasted gently, all too aware of the tension that was growing within her. She was so responsive, it was almost too easy, and so the challenge would be to make her pace herself. With that in mind he rolled onto his back and pulled her onto his chest. "Let's talk."

Her thighs imprisoned his shaft instantly. "I like this," she admitted, raising herself slightly so that her breasts were exhibited before his admiring eyes. "I think we did this in my dream."

"Yeah?" He was intrigued despite his plan to proceed slowly. "What happens next?"

Cassie's pulse quickened. She was now fully awake and enjoying the hunger in Alexander BlackKnife's sparkling ebony eyes. And she was regretting having slept for so long, wasting so much valuable time. The hard bed of muscles that made up his chest was a tantalizing sight, and as she brushed her erect nipples over him again and again, she tried to imagine what this lusty man would do if she were to suddenly straddle him and take him into herself. She hadn't actually dreamed that, but the image was so vivid in her mind that she ached for an accompanying sensation. Would he let her stay? Or would he roll her under himself and take command? Either way, she would love it, and so, with her most confident smile, she opened her legs and positioned herself over him, pulsing gently and repeatedly until he was almost completely devoured.

Alex's eyes had widened and his breathing had grown instantly more labored. When his strong hands grasped her hips, she knew he was going to assist her without trying to dominate and she moistened her lips, suddenly uncertain. He felt so good, swelling within her. She didn't want to disturb that delicious balance. She wanted him to stay inside her, hard and fulfilling, forever, and if she began to move, they would begin to lose control.

"You like that?" Alex teased. "Come on, Cassie. I'm not made of iron."

"Interesting choice of words," she breathed. "You feel like iron."

He grinned and lifted her with his hips. "Yeah?"

"Alex," she protested weakly. "Oh, Alex . . ." She raised herself again, without his help, and then lowered, and raised, again and again until she was weak with arousal. Then she leaned forward, massaging her breasts against his chest in a futile attempt to momentarily calm her thundering heart. Alex's impatient hands left her hips and moved under her buttocks, urging them to lift once more, then his fingers slipped between her thighs and began to tease at the folds, electrifying her. She was immediately riding him, with long, appreciative moves, and then his hips were raising again, hungry and demanding, as their passions swelled toward the inevitable climax. When it came, it was stronger and wilder than ever, and when it was done, she was limp with satiated relief.

Alex was muttering, as he always did when the ending came, and she stroked his hair, knowing he, too, had wanted it to last forever, despite the obvious flaw in any such plan, given the exquisitely satisfying nature of those final thrusts and their accompanying release. "That was exactly like my dream," she cooed. "You're my hero."

"If you have dreams like that, I'm the luckiest man on earth," he chuckled reluctantly. "Sex with you is like making love in a furnace." His tone grew tender. "Do you need a little more sleep before we start walking again?"

"I'm energized," she admitted, reaching for her clothes. "I could probably run all the way to the

We've got your authors!

If you seek out the latest historical romances by today's bestselling authors, our new reader's service, KENSINGTON CHOICE, is the club for you.

KENSINGTON CHOICE is the only club where you can find authors like Janelle Taylor, Shannon Drake, Rosanne Bittner, Sylvie Sommerfield, Penelope Neri and Phoebe Conn all in one place...

...and the only service that will deliver their romances direct to your home as soon as they are published—even before they reach the bookstores.

KENSINGTON CHOICE is also the only service that will give you a substantial guaranteed discount off the publisher's prices on every one of those romances.

That's right: Every month, the Editors at Zebra and Pinnacle select four of the newest novels by our bestselling authors and rush them straight to you, usually *before they reach the bookstores*. The publisher's prices for these romances range from $4.99 to $5.99—but they are always yours for the guaranteed low price of just *$3.95!*

That means you'll always save over $1.00...often as much as *$2.00*...off the publisher's prices on every new novel you get from KENSINGTON CHOICE!

All books are sent on a 10-day free examination basis, and there is no minimum number of books to buy. (A postage and handling charge of $1.50 is added to each shipment.)

As your introduction to the convenience and value of this new service, we invite you to accept

4 BOOKS FREE

The 4 books, worth up to $23.96, are our welcoming gift. You pay only $1 to help cover postage and handling.

To start your subscription to KENSINGTON CHOICE and receive your introductory package of 4 FREE romances, detach and mail the postpaid card at right *today*.

We have 4 FREE BOOKS for you as your introduction to KENSINGTON CHOICE

To get your FREE BOOKS, worth up to $23.96, mail the card below.

FREE BOOK CERTIFICATE

As my introduction to your new KENSINGTON CHOICE reader's service, please send me 4 FREE historical romances (worth up to $23.96), billing me just $1 to help cover postage and handling. As a KENSINGTON CHOICE subscriber, I will then receive 4 brand-new romances to preview each month for 10 days FREE. I can return any books I decide not to keep and owe nothing. The publisher's prices for the KENSINGTON CHOICE romances range from $4.99 to $5.99, but as a subscriber I will be entitled to get them for just $3.95 per book or $15.80 for all four titles. There is no minimum number of books to buy, and I can cancel my subscription at any time. A $1.50 postage and handling charge is added to each shipment.

Name _____

Address _____ Apt. _____

City _____ State _____ Zip _____

Telephone ( ) _____

Signature _____

(If under 18, parent or guardian must sign)

Subscription subject to acceptance. Terms and prices subject to change. KC1194

We have
4
FREE
Historical
Romances
for you!

(worth up
to $23.96!)

Details inside!

KENSINGTON CHOICE
Reader's Service
120 Brighton Road
P.O. Box 5214
Clifton, NJ 07015-5214

village. I'm also starving. Is there any of that dried meat left?"

"Don't get dressed yet. I'll feed you some grapes and some meat." He was strapping his breechcloth around his waist. "You should bathe in the stream before we go. The water will be warm."

"That sounds like heaven. I've been getting washed in a bowl for almost a week," Cassie recalled, scrambling to her feet. "Let's do that first."

Alex was openly admiring her high, firm breasts and her pale, shapely legs, as well as all that fell between them, and she imagined him caressing her in the warm waters of the nearby creek. It was as though every moment, from this day forward, would be fraught with occasions for carnal desire and satisfaction, to the exclusion of all other needs. Meals would be foreplay, baths would be orgies, conversations would be invitations . . .

His next words echoed her thoughts. "You're so sexy, Cassie. How am I ever going to concentrate again?"

She reached for the soft gray blanket that Shannon had included for their picnic, draping it around herself modestly. "Is this better?"

"No." He pulled it from her and leered. "You've done great things with that body, Cassie. Do you work out?"

"Are you serious? I play a little tennis, and I sail." She stretched provocatively. "I don't go for mindless exercising, like weightlifting or running. No offense." She reached out her hand and traced along his pectorals appreciatively. "The women in the village must have drooled over these muscles, Alex. I'll bet they've never seen anything like them."

"Kahnawakee has me doing more practical exercises," he laughed, reaching down to retrieve the black-hilted knife. "Like this." With quick, focused grace he sent the blade hurling toward a tree.

"Wow. Nice shot."

"Except I was aiming three inches higher," he grumbled. "I used to be good at this, as a kid, but it's been years . . ."

"Tell me about that knife. Is it the one John gave Kahnawakee?"

"You heard about that? Yeah, it's the same one. I'm supposed to practice with it while I'm here." He shook his head. "Three inches off. The Visionary says three inches can make the difference between killing your enemy and just making him angrier."

"Did you tell Kahnawakee that diplomats don't have enemies?" Cassie sniffed, annoyed by the violent image.

"What do we have?" Alex grinned. "Moody friends? Like Orimha?"

"Don't mention his name. It makes me so mad! He's the one man on earth I'd like to see you throw that knife at."

"Get a grip," Alex chuckled. "I liked you better as a pacifist. Come on. Maybe a bath will cool that temper of yours." Lifting her into his arms, he carried her over a mass of vines until a slender ribbon of silver water came into view.

"Ooo . . ." She scrambled free of him and was soon waist deep and refreshed. "This is more like a river than a stream. I love it!"

"It's usually shallower," Alex smiled, wading to her side and pulling her close. "Want me to wash you?"

"Yes, please." She closed her eyes as he sprinkled water over her shoulders and back. Then he knelt, and pulled her down, submerging her to her shoulders and cradling her against himself. "Lean back," he instructed.

She complied, allowing the water to soak her curls as she half floated, with Alex's hands always bracing and caressing in gentle, erotic patterns. When he pulled her close again, she was tingling with desire, and her hands were drawn to his manhood as his mouth moved to kiss her. For a long, desperate moment the kiss and the erotic massage escalated and then he was urging her thighs apart and lifting her for his entry. Their lovemaking was hot and wet and quick, with Alex almost mindlessly enjoying her, and when it was over, she didn't need to ask if this was the stuff of which *his* dreams were made.

His sheepish smile told her everything, and she giggled with delight. "Glad I could help," she teased.

"I like washing you," he grinned, "and I'm going to love drying you, too."

"We have to get going or we'll be stuck out here together all night," she reminded him with mock concern. "What will Djisgaga say about that?"

"I'll dry you with that blanket Shannon wrapped our lunch up in," he continued, as though she hadn't blasphemed, then he hoisted her back into his arms and carried her to their makeshift bed. "Lie back, now, and close your eyes."

"Why does this suddenly sound familiar?" she grinned, remembering the "texture game." "Let me guess: you think you owe me something? I thought we were past all that, Alex."

"I just want to dry you, and feed you," he shrugged. "I don't know what you're talking about."

"Oh." She studied his innocent face. "Okay. I really am starved."

"I know. Let's get you dried." He worked the soft

woolen cloth over her shoulders and breasts until they were warm with a pink-tinged glow, then he dried each leg, thoroughly and expertly, lingering over her feet for longer than she could ever have expected. It felt wonderful, and she was fully relaxed when he parted her thighs. With her eyes still closed, she imagined the damp rag being gently drawn, again and again, over her and she arched just a bit in anticipation.

When it was Alex's hungry mouth, rather than the soft fabric, that was drawn to the spot, Cassie froze in disbelief, then warmed almost immediately, surrendering to the benefits of his love.

"You were supposed to feed me grapes and meat."

"You're complaining?" Alex chuckled. "This is a first. Traditionally women complain if they *don't* have what you just had."

"Well, I never claimed to be traditional. Did Leah complain? She's pretty traditional."

"You're so jealous," he scolded. "Leah and I broke up almost six years ago. She's hardly a threat. Come here." He gathered her into his lap. "You're a wild woman, Cassandra Stone."

"You broke up with her six years ago?"

"Yeah. The day I decided to go to Harvard Law School."

"She disapproved?"

"Right."

Cassie scowled. "So *she* broke up with *you?*"

"Right. Six years ago. It's over, believe me. We've been good friends since childhood and that'll never change, but the rest is ancient history. It's like I told you yesterday. You're the only woman for me. And," he grinned mischievously, "I think we've established that I'm the only man for you."

"We've established that you're a sex maniac."

"You were the maniac in the stream," he reminded her. "I just returned the favor."

"Still," she jumped free and began to wriggle into her jeans, "you have to stop keeping score. It's inhibiting."

"You didn't seem inhibited and, if my scorecard is accurate, you now owe me big time."

"Oh, well . . ." With a playful pout, she slid the jeans back down her legs and kicked them into the underbrush. "Let's even it up, shall we?"

"You're a brilliant man, Alex BlackKnife."

"Am I?" He cuddled her closer, enjoying the way the moonlight danced across her golden curls. "Why's that?"

Cassie sighed. "You knew the best part of this would be the simplest part. Just holding one another, and sleeping in each other's arms. This has been the most glorious day." Her voice was soft with wonder. "I've never been happier in my life, Alex."

"Neither have I. It's so peaceful here. And you," he insisted, "are the sexiest woman on earth. A man couldn't ask for more."

"See? You *are* brilliant." She snuggled against his chest. "Did you study a lot of history, Alex?"

"A fair amount. Why?" The wistful quality to her question intrigued him. "Is something bothering you?"

"It's something Shannon said yesterday. She was telling me all about the awful things that happened once, when Kahnawakee's vision never united the

North Americans against the Europeans. She compared it to Hitler's Germany, Alex, and even though I guess that's true, it's so . . . unbelievable. And what's worse, she didn't believe it was the fault of one or two leaders. She actually feels that it was widespread racism and hatred." Pulling away, she propped herself onto one elbow and insisted, "That doesn't make sense, right? You and I know there were hardships and battles along the way, but basically, isn't the history of North America—*our* North America—a story of cooperation and mutual respect? There were individual cases of greed, and lots of misunderstanding, but . . ."

Alex nodded. "You're saying you think people are basically good. And Shannon doesn't agree? She must have her reasons, Cass."

"You'll have to talk to her about it before we go home." Cassie shuddered visibly. "Her story is bizarre."

Alex stroked her curls. "Then it's true? Without UNAP, the Susquehannocks were once annihilated?"

Cassie nodded. "It's unimaginable, isn't it? You would never have been born. So many, many wonderful men and women and children . . ."

Her sincere distress touched his heart. "The Visionary has described some incredibly chilling instances of European greed and corruption here, Cassie. Worse than we ever dreamed. In less than a century, there has been a real decline in native self-sufficiency—all because of rampant trade with the invaders—and Kahnawakee sees the danger."

"Invaders?"

"Sure. What would *you* call them?" When her wide blue eyes pleaded with him, he relented, but just a bit. "It's different in our time, Cass. By now, our people have coexisted for centuries, and you're as quote-unquote 'native' as I am. But here and now, your ancestors are interlopers."

"Bringing good things, too," she insisted, "not just bad. What about scientific advances? And Shakespeare!"

"And gunpowder? And smallpox?"

"Chocolate and roses."

"Chocolate is from South America," he grinned.

Cassie bit her lip. "In other words, you agree with Shannon? You think my ancestors are greedy bigots?"

"I believe if too much power is accumulated behind one group of human beings, they'll abuse it."

"So?" Her blue eyes sizzled with inspiration. "If Kahnawakee was suddenly given infinite power, even *he* would abuse it? He's only human, too."

"Some men are extraordinary."

She smiled triumphantly. "Some men are extraordinarily good, and some are extraordinarily bad."

"That's true."

"I have to believe the majority of men and women are decent and honorable. Which means if what Shannon says happened really did, it was because of a few powerful, extraordinarily evil leaders. Not because the French or Dutch or English or Spanish were greedy or cruel as a culture." Her eyes dared his to disagree. "Shannon makes it sound like it was widespread racism, but I have to believe it was a few despicable men."

Alex shook his head. "You're being naive. The average man fears what he doesn't understand, and fear is just one step removed from hate."

"No," she countered confidently. "The average person is curious—maybe wary, but not negatively so—about other worlds and other customs. I've seen that over and over. We thirst for knowledge and variety, and it's all positive. It's part of our nature."

"You're an optimist. That's good."

"And Kahnawakee's a pessimist. If he was ever given unlimited power, he'd protect your people from any contact with Europe and you'd be deprived of so many beautiful, positive things. So much art, and literature, not to mention shiny black Mustang convertibles."

"And beautiful blondes?" Alex chuckled. "You'll get no argument from me, Cassie. I like history just the way it happened." His hand slid along the smooth curve of her naked hip. "I wouldn't change a thing."

"You're changing the subject," she noted mischievously. "Pretty soon you're going to start talking dirty again."

"I beg your pardon?" He had to struggle not to laugh. "I never talk dirty."

"Sure you do. You've got this great, multisyllabic Harvard vocabulary, but when you start getting amorous, it's all 'hot' and 'baby' and 'crazy' . . ."

"Watch it," he warned, "I'm getting ideas."

"I wonder if Kahnawakee talks to Djisgaga that way when they're making love," she grinned.

"Huh?" It was an absurd, almost annoying image, and Alex resisted it firmly.

"I'll bet he uses little tiny Susquehannock words," she was continuing gleefully. "You'll have to teach me some." Then she eyed his frown and scolded, "Did you ever notice how you lose your sense of humor when Kahnawakee's name comes up?"

"If you noticed that," he retorted, "why do you keep making jokes about him?"

"Well, excuse me. Maybe I just shouldn't make any more jokes at all."

Alex sighed. "I'd miss them," he said, nuzzling her neck contritely, "so don't stop. Are you mad?"

"No." She cuddled against him. "I'm sleepy and happy. I won't tease you about Kahnawakee anymore, but," she yawned and snuggled closer, "I can't make any promises about Djisgaga."

"That's fair enough." He brushed a curl from her forehead, then kissed her gently. "Get some rest."

"You, too?"

"Yeah. In a minute." He could feel her relax almost immediately into a deep slumber. She was so trusting and innocent, and her words concerning human nature had touched him, although he couldn't find it in his heart to agree. There had been too much in history to disprove it. Even those lurid headlines in the papers after Shannon's disappearance had furnished proof of latent fear and distrust.

"But at least Shannon's safe for now," he reminded himself philosophically. "She and John will have a few years, at least . . ."

But not a lifetime. Alex had been warned, by both the Visionary and by John Cutler, to put any knowledge of their eventual fates from his mind, but one detail had nagged at him, each night around this time, as he'd tried to find some sleep. Somewhere in the deep recesses of his memory was a casual comment by a scholar named Michael Odeka, whom Alex had interviewed shortly after the Shannon Cleary scandal had erupted.

Odeka was the leading authority on Kahnawakee and John Cutler, and he had spoken to Shannon on the telephone just hours before her disappearance. While the man had seemed nervous during the entire interview, claiming that Shannon had babbled without leaving any true clue as to her plans, he had admitted that, while the history books recorded John Cutler's life as one of a confirmed bachelor, there were some indications, in some primary sources, that Cutler had been married, briefly—possibly to a Susquehannock woman. According to those sketchy sources, the nameless woman had given Cutler a son and a daughter, both of whom had been killed during a botched attempt by two European agents to stage an abduction. Apparently, the intent had been to create the appearance that renegade Iroquois warriors from several nations had stolen the children. If believed, this would have led to bloodshed between the Susquehannocks and the League, or to a falling out between Kahnawakee and Cutler if the Susquehannocks had refused to assist him in avenging the insult.

Tragically, Cutler had thwarted the agents and had learned their identity, but not in time to save his family. The wife had struggled valiantly and had been killed, as had both children. The calamity further estranged Cutler from the European community, and any danger to the vision had been averted, but at so very high a price.

"Too high," Alex mourned silently, pulling Cassie more solidly against his chest. "I'll find a way, before we leave, to warn John. I can't just leave without doing something to even the odds. Not after all Shannon and John have done for us." Kahnawakee would say that any such warning was an abuse of this miraculous opportunity that fate had given them. Perhaps that was true, but Alex knew, in his heart, that Kahnawakee would understand and forgive.

*   *   *

"Before we begin this enterprise, I feel we should establish some rules of order—some conventions, as it were—to simplify things. After all," the fair-haired, gray-eyed speaker hesitated pointedly, "an Englishman and a Frenchman—you do consider yourself to be a Frenchman, don't you?—well, to think of us forging this unusual alliance . . . it's quite remarkable, don't you agree?"

Jean-Claude Rubrier nodded, more than a little amused by his new ally's pomposity. He had heard that this man—this Benedict Fowler—would be insufferable yet indispensable to their task, and so he had decided to enjoy, rather than to detest, the man's character and habits. "It is remarkable, my friend," he agreed lightly. "And yes, to answer your question, I consider myself a Frenchman, although I have never seen my father's homeland."

"Your English is more than passable, but then," Fowler grinned, "that's why you're here, is it not? You speak a multitude of languages, all of which we may find ourselves employing before we reach the end of this little venture. Which brings us to the first of the rules I'd like to propose. Between ourselves, we should speak English. My French is adequate for most purposes, but English is by far the more precise of the two languages, and I believe organization and precision will be vital to our enterprise. Don't you agree?"

Jean-Claude bit back a scathing rejoinder. He certainly didn't need to defend the language of poets and lovers from this blustering fool, and the thought of listening to Fowler mutilate that exquisite tongue was enough to make any true Frenchman cringe. "By all means," he agreed, "I am fluent in your language, and we must be precise, as you so wisely explained."

"Excellent! And now, for the sake of expediency, I believe I should take the lead in this matter. You will communicate to outsiders, and of course, to your band of natives." He gestured toward the four native mercenaries who had been hired to assist and guide them. "But I will decide our strategy—with your help, of course."

"I cannot agree to that."

"It's simple. I'm an Englishman, and John Cutler is an Englishman. Everyone knows Cutler advises Kahnawakee. I can think like him, and so I can anticipate him."

"I see." The Frenchman pretended to consider this. "In the same way, I am half Indian, through my mother, who was pure Montagnais, and so I will anticipate Kahnawakee. And John Cutler is a European who came to love this place, and so he is more similar to myself, and my father before me, than to you. And so, my friend, it would seem that I should lead, but I refuse." His smile was only faintly mocking. "We will make our decisions together, and I am confident we will succeed. We have a full week of travel ahead of us, with much time to share our knowledge and plot our course. During those hours, Kahnawakee's downfall will be precisely determined—in English, of course—and when we return, there will be accolades enough for both, wouldn't you say?"

Fowler's expression had twisted with displeasure, and Jean-Claude found himself marveling at the irony of this predicament. In the name of civilization the English had sent a boor to deal with a supposed savage. From all reports, however, Kahnawakee was a man of peace, eloquence, and remarkable humility—he was superior in every sense to this brutish killer and, quite possibly, the most highly respected leader the century had produced thus far. While Jean-Claude fervently believed that the so-called Visionary had to be destroyed, he bristled at the thought of so great a figure dying at the hand of so unworthy a man as Benedict Fowler and he vowed on the spot to find another way to accomplish their task.

Chapter Twelve

One of Cassie's fondest dreams as an only child had been to belong to a warm, boisterous extended family, preferably all living under the same roof. When she walked back into the Susquehannock village with Alexander BlackKnife she got her wish, being almost instantly whisked away from her lover into a smoky longhouse filled with wide-eyed children and skillful women, all of whom seemed eager to welcome her. Once they had thoroughly examined her, they had furnished her with a butter-soft dress of fringed deerskin that wrapped like a tunic and hung to just below her knees. Then she was ushered to a compartment all her own, consisting of a wide platform bed with a narrow loft overhead and a small storage area below. It was too warm to stay indoors, however, and as soon as her belongings were stowed, she was being urged outside to join her new family in the cornfields. Overwhelmed, Cassie did her best to communicate her appreciation despite the language barrier.

Her longhouse, with its carving of a bear over the doorway, was not the same building in which she had slept the previous week with John Cutler at her side and Alex close at hand. That particular longhouse, with its wolf figure guarding the entrance, was the home of Kahnawakee and Djisgaga, and it was there that Alex was clearly expected to sleep. Despite Cassie's immediate fondness for semicommunal living, she was disappointed by the separation. Not that she was lonely, even in bed. As soon as she slipped under her light woven blanket that first night, the children of her longhouse piled on top of her, filling the platform and the loft with their snuggling, giggling forms, and Cassie ruefully welcomed them. Sleep came quickly that night and each succeeding night thereafter, evidencing the full, active nature of her days in the fields and at the looms of her hostesses, whose craftswomanship she was avidly attempting to emulate.

Her days were filled with learning and laughter. When she occasionally caught sight of Alex, he was walking or sitting with Kahnawakee, completely engrossed in conversation and oblivious to Cassie's presence. Occasionally Kahnawakee would acknowledge her with a nod and a playful smile, but the only man who consistently responded to her was Orimha, who was often present with the other men, arguing with Kahnawakee or listening to Alex in stony-faced silence. Should Cassie come into view, however, the renegade Mohawk would focus his attention on her to the exclusion of all else, although he dutifully kept his distance.

At sunset, Alex would come searching for her, brimming with enthusiasm over the wonders of his day, while plying her with questions and compliments over her easy assimilation into longhouse life. Then they would join Kahnawakee and Djisgaga and others in the main longhouse of the Wolf Clan, and Cassie would sit as near to Alex as she dared, listening to the laughter and boisterous, good-natured arguing.

Sometimes Alex would translate for her, but the humor was beyond her experience and she was often too weary to try to actually understand. It was more enjoyable to simply listen, with no translation or attempt at concentration. The love and camaraderie among the group was a sensory delight with no need for actual participation. It would have been enough, in fact, simply to sit by Alex's side. He was more attractive than ever, here among his people, exuding warmth and energy, winning the admiration of one and all with his cautious brilliance.

Then it would be time for bed and Alex would walk her home, stealing a kiss or two along the way, although he never tried to take the intimacy further than just that. He would leave her with reluctance, but leave her just the same, and she knew he was eager to return to his own longhouse with plans to stay up half the night in council with Kahnawakee and a few of the elders. He was in heaven in this world, and seemed almost to have forgotten the more amorous world they had visited in the smithy and at their hideaway beside the stream. He conducted himself as her friend and escort, but nothing more, and she hoped it was the distraction of Kahnawakee's presence, rather than embarrassment or second thoughts, that prompted the benign neglect.

"You told me you walked four hours on burned feet so we could *sleep* together," she reminded him on their third night in the village, as he walked her home.

"Yeah, I remember." He pulled her deeper into the late evening shadows and murmured, "I miss you too, believe me. This didn't work out the way we planned, but in a way, it's a compliment to you. I think Djisgaga and Kahnawakee put you into his father's sisters' longhouse to protect your reputation."

"According to Kahnawakee's aunt, Djisgaga wants to protect you from me until your wounds heal," Cassie countered, remembering the skepticism in her hostess's eyes as she had communicated this lame excuse to her guest by means of sign language. It had been painfully evident that, absent the language barrier, this warm-hearted woman, whose name was Kanasa, would have been more than willing to gossip with Cassie about the possible motives behind Djisgaga's cold treatment of the blonde visitor.

Alex deferred with characteristic innocence to the motives of his nurse. "That's probably it. Djisgaga spoils me, Cass. Every night she brings me a special concoction of herbs to drink. And she dresses my burns, even though they're almost completely gone."

"She likes having you all to herself," Cassie agreed. "Doesn't that seem a little odd?"

Alex shrugged. "Remember how John Cutler appointed himself the official head of your family? Well, that's exactly what's going on here, too. She's the female head of my family in the seventeenth century, and so she's my nurse. When you think about it, it makes perfect sense." When Cassie grimaced, he added teasingly, "I hear there's no room in your bed for me, anyway."

"You mean the kids?" Cassie thawed easily. "They're so cute, Alex. They compete over me, because of the novelty, I guess."

"How do you communicate with them?"

"Kanasa's grandchildren all speak French, and even though I'm not fluent, I learned some key phrases when I went to Quebec last summer. Also, they're eager to learn English, so I teach them and they teach me." She smiled fondly. "They use sign language, too, and you'd be surprised how expressive it is." Her hands slipped around his neck. "I'm not really complaining, Alex. I actually love it here. If we could be together a little more, it'd be perfect."

"I know." His hands settled on her waist, pulling her flush against himself. "Maybe we can get away together, tomorrow or the next day, and go for a walk. Would you like that?"

"Mmm . . . ," Her lips parted in expectation of his kiss, which was warm and tender and tinged with need. She knew his control was slipping, and wondered if he could be persuaded to take that walk right away, in the moonlight. Only her pride kept her from asking directly and then it was too late and he was releasing her, his smile almost apologetic.

"I guess we should save all that for tomorrow."

"Right." She moved one step away. "I'll see you in the morning. Sleep well, Alex."

He nodded, touched her cheek, and then disappeared toward the longhouse of the Wolf Clan.

Having finished instructing his subordinates for the night, Jean-Claude Rubrier turned reluctantly to his supposed equal, who was sitting by the campfire meticulously cleaning his firearm. Even seated, Benedict Fowler was a menacing sight, both taller and broader than any man Jean-Claude had ever seen. It was as though the English had bred this specimen for the sole purpose of killing well and often, and with no remorse. This animal would murder with great relish, and Jean-Claude would be by his side when he did. It was a repulsive thought—identical to those the Frenchman had had each time, over these last three days, that he had laid eyes anew on this brute.

He wondered how women reacted to Fowler. They

would be impressed, undoubtedly, by the bulging muscles and thick, wavy hair. But wouldn't the cold, iron-gray eyes frighten them away? Or would they be drawn, like the moth to the flame . . . no. The flame, at least, used warmth and light as lures. This man was cold and dark and dead inside, and women would shrink from him. Even assuming he would be wealthy as a result of this mission, female companionship would never be his reward.

Jean-Claude missed the company of women. His pretty, dark-haired wife in Trois Rivières, whom he adored with all his heart, was expecting their first child. His auburn-haired mistress in Quebec, whom he also adored, would be restless without him, and there were so many men there without wives or mistresses that she'd be tempted to stray. If it weren't for the presence of Fowler, he'd have long since asked the Shawnee and Delaware mercenaries to arrange a short stay in a friendly village along the river, where a willing maiden might have been lured to Jean-Claude's side by his melodious voice and pouchful of beads. Alas, this was impossible under the present circumstances.

Fowler had made his own tastes abundantly clear. The "savages" disgusted him. He considered the men lazy, the women vulgar, and the children larcenous— all of this without having ever had commerce with them beyond abusing them as servants when there was no one else available. He undoubtedly would refuse to bed the native females, preferring to wait for a golden-haired, ivory-limbed European beauty. In these parts, it would be a long wait. If that bothered Fowler, he didn't show it. When he spoke with longing, it was for England and civilization, but the subject of women had not been raised by either man. It would be amusing, and perhaps a little frightening, to know what a man like Benedict Fowler craved in the lonely, dark hours before dawn.

The four mercenaries who were accompanying them on this journey detested Fowler, and Jean-Claude suspected that they would have deserted by now had he himself not been there to constantly soothe and placate. But who was there to soothe and placate poor Jean-Claude? He missed his wife and his mistress, and ached for their arms, or the arms of *any* willing female. As the campfire blazed in the dark August night, Jean-Claude Rubrier prayed that this venture against the Susquehannock Visionary would end soon, successfully or not.

Alex was nowhere in sight the following day. Once Cassie had washed and dressed and done her few chores, she went in search of him. When she found Kahnawakee alone, apparently lost in thought, she took it as an omen of hope. Was school out for the day? Was Alex searching the cornfields for his woman at this very moment? Was Orimha gone for good?

Reminding herself that Kahnawakee was a venerable historical figure entitled to great deference and respect, she approached him cautiously, then giggled under her breath at his reaction.

It was just a smile, but a provocative one, and one which often graced his features when he greeted her. She had observed the way he greeted the other women of the village, his expression always respectful, mature, and slightly preoccupied. He smiled for Djisgaga, of course, and that smile was quite expressive, but it was never whimsical or naughty. As far as Cassie had been able to tell, the charming, devilish grin he now wore was seen by herself alone and it flattered her enormously.

It also confused her. This great chief had responded to her in this way from the very first moment they met. She could only guess that her kinship with John and Shannon Cutler placed her in a special category for Kahnawakee, outside of duty and responsibility, and securely in the world of friendship and relaxation. Whatever the reason, it pleased her and she longed to return the playful smile, but she had promised Alex she would be more reserved and less familiar with the leader and so she cleared her throat and attempted a suitably formal demeanor.

"Kahnawakee? Am I disturbing you?"

"Please join me." He gestured for her to sit beside him on a log.

"That's a beautiful bow. Are you oiling it?"

"I am seasoning it, as John would say. It is my habit, when I wish to clear the clouds from my mind."

"Clouds? Are you sad?"

Kahnawakee's ebony eyes danced. "Are clouds sad to you, Cassandra? I enjoy them and value them. They bring rain, and protect us from the wrath of the thunder."

"I like clouds too, but not thunderclouds. Thunder always sounds like the end of the world, although . . ." she smiled tentatively, "there are other Indian nations, southwest of here, that believe the world was created during a thunderstorm, and so they think it sounds like the *beginning,* rather than the end, of the world. My father told me about that when I was little, and it helped me to learn not to be frightened." It was a pleasing memory, and Cassie was tempted to confide the rest—how the dedicated meteorologist had first attempted to explain thunder as a sonic shock

wave caused by the fiery, positively charged current
that we call lightning as it burst through a channel of
ionized air. Only when four-year-old Cassie had covered her ears and screamed with irrational, unsootha-
ble hysteria had the desperate father resorted to an
Apache creation story.

"Your father is a good man?"

"He's terrific." She blushed and glanced about herself nervously. "Do you know where Alex is? I need
to ask him something."

"I have sent my little brother hunting," Kahnawakee apologized. "He has watched the others return with their bounty, and I saw interest in his eyes.
It is different in his world, he tells me. The weapons,"
he stroked the bow fondly, "make such tasks too
predictable." His eyes locked with hers. "You wished
to ask him something? Can you ask me? I will try to
answer for you. Or," the playful smile returned, "is
the question one of love?"

"You're a flirt, Kahnawakee," she laughed. "Actually, I do have a question for you. It's about Orimha."
She paused, remembering that she hadn't seen her
brutish admirer since the previous afternoon. "He
didn't go hunting with Alex, did he?"

"You would be angry with me," Kahnawakee
chuckled, "and my wife would strangle my neck and
so. . . . No, I did not send him hunting with Couteau.
Orimha has traveled east, to speak with his men. He
will return tomorrow."

"Why? He seems pretty well rested to me. Why
hasn't he gone home for good?" She lowered her voice
and confided, weakly, "He stares at me."

"He is in love with you."

Cassie winced. "So I gathered. I still don't see why

he hangs around. He must know how I feel about him, after the way he hurt Alex."

"He knows you have feelings for Couteau. He also knows you and Couteau are not married, and do not share a bed. And so," Kahnawakee shrugged, "he waits."

"Send him away. He was only supposed to stay until he was well rested and well fed, right? Tell him to get lost."

"In truth, I have suggested he should leave," Kahnawakee sighed. "He has asked my permission to stay and to learn."

"To learn?"

"It is of benefit to me. If Orimha can understand my vision, he will cease his resistance and will become an ally. It would be good."

"Do you think he's sincere?"

"No," Kahnawakee smiled. "I believe he stays to wait for you. But he sits with Couteau and myself, and listens to my words, and to Couteau's questions, and he learns. For this, I am grateful to you, Cassandra. He would not have listened for any other reason."

"I don't trust him. I'm surprised you think he can ever understand what you're trying to do. He's such a brute."

"He is not." Kahnawakee's eyes rebuked her. "You hate him because he tested Couteau, but you must remember, Couteau offended him. He challenged him."

"Alex told me about all that war paint," she admitted, "but that was no reason to break his fingers and to set him on fire. And did you see that huge slash on his thigh?"

"Orimha was careful to cause great pain without

true injury. That was admirable of him. When he tested Couteau, he tested me. I will always be humbly grateful to Couteau for behaving with such great dignity and pride. I envy him that success, I should confess." His tone was now quite earnest. "Every man craves the opportunity to have his manhood tested, Cassandra."

"I have a feeling Alex craved a more civilized test of his manhood," Cassie grinned, "like having to satisfy three women in one night, or something like that."

Kahnawakee burst into laughter, drawing curious stares from several villagers. "You are very amusing, Cassandra. Do you see why Orimha waits? You are a woman of great fascination."

"Thanks."

"Orimha wears many strands of beads around his neck, have you noticed?" When Cassie nodded, the chief explained, "Those are very valuable, especially the dark ones shaped from the quahog shell. He wears them to show his great wealth, so that you will see worth in him. And in that same way, he sees great worth in Couteau, because Couteau has earned your heart. In that way, he respects Couteau. Not only did my little brother earn respect by his bravery, but also by his conquest of your heart."

"If Orimha knows my heart belongs to Alex, why does he still wait for me?"

"You and Couteau are not married. You have no children. You sleep in separate longhouses. And while he waits, he learns to trust my words and so, one day, perhaps he will convince the renegades to join with me. That would be a great day, and you would be worthy of credit."

"If that happens, the credit goes to your vision,"

Cassie protested. "Anyway, if you're sure he's harmless, I guess I don't mind having him stare a little as long as he doesn't touch me or talk to me."

"You fear him? That is not reasonable. He would give his life to protect you," Kahnawakee declared. "Of this I have no doubt. He wishes to marry you one day. If it could be otherwise, perhaps he would purchase you, but he would never abduct you from Couteau, and he would never injure you." His rough hand stroked her cheek. "I will send him away if you fear him."

"I don't," she lied, adding honestly, "I feel very safe in the longhouse of your aunts."

"They love you greatly, after so short a time together. Kanasa treasures your presence. She claims your talent, with weaving and with beading, is boundless."

"She's been teaching me," Cassie blushed.

"She says you learn quickly, with fingers that fly and an eye that catches every detail."

"I just copy what she does. But I'll never be able to do it so effortlessly. I have to concentrate completely. Kanasa and the other women can weave and talk and cook and mind the children, all at the same time. I can't handle that."

"You are similar to Couteau." Kahnawakee's smile was unexpectedly tender. "When he concentrates on one task, he neglects the rest. When he studies with me, he neglects you. I have noticed, and I have considered scolding him for it."

"Please don't! His time with you is limited," Cassie insisted. "I understand that completely. And I'm happy and busy with Kanasa and her family."

"You are certain? And you do not wish for me to send Orimha away?"

"Just find him a new girlfriend," she suggested, then winced when Kahnawakee's laughter again attracted stares. It seemed prudent to leave before Djisgaga appeared—possibly armed!—and so she jumped to her feet and straightened her deerskin dress. "I'd better be going."

"I will try to find another woman for Orimha, but it will be difficult," the chief grinned, standing also and reaching for her hand. "You are the one he desires, and you are unique."

"So are you." Pretending not to notice his attempt to touch her, she scurried back toward the safety of the Bear Clan's longhouse. To her delight, Alex had returned from his hunting and was talking with two of Kanasa's grandchildren.

"Alex?"

When he turned to her, his eyes were twinkling with anticipation and she knew he hadn't forgotten their date. The children giggled and ran off, presumably to tell Kanasa the news, and Cassie flushed with excitement. "How was your hunting?"

"I couldn't concentrate. I was thinking about you."

"Good." He had made no move to touch her, and she suspected he didn't want to attract any more attention to their affair. "Should I bring some food for us on our walk?"

"I ate with the others. But if you're hungry . . ."

"I ate too. Shall we go?" Out of the corner of her eye she saw Djisgaga, frowning and watching, and she wondered if Alex had noticed her, too. If so, it was flattering and reassuring that he was still willing to disappear into the woods with her.

"I thought about you all last night," he began, then his mischievous grin faded into a respectful smile and Cassie knew he had caught his first glimpse of their chaperon. "There's Djisgaga with the baby," he announced. "He's a great kid, Cassie. Have you ever held him?"

"Little Couteau Noir?" Cassie eyed him with reluctant amusement. "You were named after him. Isn't that bizarre? He's so tiny, but he's three hundred years older than you, right?"

"It's weird," he agreed. "Come on over and take a close look at him."

"Alex . . ." She wanted to warn him that their rendezvous was in jeopardy, but he was so naive and adorable that she couldn't find the words. Hoping that perhaps Djisgaga wouldn't interfere, she sighed, "I've been dying to see that baby close up. Just protect me from your nurse."

Alex's eyebrow arched, as though he was amused but belatedly wary. "Are you going to embarrass me?"

"I'll be charming and polite."

"Just let *me* do the talking. The truth is, you two need to get better acquainted. If you could just talk the same language, you'd be friends, I'm sure."

"Maybe so." She took his hand in her own. "You do all the talking, and I'll just be charming and silent."

Djisgaga greeted Alex warmly, dismissing Cassie with a quick, impersonal nod. After a brief conversation in Susquehannock, the mother reluctantly surrendered her child to Alex, who handled the one-year-old with casual expertise. "Cassandra Stone, meet the first Couteau Noir."

Her heart melted despite her wariness. While the baby had his mother's eyes, his jawline and cheekbones were already echoing those of his visionary father. He was alert and good-natured, accepting

Cassie's caress of his shoulders as she cooed, "He's
the most beautiful baby I've ever seen. Tell her for me,
Alex. Tell her I think he looks a lot like her, and also
a lot like you."

After listening intently to Alex's translation of the
praise, Djisgaga murmured something in return,
stroking Alex's cheek as she spoke. He seemed to
flush slightly, either from the gesture or the words,
and Cassie teased, "What did she say? That you're
handsomer than her own son?"

"No." His smile was wistful as he handed the boy
back to the mother. "She agreed that this baby looks
like me, but she's afraid if you and I had kids, they
wouldn't look anything like me at all, and that makes
her sad. But," he shrugged, "she's wrong, don't you
think? Our kids would look a little like me and a little
like you."

"She said that?" Cassie glared indignantly. "Don't
you see she just tried to insult me? And tried to discourage you from being interested in me?" When he
seemed about to disagree, she waved her hand in disgust. "Never mind. You're hopeless. And *she's* a
bigot!"

"Cassie!"

The baby had begun to fuss, and as Djisgaga
soothed him, she spoke with cool authority toward
Alex.

"She wants to know what you just said," he muttered. "Thanks a lot, Cassie."

"Tell her I said she's a *bigot.* She probably knows,
anyway. She probably speaks perfect English, Alex.
You're so naive!"

He shook his head and answered Djisgaga in Susquehannock, then winced when she responded
sharply and departed in a huff.

"Tell me," Cassie demanded.

"I told her you think she doesn't like you," he explained wearily. "And she said you have a sharp tongue."

"And you didn't defend me?"

Alex was visibly holding his temper in check. "Let's just go for our walk. Forget about Djisgaga. In a few weeks, you'll never have to see her again."

"Then, in a few weeks, we can go for our walk."

His anger seemed to fade, replaced by amusement. "Oh, yeah? John's right, Cassie. You're the stubbornest woman on earth. And," he drew closer and cajoled, "the prettiest. Don't be mad."

"I'm not. You'd better go talk to Djisgaga. She's the one who's upset. And you should report in with Kahnawakee. He thinks you're still hunting." She raised her chin defiantly. "He and I had a long talk, but don't worry, I didn't say anything to embarrass you. We talked about Orimha, my devoted admirer, the whole time."

Alex was laughing sheepishly. "Okay, punish me. I'll get this thing between you and Djisgaga figured out before I come to pick you up for dinner. And maybe, in a day or so, we can go and visit John and Shannon. Would you like that?"

"Dinner?" Cassie studied her fingernails in feigned disinterest. "If you plan on eating dinner with me, I'll be dining in Kanasa's longhouse and I'm sure she'll welcome you."

His grin disappeared. "Pardon?"

"The male suitor is supposed to come to the female's longhouse. You should know that. Even after they get married, it's the man who leaves his mother's longhouse and goes to live with the wife's family."

"Yeah, I know." He cleared his throat and then

reached for her hand. "You've learned a lot, Cassie. That's nice. But the fact is, there are exceptions to that general rule. When Djisgaga married Kahnawakee, for example, she went to live with him."

"Well, we've established that she's special," Cassie retorted. "I'm just an ordinary maiden and my suitors are supposed to come to me, unless," her eyes grew bright with challenge, "you're comparing yourself to Kahnawakee. That's awfully grandiose, Alex." Before he could respond, she added, "I know you need to spend as much time with your Visionary as possible, so just do whatever's right. I'll be fine either way." Spinning on her heels, she strode into the long-house.

Djisgaga's insults were still fresh and stinging, and while Cassie wasn't honestly angry with Alex, she was furious with life in general for having forced her into so frustrating a situation. Sitting cross-legged on her platform with two toddlers in her lap, she managed to calm herself down enough to realize that it wasn't simply Djisgaga's prejudice that was disturbing her. It was the knowledge that the cultural conflicts and suspicions would not end here. If anything, they would intensify in the twentieth century. After all, Alex had proven himself here, and was accepted as a brave and phenomenal hero, at least of sorts. Back in his old world, he was regarded simply as "promising," and there were those among the twentieth-century Susquehannocks who had expressed outright disapproval. Even Leah Eagle had dumped him for choosing Harvard. What would happen if he chose Cassie?

"If . . ." The word rang in her ears. He hadn't chosen her yet, and *she* certainly hadn't chosen a lifetime of apologizing or treading softly for fear of offending the power structure. If Alex couldn't even bring himself to visit her family—her Susquehannock family, no less!—for a simple dinner, how would he ever find the time for her biological family, or her friends, or her world at all? She didn't need to be part of his every waking moment—she had her own career and hobbies, after all, and would probably feel suffocated by a man who had to be with her night and day without a break—but she didn't want to be relegated to a second-class status in any man's life. If that was all Alex could offer her, she would rather revert to the two-torrid-weeks-on-a-desert-island scenario and be done with it.

Pulling the children closer, she murmured, "We were better off before we made love. Now I'll always know what I'm missing, after he's gone from my life. I thought this was such a great arrangement, but it's awful. I want what we had by the stream, laughing and talking and making love . . ." When the elder of the children began to whimper, Cassie blushed and reprimanded herself sharply. Feeling sorry for herself was not usually her style, and if this affair was reducing her to so low a state, it was all the more reason to deal with it quickly. In the meantime, she reached under her platform and found the whimsical cornhusk puppets she had made to entertain the children. Soon the two toddlers were giggling happily.

For the rest of the day she resisted thoughts of Alex, concentrating on learning to scrape the hair from a stretched deerhide with a sharp piece of rock. Kanasa seemed to be the resident expert in all techniques concerning the leatherworking process, and as she sat by Cassie's side, monitoring her progress, the old woman occupied her hands by reshaping the moccasins Alex had given to the younger woman as a farewell present less than two weeks earlier.

Cassie could feel her cheeks flushing with embarrassment as she informed her mentor, in as casual a way as possible, given the language difficulties, that she would be dining that evening with her family, rather than with the Wolf Clan. Her embarrassment was compounded by the raised eyebrows this information caused as it passed from woman to woman, but to her relief, they offered no sympathy or advice, but simply made her feel even more welcome than usual, preparing special corn cakes with berry sauce in addition to their regular fare.

As the sun began to set, Cassie remembered the three previous evenings, when Alex had come to meet her outside the longhouse. His smile had always been so handsome and confident, as though he considered them, at that moment at least, to be the perfect couple, and Cassie had responded with a rush of pure love that had assured her he was correct. Now she knew better and, as she settled inside the longhouse of the Bear, with children climbing in and out of her lap while Kanasa served the delicious meal, she wondered how she could have been so naive.

Then a hush fell over the diners and Cassie, who had been wiping berry juice from a tiny mouth, turned and almost gasped aloud at the sight of Alexander BlackKnife, filling the doorway of the longhouse with his tall, lean, muscular form. He was wearing his jeans for the first time since their arrival, and the vest he wore with them was suspiciously reminiscent of the black one that was his sexy trademark in the twentieth century. Worn as now, with no shirt to obscure his broad, tanned chest, it was more provocative than ever, and Cassie listened with nervous approval as the young girls whispered behind their hands to one another and sighed with longing at the sight of him.

He crossed to Kanasa and greeted her respectfully, then came and sat beside his woman, a sly smile on his face. "What's for dinner?"

"You came?" she murmured in breathless wonder.

"Yeah." Accepting a clay bowl filled with soup and bread, he began simultaneously to eat and to field the barrage of questions that Cassie's "family" was throwing toward him. Unable to comprehend the Susquehannock banter, Cassie could nonetheless understand exactly what was happening. He was charming them—entertaining them with his stories and impressing them with his sincerity. He was playing the suitor, earning permission to court the golden-haired maiden who'd caught his eye. By the time the meal was drawing to a close, Cassie had cuddled so close to him that she was half in his lap and totally in his power.

More than anything, she was enchanted by the fact that Alex was so clearly enjoying himself. Whereas in the Wolf longhouse he had always been alert and attentive, he seemed now to be totally relaxed, laughing without the self-consciousness that characterized his behavior in Kahnawakee's presence. He particularly seemed to enjoy the children, who examined his jeans and climbed on his strong back in endless exploration, and who, he claimed, reminded him of his own cousins, as well as the two little nephews his eldest sister had provided thus far.

"Everyone adores you," Cassie whispered in proud defeat as the meal came to a close and the families drifted toward their compartments to bed their children down for the night. "Thanks for coming, Alex. It really meant a lot to me."

"You honestly thought I wouldn't?" He shook his

head, plainly bemused. "Don't you know how I feel about you?"

"No." She waved one hand quickly to discourage a facile reply. "It's like you said: after only a week or two, we can't know for sure how we feel. We can only suspect, and hope and enjoy, and I'm doing all those things tonight." Her tone grew husky. "I know you have to spend time with Kahnawakee, and I know you want to make a great impression on him. Believe it or not, I understand completely."

"You're the one making a great impression for me," he insisted. "Kanasa just told me you're the best weaver they've ever met. They're proud to have you in their family, and I'm proud to have you as my woman."

Cassie flushed at the praise. "I'm teaching them all my camouflage tricks. They hardly make mistakes, so they don't have much practice hiding them, but I'm a pro."

"You're being too modest. They say your fingers are so fast, they seem to fly."

"I'm fast because I don't have distractions, like they do. But tonight," she ran her fingertip over his lips, "I have a distraction, and it's wonderful. I wish the night wasn't ending so quickly." As she spoke, she noticed that Kanasa was replacing the light blanket on Cassie's platform with a large, soft rabbit-fur throw, and she gasped, "Are you sleeping here tonight?"

"Do you think your little bedmates will mind?"

"They're history, believe me." She knew her cheeks were scarlet with delight. "Are you sure the Wolf Clan won't come looking for you?"

Alex chuckled. "Actually, this was Kahnawakee's idea. He thinks it'll discourage Orimha."

"Oh." Her heart shuddered to a near halt. "All of this was Kahnawakee's idea? I should have known."

"The dinner was my idea, believe me," Alex scolded, "and when I went to tell the Visionary, I was all prepared for disapproval. But like I said, he approved." Nibbling hopefully at her earlobe, he confided, "Kahnawakee says, if I neglect you, Orimha will never stop pursuing you, so I'm here to meet your every need."

Cassie's heart resumed its frantic pounding. "I usually help Kanasa clean up for a while before bedtime."

"Go ahead. I'm not going anywhere. Whenever you're ready . . ." His eyes twinkled with desire, and she carried that image in her tantalized imagination as she hurriedly scraped bowls and ushered children into the lofts for the night. Then she sifted her fingers through her curls, kissed Kanasa's cheek, and returned to her compartment.

The longhouse was dark, and while it was not yet ten o'clock, the inhabitants had all retired by the time Cassie had slipped under her blanket and begun to wriggle out of her dress. Within seconds, Alex was greedily caressing her naked body while they traded kisses, and softly whispered compliments, and mutual apologies for the afternoon's quarrel. "You feel so strong and warm," Cassie gushed, running her fingernails down his back and over his buttocks, then sliding her hand around to shyly explore his manhood.

"You feel great too," he groaned, moving his mouth to her breasts and enjoying them hungrily. "I can't believe I've been sleeping over there, all alone, when I could have been doing this."

"Alex," she sighed, a bit too loudly, and a spattering of gentle laughter echoed through the dark recesses of the longhouse.

"Shh," he warned, returning his mouth to hers and kissing her in gentle reprimand. "This semiprivate stuff is tricky."

"I'll be quiet," she promised. "We'll use sign language, like this." She wrapped her long legs around his torso. "Get it?"

Alex chuckled ruefully, then caught himself and shook his head. "I'm not so sure about this," he hissed. "It's inhibiting."

"What?" Cassie found his hand and guided it to her inner thigh. "It's great, Alex. Just forget they're there."

"You've adapted better than I have, Cassie. It's been over a century since we lived in communal houses. I like my privacy." Pulling his hand free he added mournfully, "I *need* my privacy."

"What?" She struggled to regain her equilibrium. "Are we stopping?"

"I can't do this with an audience."

"Oh." With reluctance, she unwrapped herself from him and tried to find a silver lining. "At least we can sleep in each other's arms, right? And maybe tomorrow we can go for that walk in the woods."

"There's a bright moon tonight," he cajoled. "We can go as soon as everyone's asleep."

"Alex! They'll know why we left. I'll be mortified."

He laughed under his breath. "You're too much. You're willing to make love under their noses, but you're embarrassed to sneak out with me?"

"Exactly," she teased. "What kind of a girl do you think I am?"

His hand returned to the soft, velvety reaches between her thighs. "Come on, Cassie. Just for a short walk?"

"Mmm, keep talking. I'm almost convinced."

Chapter Thirteen

She wondered if the villagers could tell how serenely content she was, the following day, as she hummed over her weaving and gathered grapes with the children in the woods that had provided cover for her torrid rendezvous with her lover only hours earlier. They had made endless love, returning to the longhouse only minutes before the elders and infants had begun their predawn stirring. Now Cassie felt as though her body might actually be glowing with rosy contentment and she prayed that the day would pass quickly and the night would last forever. Alex hadn't actually said he would come to her again, but some things did not need to be spoken aloud.

Djisgaga had given her a scathing glare earlier that day when they'd met beside the river, but Cassie had just grinned victoriously. She was suddenly invincible, and even when Orimha returned, early in the afternoon, and resumed his staring, she was unconcerned. He would hear the rumors soon, and would know that Couteau Noir had laid claim, once and for all, to the golden-haired weaver. Hopefully, for Kahnawakee's sake, the Mohawk would decide to stay and continue his lessons, but Cassie doubted whether that would be the case, and she was much too happy to worry over one broken-hearted malcontent.

"You seem fanciful today, Cassandra. You are well rested?"

She hadn't heard Kahnawakee come up behind her, and when she spun to respond, she was prepared for the devilish grin. "I love weaving," she quipped. "Would you like me to make something for you, Visionary?"

He chuckled. "My little brother is exhausted, but you are filled with spirit. Our humble village life pleases you?"

"I love it here," she agreed. "I love everything about it."

Kahnawakee nodded. "I see that. Do you not miss your own family? The father who told you stories of the thunder?"

"I don't see my parents very often," she smiled, returning her eyes to her work as she spoke. "They're working on a ship, in the middle of the sea, taking measurements and developing theories about the weather. I'll see them at Christmastime. I love them, but we don't hang around together."

"They will approve of Couteau?"

"Absolutely. They've always been afraid I'd marry an artist." She paused, wondering if talk of marriage seemed presumptuous, but after that passionate night in the woods with Alex, the future seemed crystal clear. "Anyway, they'll love him."

"You do not live with them?"

"I live alone. In a pretty little house by the river."

"Alone?" He seemed shocked by the notion. "Your father permits this?"

"My parents are hardly permissive," she grinned. "They just finally gave up on me. When I was growing up, they read every childrearing book on the market, and they decided to give me the finest education and tons of preparation for the so-called real world. They were confident I'd be the first female president of the Commonwealth. Instead, they got a full-time texture junkie whose most valuable possession is a potter's wheel."

"They wanted you to be a leader?"

"Exactly, and for the right daughter, it would have been great, but it was wasted on me. I was a day-dreamer right from the start. My mother was stocking me with calculators and organizers and self-improvement books from the time I was old enough to read. She even gave me a supply of condoms when I was only fifteen years old! Can you believe that? She wracked her brain trying to keep me from making any mistakes and ruining my chances for success, all because she wanted me to be happy. She just couldn't see," she added fondly, "that I was already happy just the way I was."

Cassie had become so lost in her own words that she'd almost forgotten her listener, whose earnest confusion was apparent in his face. With an apologetic grin, she sympathized, "You're lost, right? That's probably just as well. Calculators and condoms weren't the only things they gave me. They also gave me tons of love, and that's what's important."

"I can hear the love in your voice," Kahnawakee assured her. "And I can have sympathy for your father. You are very lively, Cassandra. To be your father must have been a difficult task, but also a source of great amusement."

"He'd agree with that," she laughed.

"I believe," he added slyly, "that you will be an amusing mother to Couteau's children."

She suspected from his expression that he had heard about the scene with Djisgaga. "If we had children," she nodded, "they'd look like you, I guess, since Alex looks so much like you."

Kahnawakee grinned. "He resembles me, but he is taller."

"And Shannon's taller than me," Cassie smiled. "It's obnoxious of them, don't you think?"

Kahnawakee burst into appreciative laughter, then patted her knee and ambled away. Cassie tried to concentrate on her weaving, but the events of the last twenty-four hours were preempting her thoughts. She and Alex were so clearly in love! Even the Visionary himself was openly speculating about an eventual marriage and a horde of adorable children. Perhaps he had scolded Djisgaga! That would explain her glare at the river that morning. Or perhaps she had simply seen Alex's face, when he had returned to the longhouse after a night of love, and had realized her campaign against the blond invader had failed.

Sometime during the passion-filled night, Alex had renewed his offer to take her to see Shannon soon, and Cassie was now eager to make the journey, not only because it would give her time alone with her lover, but also because she knew her cousin would be excited and supportive over the rapid progress of the love affair. And of course, the baby could come any day, and so it was wise to return to the Cutler cabin soon in any case.

The one thing Alex hadn't mentioned was whether they would be leaving the village temporarily or for good. How much time, she wondered, did he need to spend with his teacher before he felt confident to return and lead his people? Or did it really matter what Alex wanted? Wouldn't destiny simply hurl them back to the twentieth century when the time was right? Which was probably for the best, given the fact that Alex would probably never be able to tear himself away from his mentor any other way.

Due to her blissful preoccupation, she had made innumerable mistakes in her weaving project and so, with a rueful smile, she unraveled the strips of rabbit fur and stuffed them back into her pouch for another time. She was almost ready to seek out Kanasa for a more mindless assignment when Alex appeared before her. Something in his expression warned her he was angry, but that seemed impossible, and so she greeted him with innocent enthusiasm. "Hi, Alex. I've been thinking about you all day."

"Really?" he seethed. "Haven't you been thinking about calculators and *condoms?*"

"Huh?" She shrank from his angry glare, then laughed uneasily. "Oh, no . . ."

"I can't believe you, Cassie. You have the privilege of meeting the most revered figure in all of history, and you talk to him about condoms."

"I didn't talk to him about condoms," she protested, amused despite his frustrated tone. "That's silly, Alex. I was just rambling on about my parents, in answer to *his* questions."

"He *asked* you about condoms?" Alex's dark eyes flashed. "You're never serious, are you? Jokes about Djisgaga, jokes about the Visionary. Everything's a joke to you."

"That isn't true," she retorted, more annoyed by the mention of Djisgaga than by his ridiculous accusations. "Lighten up, Alex. He didn't understand a word I was saying."

"That's right. He didn't understand, and so he asked *me* to explain it to him."

"He asked you to explain what a condom is?" she winced. "Sorry, Alex. I guess that was a little embarrassing."

"Embarrassing?" he growled. "It was no more embarrassing than having you call Djisgaga a bigot in front of half the village."

"Half the village?" Cassie shook her head. "I don't remember that part. Anyway, I'm sorry about the mix-up with Kahn. What did you say to him? Do you want me to go and apologize to him?"

Alex was staring in open-mouthed horror. "Kahn?"

Cassie flushed. "Don't go crazy, Alex. I never call him that to his face, believe me. Do you think I want to get struck by lightning?" When he didn't respond, she tried for a soothing tone. "I'm sorry I embarrassed you. Let's just drop it before we say anything else we regret."

"Just don't say anything else at all," he countered coldly. "To anyone, anymore, until we leave. Do you understand me?"

Cassie took a deep breath, struggling with a wave of anger. "We'd better leave right away, then," she suggested carefully.

"I can't leave right away. Do you think I want my last talk with Kahnawakee to be about *condoms?* Do you think that's how I want him to remember me?"

"He probably isn't giving it another thought, Alex," she sighed. "Honestly, you're overreacting, and it's getting on my nerves. Just tell me what you said to him. I'm sure you explained it tactfully and there's no damage done."

"Believe me," Alex drawled, "you don't want to know how I explained condoms to him."

Her eyes locked with his and she knew, to her horror, that he was implying he had used *her*—or rather, his inconvenient relationship with her—as an example of a situation in which condoms might be prudently employed. Whether that was true, or whether he was just baiting her, she reeled at the unfairness of such a tactic. To make the insult more stinging, she was re-hearing the innocent banter between herself and Kah-nawakee over the subject of the children Alex would father with her. Alexander BlackKnife had appar-ently decided such children would be a disaster!

"We'll leave tomorrow." His tone had become less caustic. "Just stay with Kanasa, and don't talk to anyone else, especially not Djisgaga or Kahnawakee. Is that clear?"

"Absolutely."

"I'll come and get you for dinner, and we'll eat in my longhouse, and you'll just listen politely, right?"

"Right."

He seemed relieved and slightly mollified. "I can't expect you to take all of this as seriously as I do, but . . . it's important to me, so just respect my wishes, okay?"

She nodded woodenly.

"I shouldn't have raised my voice. I apologize for that."

"No problem." She knew that if they stood there, face to face, one minute longer, she would explode, and so she turned away, murmuring, "See you at dinner."

"Cassie?"

With her back to him, she managed to hiss, "Yes?"

"Are you angry?"

It was priceless—he had dared to give her orders and now wondered if she was "angry"!—and it gave her the inspiration to turn and smile with gracious composure. "No, Alex. I just promised Kanasa I'd help with the children, and I'm late. See you at dinner." At that moment, one of Kanasa's grandchildren ran to her and she scooped him into her arms, cooing and rushing away, pretending not to hear Alex calling goodbye to her. Once inside the longhouse, she quickly sent the little boy away, unwilling to expose him to her angry trembling for even one second longer. She had never been humiliated in quite so effective a way, and while she knew she would eventually begin to see Alex's side, and perhaps even to forgive him, she wanted to be miles away from him before that absurd process began. For now, she savored her fury, hoping only that it would burn away the hopeless love she knew still lurked in her heart.

Fortunately, the longhouse was deserted and Cassie dressed quickly, choosing her jeans and tennis shoes, along with John's roomy shirt over her leotard, as the most comfortable outfit for the four-hour walk confronting her. If she rested only briefly, halfway there, she could easily reach the cabin before nightfall. Shannon would be glad to see her, and would agree that this love affair had been a gross mismatch from the start. And she would understand that Cassie couldn't wait around for the baby to be born. The birthing sling would have to do.

She would leave the Cutler cabin at dawn, would trudge to the burial ground, and this nightmare would be over. With her purse bulging with mementos, Cassie slipped from the longhouse and made her way to the cornfields, imagining with dark delight how embarrassed Alexander BlackKnife would be when he discovered that his former lover had deserted him. Kahnawakee would ask questions, and Djisgaga would probably throw a party . . .

"And Kanasa will be hurt," she reprimanded her-self, as she found her way to the river and began the long walk to the cabin. "Even poor Kahnawakee will be a little hurt, I'll bet. Even if I am an infidel invader who talks incessantly about birth control, I *know* he liked me." Of course, it was always possible that Kah-nawakee had simply been cordial to her because she was Alex's woman and John Cutler's friend, and so maybe he'd be a little pleased himself at the breakup, knowing that a more suitable wife for "Couteau" could be found.

"They'll *all* go to the party, then," she seethed. "And they'll be right! We *should* celebrate! This rela-tionship has been a disaster from the start. Alex tried to tell you that, Cassie, the first day when you stupidly invited him to dinner, and nothing has changed since then."

A twig snapped behind her and she spun, aghast at the thought that Alex might have followed her to demand an explanation for this latest stunt. But there was no one there, and she summoned a nervous laugh. "You're hearing things, Cassie. You're so ticked, you're actually hearing things. You'd better calm down."

Her temper had always been quick, but this white-hot wrath was something she'd never before experi-enced, and she realized sheepishly that she'd better get it under control. While it would be convenient to stay angry forever, so that she could deal swiftly with Alex should he ever seek her out for an explanation, she knew it was a futile plan. She would calm down—not that he deserved it!—and then she would be forced to deal with the heartache that was being so effectively masked by the whirlwind of emotion.

"You love him, and it can never work out. He did

his best, and," the anger resurfaced, "his best was incredibly lame. Still, that doesn't change the fact that it was a mismatch from the start, and he tried to warn you, and *you* had to ask Uncle Matt to make him your escort anyway, so it's really all your own fault."

Someone was watching her—this time she was certain!—and so she whirled again, only to find that her imagination had fooled her once more. There was no one there. She was all alone, among black-barked trees and low-hanging vines, but the eerie sensation of being watched by curious eyes continued.

She couldn't shake the feeling, which slowly replaced her anger as she scurried along the trail. More than once she considered returning to the village. They probably wouldn't have missed her yet and so she wouldn't have to explain herself, and at least she would be physically safe. Out here, with renegades and bears and snakes, she was considerably more vulnerable. As she trudged along she remembered all too clearly the true reason why she had always hated camping. It wasn't the lack of restrooms or the dirt, it was *this*—bears and darkness and danger from so many sides one couldn't possibly guard against it all.

Alex had told her that the path along the river, while somewhat longer, was the more sunny and the more easily negotiated, and so she followed it despite the fact that she remembered her way through the trees. He had also told her, while they had lounged naked alongside the bubbling stream during their scintillating afternoon of love, that the burial ground was across the river, almost directly opposite their love nest. As she hurried along in uneasy silence, she considered going directly to her uncle's resting place and demanding transportation home. Only loyalty to Shannon prevented such a course and so she continued toward the cabin, occasionally cursing all things natural under her breath.

"What would Shannon do in this situation?" It was an interesting question and she tried to focus on it, but the sensation of being followed was growing stronger, and she knew that even a nature-lover like Shannon Cleary Cutler would be frightened under these circumstances. Frightened but brave, she would probably turn around and calmly demand that the renegades come out of hiding and begin their torture, so that it could be finished and she could be on her way.

"That's crazy, Cassie," she laughed nervously. "Shannon would just keep running, exactly like you're doing." Although she had no skill at telling time from the sun, she guessed that at least two hours had passed and knew that she would have to rest soon despite her fear. If she didn't, exhaustion would make her faint, and then she truly would be at the mercy of her stalker.

Finally, exhaustion won out and she collapsed near the bank of the river, cupping her hands to bring water to her parched throat, all the while glancing about for any sign of intruders. Instead she saw a canoe, hidden partially by brambly bushes, and for the first time in hours, a glimmer of optimism warmed her heart.

The river current would carry her, and she would be free to scan the woods for any sign of the creature that was following her. Once she had traveled an appreciable distance, she would begin to whistle for Prince, the only true hero on whom she could depend. The thought made her smile, and with a final drink of cold, clear water, she jumped to her feet and began to wrestle the heavy dugout canoe from its hiding place.

Just as she had begun to make some progress, a huge hand fell heavy on her shoulder and spun her around.

Orimha! Cassie recoiled, trying to shriek but succeeding only in gasping his name. The water was behind her, Orimha was blocking her path, and she knew she was doomed. There was no hope for escape, and no chance that Prince or Alex would find her in time, and despite Kahnawakee's naive belief that this man was honorable, she knew that reason or resistance were useless options.

He hadn't spoken a word or budged an inch. Instead, he was staring at her with the same dogged interest that had characterized his stay at the village. As Cassie's panic subsided just a bit, she remembered what she had been told by both John and Kahnawakee: this wasn't a simple case of lust. This frightening man believed himself to be in love with her. If so, he wouldn't kill her or injure her beyond the unspeakable injury she knew he was now contemplating. "No," she whispered stubbornly. "No, no, no."

"John Cutler," Orimha replied.

Cassie's eyes narrowed. Why on earth was he mentioning John? Was he bringing her a message? Was John hurt? Was the baby coming? "Are you crazy?" she taunted herself aloud. "Do you think they'd send *Orimha* with a message? Get a grip, Cassie."

Orimha smiled slightly and touched his own chest. "Stone," he reminded her, then he gestured toward Cassie, without any attempt at physical contact, and repeated, "Stone."

She nodded, encouraged by the attempt at civilized conversation. "We have the same name. Stone."

Orimha nodded in return, then gestured to the south. "John Cutler."

"Pardon?"

Orimha gestured once more, this time toward the river, and explained, "No John Cutler."

"Oh!" She exhaled in relief. "You're telling me I was going the wrong way? Really? Oh, gee . . ." Her knees buckled under her and she sank to the ground. "You scared me half to death, Orimha. Have you been following me this whole time? And you knew where I was going? And . . ." *And you wanted to be sure I got there safely?* she finished in silent amazement.

"John Cutler."

"Okay," she groaned, "just give me a minute. My legs are shaking." Although she was still too dazed to completely trust his motives, he seemed intent upon reassuring her, both by keeping his distance and by repeating John's name. In fact, he was being a perfect gentleman and she needed to encourage that behavior, so she struggled to her feet and smiled. "Let's go see John Cutler."

He motioned for her to follow, then he was disappearing down the path. She trailed after him for a few minutes, then jogged to his side. "Orimha, wait." The look of complete surprise on his face touched her and she was finally certain she was in safe hands. Apparently Kahnawakee was a good judge of character. "Thanks for coming after me. Let's walk together, okay?"

He cocked his head to one side, studied her for a moment, then stooped to the ground to pick up a rock. "Stone," he announced hesitantly. "Orimha, stone."

"Right. Do you know any other English?" His blank stare amused her. "The only word you know is stone? That's pretty egocentric, Orimha."

Her smile seemed to encourage him, and he began

to speak rapidly in his Iroquoian dialect. She caught only a few names—Kahnawakee's once or twice, and "Couteau Noir" over and over again—and she began to suspect he had witnessed their argument and was asking her if her departure from the village signaled the end of her love affair with Kahnawakee's student. Despite her lingering confusion toward the Gahnienca, borne of the fact that he had tortured the man she loved, she was beginning to sense the honor that Kahnawakee had perceived in the man and her heart went out to him. She needed to clear this up immediately, so that he wouldn't entertain futile hopes. "Do you speak French? Français?"

"Oui, seulement un peu."

"You're saying, not much French?" she guessed. "It's bound to be more than I know. I should have time traveled to *South* America so I could use my Spanish a little."

She had had three weeks in Quebec, for an embroidery and weaving clinic, and had learned a spattering of French tailored to enable her to find her hotel, order food from a menu, and discourage amorous locals. This last category of phrases might make the long walk with Orimha less painful, and so she explained, *"Vous êtes très gallant, mais je ne suis pas pour vous.* I'm just not for you." She paused to see if she was making any sense at all to him.

"Aimez-vous Couteau Noir?"

"Oui," she sighed. "It's hopeless, but I still love him. Probably forever. *Toujours* Couteau Noir. And," she touched his arm in apology, "it can never be you, Orimha. *Jamais,* Orimha. Never. Do you understand?"

"Jamais? Nev-er?"

"That's right. *Comprenez-vous?"*

He nodded, his expression stoic, then turned and continued down the path. Cassie had to hurry to keep pace with him, and she wondered if his heart was now breaking or if he was simply anxious to complete his errand and return to his men. In any case, she was convinced of continued courteous treatment and so she decided to try to lift both their spirits. "I've used up all my French," she chatted breathlessly, "but I know some songs. We could sing. How about *Frère Jacques?* Do you know that?" She sang a few lines, and when he didn't join her, she laughed lightly. "Your turn."

Orimha stopped again, studying her with renewed interest. When he spoke, his voice had a sing-song quality. *"Boddelsa boddelsa beer onawa . . ."*

"What? Is that a Mohawk song? I mean, Gahnienca?"

Orimha chuckled and repeated the line, this time singing it with gusto. Cassie stared in amazement and then burst into laughter. "Where did *you* learn *that?* Ninety-nine bottles of beer on the wall, right? Where did you hear it, Orimha?"

He seemed a bit offended by her laughter and explained, somewhat haughtily, "Couteau Noir."

"Alex? He sang *that?* Good grief!" She didn't know whether to laugh or cry. Had Alex sung this ridiculous drinking song while being tortured? Had it been a gesture of defiance, or simple delirium? "Or really bad taste?" she added aloud, then she grinned toward Orimha. "Okay, sing it again. Boddelsa boddelsa beer onawall? Great, let's go."

The song served the dual purpose of helping Cassie keep pace with the warrior and cementing the bond of camaraderie between them, so that she was almost wistful when the Cutler cabin came into view. She would be gone in less than a day, and Orimha would never understand precisely what had happened. Perhaps in his own way he really did love her. If so, then he would be sad for a while, and the thought flattered her.

Orimha paused on the ridge overlooking John's "estate," apparently expecting her to continue down to the cabin without him. While it seemed rude not to invite him, the cabin was not her home and Orimha might not be the most welcome of guests. John would understand, but wouldn't poor Shannon be shocked if she brought a torturer home for dinner?

"Come with me, Orimha," she decided aloud finally. "You should have a meal and rest before you start back."

He shook his head and motioned for her to go on ahead.

"Are you sure?" She was tempted to kiss him, but resisted, patting his arm briskly instead. *"Merci, mon ami. Au revoir."*

He grinned but made no motion to leave, and she realized he intended to watch her until she had arrived safely on the doorstep. With a grateful smile, she turned away from him and began her descent, whistling for the dogs as she went. Almost immediately Duchess scampered from the cabin and planted herself in the yard, howling frantically toward Cassie.

The dog's panic had not been lost on Orimha, who now joined Cassie hastily, propelling her down the path by her elbow. Prince had still not appeared, and John was clearly not on the premises, but Shannon . . .

"Shannon doesn't ever leave! Not in her condition," Cassie whispered. "She's in that cabin, Orimha. I just know it!" Almost as though in answer, Shannon stumbled onto the porch, gripping herself about the middle, and raised her eyes toward Cassie. She was in obvious and absolute agony, unable to call out.

"Shannon!" Cassie wailed, racing across the yard and gathering the sobbing cousin into her arms. "Where's John? What's wrong? Is the baby coming?"

"The baby," Shannon gasped. "John isn't home . . . Prince never came back. We have to go look for them—*Aaugh!*"

The contraction seemed to swallow her whole, preventing any attempt at communication. Cassie continued to cradle her, whispering reassurances and scanning wildly for John or Prince. When the pain seemed to have subsided at last, she whispered, "Shannon? Where did John go?"

"Fishing . . . just fishing, and he should have been back by now," Shannon sobbed. "And the contractions started, and so I sent Prince, and now *he's* gone, and what if they're dead? What if they need help?"

"Shhh, they're fine," Cassie insisted. "We have to get you back inside."

"You have to go look for them!"

"No, Shannon, I need to stay with you. The baby's coming, remember? We have to get the sling—"

"Forget the stupid sling!" Shannon hissed. "I want John. *Aaugh!* Cassie, help me!"

"I'm trying! Orimha!" She turned desperate eyes to the Gahnienca. *"Cherchez* John Cutler! Please!"

He nodded, then glanced about himself, as though trying to decide which direction to pursue. Cassie grabbed his arm, signaling for him to wait, and when the contraction had finally released the exhausted Shannon, she coaxed gently, "Shannon? Do you know which way John went? Orimha will go after him, but he has to know which way to go."

"Orimha?" Shannon stared with hollow, disbelieving eyes. "This man is Orimha? Are you *crazy?*"

"I know it sounds bad, but he's okay. Trust me."

"He almost killed Alex!" Shannon shrieked. "Get him out of here! Now!"

"You'd better go," Cassie murmured. *"Allez,* okay? She's getting too agitated. Just do your best, Orimha."

He nodded and sprinted away.

"Are you crazy?" Shannon repeated hoarsely. "Is he gone?"

"He's gone. Please come back inside." Cassie tried to find a cheerful tone. "We have to get you into bed while I hang up the sling."

"Would you stop? John's out there dying and *you're* talking about *slings!"*

Cassie almost welcomed the next contraction, which redirected Shannon's hysteria for a moment. The only logical move seemed to be to leave the patient on the porch—in her condition she couldn't go far—and to find the birthing sling. Hopefully, John had kept his promise and had secured a hook in an overhead beam so that the harness could be easily mounted.

Which will be useless if you can't convince her to get into the stupid sling, Cassie mocked herself. *You're going to end up delivering this kid the old-fashioned way, Cassie, and then we're all in trouble.*

Shannon's hostility had disappeared for the moment and she began to weep. "I need John, Cassie. I'm sorry I yelled at you, but I'm scared. He's been gone for too long, and Prince . . ."

"I know," Cassie soothed, seizing the opportunity to urge her successfully back into the cabin and over to the bed. "I'm sure he'll be back any minute,

Shannon, and these contractions are just going to get worse."

"I know," she sniffled pitifully. "I'm scared."

"There's nothing to be scared of," Cassie bluffed. "Women have babies every day. It's the most natural thing in the world, right?"

"It's killing me! *Aaaaugh!*"

Cassie stared in horror as her cousin's yowl resounded through the cabin. For the first time, she was wondering what they would do if there was a complication with the delivery. Even if she could get Shannon into the sling, it wasn't any guarantee. What if she needed a Caesarian section, or oxygen for the baby? What if this wasn't "the most natural thing in the world?"

"Shannon? I have to go find the sling. You just lie here and relax until the next one comes, okay? Try to rest while you can."

"I want John."

"Don't think about John. You have to concentrate on having the baby."

"If John's dead, I don't want the baby! I want to die, too!"

"No one's going to die," a firm voice interceded. "Cass, go and find the birthing sling. Shannon, let's have a look at you."

Cassie spun toward Alex and groaned with relief. "You followed me?"

Alex raised one eyebrow sharply, as though wondering what to do with her. "Find the sling and try to stay out of trouble." Seating himself on the edge of the bed he stroked Shannon's face. "You look pretty good, Shannon. How far apart are the contractions?"

"Alex!" Shannon gasped. "I think John's in trouble! Go and find him!"

"Sure I will," he soothed, propping a pillow behind her head. "As soon as you're in the sling, I'll go and find John. I promise."

"I don't *want* to go in the stupid sling!" she sobbed. "I hate it!"

"We'll just try it for a minute, and if you still hate it, I'll take you back out of it." His tone was firm yet tender. "We won't do anything you don't want us to do, Shannon. I promise."

"I want to die," she sobbed. "John's dead, and I want to die, too."

"He's not dead," Alex promised. "He's been delayed, but he's not dead."

"How do *you* know?" Shannon's shriek reached a new high. "You're *lying* to me! *Auugh! Auugh!*"

Alex held her hands tightly and talked her through it, his voice resonant with confidence. "You're doing great, Shannon. Just take a breath and look at me. Try to focus on me."

"You should be looking for John!" she accused, as soon as she could speak. "He could be dying and you're just sitting here!"

"Calm down, Shannon."

"Don't call me that!"

Alex grinned in frustration. "Don't call you Shannon? What should I call you?"

"Don't *speak* to me! You're letting John die and you won't help him!"

"Okay, listen to me." Alex cupped her chin in his hand and spoke rapidly. "I know for a fact that John Cutler lives past the age of sixty-one. I've seen the records with my own eyes."

Shannon's eyes locked with his, incredulous at first, and then brimming with tears of gratitude. Finally, she slumped back into the bed and whispered, "Thank you, Alex. Thank you . . . thank you . . ."

"Cassie?" Alex turned to the wide-eyed onlooker with a patient smile. "Did you find the sling yet?"

She stared, wondering if he could possibly be as calm as he seemed. "I'll find it right away," she murmured, then flew through the door and into the yard. With Duchess on her heels, she reached the smithy, located the ornate contraption, and raced back to the house, never once pausing for a decent breath. She was gasping for air as she presented the sling to Alex, who had apparently just weathered a contraction with the nearly hysterical mother-to-be.

"You'll have to hang it up, Alex. I can't reach the hook," Cassie panted. "It's too high."

"We need it to be high," he reminded her, jumping from the bed and positioning the long leather thongs overhead. "You did a great job on this, Cass. It's a beauty."

"Alex!" Shannon wailed. "What if John's hurt?"

"Hey!" He rejoined her quickly, cradling her face between his hands once more. "Look at me, Shannon. You're panicking again. Is that what John would want you to do?"

She shook her head, tears streaming down her face.

"Now, take a breath," he instructed firmly. "Good girl. You're going to have another contraction now, and I want you to be sure to breathe with me. John's baby needs air. Understand?"

The contraction came, and to Cassie's amazement, Alex guided Shannon through it. While the pain was clearly still intense, there was an element of control, and she could finally dare to believe that it was all going to be okay . . . thanks to Alex.

"Now, we're going to stand up, Shannon. Here we

go. Good girl." His tone was masterful and soothing.
"You're doing great, Shannon. Everything's going
great. Your color is perfect, and the contractions are
strong. That means it'll be over faster."

"I can't take many more of them," Shannon murmured, but the edge of panic was gone from her voice.
"I thought there wouldn't be any problem . . ."

"Problem?" Alex scoffed. "This is textbook labor,
Shannon. Okay, here it comes. Put your arms around
my neck."

"Ohh, Alex, it hurts . . ." The pain overcame her
and she leaned against him while he held her tightly
under her arms and continued his low, patient cheer-
leading. Cassie was mesmerized by him, acutely aware
of the awesome strength that seemed to be consistently at his command. He had drawn on it most notably when Orimha had tortured him, yet that very
same endless supply of strength had emerged, again
and again, during these tumultuous weeks since
they'd first met. His strength fueled his lovemaking
with Cassie, his dedication to Kahnawakee, his dogged search for a missing woman. . . . In fact, it per-
meated everything he did, as though he could actually
will himself to be successful in the face of overwhelming odds.

She had witnessed this strength so often, and had
felt its power deep within herself, but never before had
she seen it so purely and unselfishly at work as he
calmed and soothed this frightened young woman
and somehow, magically, convinced her to allow Cassie to hook her into the birthing sling. It seemed to
help relieve some of the pressure immediately, and
Shannon even began to doze between contractions
while Alex made the final adjustments to the thongs.

"Can you handle this now, Cass?" he whispered

into her ear. "She'll be able to concentrate better if she knows I'm out looking for John."

"I think I can manage," she smiled with shaky confidence. "Did you mean what you said? Is it going smoothly?"

"Sure. Just keep talking to her, and get her to tell you where she feels the pressure. If it's along her spine, adjust the sling like this. If it's across her middle, move it like this, so that there's no pressure on her stomach. See?"

"Alex?" Shannon interrupted groggily. "Tell John I love him."

"You'll tell him yourself, any minute now," Alex assured her. "Here it comes now, Shannon. Let's see if this harness of Cassie's does its job."

Cassie had constructed almost two dozen of these harnesses but had never seen one put to use until now, and she beamed with pride as the laboring woman rocked herself into the most comfortable position and then seemed to use the contraction rather than to fight it.

"Any minute now, she'll be pushing," Alex marveled. "You need to sit on the floor for that, Cass. When you see the head, that's the time for real action, or at least," he grinned self-consciously, "that's how it was with my sister, and everything turned out fine. Just try to keep her from pushing when it won't do any good. We don't want any more ripping than necessary."

"Ripping?" Cassie winced. She was *never* going to have a child, she decided grimly. And she was never, ever going to blithely agree to assist at a birth again. She would make the slings, but would sell them by mail order and that would be the extent of her involvement with childbirth after this was over.

"They still hurt," Shannon moaned, "but I feel like it's really happening. It's going to work . . . if only John were here."

"I'm going to take a quick look around," Alex soothed. "Just tell Cassie where it hurts, and she'll help you. And if it helps to scream or cuss," he added fondly, "go ahead. You won't say anything we haven't heard before, I guarantee."

Cassie bathed her cousin's face in cool water, then sat onto the floor to begin her watch. "Go ahead, Alex. We're fine."

He nodded, kissed each female's cheek, and hurried from the cabin.

"He's so wonderful, Cassie," Shannon whispered. "Don't you just adore him?"

"Yes. Brace yourself, Shannon. It's time for the next contraction . . . oh, good grief! Don't push!"

"Cassie!" Shannon's entire tone had changed. "I feel the baby!"

"I can top that," Cassie giggled nervously. "I *see* the baby, or at least, the top of his head. Don't push yet, please! Just pant, like a dog."

"Aaugh! Oh, oh! Cassie—"

"Don't!" Cassie pleaded, her eyes glued to the aperture that was straining at the force of the head. "I don't think it's time! You have to wait, and pant, and . . ." As she watched, the head began to emerge, Shannon instinctively bore down, and a new life was expelled into Cassie's trembling hands.

Chapter Fourteen

"You know what my favorite part was?" Shannon's voice was groggy as she nestled in her bed and cuddled her baby girl to her breast. "When Alex told me John's going to live for years and years and years. And the worst part was when I dreamed you were crazy enough to bring Orimha here with you. I really must have been delirious."

Cassie chuckled with delight. "My favorite part was when you proved, once and for all, that Djisgaga doesn't know everything. After all," she finished bathing Shannon's newborn son and cradled him lovingly in her arms, "she said it couldn't be twins, and you proved her wrong. You're a great cousin, Shannon."

"So are you," Shannon echoed solemnly. "What was the worst part for you?"

"I guess that was when I said, 'I'm glad that's over,' and you said, 'There's another baby coming, Cassie.'" She laughed ruefully. "But that's also my favorite part, because little Philip here was born just two minutes later. He's so adorable, Shannon. Take him for a while and let me look at Robin." She clucked her tongue at the baby girl and cooed, "Hello there, Robin Cutler. You're sooo pretty."

"I wish John would hurry. His children are almost an hour old and he still hasn't met them."

"Alex was pretty sure that leg is broken in two places," Cassie reminded her. "Maybe they're having trouble splinting it. I guess we should just be thankful he found him at all."

"Poor Alex. We've run him ragged today, haven't we? First he had to come chasing after you, then he had to calm me down, then find John *and* drag him out of a bear pit, then run back here to report, then back to John. I'm exhausted just thinking about it."

"You're exhausted because you just had twins, so go to sleep. I promise I'll wake you as soon as John hobbles in."

She watched in weary contentment as her cousin hugged her two children tightly and snuggled in for a much-deserved rest. The Cutlers were a perfect family, loving and self-sufficient and safe in their idyllic corner of the backwoods. John's decision to make his home away from both colonial town and Susquehannock village had been a good one. Unfortunately for Cassie, such an option was not open to Alexander BlackKnife, whose life was firmly centered in the village. Life with Alex would never be simple or idyllic, but in its own way, it just might be perfect.

Catching a glimpse of the two men through the window, she pulled a lightweight coverlet over the sleeping mother and babies and ran to lend her shoulder for John's support. "Poor John," she crooned, slipping her arm around his waist. "Does it hurt?"

"How's my family?" he demanded gruffly. "It took us forever to get here. Is Shannon upset?"

"She's sound asleep, and so are the kids, so stop

complaining," Cassie scolded. "Shannon thinks it's
romantic that you broke your leg, because it was
broken when you two first met. So," she sent Alex an
amused glance, "stop whining and be a man. You
have to set an example for your son, John Cutler."

John chuckled. "Alex tells me that contraption of
yours worked like a charm, missy. I suppose now
you'll be bragging?"

"That's right, so get used to it."

They had reached the porch and John took a deep
breath. "I can make it the rest of the way on my own.
I want to see her, and the babies, for just a minute."

"Sure," Alex nodded, slumping wearily against the
porch rail. "I'll just collapse out here for a while."

"Wash your hands before you touch those babies,
John." Cassie patted his shoulder and added sweetly,
"Little Philip looks just like you, you handsome bully.
Just call us when you need us. And elevate that leg as
soon as you can."

Alex sat down on the step, yawning loudly. "Will
you sit with me for a minute, Cassie?"

She joined him quickly, slipping her hands around
his neck. "You were so magnificent, Alexander Black-
Knife. I'll never forget the moment you walked in and
took my hysterical cousin off my hands. I think you
saved my life."

"So? You're not still mad at me?" He yawned
again. "That's good news, because I don't have the
energy to argue with you right now. I apologize, but
you'll have to wait until tomorrow for the actual
groveling."

"I can wait. You should sleep now, Alex. You definitely earned it."

"Yeah . . ." He stretched out on the porch and was
snoring softly within seconds.

For the next two hours, Cassie hovered over the four Cutlers, all of whom seemed to need rest more than anything else. Finally, when all was clearly under control, she lit a lamp, stepped carefully over Alex's slumbering body, and made her way through the darkness to the smithy, hoping to grab a few minutes' sleep on the bed of rushes that held such fond memories of her first lovemaking. To her delight, she was no sooner undressed and in bed than Alex had joined her.

"Can I sleep here with you, Cass?"

"Mmm, I would have invited you, but you were sound asleep." She laid her head on his chest and sighed with weary contentment. "What a day."

"Yeah. It all worked out. But it all could have been a disaster, especially," he stroked her back gently, "running off with Orimha, of all people, that way. I know you were mad at me, Cassie, but that was still foolhardy of you."

"I didn't run off with him. He followed me."

"Oh."

"Did he go back to the village?"

"I doubt it." Alex pulled her closer. "I set him straight about us after we got John out of the pit."

"Pardon?" Cassie raised her head and tried to discern his expression. "I hope you weren't rude to him."

"Rude?" He paused for a moment to stare in disbelief. "I told him if he ever came near you again I'd break his neck."

"Alex! He didn't lay a finger on me, and he helped you find John!"

"He didn't lay a finger on you because he knows you're mine," Alex countered. "If he had thought you were available, he would have been all over you, I guarantee it. It's a good thing he didn't know about our argument."

"Argument?" Cassie murmured. "We didn't argue. You blasted me, and Orimha knew *all* about it."

"Did he make a play for you?"

"Yes, but I turned him down. In French. We got along really well. I wish you hadn't been belligerent with him, Alex."

"Belligerent?" he chuckled. "Do you know how hard it was to resist challenging him to a full-fledged duel? Ever since that . . . experience in his camp, I've wanted a chance to pay him back, a little."

"I guess I can't blame you," Cassie sighed. "Let's get some sleep now. Shannon's going to need my help with the twins soon."

"The babies are probably exhausted, too," Alex smiled. "Hopefully, they'll spend most of their time sleeping for the first few days. When Kahnawakee hears that there are two of them, and that John's laid up, he'll send them some help, I'm sure."

"Maybe one of Kanasa's daughters could come," Cassie nodded. "They're wonderful with their own babies, and they could be more help than I could. And then," she snuggled closer, "we could go home."

"Home? Are you homesick?"

"A little. Are you?"

"I keep wondering what's going on back there," he admitted. "I don't like to miss out on important developments. I need to be there, but I also need to be here. It's frustrating."

"You need to sleep," she cooed. "You've been playing hero for hours, and I'm so proud of you. I'm going to sing you an Iroquois lullaby."

"Really?" he beamed. "That's incredible. Let's hear it."

"Boddelsa boddelsa beer onawa," she crooned gently, *"boddelsa boddelsa*—Alex!" Her laughter rang through the smithy as he silenced her with a fiercely passionate kiss that could only lead to more.

"I still say we just kill the Susquehannock troublemaker and be done with it," Benedict Fowler was insisting to his companion, as they paddled together in the first of three birchbark canoes that had been provided for their expedition.

Jean-Claude Rubrier groaned. This argument had been raging, on and off, for days, and this new dawn was no exception. Soon they would arrive within killing distance of the Susquehannock village, and if something didn't change, Benedict Fowler was going to commit the biggest mistake of his short, ill-conceived career as an assassin. "Can you not see the potential for disaster, my friend?" Jean-Claude tried for the hundredth time. "At this moment, Kahnawakee is a mystery. The Susquehannocks admire him, but most of the other natives distrust him. The Iroquois find him attractive, yet his nation will not submit to them and so they listen to him, but with strong reservations. The Hurons listen also, and the Delawares are intrigued, but . . ." The French agent shrugged. "They are slow to accept him. If you murder him, all that will change. He will be a martyr, my friend, and his message will travel faster than the wildfire. We will not be able to deal with that so easily."

"We'll make it look like the Mohawks did it. You told me yourself a group of those cut throats are protesting their leaders' endorsement of Kahnawakee."

Rubrier nodded. "Renegades, roaming through the woods."

"Exactly. We'll make it appear as though the renegades killed him, and the traditional hostility between the League and the Susquehannocks will flare into war."

"Kahnawakee has trained other young men," Jean-Claude countered, "and they might just be able to continue to keep the peace. They would say the Visionary died for his beliefs and now it's their place to see that his vision is implemented. He has welcomed the finest young men from many villages to come and study with him, for a month or more at one time, and more than a dozen have done this. They then returned to their own people, and they counsel the elders, and the results have been very successful."

"Then what do you suggest?"

"We cannot defeat him by killing him. We must be more clever than our prey. We must make him defeat himself. Either we must bribe him, or enrage him, so that he abandons his talk of peace and attacks one of the nations he now calls 'brother.' Do you see?"

Fowler nodded. "That makes sense. From what I hear, he's not interested in bribes of any kind. That's been tried. So, we'll enrage him." His steely eyes glistened at the thought. "We'll murder his children, or one of his wives, and make it appear that the Mohawks did it."

"He has only one child and only one wife. My informers tell me they cannot be touched. They do not leave the village."

"I could sneak in, at night, and cut the black-eyed bitch's throat."

Jean-Claude felt an icy chill run down his spine, all too aware of the fact that his companion would love nothing more than to draw his razor-sharp blade across the neck of any innocent native who stumbled across his path. "If you were caught, Kahnawakee's warning against all European colonists would be validated. If the other Indians realized we saw their unity as a threat, they would wonder if his warnings are not justified. They would begin to believe we have come to this land to eradicate all that has been here, and to replant Europe in its stead."

"And the sooner, the better." Fowler noticed Jean-Claude's wince. "You don't agree?"

"My father came here to live in peace. To hunt and to fish and to raise his family, in peace, alongside the native dwellers. He considered it an honor to be accepted by them, and in return, he offered them the one priceless treasure they did not yet have. He offered them salvation. We are here to save their immortal souls, Fowler."

"And you're willing to murder them in order to save them?" Fowler mocked. "Typical Papist illogic."

"I do not consider it murder. It is a holy war."

"You honestly think these savages have souls to save?"

Jean-Claude nodded.

"You'd better hope they don't." Fowler pulled his hunting knife and ran his finger along the blade. "If Kahnawakee has a soul, and you cut his throat, I don't think the Almighty will be too pleased with you. Thou shalt not kill, and all that."

"If one man must fall to save a continent of souls . . ." Jean-Claude coughed nervously. When he had first been asked to participate in this scheme, he had asked the very same question of his confessor and they had decided, with great sadness, that Kahnawakee could no longer be allowed to interfere with

the holy work being done on this continent. If there
was a bloodless way to accomplish this, Jean-Claude
would find it. If bloodshed was necessary, Jean-
Claude would moderate it to the full extent of his
abilities.

"You admire Kahnawakee," Fowler complained.
"I can see it in your eyes."

"He fascinates me," Jean-Claude shrugged. "For
the same reason that he fascinates his people, I suppose. He was born under an eclipse, alongside rapids
of this very river—did you know that is the meaning
of his name in Susquehannock?—and he rose to
power as a great war chief only to speak words of
peace and unity and strength. He lives a life of tem-
perate purity, they say. Using few conveniences, resisting wealth, practicing forbearance and kindness.
And with all this, he is also clever. He uses words as
weapons, to capture and hold even the most unwilling
of listeners."

Fowler shook his head. "Why destroy him, if you
believe all of that?"

"He is a devil. A clever and fascinating one, but a
devil. He thwarts the work of the Jesuit Fathers. I ask
myself why. If Kahnawakee has such love for his
people, why does he keep them from salvation?"

"I had heard just the opposite," Fowler mused. "I
heard he allowed a missionary to stay in his village for
a month last year, unmolested. I heard he allows
preaching and conversion without interference."

"He is clever," Jean-Claude repeated. "He allows
the Fathers to visit the villages, but cautions the Indians not to go to the French communities. He has sent
word to the Fathers that their God is welcome among
his people, but that their customs and criticisms are
not. In this way, he cleverly subverts us."

"Us?" Fowler mocked. "You'd make a strange priest, Jean-Claude. Didn't my superiors tell me you enjoy breaking your vow of chastity at every opportunity?"

Jean-Claude flushed. "Each man worships in his own way. This . . . distasteful assignment is my contribution to the Lord's work." He hesitated, then added, "Tell me something, my friend. Why did you take this assignment? Was it for the reward, or for the pleasure of killing Kahnawakee?"

"You talk about bringing salvation to this continent. England brought something a bit more substantial, wouldn't you say? We were civilizing this place, and making some progress with it, when this Kahnawakee began to incite the primitives. After all we had given them, they now consider turning on us and following him. Every day, throughout New England, word of his blasted vision spreads. He has to be stopped." Fowler's eyes flashed. "When I return home, I'll be greeted as a hero. The man who eliminated Kahnawakee and restored safety to the Colonies."

"By admitting he is a threat, you admit he has some worth," Jean-Claude taunted.

"Don't fool yourself," Fowler laughed. "Kahnawakee's effective because he has John Cutler behind him. The Susquehannock is just a puppet for Cutler, and why not? Cutler's an Englishman, and well educated, and the son of a disinherited wanderer. There's nothing in England for him and he believes he can set himself up here as a monarch in the eyes of these primitives. I can almost admire that," he added sincerely, "but he goes too far. He's not content to build his own empire. He wants to destroy the one that ejected his father."

"I have heard Cutler is a good man, but misguided. He advises Kahnawakee, but it is the vision that leads them both."

"The vision?" Fowler scoffed. "You believe that heathen honestly had a vision?"

"I believe it is possible." Jean-Claude's voice lowered ominously. "He is the instrument of the devil, whether he knows it or not. We must stop him."

"I'm beginning to think we should eliminate John Cutler," Fowler mused. "Kahnawakee would be lost and ineffective without him."

"Do not underestimate the Visionary, my friend."

"If someone in that pair has a vision, it's Cutler. Take my word for that." Fowler was warming quickly to the new plan. "We'll make it seem as though Cutler was butchered by the renegades. Kahnawakee will make war against the Mohawks in retaliation."

"We cannot know how Kahnawakee might react to the death of his adviser."

"That's true." Fowler grinned reluctantly. "He might be believing his own stories, and thinking he can survive without Cutler's guidance. I doubt whether these savages feel loyalty to their friends in the civilized sense."

The Frenchman seethed inwardly, doubting whether Fowler had ever had a friend in the world. His bigotry and slurs were doubly painful, given Jean-Claude's Montagnais blood and the many true friendships he had forged over time with men from a myriad of cultures. He had no doubt that John Cutler and Kahnawakee would give their lives to save one another willingly, but would the survivor of the pair endanger the vision to avenge the murder of the first killed?

"I still wish we could kill the wife," Fowler was

complaining. "Even a savage would be loyal to his woman."

"She stays in the village," Jean-Claude repeated firmly. "She does not live in a cabin or house, like the wife of John Cutler. She lives in the longhouse, with dozens of others."

"Cutler's married? I didn't know that. Is she a Susquehannock?"

"Some say she is Susquehannock. Some say she has golden hair and blue legs."

"Blue legs?"

Jean-Claude chuckled. "The rumors that run wild through these woods would amaze you. I have heard she has blue legs, but I have also heard that she wears breeches. Some say she is carrying Cutler's first child. No one knows her homeland or name."

"Perfect," Fowler whispered, as though in awe of the opportunity to wreak havoc on this new victim. "We'll find out when the child is due. With any luck it's born by now. You told me the Mohawks steal babies and adopt them as their own. We'll make it seem as though they've taken the child."

"And Kahnawakee and Cutler will try to regain it?"

"Kahnawakee won't endanger his vision over a white child. But John Cutler is an Englishman at heart and he'll move heaven and earth to recover his offspring." His silver eyes were beginning to shine. "When Kahnawakee refuses to aid him, it will cause a break between them."

"That would destroy them," Jean-Claude agreed quietly. "No friendship, not even theirs, can survive such a test."

"Tell your Indian friends to stay behind. We can reach the vicinity of Cutler's cabin by nightfall. When we return, we'll have a valuable prize for them to barter to the renegades, and while they're bartering, we can be returning to the safety of Quebec before the hostilities commence."

Jean-Claude struggled against a wave of revulsion at the thought of tearing an infant from its mother's breast, but it was a bloodless solution, at least on their part. The child would be raised with love by the Mohawks, whose ferocity in battle was equaled only by their commitment to family. It was a shame, and would weigh heavily on him always, but the alternatives, including the thought of slitting someone's throat, were much worse, and so he would cooperate with Fowler's plan, praying that it would all be over soon.

"You mentioned something about groveling last night?"

Alex laughed and pulled her into his arms. "So? You finally have time for me? It's almost noon, woman, and I haven't seen more than a glimpse of you all day."

"Between John's leg, Shannon's appetite, and the babies' diapers, I'm feeling very indispensable. I'm also a mess." She fluffed her matted curls ruefully. "It's nice and cool out here on the porch, isn't it? Maybe I should move Shannon out here for a while."

"Later. For now," he nuzzled her neck eagerly, "I'm ready to grovel."

"I was just teasing," she sighed, curling her arms around his neck. "I embarrassed you in front of your idol. I'm going to be totally serious about Kahnawakee from now on." Memories of his accusations resurfaced fleetingly, and she added, "I *am* capable of being serious, you know."

"John thinks your warped sense of humor is good for Kahnawakee," Alex admitted. "We had some time to talk, while I was bringing him home yesterday, and he says it's been a rough year. The Visionary suddenly has an image to protect, and it's hard for him to have a good time or relax. I guess it's the burden of fame, or whatever."

Cassie nodded. "He has to measure every word and every expression. I've noticed that."

"But with you, he just laughs right out loud. John thinks it's some sort of stress reliever for him. He says the Visionary responded that way to you almost instantly."

"I think it's true," Cassie blushed. "I've seen a whole different side of him than you have, Alex. He teases me, and he seems to want me to tease him back. I think he's wonderful, and I respect him, but . . ." she smiled fondly, "he doesn't want me to be *too* respectful. He gets enough of that from the other women, and, of course, from you."

Alex winced. "I can't just see him as a regular man, Cassie. I've spent a lifetime trying to emulate him. I know he and I resemble one another, and we're close in age, but he'll always be bigger than life to me. My mentor, not my equal."

"Yesterday, when you appeared out of nowhere, and calmed Shannon down, and helped me get her into the birthing sling," Cassie smiled, "you were *my* hero. You're a lot more like Kahnawakee than you realize."

"Thanks." He shrugged to his feet and stretched. "These last two weeks have been incredible, haven't they?"

Cassie nodded. "Especially for you. You've been dragged through time and tortured, and you've had to walk on burned feet and deliver babies and haul a big, bearded man out of a bear pit."

"It's been wild for you, too. You delivered those babies, you've had to adapt to backwoods life *and* longhouse life, and . . ." he reached down and pulled her to her feet, "you made love for the very first time. And I repaid you by losing my temper. I apologize for that, Cassie."

"If that hadn't happened, I wouldn't have left in a huff, and we wouldn't have been here to help Shannon. It's like I told you a long time ago: things always seem to happen for a reason. No matter how bizarre life seem at any moment, eventually, it makes sense."

"Just the same, you could have been hurt. Running off into the woods with a maniac like Orimha hanging around." He shook his head. "Hopefully he and his band of merry men will be far away by the time we reach the village tonight."

"We?" Cassie laughed. "I'm not going anywhere. Shannon needs me, Alex. Anyway, Orimha's not so bad. I told you he was nice to me, and even if he wasn't, you shouldn't offend him. Your feet are just beginning to recover from the last time you challenged him."

Alex wasn't smiling. "I need for you to come back with me. We could leave early tomorrow morning, and reach the village by noon. Then Kahnawakee could send someone here to help with the babies until John's leg is better." His jaw tensed slightly. "This is an important time, Cassie. The Five Nations have invited the Visionary to address their Council. It's a rare honor, totally unheard of these days. They never allow outsiders that privilege. It's a sign they really respect his message. He's preparing for that, and somehow it seems to help him to talk to me about it." His eyes were suddenly shining, with pride and with excitement. "Of course, for me, it's incredible to be able to study his thought processes. I feel like I'm watching history being made, and learning how to help make a little myself, when I go home."

The fire in his eyes warmed her, and she insisted, "You should be there, Alex. Feel free to go."

"But I want to be with you, too." The tensed jaw had returned. "I feel like I'm being torn."

"Well," she teased gently, "I never said it would be easy being my escort. On the other hand, if it wasn't for me, you would never have met Kahnawakee, right?"

Alex chuckled. "I don't believe that anymore. The truth is, I think I was supposed to come alone."

"Pardon?"

"I've been giving it a lot of thought. I stood there, in full war paint, and asked to be tested. That's what triggered this. Your coming was just a fluke."

"No, Alex, that's not true." For some reason, she found the theory fundamentally intimidating. "Shannon's my cousin—"

"And when you burned the cabin, nothing happened," he reminded her gently. "You were never supposed to come. If you hadn't wandered in the woods and run into that snake, you'd be safe and sound, back in the twentieth century, and I'd be able to concentrate completely on Kahnawakee. That's how it was supposed to be."

It was as though all the joy and energy was escaping rapidly from her heart through a tiny wound inflicted by his words. This love affair that had meant the world to her had been a regrettable distraction for him. She had accepted the fact that she and Kahnawakee had needed to compete, good-naturedly, for Alex's time. Now, apparently, she needed to accept the fact that there had never been any real contest.

"Cassie?" Alex studied her warily. "Is something wrong?"

She shook her head and turned away, squinting to study the tree-lined ridge. "I appreciate the honesty, Alex. And I think you should go, right away, to the village. Kahnawakee will be anxious for news of the twins, and you need to study with him, so . . . go ahead. I'll be busy here with Shannon."

He turned her toward himself. "Tell me what's wrong. You're not jealous, are you?"

"I have to be honest with you, Alex," she murmured, refusing to meet his gaze. "I wouldn't have missed this time with you for anything in the world, and it hurts a little to hear you say you wish I hadn't come."

"Is that what you heard?" He whistled softly. "We'd better get married right away, Cassie."

She stared for a long moment, then managed to whisper, hoarsely, "Excuse me?"

Alex shook his head. "Somehow, I'm screwing this up, and I'm not going to allow some misunderstanding to come between us this late in the game. So, let's get married. Then you'll know, once and for all, how I feel about you, and how committed I am to you, and then we can both relax."

"And you can concentrate on studying with Kahnawakee?"

"Right. It's a once in a lifetime experience."

"So is falling in love." She immediately regretted the wistfulness to her tone. "I guess I shouldn't have said that."

"Why not?" he demanded.

"Because we agreed we'd use this time to explore our feelings, and we wouldn't decide until it was time to go back . . ."

"I was wrong." He grasped her by the shoulders and caught her gaze in his own. "I've known from the start how I felt about you. I didn't need the lovemaking in the smithy, or by the stream, or any of that to know I wanted to marry you. That realization came to me during the torture, when I saw how short life could be, and how profoundly you had affected me in just three short days."

"Alex—"

"If you hadn't time traveled with me, I would have come looking for you as soon as I got back to the twentieth century. There's no doubt about that in my mind." When Cassie simply stared, hungry to believe him despite her growing doubts, he added firmly, "I never would have given this up, but I'll admit, I would have postponed it. I need to spend this time with Kahnawakee. And then," his lips brushed hers, "I need to spend the rest of my life with you."

"I need you, too," she whispered, resting her cheek against his chest. It was a beautiful moment, yet tinged with the hopelessness that had plagued this love affair from the start. She wanted to ask him *When?* When would the time be right? He spoke of "postponing," and claimed he would have come looking for her as soon as he got back, but how could that be? He would have been pumped full of visionary fervor, all the more intense given the fact that there had been no distractions in the seventeenth century to keep him from his study, and he would have needed to meet with the elders and the chiefs, to instruct and amaze them, and to implement all he had learned. He would have been nominated for office, and would have campaigned, and his image among his people, and in the media, would have become a sensitive issue . . .

He would have waited for the right time before running to her, and the right time would never have come, and the love would have slipped away. The fact that he couldn't see this frightened her, and the fact that it didn't frighten him, too, just a bit, hurt more than she ever could have guessed.

"I love you, Cassie," he was proclaiming confidently. "We can get married today, if you want. And I'll stay here, with you, until you're ready to return to the village with me. I can't get anything done there without you anyway," he grinned, kneading her waist suggestively. "I think about you all the time. I can't imagine living without you. I used to watch other guys going crazy over some girl and I'd wonder what all the fuss was about, and now," his grin widened, "I know. You've spoiled me for any other woman."

"That's sweet, Alex."

"Sweet?" he scoffed. "Come to the smithy with me, and I'll show you how sweet I'm feeling."

Cassie stiffened at the thought of making love when her heart was so confused. "I promised Shannon I wouldn't be gone long," she lied desperately. "I'll be busy the rest of the day, Alex. This is time you should be spending with Kahnawakee."

He nodded. "I want to make love to you but I guess you're right. We'll be lucky to grab any time together around here for a while, and the Visionary will want to know about the babies, and about John's leg. Maybe," his eyes brightened with inspiration, "he'll come back with me! That would be the perfect set-up. He and John can plan their strategy, and I can listen, and you can help Shannon, and at night . . . ," he reached for her hand, "we can be alone together. How about that?"

"It's a wonderful compromise," she murmured.

"If I leave right away, Kahnawakee and I can be back by suppertime. It makes sense, except," he lowered his mouth to explore her neck, "I won't like being away from you."

"We'll survive." She tried for a lighter tone and added, "After all, we have the rest of our lives to make love, right?"

"We'll need it," he chuckled. "I'm feeling very amorous, Miss Stone." When one of the twins began to wail, he added, "Is this what it's going to be like when we have *our* kids? Crying every time I'm trying to make a move on you?"

"We'll see." Cassie pulled away quickly and headed for the doorway. "I'll tell John your plan. I'm sure he'll approve."

"Tell him the whole plan," Alex insisted, pulling her back into his arms and bestowing a long, lingering kiss on her lips. "Tell him I'm bringing Kahnawakee back here for two reasons. To prepare for the Council, *and* to marry us. There's no point in waiting another day, right? Maybe once *I'm* the male head of your family in the seventeenth century, big John can finally relax."

Chapter Fifteen

"Cassie? Did Alex finally leave?" Shannon's smile was a tender tease. "He kept giving you 'one last kiss.' It was so romantic."

"He's a wonderful man." Cassie nodded, struggling to keep her own smile in place. She had been fighting this struggle for hours, and losing often, and soon she would be weeping openly. Hopefully, she would be deep in the woods, on her way to the burial ground, by that time.

"He'll be back here with Kahnawakee by nightfall, missy," John Cutler assured her. "He's anxious for the wedding, or should I say, the wedding night?" He grinned impishly. "I'll be relieved to have you properly married."

Cassie nodded. "You've been a wonderful protector, John. I'll always cherish your concern for my welfare."

"Well," John coughed, subdued by the unexpected praise. "My pleasure."

"Cassie?" Shannon carefully settled her newborn daughter into the cradle beside her baby brother, then hurried to Cassie's side. "If you miss him already, why don't you run and try to catch up with him? John and I will be fine alone . . ."

"No, Shannon. I'm not missing Alex. I'm just feeling sentimental, I guess. Seeing you and John and the babies—like the perfect family . . ."

"You and Alex will have all of this one day, too."

"No." Her voice was wistful but firm. "We were lucky to have any time together at all. In the twentieth century, our relationship would have been doomed, but here . . ." She noticed the worried looks exchanged by her host and hostess and rallied quickly. "This has been the most wonderful two weeks of my life."

"You keep saying everything's 'wonderful,' but you look like you're going to cry," Shannon accused. "Tell us what's wrong. Did you and Alex have an argument?"

"No. No argument." Cassie's smile was rueful. "It's nothing. Go back to bed. And, John," she put her hands on her hips and pretended to scold, "elevate that leg."

He chuckled and complied. "Alex is marrying a feisty woman. I warned him about you, missy, but he's determined to have you."

"Is that what you two were whispering about on the porch?" Cassie demanded. "Every time I asked Alex about what you two were discussing, he changed the subject."

John cleared his throat. "Never mind about that. It was man talk."

"Man talk?" Shannon rolled her eyes. "You're a bad influence on little Philip . . ." She gathered her baby boy into her arms and cooed, "You're not going to be a chauvinist like your daddy, are you, honey?"

Cassie backed toward the door. "Can I take Prince with me for a little walk?"

"Don't go too far," Shannon cautioned, without looking up from her baby's face. "We'll have lunch soon, and then you should take a nap, so you're fresh for your wedding."

The sound of John's knowing chuckle followed Cassie into the yard as she hurried toward the workshop to gather her belongings. "Just take one step at a time," she cautioned herself grimly. "Don't think about Shannon or the babies or Alex. Just think about what you need to bring with you, and what you need to leave behind. And how you're going to get to the burial ground." She thought of leaving a note for Shannon on her workbench, but her fear that her cousin might find it prematurely, and might be foolish enough to come after her, even in her weakened condition, precluded such a course.

If only she could face John and Shannon and simply explain her need to depart immediately, but she could not. They would want to reassure her, and persuade her to give love a chance. They would point to the success of their own relationship, which had blossomed and flourished despite unimaginable odds. They would call it a miracle, and they would be right, but would refuse to accept the simple fact that Cassie's arrival in the seventeenth century and her affair with Alexander BlackKnife had been a fluke, not a miracle.

You were never supposed to come. . . . Alex's words rang in her ears. She had struggled to disprove them, but had finally been forced to see the truth. Had she not gone walking in her new moccasins that fateful afternoon . . . had she taken his car to the border, as he had directed her . . . then she never would have been menaced by the snake and destiny would never have been required to snatch her from danger and deposit her on Shannon's doorstep. Alex would have come alone, in full war paint, to be tested and then to be groomed by Kahnawakee as his successor. *That* was the way it was supposed to have happened.

Would he have come for her, one day, upon his return to the twentieth century? It didn't seem to matter anymore. What mattered were her pride and her self-respect. She had a full life to lead in the twentieth century. She was neither a fluke nor a pest, nor a lovesick female who needed to be humored by a man who needed to be giving his full attention to the awesome task of becoming a philosopher/warrior.

"Now he'll be able to focus completely," she reassured herself, as she stuffed fur and sinew into her purse. "He'll complete his training and then he'll come home, and then, somehow, we'll know what's right. He'll thank me, eventually, for leaving like this."

She left her tennis shoes for Shannon, whose own pair had worn away months before. For the babies she left the woven hammock and a rattle donated by the hapless snake that had caused all of this grief. The snake's skin had been fashioned into a collar which Cassie now fastened carefully around Prince's neck. "My hero," she murmured. "You were the one who found me, and now you're the one who's going to take me to the burial ground." With a wry smile she added, "I guess *you're* my escort."

The ensuing hours were a blur, with Cassie only dimly aware of the spectacular display of color and texture along the river path. She was composing the farewell letter in her head while diligently refusing to reminisce, even when she neared the spot between the river and the creek where she and Alex had spent a night of love and wonder. It was there that she bathed, committed her notes to paper, and took her leave of Prince. "Take this to John," she instructed, tucking the letter securely under his new collar. Then she buried her face in his fur and whispered, "You're such a great dog. I really love you. Take care of everyone for me." Pulling away, she finished, "Hurry back to the cabin. Go to John." When he cocked his head and whimpered, she lowered her voice to a soft, ominous command, as she had heard John do when pulling rank on his dogs. "Go home, now. Go!"

He was gone in an instant, running at top speed, and she imagined he intended to return to this spot with the same stubborn alacrity once his mission had been performed. Hopefully, she could find the heavy canoe in the bushes—it made her think of Orimha, which made her smile for a brief moment—and then she would cross the river to the burial ground. Her matches were handy and her determination growing by the moment.

For all that she had loved being here with Alex, and for all that she had adored the days spent with Shannon and with Kanasa, the truth was that she missed her old life—her dye garden, her view of the river, her cluttered workroom, her potter's wheel. Life in the twentieth century had been cruel to Shannon Cleary, but to Cassie Stone it had been a celebration. She longed to share it with Alex, but not to give it up entirely, and so as she paddled clumsily toward the burial ground, she forced herself to remember hot showers, and rock-and-roll on the stereo, and her state-of-the-art sewing machine, and her parents and friends.

Finally she reached the riverbank and from there

easily found the wide path that led to the spot at which her uncle would one day be laid to rest. She had visited it only once, and the visceral impact she experienced as she stepped into the clearing stunned her. It was like being welcomed to the home of a loving friend, and for the first time since she'd left the cabin she was certain she would be allowed to leave this time without recrimination or further delay.

Because *you were never supposed to come. . . .* Those words, in Alex's voice, continued to echo in her head. Not the protestations of love, or the talk of marriage, or the soft cajoling and confident promises—all of these had lost their value the moment she'd understood that they should never have been spoken. They were flukes, not miracles. Perhaps when he came home he would repeat them and they would regain their force and beauty, but for now they were dormant, like their love itself, waiting like Sleeping Beauty to be either awakened with a kiss or doomed forever to be silent and still.

As Shannon had noted, Alex had kissed Cassie goodbye countless times before leaving for the village and even that had seemed portentous. Perhaps on some level he'd known what needed to be done, and now she would do it. With a heavy sigh, she sank to her knees and pulled her supplies from her purse. Twigs, and sinew, and bark . . . and matches.

She built herself a dream house, imagining it filled with love and warmth and the sounds of laughter and passion. It was a place she could live with Alex, if only he were free. It was a place she could live without him, if only she could catch a glimpse of him from time to time, and speak to him on occasion, and make love with him once in a while. . . . It was a place she could wait, perhaps forever, if only she had forever to wait. Sadly, she did not.

The pain was consuming her, as though it were a flame and she a rustic replica of a dreamhouse. Her tears were flowing freely, fueling rather than extinguishing the agony, and she reached for the matches, struck one forcefully, and pleaded through her anguish, "I was never meant to come here, so take me home."

The tiny structure resisted the fire once, then twice; then a spark took half-hearted hold. Rocking back onto her heels, Cassie tried to remember the sensation of being embraced by an unknown benevolence and escorted gently through the centuries. She had almost forgotten how serenely soothing the experience had been, and she suddenly craved it. Her tears disappeared as she stared into the struggling flame and willed herself to be home.

For the longest of moments there was nothing, and then, without warning, she felt herself seized, and it was terror rather than tranquility that engulfed her as strong, unloving hands forced a gag into her mouth while a viciously gleeful voice commanded her to be still, lest he indulge himself at her expense on the spot. Immobilized both physically and emotionally by the unseen brute, Cassie struggled with her panic, desperate to prepare herself for the horrors a man such as this could inflict in any century.

Alexander BlackKnife gazed with fondness at the Cutler cabin, enjoying the curl of smoke that rose so lazily from the chimney. Peaceful, tranquil . . . safe. He had needed to see this, so much so that he had turned back, when more than halfway to the village, and had run at top speed—back to his beautiful Cassie. Now, as he paused to savor the sight and to catch his breath, he remembered his conversation with John Cutler, just minutes before he had left the cabin.

He had wanted to talk to John about the lessons of history. To warn John of the dangers that lurked, somewhere in the indeterminate future, from European agents who would descend upon this peaceful cabin to simulate, with deadly thoroughness, a Mohawk attack. But John Cutler had refused to listen, echoing Kahnawakee's sentiment that such a warning would constitute an abuse of the rare privilege which destiny had granted them. John had added his own personal caveat, claiming that advance knowledge would render every ensuing moment sour and somewhat anticlimactic. He simply did not want to know his future—he wanted to live it fresh and in innocence.

And so Alexander BlackKnife had kissed Cassie with insatiable frequency, and had taken his leave of the Cutlers, but the foreboding had become too intense, despite John's protests, and so he had returned to insist, clearly and definitely, that great care must be taken over the months and years to come, lest Shannon and the babies be lost. After all, there now existed the requisite son and daughter who would purportedly be killed along with Shannon one day. The agents could come at any time. If nothing else, Kahnawakee's upcoming address to the Iroquois League would alert the invaders to the fact that this so-called Visionary was becoming a real and substantial threat, and perhaps it would be only a matter of weeks before a plan for subverting him would be devised. That plan was doomed to failure, as Alex knew, yet it would destroy all that Shannon and John had found together and could not be allowed to proceed.

The beagle was howling a greeting as Alex descended into the yard, while the other dog—the wolf-shepherd with the overprotective imagination—barked a sharp warning. "Prince, right?" Alex grinned, striding over to confront the rival. "Why does John have you tied up, boy? Have you been causing trouble?" Ruffling his hand through the dog's heavy fur, he added, "Have you been taking good care of Cassie for me?" Then he turned eagerly toward the cabin and sprinted onto the porch.

"Where's my fiancée?" he demanded cheerfully, stepping through the open doorway. "Why's the wonder dog tied up?" His good humor faded as the expressions on the Cutlers' faces registered. "What's wrong?" His tone was calmer, almost ominous, as he repeated, "Where's Cassie?"

"We didn't expect you back so soon, Alex," Shannon murmured. "Come in and sit down. We need to talk."

John was struggling to his feet despite the cumbersome splint. "She's not hurt, Alex," he insisted, extending his hand awkwardly. "It's good to see you . . ."

"Not hurt?" Shannon sniffed. "How can you say that? Her heart is broken."

"Her heart?" Alex shook his head. "Sit down, John. Tell me what's going on."

Shannon moved to the sideboard and retrieved a fold of paper from the drawer. "I'll let Cassie tell you herself."

"A letter?" Alex accepted it warily. "She wrote me a letter that says her heart is broken? That doesn't make sense." His eyes were beginning to scan the neatly printed words even as he spoke.

"She didn't write *you* a letter. She wrote it to me. I'm not supposed to show it to you, but—"

Alex held up one hand to silence her so that he could give his full attention to the heart-rending message.

Dear Shannon,

By the time you read this, I'll be back in the twentieth century, probably soaking in a bubble bath and wondering if I imagined all of the magic and heartache of the last two weeks. Please don't try to come after me. If I'm not successful, I promise I'll come right back to your cabin, but I know I'll be successful because I was really never supposed to be here in the first place. You came for a purpose, which was to keep Kahnawakee from being killed before he could establish UNAP. Alex came for a purpose, too, which was to learn how to handle the twentieth-century crisis—I guess because the members are threatening to withdraw or make radical policy changes.

I didn't come for a purpose. I came as part of a series of flukes, and I'd be lying if I said I wish I'd never come, but I'm a distraction to Alex, who's doing his best to fulfill his destiny. Believe me, I'm not being noble. Without me here to distract him, I'm hoping Alex can finish quickly and return to our time.

Forgive me for not saying goodbye. It would have been so difficult, for all of us, because you and John have become such close members of my family. This way is best. I'll always remember you, Shannon. Take care, and kiss John and the babies for me. And please try to find the words to convince Alex that I left because my time had come. Reassure him, Shannon. Tell him I'll wait patiently for him and that I'll marry him as soon as he returns. Once he accepts that, he can put me out of his mind and concentrate on Kahnawakee.

The truth is, I had this short time with him, but it's naive to assume we can make a marriage work. If he sees me as a distraction now, can you imagine how inconvenient I'll be when he's running for office or planning the future of his people? If by some miracle we end up together, I'll be the happiest woman in the world, but if not, I'll survive, so please don't worry or be sad. You've got it all, Shannon, and I envy you, but only in the most loving of ways, because you deserve it after all you went through. You're a great cousin! Take care of John and the twins, but most of all, take care of Alex, please? This will be rough on him, but it's the only way.

Love, love, love,

Cassie

"How long ago did she leave?" Alex demanded finally.

"She's gone, Alex." John's tone was firm and final. "She would have been back by this time."

"Not necessarily. She uses the trail along the river—"

"She's gone. That's why we had to tether Prince. He would have searched himself into exhaustion with no hope of finding her."

Alex took a deep breath. "I can't believe it. How

can she think . . . ?" He stopped himself grimly. If Cassie believed he saw her as an inconvenient distraction, it was because he had used those very words, or perhaps even stronger ones, earlier that day. He could *hear* himself, and the words staggered him. Had he shown so little respect for their love? She was always so playful, so lighthearted, so resilient, that he hadn't seen the need to nurture and court. Instead, he had dared to crush her with his thoughtless musing, relying on a casual, presumptuous marriage proposal to cushion the insult.

"She's gone home, Alex," Shannon insisted. "You're going after her, aren't you? If you don't," she paused dramatically, "it means she was right. You'll never find the time if you can't find it right now when it really counts."

"I don't agree," John interrupted. "If you go after her now, when your work with Kahnawakee is unfinished, you're admitting you can't have both. Once you leave, your access to Kahnawakee is gone forever."

"And if you stay," Shannon warned, "Cassie is lost to you forever. I'm a woman, Alex. I know exactly how she feels. If you hesitate now, she'll never trust you again."

"And if you go back now," John countered, "you'll resent her one day for manipulating you."

"Manipulating?" Shannon's angry eyes filled with tears. "Is that what you think she's doing, John Cutler? *He broke her heart!* I'm sorry, Alex—you know I'll never forget all your help with the twins, but . . . my cousin fell in love with you and you practically threw it back in her face."

"He was bringing Kahnawakee back here, tonight, to marry them," John reminded her swiftly.

"For his own convenience! So he could concentrate on the stupid vision without worrying about losing her in the process."

"That's enough." Alex shook his head, still slightly dazed at the thought Cassie could be beyond his reach, either physically or emotionally. "Shannon's right, John. I blew it. I stood on that porch and told her I wished we could have postponed our time together. The most perfect days and nights of my life, and I dared to call them inconvenient."

"Go after her, then," Shannon whispered. "Please, Alex?"

"I have to think." His jaw tensed slightly. "Either way, I need to go to the burial ground. Maybe I'll find her along the way, and I can tell her . . ." Forcing himself to take a deep breath, he repeated, "I have to think this through. Can I take the letter, Shannon?"

She nodded, cuddling her babies close to her breasts. "Read it again before you decide. You're the one who hurt her, Alex. You're the only one who can make it better."

"Alex?"

He turned to John Cutler. "Yeah?"

"If Cassandra was correct—if there isn't room in your world for your duty to your people and your love for her—"

"There's room," Alex growled. "I'll *make* room. There's no way I'm giving either one of them up."

"Good."

"Now all you have to decide," Shannon declared coolly, "is their order of importance. Are you going to ask a woman like Cassie Stone to stand in the shadows of your life and wait for crumbs? Because if you are—"

Alex stopped her with a kiss to her cheek. "I've got

to go. Don't worry about Cassie. I'll make things right with her, I promise." Turning to John, he extended his hand. "If I don't see you again, thanks for everything."

"I'll walk you out." John dragged his splinted leg toward the door before anyone could protest. Once on the porch, he motioned for Alex to close the door, then insisted, "If it's any consolation, my friend, I think Cassandra put you in an impossible situation. She *was* a distraction. A beautiful whirlwind, and you wanted to be caught up in her passion, but you feared your time with Kahnawakee was limited. This opportunity you have been given is also a responsibility. As much as you were tempted to play with Cassandra, you needed to take that responsibility seriously."

"Thanks, John. If I don't see you again, it's been a tremendous honor—"

"The honor has been mutual," John interrupted. "You'll be a fine leader, Alex. You're Kahnawakee's equal in all things. Never doubt that." When Alex attempted to object, John growled, "I've known him for years. He can be overzealous and overcritical of himself, but he has never failed to rise to a challenge. In two short weeks with us you have demonstrated those same weaknesses and that same indomitable strength. If you choose to go after Cassandra, never doubt that you're ready for leadership. More time with Kahnawakee might be desirable, but not because of anything you lack. You were born with all you needed to fulfill your destiny."

"Thanks, John." To leave with such praise ringing in his ears was a temptation, but there was one last loose end, and so Alex insisted quietly, "Never leave Shannon and the babies unprotected, John."

"Huh?" The big man seemed confused by the apparent non sequitur, then his eyes widened slowly. "The danger is to *them?* I had assumed, if someone were to become a target, it would be Kahnawakee or myself."

"There were unsubstantiated accounts, fairly non-specific, and nothing that affected the course of history, but . . . just don't leave them unprotected."

John grasped Alex's hand in his own and pumped it vigorously. "You've been a good friend, Alex. You helped birth my children, and maybe now, because of you, they'll have the life I've envisioned for them. I wish you the same, with Cassandra and your own sons and daughters. Good luck to you."

Alex exhaled sharply. He hadn't realized how heavily this foreknowledge had weighed upon his heart, but his relief was tempered by the loss of Cassie's nearness and trust. He wouldn't be able to rest until he had verified, and come to terms with, her leaving, and so, with a rueful smile toward his bearded friend, he began the long run toward the river.

Bound at the ankles and wrists and silenced with a gag, Cassie passively studied her captors from her lowly position on the floor of their canoe. Once the initial wave of panic and fear at having been abducted had passed, she had begun to catalog and appreciate the many clues as to these men's intentions. While far from honorable, those intentions were also not sexual or violent, at least not overtly. The one called Fowler had manhandled her quite thoroughly while carrying her from the burial ground to the river, but he had neither attempted to undress her nor to inflict any wounds. She had the distinct impression the other man, who was called Rubrier, would have objected forcefully to any such conduct on Fowler's part.

They believed she was Shannon Cutler and somehow this stunt was a means of getting to John. While the nature of their hostility toward John had not yet been revealed, Cassie was taking great comfort in the knowledge that due to the case of mistaken identity, Shannon had been spared this bizarre mischief. In fact, had these men not chanced upon Cassie at the burial ground, they would have proceeded to the cabin, where resistance and bloodshed might have ensued.

Cassie was more than willing to take the place of newborn babies or a weakened mother in this little hostage drama. Once these men sent their ransom demand to John, the Cutlers would realize what had happened and would rescue her, either by paying or by sending the Susquehannocks to her aid.

And Alex will be embarrassed and distracted again, she taunted herself in disgust. *You really* are *a burden to him.* Of course, he'd also be glad to see her, and relieved she was alive and in one piece and hadn't run off to the twentieth century, but now she would have to face the endless protestations and reassurances from Alex and from the others, when all she wanted to do was retreat to her little A-frame by the river and lick her wounds.

But you can't get back there anyway, she reminded herself. *Nothing happened when you lit the match. You'll have to face them all, and you'll have to be strong. For now, just be grateful these creeps grabbed you instead of sweet, innocent Shannon. Just tough it out until the ransom is paid.*

For a moment she envisioned the many strings of lovely wampum that adorned Orimha's neck. Would

he contribute to her bounty? After all, he had claimed
often enough to love her. Then she remembered the
look in Alex's eye when he had described his last
encounter with the Gahnienca. Alex had offended,
perhaps even enraged, the renegade leader. It would
be left to the Cutlers and the Susquehannocks to bail
her out of this ridiculous dilemma, and she would be
mortified to have cost them so dearly when she'd been
able to contribute so little in return.

Although the long run to the river had winded him
and the swim across to the other side was an arduous
one, Alex was too pumped to rest, even for a few
minutes, before covering the two miles remaining between himself and the burial ground. While playful
images of Cassie, laughing and teasing and flirting,
had propelled him forward until now, he had suddenly begun to recall a more vulnerable woman, lying
in his arms on a warm summer's night and hesitantly
confiding her immense trust in the nature of man. She
saw the human race as a font of curiosity and positive
energy, and was disturbed by Shannon's belief that
genocide, or worse, could be the result of culture
clashes rather than individual, isolated episodes of
megalomania.

He loved that woman so intensely it almost hurt.
Her every thought was one of gentleness, her every
skill one of beauty, and her every instinct one of hope
and confidence. To imagine her now, hurting and
alone, was almost more than he could bear. What
would she think of human nature now that the person
she'd allowed closest to her heart had betrayed her
with his arrogant thoughtlessness? How trusting
could she be? Would she *ever* trust him again?

The temptation to pursue her through the centuries was strong. Nothing could be as important as reassuring and loving this incredible woman. She had said in the letter that it was naive to assume they could have a life together.

"But there's nothing naive about it," Alex announced aloud as he stepped into the clearing. "I don't just want it, I *demand* it. Just because I'm trained as a diplomat doesn't mean I always compromise, Cassie. I can be as stubborn as you. And if there's even a remote possibility I can lose you by staying here . . ."

But what if he lost her by following prematurely? Was John Cutler correct? Would Cassie take it as proof that he didn't see their relationship as strong enough to weather the demands of his career? Would he resent Cassie one day in the distant future for having forced his hand? If only he knew what she needed from him at that moment! In his heart, he believed she wanted him to stay and finish with Kahnawakee, and then to rush to her and sweep her into his arms, never allowing her to doubt his love again, but how could he know for sure?

Then he saw her half-burned dream house, and through his heartache, he knew what needed to be done. If she had built a cabin, or an A-frame, or even a whimsical castle, his quandary would have persisted, but Cassie Stone had built a longhouse. Its half-burned state was proof that she had left him, but the part that remained, strong and well built and infused with love, told him the rest.

"Wait for me, Cassie," he pleaded into the rising afternoon wind, as he made his way slowly back to the path that would take him to the village. "Wait and, when we're together again, the doubts will all disappear and I'll earn your trust once and for all time."

Chapter Sixteen

It was easy to despise Benedict Fowler, whose leering gaze and coarse language had dominated the long, sunbaked ride in the canoe. In contrast, Jean-Claude Rubrier seemed basically a gentleman despite the fact that he was currently engaged in kidnapping. Cassie longed to tell them what she thought of them, but knew it was probably for the best that they were keeping her gagged. In her righteous indignation she might accidentally reveal her true identity, and these men might be angry enough to kill her or determined enough to turn around and make another attempt at grabbing Shannon Cutler.

Still, she needed to eat and drink, eventually. Rubrier had moistened her mouth with water through her gag but had not had the guts to defy Fowler, who had proclaimed that they could not take a chance on having "Madame Cutler" call out while they were passing through Susquehannock lands.

"By nightfall, we'll be out of their territory and the little hellcat can scream and scratch to her heart's content," the Englishman had grinned. "I'll untie her personally, and maybe we'll have a little look under that preposterous shirt of hers. You'd like that, wouldn't you, Rubrier? They say you love the ladies, and this one," his eyes grew hotter, "is among the most provocative I've ever seen."

"She will not be molested," Rubrier had countered coolly, but Fowler had simply laughed his raucous, irreverent laugh and paddled more briskly, as though anxious to arrive more quickly at the moment of the unveiling.

Cassie believed Rubrier would try his best to protect her, but doubted whether the moderately sized, gentle-faced Frenchman could be even temporarily effective against a monster like Fowler. The Englishman's arms and thighs were huge with muscles, and he was at least six and a half feet tall, with every inch well-toned and alert. There was a hunger behind his silvery eyes, as though he needed to physically dominate all within his scope. She suspected Rubrier was secretly terrified of the man, and she could hardly blame him. Hopefully, Fowler's desire for ransom would outweigh his need to bully, at least until help could arrive.

Her best course for the moment was to try to pretend this wasn't happening. When she closed her eyes and concentrated on the sound of the paddles stroking the water, she could almost forget the presence of the kidnappers, remembering instead the moments she had shared with Alex over their brief, rocky, yet admittedly scintillating love affair. The thought of being touched by another lover, or perhaps even marrying another one day, was so ludicrous that she could almost believe things were going to work out for them. Hadn't Alex said basically the same thing that afternoon in the workshop? He had insisted he wanted to be married, and wouldn't consider marrying any woman other than Cassie, and so the debate over whether they should or should not be together was moot. It was a curiously refreshing piece of logic and she was more than ready to accept it. As soon as the ransom was paid, she would fly into Alex's arms and allow Kahnawakee to marry them without further delay.

The sun was setting when the two abductors finally steered their canoe to the bank of the river. Fowler's grin was wide and alarming. "Time to bed down for the night, Madame Cutler. Shall we draw straws to see whose backside you'll warm?"

Rubrier snorted. "Such talk is unacceptable. We are not animals, my friend. This woman is frightened, and hungry, and she does not deserve to be tormented. She has done nothing wrong."

"Why don't you let her speak for herself? She may be the kind of woman who doesn't like to sleep alone, and . . ." Fowler chuckled wickedly, "she's been giving you some long, warm looks, *mon ami.* You may be surprised tonight. You may wake up to find her pretty little hand in your breeches. You'd like that, wouldn't you?"

To Cassie's dismay, the Frenchman's eyes warmed, for a brief but telling moment, before he growled, "She will not be molested." Turning to Cassie, he insisted, "You are safe with us, Madame Cutler. Once you have had some food, you can sleep by the fire, and I will watch over you."

"He'll drool over you, more likely," Fowler laughed, then he jumped from the canoe into knee deep water, pulled the craft up onto the shore, and turned back to Cassie. "I'll carry you again. You liked it before, didn't you?"

She glared and cursed through the gag, which seemed to amuse him. This time, when he hoisted her into his arms, he didn't sling her over his shoulder, but held her as a bridegroom might carry his bride while his eyes traveled over her with lingering admiration, settling on her breasts, which were sharply defined, even under John's loose shirt, due to the fact that her hands were bound so tightly behind her back. "Why were you wearing a man's shirt?" he murmured softly. "I'd like to see you in a satin gown, with petticoats and lace. These," he inclined his head until his lips were brushing her nipples through the soft fabric, "are inspiring, Madame Cutler."

Cassie's stomach was churning instantly, with fear and with disgust, and she turned pleading eyes to Rubrier, who muttered, "That is enough. We'll make our camp here. Put her down, my friend."

Fowler raised his head reluctantly. "Later, perhaps," he whispered, setting Cassie carefully onto the ground. To his companion, he added, "She'll scream like a banshee if you take that gag away. And she'll scratch your eyes out, or kick, if you untie her. Leave her to me. I'll feed her, and believe me, she won't dare to utter a sound, will you, my sweet?" His voice grew suddenly cruel. "Are you going to be a good little girl and keep perfectly quiet, or do I need to teach you a lesson?"

She was trembling as she shrugged her shoulders, wondering if he knew that she was too terrified to make even the slightest of sounds. She had assumed this would all go so smoothly, with her status as hostage ensuring that she would not be molested. Now it was clear that Benedict Fowler had no problem with returning her to John in a damaged condition and she had only ineffective Jean-Claude Rubrier to whom to turn.

Rubrier, however, feigned confidence despite the

disparity in size and temperament between himself and his companion. "I will feed Madame Cutler, and she will be very quiet for me, will you not, Madame?"

She nodded gratefully.

"You must remember, my friend, that she will be less valuable in trade if she is molested," he continued quietly.

"I don't care how much she brings in trade," Fowler scoffed. "The reward comes later, Rubrier."

"Yes, but . . ." The Frenchman shrugged. "It must appear that she is valuable, do you not agree?"

"I suppose so." Fowler eyed them with disgust. "Feed her, then. I'll have a look around. Those damned Indians you hired were supposed to meet us, weren't they?"

"We specified no particular time or place," Rubrier reminded him, "but they will find us soon, I am certain. We should be well rested, do you not agree? It may be necessary for us to move quickly tomorrow."

Fowler grunted, then moved away into the brush, leaving his companion to sigh aloud with relief. "Were you frightened, Madame?" he sympathized. "I must admit, I myself was feeling intimidated. I can only assure you that I will do what is necessary to protect your honor from that lout, but he is twice my size, and so . . ."

Cassie nodded. He was telling her he would give his life to protect her, but if it came to that, his life would be given in vain, because Fowler would be certain to win. Hopefully, this idea of conserving her "value" in the upcoming "trade" would keep Fowler from acting on his despicable urges.

Trade. It was an odd expression to use in connection with a ransom situation. Was it possible Kahnawakee was holding someone prisoner, and these

men intended to trade "Madame Cutler" for that
hostage, rather than for a simple ransom? It made no
real sense. Alex had told her the Susquehannocks
were not currently at war with any group, and so why
would they have a prisoner? And what prisoner would
interest a Frenchman *and* an Englishman?

"You are confused?" Rubrier soothed. "You wonder why we have taken you in this cruel manner?"
When Cassie nodded, he smiled. "If I remove the gag,
will you promise not to scream?" Again she nodded,
and the gag was blessedly removed. Then the Frenchman pulled a pouch of dried fruit from inside his shirt
and offered her a taste. "You will like this. My wife is
very fond of it."

"You're married?" Cassie murmured.

"To a beautiful woman, but not more beautiful
than yourself, Madame. John Cutler was a fortunate
man to have found so lovely a mate."

That's right, Cassie, she reminded herself sharply.
Don't let him know you're not Shannon. "Why do you
hate my husband enough to kidnap me?" she asked
softly.

"I do not hate him. I do not hate any man, not even
Kahnawakee, although it is Kahnawakee who must
be destroyed."

"Destroyed?" Cassie's heart began to pound. Was
it possible that these men were hoping to trade Shannon Cutler's life for Kahnawakee's? It was ludicrous,
and frightening, and she shook her head vehemently.
"They will never trade the Visionary for me. And if
you don't let me go, the Susquehannocks will come
after you and kill you."

"Trade you for Kahnawakee?" The Frenchman
seemed reluctantly amused. "That would have been a
daring plan. Now that I have seen how beautiful and

desirable you are, I think perhaps it may even have succeeded. But no, *chérie,* we will not be trading you to the Susquehannocks."

Cassie sighed with audible relief. The thought that Alex might have been placed in so impossible a situation had scared her more than she dared admit. To be not only a fluke and an inconvenience, but an actual danger to Kahnawakee's success and Alex's entire future, not to mention his self-respect and sanity, was a fairly staggering fate! "You're going to trade me back to my husband, then?" she whispered gratefully. "Thank you. That's all I want." She glanced about herself, wary of Fowler's eventual return, and then dared to smile. "What will you trade me for? My husband is not a wealthy man."

Rubrier's eyes clouded with regret. "I do not know which is the more cruel, to tell you of your fate, or to allow you to be ignorant, and filled with hope, for one last night. But I will not be able to rest until I have explained myself to you, so that you will understand and forgive."

"My fate?" Cassie winced. "You're not giving me back to John, and you're not giving me to the Susquehannocks, and so . . ."

"And so," Fowler's voice jeered from behind her, "you had better hope your new suitors are half as gentle as our Jean-Claude here is. Tell me, Madame Cutler," he added, coming up behind her and leaning until his lips were against her ear, "would you like Jean-Claude to make love to you, or would you like your last night with a white man to be a more memorable one, with myself?"

Cassie turned toward the hot breath, and without pausing to think, buried her teeth into the flesh of his cheek with all the force she could muster. The man cried out, and then in an instant his huge hands were on her throat, squeezing the air and the life from it while Rubrier struggled in vain to stop him.

"Little whore!" Fowler snarled. "You'll regret that, I promise you." One hand stayed on her throat, restraining and silencing her, while the other began to paw at her breasts through her shirt. "You'll remember the day you dared bite Benedict Fowler."

"Take your hands from her," Jean-Claude Rubrier insisted, his voice calm but menacing, and Fowler turned to see a hunting pistol aimed directly at his head. With a grunt of disbelief he stopped his assault, but not before he had grabbed the gag and forced it back into Cassie's mouth.

"You're insane, Rubrier," he muttered, wiping at his bloody cheek with his coat sleeve. "The whore bit me. She's not the innocent angel she appears to be. Let's hope," a dark smile played across his lips, "her new owners know how to discipline her."

"Your new owners will adore you," Rubrier assured Cassie tenderly. "You must try to rest now, Madame, and do not worry. Put your trust in God, and He will ease your mind."

Cassie stared in mute horror as the words finally began to register. *Your new owners . . . your new owners . . . your last night with a white man. . . .* Curling into a ball, she tried to blot out the sound of the phrases, but they echoed in her confused brain long into the night.

"Couteau?"

Alex pulled his gaze away from the endless expanse of forest that separated him from the burial ground. "Is it time to leave for Onondaga, my brother?"

Kahnawakee's grin was almost wistful. "You no longer feel the need to address me by my illustrious title?" Waving away any protest, he added, "I am pleased to be called your brother, which is perhaps the *most* illustrious of titles. You are thinking of Cassandra?"

"Yes."

"You should go after her now. You have learned all I have to teach you. I confess I looked forward to having you by my side at Onondaga, but only because I am so proud of you. You may leave, Couteau, and you will be missed, but all will understand."

"Cassie would never understand," Alex corrected wryly. "She knows how important your address to the Council is, historically. If I leave without witnessing it, she'll always be sure I was deprived of something because of her and I suppose she might even be right. I'm here to learn, and I'll learn an incredible amount from that experience, so . . . ," his voice grew mildly impatient, "let's leave right away."

Kahnawakee chuckled. "You are restless. You need to walk. I think perhaps you need to walk alone. Go on ahead. Take time to fish and hunt and practice with the black-hilted knife. I will join you along the way, in a day or two."

Alex shook his head. "I'll wait. You shouldn't travel alone, Kahnawakee. Orimha's out there somewhere, and we can only guess how angry he is."

"He is a disappointment to me." Kahnawakee's jaw had tensed, making his resemblance to Alex all the more dramatic. "The moment he heard Cassandra had disappeared, he left us. I thought he had begun to listen."

"It's probably my fault. I threatened him, back at

the Cutlers' cabin. Do you think he's going to cause trouble?"

"I do not know what to think," the chief sighed. "His support would have been so valuable, and his opposition could prove equally disastrous. But," his tone grew more confident, "I do not believe he would attack me, or even you, Couteau. He may use his anger to ruin us, but he would not be cowardly enough to murder either of us."

"I hope you're right. I guess he and I have something in common. We both wanted Cassie, and we both blew it. Luckily, I'll have a second chance, and I'll make it count."

Kahnawakee's hand settled on Alex's shoulder. "You have learned your final lesson, Couteau. It is regrettable that you learned it through the loss of Cassandra, but that will be remedied when you return to your home."

"You mean, I learned that love is as important as destiny and politics?" Alex shook his head. "I always knew that. I don't know why everyone thinks I didn't."

"You knew love was important to you as an individual. To your heart, and to your personal happiness. But you saw it as a danger to your nation, as though your attentions to her could weaken your commitment to us. Now you have learned the truth. The loss of Cassandra has weakened us all."

"That's true," Alex mused. "I thought it was tough to concentrate when she was here, but now it's impossible."

"Our nation is important, and your UNAP is important, but there is nothing more important than the unity of a man with his woman. The Europeans preach the importance of the individual man, with his

many 'divine rights,' but what use is he without his
woman? And what use is she without her man? Together, as a family, they can be strong in a way that
is impossible for one person alone. It is that strength
that a man should value, as dearly as he values the
strength of his nation. Without that strength," he
exhorted passionately, "how can the nation ever be
strong? You have come to value both equally, and
that is good." His tone softened as he added, "Cassandra knows this also, in her heart. She will wait for
you, little brother."

Alex nodded. She would wait for him, and he
would win her heart again and forever, but in the
meantime there was something wrong, and it haunted
him, although he dared not share the sensation with
his mentor. It was too vague, too undefined, too melo-
dramatic in its scope, and it would confuse the Visionary when he needed to have clarity of mind, and so
Alex reluctantly kept it to himself.

It had been haunting him relentlessly since the previous evening. Every time he tried to picture Cassie,
wistful but busy at her potter's wheel or in her garden,
he saw her instead curled into a tight ball of apprehension and distress, afraid to speak or to cry out. It was
so unlike her, yet the image was sharp, and it tortured
Alex in a way Orimha's paltry jabs never had.

Don't flatter yourself, BlackKnife, he mocked himself half-heartedly. *You think she's pining away for
you, when she's really probably laughing that sexy
laugh and tossing that golden hair. . . .* But he knew it
wasn't so. She was miserable, and as soon as the
Council had adjourned, he would rush to her side
with no further delay.

* * *

Cassie was shivering, although the weather was warm, as she lay curled into a tight ball by the camp-fire on the second night of her captivity, listening to the terrifying philosophies of her captors—Fowler, with his unbridled contempt for human life, most specifically the lives of the natives of North America, and Rubrier, with his misguided missionary zeal. It was all true, everything Shannon had described!

The stories and examples from her cousin's version of history now loomed in Cassie's tortured imagina-tion, overshadowing all else. Broken promises, bro-ken treaties, massacres . . . insatiable lust for land and for scalps . . . it was all true! Even the horror story of "gifts" of blankets, infected with smallpox, given by the military to the Indians! Of all Shannon's horror stories, this one had been the most incredible and was now the most believable, given the intensity of Fowler's contempt for the native dwellers. Disease, warfare, dispossession, and genocide—it was all true . . .

And for the Susquehannocks there had been com-plete annihilation. Alexander BlackKnife had never been allowed to be born in Shannon's version of the twentieth-century world. Hatred had killed Kah-nawakee before UNAP could be formed and strengthened. And now these hideous men—these damnable invaders!—were hoping they had found an-other means of ensuring that grisly fate for the conti-nent and its legitimate inhabitants.

As soon as the Indian mercenaries arrived at the camp, Cassie would be spirited away and sold to some unknown owners who would rape and beat her. Fowler and Rubrier would then send anonymous word to John Cutler, whose outrage would cause the forests themselves to tremble. He would mount a res-

cue, despite his injured leg, and he would avenge the
humiliation and abuse that had been heaped upon
her. Alexander BlackKnife would rise up in horrified
fury, stunned by Cassie's fate and temporarily blind
to the impact upon history of any rescue. Perhaps
Kahnawakee would see the truth and would advise
against bloodshed, but he would be unable to prevent
the confrontation that would shatter the fragile peace
in which UNAP had been gestating over these crucial
months.

You were never supposed to come. . . . She was now
more than an inconvenience or distraction or fluke.
She was the downfall of the Susquehannocks. She
thought of escape, but her bonds made that impossible. She thought of reasoning with her captors, but all
her faith in the goodness and positive energy of
human nature had been dashed by the men's unholy
conversations. She even thought of destroying, or at
least disfiguring, herself. Did she have the means, or
even the guts? Not that it really mattered. Her body,
even if lifeless, could be used by these fiends quite
nicely. They could molest it and deform it, then toss
it on John Cutler's doorstep with a Shawnee or Delaware blade stuck into her back.

For the past twenty-four hours Fowler had left her
relatively unmolested. Rubrier, in a staggering feat of
illogic, had appointed himself her protector, with his
pistol always close at hand to reinforce his position.
He had removed her bonds every few hours so that
she could slip behind a tree and see to her own personal needs in makeshift privacy, and had tried in
countless other ways to make her comfortable. She
knew she should try to summon an occasional smile,
for her own safety, but her hatred for him was sharp

and uncontrollable. How could he believe, as he claimed, that loss of life, even on a massive scale involving innocent women and children, was a small price to pay for spreading the "glory" of his God? His favorite example was St. Joan of Arc, whose fate he often compared to Cassie's, explaining, "You do not realize the truth, Madame, but you are a spiritual sacrifice to the salvation of an entire continent. In a small way, you have been honored by fate as surely as Jeanne D'Arc."

Now, as she lay by the fire, despair threatened to consume her. Through no fault of her own other than a rash of poor decisions, she was about to undo all that Shannon and John and, most of all, Kahnawakee, had managed to accomplish. And she was going to be brutally raped, and perhaps also tortured in the process, all because these men, and the rest of their kind, felt threatened by a lifestyle they could not or would not understand or respect.

"I envy those bastards," Fowler was chuckling. "To have a wild beauty like our pretty Madame Cutler thrown into their midst . . . they'll have themselves a time with her, I'll wager."

Rubrier, ever the gentleman, glanced over to see if Cassie was listening, then added for her benefit, "They will stand in awe of her beauty, and will take care with her. She will be spared the torture most captives endure. One of the leaders will take her as his wife and will provide well for her."

"Or they'll share her until there's nothing left but those teeth she bit me with," Fowler chuckled. "If you're right, I pity her new husband. Let's hope the poor man knows how to discipline a wench like this."

Cassie shrank from his loathsome expression, but

as his words registered in her unhappy brain, she
weighed them tentatively, seeing in them a germ of a
solution, if only she could be strong enough to implement it.

Chapter Seventeen

The four mercenaries had arrived. As they conversed with Rubrier, Cassie forced herself to study the situation calmly, hoping for new information that would enable her to refine her bizarre plan. She could glean little from the rapid interchange, which was being conducted in a language she had never heard, and which did not even remotely resemble Susquehannock or French. The four newcomers were of medium size and build, with shaven heads and bodies smeared with red coloring. Their faces were basically expressionless, yet it was apparent, from their body language, that they were fond of Rubrier and despised Fowler.

"We have something in common," Cassie told herself with a futile attempt at finding some respite in humor. She had always been able to find that tiny ray of silly sunshine in even the most dismal of situations, but this one was beyond her, even assuming her plan proved successful.

That plan was relatively simple, hinging on one small scrap of logic. The Indians to whom she would be sold would not be foolish enough to trade valuable belongings for her for the mere pleasure of killing her.

The purchase, or trade, would be based upon a desire to put her to work, either sexually or otherwise. Fowler had jeeringly referred to her "new husband." Could she hope for that? One man, looking for a healthy, pretty, cooperative wife. And if she cooperated, there would be no need for rapes or beatings, and when John and Alex arrived—as she knew they eventually would —they would find her healthy and happy, with no need for vengeance of any kind.

Thereafter, if her "new husband" was willing to sell her back to John, she would be joyful and grateful forever. If he insisted that she stay with him, she would stay, convincing John and Alex that she had chosen this life freely and had fallen in love with her spouse. They would be astounded and argumentative, but she would convince them. Under no circumstances would she permit either rescue or retaliation. The fragile peace would be maintained, the vicious invaders would be thwarted, and history would be back on track.

And Cassie Stone would no longer be a threat. Instead, she would once again be a mere fluke, a status she had earned through her many faulty decisions. "But *this* decision is wise," she consoled herself as she studied the mercenaries. "A person can only do their best, Cassie, and if you can carry this off, you'll have to forgive yourself the rest. Remember, Fowler and Rubrier and their kind are the real villains, not you. Alex and John and Kahnawakee are the heroes. You—you're just doing the best you can."

Rubrier left the mercenaries and joined Cassie, stooping to unbind her ankles, then pulling her gently to her feet. "It's time, *chérie*," he sighed. "One day you will forgive me—if not in this life, then certainly in the next."

The gag prevented any reply, but she hoped her
eyes were communicating her disgust. Misunderstanding the glare, Rubrier counseled softly, "Do not
become defiant, Madame. It was foolish to bite that
bastard Fowler, and it would be even more foolish to
use your claws or your teeth on your new owners.
Cooperate with your escorts. I have instructed them
not to molest you. Once the trade has been made, you
must try to appear sweet and docile, so that a powerful man will choose you and offer you his protection.
Do you understand?"

I'm miles ahead of you, she taunted silently.

"It will be difficult at first, but you must submit or
he will beat you. You can survive this, *chérie,* but only
if you trust in your God and abandon yourself to your
fate. Be proud that you have been chosen as the instrument for the destruction of the devil Kahnawakee."

I'm not just going to survive, Cassie vowed. *I'm
going to make sure my marriage is so gentle and peaceful that it doesn't even cause a ripple in Kahnawakee's
vision.*

"John Cutler will come for you soon," Rubrier
predicted ruefully. "Either he will come alone, which
will mean Kahnawakee has refused to help him, and
their alliance is destroyed. Or the Susquehannocks
will arrive en masse, and the Mohawks will refuse to
allow Kahnawakee to address the Council, and war
will be declared between the League and the Susquehannocks. Either way, Kahnawakee's vision will
have ended. I sincerely pray you will live to see that
day."

*And I sincerely pray I live to see the day you and your
kind are driven away from these shores and back to
Europe, where you belong,* Cassie wanted to growl, but

she could only stomp her foot and glare. Then she caught sight of Benedict Fowler, standing in the distance and enjoying her tantrum. With a more dignified air, she moved away from Rubrier to join her new escorts.

"Au revoir," Rubrier murmured. "We are returning to Québec this very morning. I will pray for you, Madame Cutler. Be brave, and be proud."

"And smile," Fowler called after her cheerfully. "In a few hours you'll find you've become the most popular whore in the backwoods."

Alex tried in vain to relax and enjoy his meal of roasted rabbit as he sat by his campfire after a full morning of hunting and fishing. He had left the village the previous afternoon and had found this spot along the path toward Onondaga. His efforts at keeping himself occupied had not been successful in distracting him from his misgivings over Cassie, but had at least drained away some of the nervous energy that had possessed him since her departure.

Still, he was haunted. First and foremost, he was tortured by the relentless vision of her, huddled and shivering and pale with despair. It was a painful omnipresent sensation which paired eerily with his bitter memory of the fact that Cassie had refused to allow him to make love to her that final morning at the cabin. She had known at that moment that she wouldn't see him again for a long while, yet she had resisted his affectionate advances. Why? Because she was angry? No . . . there was no anger in her note, only hurt. It was because she truly believed their affair had ended, or worse, was never meant to be. He ached for her, and for himself and the loss he refused to accept.

There was a faint rustling in the underbrush and he tensed, waiting to see if it was Kahnawakee or some less welcome guest. When two braves stepped from behind dense cover, he was ready for them, greeting them in peace but prepared to kill them without hesitation, should it become necessary.

"You are the brother of Kahnawakee?" one man inquired, studying him intently.

Here we go again, Alex thought in grim amusement. Orimha must have been this guy's teacher. "I am the brother of Kahnawakee," he confirmed patiently.

"That is good," the second newcomer proclaimed, and his companion nodded his agreement, his eyes settling hopefully on the meat roasting over the fire.

Relaxing slightly, Alex invited them to join him, although he himself had lost his appetite. It sickened him to realize how comfortable he had become with the thought of taking a pair of human lives. The experience in Orimha's camp had warped him, he decided sadly, and as soon as he returned home, he would consciously regain control over this unbridled ferocity. On the other hand, it was a necessary evil in *this* world, and so he would be content simply to be aware of and to moderate it for the time being.

Between noisy mouthfuls, the two Delaware braves explained that they had heard Kahnawakee would be traveling along this path toward Onondaga and they had hoped to meet and to talk with them. They were pleased to learn that Alex was one of the Visionary's students and plied him with questions, which served the dual purpose of cementing their mutual trust and distracting Alex from thoughts of Cassie.

"We will wait here, together, for Kahnawakee?"

Alex nodded. "He'll be along by tomorrow at the latest. In the meantime, I appreciate the company." Noticing that they were intrigued by his jeans and tennis shoes he explained, "I came here from another village, far away."

"You wear the colors of the golden-haired captive?" one guest suggested, and the other man chuckled as though a fine joke had been made.

"The golden-haired captive?" Alex smiled. "Who is he?"

"It is a woman, or so we have heard. One of our brothers claims to have seen her in a canoe with two Français. She had blue legs, and her hair was shining in the sunlight."

It sounded too much like Shannon or Cassie to be dismissed as baseless. "When did he see her?"

"On the day before yesterday."

"And you say her hair was golden and shining? Was it long and straight? Or braided?"

"I did not see her, and I do not know if my brother's eyes deceived him, but he swears her hair was a tangle of curls, across here," he drew his hand across his forehead, "and around a face that was pale with beauty and fear."

Jean-Claude Rubrier had apparently instructed the mercenaries not to molest Cassie along the way but had failed to insist that she be treated with anything other than complete disinterest, and so it had become necessary for her to maintain a half-run in order to keep pace with their long, even strides. They never paused to rest, and seemed oblivious to such mundane needs as personal convenience, food, or drink. Thanks to her newly stretched moccasins, Cassie's feet were surviving, but her lungs were feeling the strain and her throat was literally parched.

Her hands were still bound, and the gag remained in place. No one attempted to converse with her, except to scold harshly when she occasionally fell behind. Twice, when she stumbled, it drew only the most disdainful of reactions, even though the second mishap landed her in a thorny mass of vines that inflicted three deep gashes on her neck and cheek. Those wounds bled for a short time until, untended, they dried in the hot August breeze.

Keep it up, Cassie grumbled inwardly, *and I'll be so scarred up you won't get a dime in trade for me.* She knew these men, as mercenaries, were likely to be paid in proportion to the amount they received in exchange for her, and she wondered if they realized they were pawns in an unholy scheme to defeat Kahnawakee. She wondered, in fact, if they had ever even heard of the Visionary. How sad if they had not, and if they had, then their shame was great.

The discomfort from the gashes on her cheeks had made her acutely aware of the absence of physical pain from her life until now. She had been sheltered and naive for so long, and this crash course in reality was becoming more than she could bear. It made her all the more intent upon pleasing her "new husband" so that the humiliation, while great, would be psychological rather than physical.

But what if he beat her anyway? What if he and his friends *wanted* to beat and rape her? Maybe that was part of the allure of this particular trade. She had no more illusions about the fundamental nature of men—they were base and destructive. Due to her sheltered life, she had met such noble exceptions as her father, and Philip Tremaine, and John and

Kahnawakee, and, of course, Alexander BlackKnife, but now she knew the truth. The Fowlers and the Rubriers of the world were the norm—a shortsighted, self-absorbed majority that feared and destroyed anything beyond their limited cultural experience.

If her new husband was such a man, she was doomed, no matter how docile and submissive she might be. Given his "ownership" of her and his distrust of her as a Eura—so strange in both appearance and speech!—he would feel free to torment her as the Gahniencas had tormented Alex. And Cassie was nothing like Alex. She lacked his strength and courage and would scream and cry and die a cowardly death.

Stop! she commanded herself. *Maybe he'll be a nice guy. . . .* The sentiment died in her heart as she stepped past her escorts into a glade and saw Orimha standing in the distance. The expression on his face was more fierce and unloving than anything she had ever seen, and when that expression failed to soften, even just a bit, at the sight of her, she knew her predicament had taken a bizarre turn toward further tribulation.

The bartering proceeded, surreal and unintelligible. Nothing in Orimha's manner acknowledged that he had ever before laid eyes on Cassie, much less that he had fallen in love with her, or had stared with love-struck admiration during those days in the Susquehannock village. The thought that Alex had so completely offended him that he now hated all blue-legged intruders occurred to her more than once as she tried to smile sweetly to him through her gag.

It should have been a lucky break that the mercenaries had chosen Orimha as their customer. Of course, it was always possible that Orimha had heard the news and had solicited this sale, anxious for an opportunity to humiliate Couteau Noir for his arrogant ingratitude.

But that doesn't make sense, Cassie mused silently. *Fowler and Rubrier and these Indians think I'm Shannon, not Cassie. They don't even know there's a Cassie Stone. Orimha knows Shannon just had a baby, so he wouldn't have ever believed she was marching through the woods for days on end. . . .*

The Gahnienca leader was negotiating rapidly, still ignoring Cassie completely, but she could see now that his disinterest was a bit too studied and his expression a bit too rigid to be natural. It was an act! He was convincing these men that this was a business deal, so that they wouldn't become suspicious.

Suspicious of what, Cassie? Of the fact that he's in love with you, for fear they'll increase the price? Or the fact that they grabbed the wrong female, and John Cutler is home with his wife, safe and sound, and out of reach of their fiendish plan?

More than anything, she needed to know if Orimha was angry. If not—if he was actually purchasing her as his bride, with the same affection in his heart that had existed that day along the trail near Shannon's cabin—then she had been blessed by a coincidence that was almost miraculous. She had seen his gentle side and could trust him, despite the brutal side that had been so active during the torture of Couteau Noir.

He could have killed Alex, but he didn't, she reasoned carefully. *He's only as violent as he needs to be, and he doesn't need to be violent with you at all. You can proceed with your plan,* her eyes filled with tears of dismay at the thought, *and Alex and Kahnawakee*

*might even believe you went willingly with this man
after you decided it was over between you.*

The negotiations ended as abruptly as they had
begun, and when the mercenaries walked away without even a glance in Cassie's direction, they had possession of every strand of purple onekorha that had
adorned Orimha's proud neck. Only when the sellers
were out of sight did the new owner move forward to
collect his prize.

His face still impassive, he removed the gag from
her mouth, then motioned to one of his fellow Gahniencas, who quickly brought water in a birch-bark
cup. She drank deeply, then tried to smile. *"Bonsoir,
Orimha."*

Orimha shook his head in warning and spoke rapidly in his Iroquoian tongue. He was agitated and
angry, and Cassie could see it was best to allow him
to vent his emotions with words, lest he decide to
employ any of the methods he had tried on Alex less
than three weeks earlier. She wanted to assure him
that somehow, John and Alex would find a way to
replace the beautiful strands of shells, if that was the
source of this frustrated rage. And she wanted to
apologize to him for Alex's rudeness, and to thank
him for sending the mercenaries away, but most of all,
she wanted to lean against his stocky chest and cry her
heart out. Fatigue, and fear, and an overwhelming
sense of confusion were bubbling up inside of her, and
she didn't know how long she could hope to maintain
her sanity under these ever-changing conditions of
danger and humiliation. If only she could make him
understand what was happening! "Listen," she insisted weakly, "the French and the English are trying
to destroy Kahnawakee. They're using me because
they think I'm John Cutler's wife. Did you get any of

that when you were bargaining with them? They think I'm Shannon. They want to destroy Kahnawakee. They—the Anglais and the Français—want to destroy . . ." she made a quick, sharp motion between her two fists, as though breaking a stick, ". . . Kahnawakee. They're using you, Orimha, to hurt Kahnawakee. *Ils sont très mal . . .* they are very, very bad men."

He was silent for a long moment and then he said one word, and that word made it all clear to her: *"Jamais."* It was the French word for "never," and Orimha spoke it in a voice charged with challenge and rebuke.

"Jamais?" Cassie whispered. "You're remembering the day I told you it could never be you? That it would always be Alex? And now you're thinking I won't be your wife, because I'll always belong to Alex?" She couldn't afford to waste any more time trying to appeal to Orimha's political interests and she turned instead to his apparently inexhaustible romantic preoccupation. "Okay, here we go." Taking a deep breath, she announced, "I belong to *you* now. *Je suis pour vous.* You bought me, right? *Vous achetéz moi*—or something like that—and that's okay with me. *Je suis pour vous,* Orimha. *Toujours.* Always."

His dark eyes widened with tentative hope. *"Et* Couteau Noir?"

"Jamais Couteau Noir," she sighed. "I promise." *"C'est fini?"*

Fini? It almost broke her heart to hear that word. Orimha was asking, quite simply, if her precious, passionate love affair with Alex was finished, and the answer, quite simply, was yes—it *was* finished. The love she had dreamed of finding . . . the love every woman dreams of one day experiencing . . . it was

over, and Cassie could feel a part of herself dying at
the loss of it.

Even if Alex found her one day soon and bought
her back from Orimha—even if he arrived at this very
moment, dressed in a suit of armor, and swept her
away on a prancing stallion—it was over, because
their priceless, poignant love affair paled when compared to the need for UNAP to be born and to thrive.
The invaders had to be stopped. Cassie had learned
that well, cringing in horror by the campfire while
Rubrier and Fowler traded countless rationales for
the suffering they were inflicting daily on the Indians.
Civilization and salvation—their twin defenses to the
charge of genocide. She would play no willing part in
their mayhem. More than ever, thanks to Cassie's
interference with history, Alex needed to study with
Kahnawakee and to return to his own time as a
leader, unencumbered by a liaison with a Eura.

Orimha was waiting for an answer and so she raised
her tearfilled eyes to his and murmured, *"Oui, c'est
fini.* It's over."

"Pourquoi?" he inquired gently.

Why? If only she knew! Why had she been asked to
experience true love only to lose it? *"C'est fini,"* she
shrugged again, wiping a tear from her cheek and
summoning a bittersweet smile. *"Vous achetéz moi,*
right? You bought me, and now I'm yours." Raising
her hand, she gently stroked his jawline and whispered, "I'm glad it was you, Orimha. I've been so
frightened." To her dismay she burst into tears, and
in an instant Orimha had pulled her into his burly
arms, murmuring softly and possessively as he buried
his face in her curls.

Chapter Eighteen

After Cassie had had a long, cleansing cry against Orimha's massive chest, the Gahnienca leader turned his attentions to his men, barking orders like a drill sergeant. Soon Cassie found herself feasting on a host of delicacies, from rabbit to duck to freshly grilled trout, washed down with a syrupy-sweet maple-flavored beverage. Two of the men had been sent off at a run, presumably to catch even more and better food for the new bride, while a third had been appointed impromptu chambermaid, furnishing her with a soft deerskin tunic to replace her soiled clothing.

Orimha himself had cleansed and anointed the deep scratches on her cheek and neck, muttering under his breath as he worked. Finally, when the fussing had ended and the others had settled down near the campfire for the night, Orimha led her a distance away, where she saw that a rabbit-fur blanket had been spread on a bed of pine needles.

She wanted to be brave—she had *promised* herself that she would respect both her own dignity and Orimha's by suffering this in docile silence—but the love nest reminded her of her times with Alex, bringing heartache that she could not bear for Orimha to

see. He had been so kind and patient, and he had
trusted her when she said it was over between herself
and Alex. *Fini.* Finished. She owed it to this man—
this husband—to honor that trust.

She turned to him and smiled shyly, then sank to
her knees on the blanket and patted the spot beside
her invitingly. "Come and join me, Orimha."

He smiled as though amused by the flirtation, and
lowered his burly frame down by her side. When he
didn't make any further move, she prodded, "It's
okay. I'm ready to be your wife. Your *esposa*—no,
that's Spanish, I guess. Your *mari?* Is that right?"

He touched her shoulders slightly, urging her backward into a reclined position, then he was tenderly
sifting his fingers through her hair while murmuring
in a gentle, seductive blend of Iroquois and French.

"That's pretty." Cassie's voice trembled despite her
efforts to sound relaxed. "I didn't understand a word
you said, but it was pretty."

He seemed to understand and explained, with exaggerated clarity, *"Je ne suis pas ton mari."*

"You're saying you're not my husband?" She
frowned, then his meaning hit her and she gasped
with relief. "You want to wait until after we're married? Oh, Orimha, that's so sweet." Her eyes were
once again swimming with tears, this time tears of
gratitude. "It doesn't change anything, I suppose, but
in a way it makes all the difference. Thank you for
respecting me, Orimha. Our marriage . . . oh!" She
was remembering the two men he had sent away. Had
they gone for a holy man to perform the ceremony? It
was so civilized.

"That awful Fowler considers himself more civilized than you, but you're a true gentleman, Orimha,
and," she kissed his hand then held it against her

cheek as she snuggled in for a much-needed sleep, "I'll always be glad they brought me to you. It could have been a nightmare, but instead, I think I can learn to appreciate you, so. . . . *Bonsoir, mon fiancé. Mon ami.* Sleep well."

She wouldn't have been surprised had he moved in close, but he settled down a few feet away instead, and, to her fond amusement, was almost instantly asleep. It reminded her of the night after the babies were born, when Alex had been so exhausted.

But not too exhausted to make love to you one final time, she reminded herself sadly. *I'm so glad we didn't know then that it was our last night together. We would have tried too hard, or been too sad. Instead, it was so much fun, and he was so loving.*

But Orimha's loving, too! she chastised herself immediately. *Try to adjust, Cassie. This is your new life, and he's your new husband, so try to get used to it. He's a good man, when you think about it. Look at him— dead to the world, like he doesn't have a care.*

Then it dawned on her that he was in fact sleeping so very soundly that if she moved away, very slowly and quietly, he wouldn't even stir. And if she crept into the woods and made her way back to the river . . .

There was a bright slice of moon illuminating the glade and she could remember the proper path, and the distance, and she could make her way quickly and silently in her soft, supple moccasins . . . but did she dare? Orimha would be livid when he woke up. She had told him she would stay with him forever. He might come after her and kill her! He might come to the village and demand her return! And what about her plan? Wouldn't she be risking the future of UNAP?

No! Until now, the danger had been from aggression by the Susquehannocks against the Gahniencas. But if she could escape on her own, the situation would be reversed. The Susquehannocks would no longer be the aggressors, nor the peace breakers. Orimha would have a valid claim against Cassie and perhaps against the mercenaries who had sold him a reluctant bride, but any warfare would be started by the renegades, not by Kahnawakee. And Kahnawakee and Alex could use their diplomacy, along with the information concerning Rubrier and Fowler, along with the sheer size of the Susquehannock Nation against the small band of renegades, to prevent loss of life or, more importantly, loss of faith in the vision of a union of Native American Protectorates.

With the vision secure, she could begin to honor other values and principles. She was a human being, not a commodity to be bought, sold, or owned! While she had been willing to sacrifice her own happiness to prevent war, she was hardly bound by the contract of purchase between Orimha and the mercenaries. She had respect for other cultures, but not to the extent of condoning or even pretending to understand enslavement under any circumstances, and now she had the power to resist and perhaps overcome such blatant indignity.

Was it possible? After all this trauma, could she regain her freedom and self-determination? Would Time then take pity on her and send her back to her own little world? With all due respect to Saint Joan of Arc, Cassie had no desire to be a martyr—or a masochist.

"I'm out of here," she announced silently, as she edged away from her slumbering 'fiancé'. With her announcement came a rush of energy and hope that

felt almost foreign to her beleaguered body. When she
had reached the cover of the forest, her spirit soared
at the unfamiliar freedom, and with a silent whoop
she broke into a run.

On that fateful afternoon, just three days earlier,
when she had stormed away from the Susquehannock
village with Orimha in silent pursuit, she had seen
these woods as her enemy, harboring bears and
snakes and villains that might leap out at any moment
to molest her. Now that she'd had a taste of true
danger, she found herself loving these trees that
seemed now to be sentries, lining the trail that would
lead her back to Shannon and John. And Alex?

No! she chastised herself one final time. *He has to
study with Kahnawakee. Haven't you learned your lesson yet? You can ruin the future for millions of innocent
people, or you can accept the fact that you and Alex
were a mistake from the start. He's the twentieth-century Kahnawakee. He needs someone like Leah Eagle
by his side, so leave him alone!*

She felt strong—stronger than ever before. Strong
enough to keep her distance from Alex despite the
temptation to run to his arms. She would concentrate
on her freedom and would savor it for years to come,
knowing that it might have gone much differently. As
Orimha's bride, life would have been bearable but
joyless. As the bride of an unknown purchaser, her
life might easily have become an instant hell. Now she
was alone and she would learn to appreciate that
without asking for the impossible.

She passed landmarks, such as the mass of bram-
bles that had scratched her, and the fork in the trail
that had taken her away from the river, and she knew

she was within sprinting distance of the spot where
Rubrier and Fowler had camped. Once there, she
would rest, on the bank of the river that would lead
her back to the burial ground and then to safety. With
luck, she would encounter another hidden canoe
along the way, but if she was required to walk, she
would do so proudly. A walk in these moccasins had
gotten her into this mess, one fateful afternoon not
long ago, and another walk would bring her back to
safety and, she hoped, back to the twentieth century.

Then she reached the deserted campsite and a chill
rippled down her spine as she pictured herself, just
one night earlier, bound and gagged and shuddering
beside the fire, the picture of humiliation and despair.
All that had changed. In fact, she would build her
own fire on that very same spot, using a miniature
A-frame stick house as tinder. She would conquer any
lingering fears before leaving at dawn. Fear had
owned her so completely, albeit briefly, and she would
never surrender to it again.

Then it was back, in full force and without warning,
as Benedict Fowler stepped into view. Cassie's mouth
gaped open and she felt her knees begin to buckle as
the futility of crying out or attempting to run overwhelmed her. This simply could not be happening,
and yet it was.

"Didn't I *tell* you she'd fight them, Rubrier?" the
huge man grinned, striding forward to grasp her by
both wrists. "Welcome back, Madame Cutler. I *told*
our friend Jean-Claude that any woman feisty enough
to bite *me* wouldn't just close her eyes and spread her
legs for a group of renegade savages."

She stared in horror, cursing herself for having
walked right into his arms. But hadn't she heard
them say, again and again, that they must put many

miles between themselves and this place before word
was sent to John? They had broken camp before
her very eyes, and loaded their belongings into the
canoes . . .

But Fowler had known, and he had come back, and
now it was all over. There was no doubt but that he'd
punish her in a myriad of unspeakable ways and then
send her back to Orimha, whose justifiable wrath
would finish her off.

"Look at our beauty, Rubrier," Fowler was grinning. "They dressed her up like one of their own. Did
you bite them, my sweet?" When she simply stared, he
demanded in raspy delight, "Did they rape you?"

"Yes," she lied, hoping beyond hope that they
would consider that sufficient indignity and would
bundle her off to John.

"How many had you?"

"Two," she whispered.

"That will anger your husband, wouldn't you say?"

"He will be furious. He won't rest until he's killed
them."

"If two will anger him, four might just drive him
mad with vengeance, don't you suppose?" He roared
with laughter when she cringed. "What do you say,
Rubrier? Shall we make it four?"

Jean-Claude moved closer, shaking his head sadly.
"You're the one who's mad, Fowler. Have you no
heart? No soul? Look at her! She's been through
hell."

"Are you suggesting we release her?" Fowler
mocked. "If she goes back to Cutler, she'll tell him
our homelands were behind this and he'll cause more
trouble than ever before."

"It's true. She must die now. But with dignity. I
insist upon that." The Frenchman stepped to within

inches of them and petted Cassie's hair. "You are an angel. Be brave."

"She is indeed an angel," Fowler chuckled. "Look at her, Rubrier. They didn't do enough damage. Her body," his eyes caressed her curves with hungry thoroughness, "has been only slightly abused. I see only a scratch or two. She must appear much, much more . . . *violated,* don't you agree?" His meaning was grotesquely clear, but still he elaborated, "We can kill her first and then do the damage, but it will be much more enjoyable with her lively little self fighting us, believe me."

Cassie shrank from his horrific leer and turned toward her supposed protector. Far from providing reassurance, Rubrier's eyes were warm with reluctant desire. "You must submit, Madame Cutler. We will be as gentle as possible."

"No," she pleaded softly. "I can't bear this. I can't take any more . . ."

"We will be gentle," he repeated, drawing a small knife from a jeweled scabbard hanging from his jacket. With careful grace he severed the ties that bound her tunic. "It will be over quickly."

"Speak for yourself," Fowler growled. "I'm planning on taking all night, but . . ." he shrugged and released her wrists, "you can have her first."

Cassie gathered the dress around herself and locked eyes with Rubrier. "You're an animal, just like him. You should be ashamed! After all your moralizing, you'd consider this?"

"If there were any other choice, I would support it, but you must die. And if you must die, why not put your death to the glorious use of destroying the work of the devil?"

"Then just kill me." She couldn't believe she had

said that, but she also couldn't retract it. In fact, she added a humble "please" that was more humiliating than anything that had yet transpired. Alex had been so brave, and she was falling apart.

"You are a lady, and I swear we will respect that," Rubrier murmured, but his eyes had traveled to the swell of her breasts beneath the tunic and his breathing had grown slightly ragged. "Come here to Jean-Claude . . ." Extending his arms toward her, he soothed, "Come to me, my angel . . ."

He wanted to make love to her! It was so completely ludicrous that it roused Cassie from her listless surrender and she dared to embrace one final, hopeless ploy. "I don't want to do this in front of him," she whimpered, gesturing toward Fowler without raising her eyes from the ground. She was the picture of submission and femininity, or as close to that picture as she could hope to come, and it proved more than enough for Rubrier, who practically hissed his companion away. Fowler chuckled and complied, reminding her as he retreated, that she was "saving the best for last."

Cassie smiled shyly. "Will you turn your back while I disrobe? As you said, I'm a lady, and . . ." Her pause was delicate and tentative. "Please, Jean-Claude?"

He moistened his lips. "You will not keep me waiting long? I have thought of you this way, and the gentle need within you, my love . . ."

"I'm glad it's you and not him. I trust you, Jean-Claude." As he turned his back, she added in the sweetest of voices, "You are truly a gentleman, and," every muscle in her body tensed and she spat, *"truly a fool!"*

She was running and shrieking in an instant, intent upon finding either safety or total exhaustion and

death rather than surrendering to fear. That part of
her life was *over!* She could dive into the river and stay
under the water until she drowned and it would be
infinitely preferable to Jean-Claude Rubrier's hot
breath, not to mention Benedict Fowler's sadism. As
she streaked through the woods, she screeched for
Orimha, and for John, and for Alex, although in her
frenzy she found herself calling him "Couteau!"

Then she was tackled to the ground, her head hit-
ting sharply against an outcropping of rock. It wasn't
enough to render her unconscious, but it blurred her
vision and seconds passed before she realized it was
the Frenchman who was viciously mounting her. She
had expected Fowler, but apparently his huge size had
one disadvantage, while the wiry Frenchman had
been able to catch her easily. And the wiry Frenchman was enraged. Gone was the would-be lover. The
gentleman no longer existed. His pride had been shattered and he was bent upon humiliating her, even to
the point of slapping her face, again and again, while
she struggled and clawed and shrieked for Couteau
Noir.

He was named for the black knife that had been
given to Kahnawakee by his closest adviser and now,
as she screamed, that same black knife came hurtling
through the air, burying itself in Jean-Claude Rubrier's back only moments before the man could rendered Cassie senseless with his repeated strikes to her
blood-red cheeks. Through the haze of pain and revulsion, Cassie had seen the amazing weapon, thrown
by an amazing man, moving toward its target. Not
three inches, or two inches, or one inch high or low.
The blade entered neatly and precisely, and Rubrier
fell dead across her chest.

Alexander BlackKnife had come for her, but he

could not come *to* her. Not yet. One last obstacle loomed in his path in the person of Benedict Fowler. Alex was a tall man—lean, hard, and agile—but Fowler was a towering mass of muscle. Alex was a true warrior, but Fowler was a weapon in human form, and from the elated gleam in his silvery eyes, Cassie knew he had always dreamed of crushing an opponent as worthy as Alexander BlackKnife.

"Tell me who you are," the huge man grinned. "What's your interest in our pretty Madame Cutler?"

"I'm the brother of Kahnawakee."

"Ah." His grin widened with anticipation. "And I am Benedict Fowler, your executioner."

"Benedict Fowler?" Alex taunted carefully. "A coward who preys upon helpless women? Except," his dark eyes flashed, "this woman is not helpless. She has the full force of two nations behind her. You chose the wrong victim, coward, and it's going to cost you your life."

Fowler nodded as though complimenting Alex's style, then reached down to his high black boot and pulled out a nine-inch blade with a jagged edge that might have glinted had there been sunlight to strike it. Cassie's hand moved quickly to the black-hilted knife in Rubrier's back and she struggled in vain to remove it. Her actions amused Fowler, who suggested, "Shall we wait until your little whore can come to your aid? Or are we waiting perhaps for the full force of two nations? Will they be arriving soon?"

"We're waiting because you're too cowardly to make the first move, even though you have a weapon and I have only my bare hands," Alex shrugged. "Any time, you bastard."

"Alex, wait!" Cassie's eye had been drawn to Rubrier's tiny dagger and, without thinking, she pulled it

from its scabbard and tossed it toward her lover. Alex
caught it neatly, then chuckled, shaking his head at
the contrast between this foppish three-inch orna-
ment and the atrocity in Fowler's grasp.

"Don't help any more, Cass," he suggested with a
reassuring wink. "Go to the river. There's a canoe
there. Take off. I'll catch up with you when I'm done
with this coward."

"I'm tiring of that particular insult," Fowler
warned, advancing slowly toward his prey. "I believe
I'll cut your tongue out and roast it for my dinner.
Isn't that the way you savages do it?"

"I'm about to show you exactly how we do it,"
Alex assured him, then he took a giant step backward
and threw the tiny knife.

Fowler blocked it, as anticipated, but in that instant Alex pounced, feet first, kicking the longer blade
from the man's hand. It went spinning into the underbrush and Cassie dived for it, then realized in dazed
wonder that Alex didn't need her help at all. He had
Fowler pinned and was slamming the big man's head
against the ground again and again. For just one
moment the advantage shifted, with Fowler lifting his
lower torso off the ground and breaking Alex's hold,
and then the Englishman's head became imprisoned
against Alex's chest and one swift, vicious twist of his
neck rendered him lifeless and still.

Alexander BlackKnife stared down at the dead
man, wanting to feel remorse or at least a hint of
regret at having taken a human life so brutally, then
his gaze shifted to Cassie—huddled and shuddering
and pale with exhaustion, exactly as he had been seeing her over these torturous hours!—and he dropped

the body to the ground with unceremonious finality. Striding to her side, he dropped to his knees and was overwhelmed by the trembling of her body as she clung to his neck and thanked him again and again.

"What did they do to you?" he mourned into her matted curls. "Cassie, darling, don't be frightened anymore. Whatever they did, it's over now."

"They just scared me," she sobbed. "I'm not like you, Alex. I couldn't be brave. I couldn't take it."

"Shhh." His dark eyes were filling with tears for the first time since the death of his father ten long years before. "I couldn't take it either, Cassie. You don't believe that, but it's true. No one can take it, some people can just bluff a little. That's all I did. Inside I was terrified, but . . ." He pried her face away from his chest and tried to catch her teary gaze. "These last few hours, since I found out you were in danger, were even more terrifying. The thought of losing you . . ." His lips brushed her forehead lightly. "I can't live without you."

"Alex, don't kiss me," she pleaded softly. "Just hold me."

"Sure, baby. Whatever you say." As he stroked her back, he tried not to imagine the trauma and humiliation that might have reduced her to this state. The thought that she could dread his kiss, when it had always been welcomed with such innocent delight . . . "I'll wait until you're ready," he vowed hoarsely.

"Never," she whispered. *"Jamais . . ."*

"Huh?" He could feel her relaxing into sleep, and there was a dazed quality to her speech that told him she might have a head injury along with exhaustion. Perhaps she was even in shock, and he wanted to let her rest, but her words had sounded so final, as though his kiss would truly never be welcomed by her again. He couldn't bear that, and so he urged gently, "You'll feel differently in a week or so, baby. Trust me."

Her eyes were closed and her breathing shallow as she shifted against him and murmured, in a low, trusting voice, *"C'est fini, Couteau. C'est fini."*

She was sound asleep and he didn't dare awaken her despite his crushing need to convince her they had a future. "It's not finished," he murmured into her hair, then he lowered her gently to the ground and stretched out beside her, his arm protectively cradling her neck. "These memories will fade, and you'll forgive me for neglecting you, and you'll love me again. I'll make you fall in love with me again."

She slept deeply, in his arms, until the first tentative rays of dawn replaced the moonlight and she began to stir. Alex had not left her side for even one instant, although sleep had been beyond him. Instead, he had used this time to design reassuring and apologetic phrases that would soothe her and win her back. Now, as she shifted against him and opened one sapphire blue eye, he smiled confidently. "Hi, Cass. Are you feeling a little better?"

"Mmm . . ." Her smile was angelic. "All better."

"Good. Are you hungry?" When she shook her head, he prodded, "You're just anxious to put this place behind you? I couldn't agree more. I can carry you to that canoe and we can travel a while, then we'll find a spot where you can rest while I catch us some breakfast."

"I can walk," she insisted, "and we really should hurry, Alex. Orimha could show up any minute, and he's bound to be angry."

"Orimha? What does he have to do with this?"

"He bought me." She frowned pointedly. "I hated that part, but luckily, they chose Orimha as their purchaser and he was a perfect gentleman. We were supposed to get married today."

"What?"

Cassie nodded sympathetically. "I have a lot to tell you, but the bottom line is, I escaped while he was asleep and we'd better get back to the village before he realizes I've left. I don't want you to fight him. He was good to me. We'll let Kahnawakee explain everything to him, and apologize and thank him."

"Whatever you say." Alex was pleased by her calm, coherent speech. And she hadn't tried to draw away from him, which he took as a sign that her trust was returning. Hopefully, the love and, eventually, the passion would return as well. If Orimha or these Euros had abused her sexually, he knew he might need to be patient, but as long as she was no longer claiming it was *"fini,"* he could adjust. "You're pretty smart, Cassie. Remember how you always told me everything happens for a reason, even if it doesn't make any sense at the time? Well, you were right. If I hadn't needed to leave the village ahead of Kahnawakee, to be alone and think about us, I never would have run into those two Delawares who told me about you in time to help you. It all happened for a reason."

"No, Alex." She sighed and drew away, sitting up and gathering her deerskin tunic about herself carefully. "Some things are not supposed to happen at all. I was never supposed to come here, just like you said."

"Now, don't start that again." His tone was playful despite the jolt of foreboding those words had just caused. "You and I were meant to be together, Cassie Stone. Don't bother trying to argue with me on that."

"You don't understand yet," she shrugged. "You didn't hear Fowler and Rubrier," she paused to glance with distaste toward the corpses, "and we grew up in a world where UNAP was a reality. We take it for granted, but Shannon was right." Struggling to her feet, she managed to retie the severed ends that had held her tunic in place and insisted, "I'll explain everything while we walk, but we really have to go now. Orimha could . . . oh!" She shrank against Alex, then relaxed a bit and almost smiled. "Look who's here."

He turned to see Kahnawakee and realized why Cassie hadn't immediately recognized the chief. His long black hair had been shorn away, with only a close cropped circle at the crown to adorn his otherwise shaven head. Alex understood all too well what this meant. The Visionary had heard that Cassie was in danger and had been ready and willing to go to war to save her. "She's okay, my brother," he smiled gratefully. "She's tired and they scared the hell out of her, but she's going to be fine." He watched as Cassie stepped toward the newcomer, her eyes fixed on his shiny head. If she made a joke, he'd be certain at last that the old Cassandra Stone was alive and well inside that still-shaky body.

"Visionary," she murmured, as though completely in awe of him. "You should go back to the village. Orimha's angry with me and I'd . . . I'd never forgive myself if he hurt you."

Kahnawakee was clearly as stunned as Alex by the unfamiliar reverence. "Orimha is no danger to us, Cassandra," he soothed, reaching for her hand and patting it awkwardly. "It was Orimha who sent word to me that you had been captured."

"What?"

Alex joined them, slipping his arm around Cassie's waist. "Orimha did that?"

"He thought we would be frantic over her disappearance, and he assured us no harm would come to her while she remained in his camp. But I see," his eyes scolded her fondly, "you did not remain."

"I thought he was going to make me marry him," Cassie sighed. "He tried to reassure me, I guess, but our communications were a little jumbled."

"He understood that this vile plan was a means of coming between John Cutler and myself. Orimha saw the danger to my work and, because of you, Cassandra, he has come to value the vision of a united continent."

"Oh, Kahnawakee!" Cassie's eyes were sparkling with delight. "That's the most wonderful news! But the credit goes to you. All of those conversations you had with him at the village."

"He heard, but did not understand. Only when he saw that you were willing to give up your love for Couteau to protect the peace did he see how valuable and noble our plan for unity must be."

"There's nothing more important right now than UNAP," Cassie agreed quietly.

Alex's discomfort was growing rapidly. While it pleased him to see Cassie valuing Kahnawakee's work, he was disturbed by the borderline fanaticism. As Cassie herself might have said, she had that "Leah Eagle" look in her eye. "Don't worry about UNAP, Cass," he insisted. "Kahnawakee's on his way to Onondaga right now, to make that address I told you about. Everything's going well."

She patted his hand as though he were a child. "We have to be careful, Alex. Don't take anything for granted. As long as you and I are here, we can inadvertently change something and history will be a disaster, just as it was when Shannon was a little girl. Believe me," she took a deep breath and blurted, "I've heard the way these Euro invaders think and it's appalling."

"These Euro invaders . . ." Kahnawakee's eyes clouded. "You must try to forget that now, Cassandra. You are safe, and these men," he walked to Fowler's body and rolled it over, contemptuously, with his foot, "are very dead. I see you have done well, little brother." He wandered over to Rubrier's corpse, pulling the black-hilted blade free with one sharp motion. "Your aim has improved."

"I was pretty motivated," Alex nodded, gratified by the praise. It *had* been a great throw. Cassandra Stone deserved nothing less than the best. "Thanks for the lessons."

"My pleasure." Kahnawakee smiled gently toward Cassie. "We will take you back now. Do you wish to return to the cabin or to the village? Kanasa will take good care of you."

"You need to go to Onondaga, and so does Alex," Cassie reminded him brightly. "I can make it down the river alone."

"No way," Alex growled. "Are you serious, Cassie? Do you think we'd let you out of our sight?"

"Now that Orimha's solidly in our camp, we can ask him to take me back to the cabin," she countered briskly. "I refuse to make Kahnawakee late for the Council address. You know how important that is historically, Alex. And," her eyes flashed with determination, "don't tell me *you're* thinking of missing it!

I won't accept that. You're here for a purpose, Alexander BlackKnife, and being my escort is not it. Right?"

"Cassandra," Kahnawakee soothed, "Couteau will be unable to concentrate. He has missed you greatly."

"Either Orimha escorts me, or I go alone. Which is it?"

Alex winced at the radical gleam in her eye. She was suddenly a zealot in Kahnawakee's "camp," as she so blithely referred to it, and he had a feeling this new dedication was going to be just as frustrating, and *much* less enjoyable, than the old irreverence had been.

Chapter Nineteen

"Robin is the smartest little girl in the world," Cassie insisted, as she finished diapering her cousin's daughter on John Cutler's bed. "She's not even one month old yet and she recognizes her name. That's not normal, Shannon. I think she's a genius. Watch." She stepped away from the bed. "Mary . . . Ellen . . . Robin . . . see? When I say Robin, she looks!"

Shannon shifted little Philip from her right breast to her left. "You're going to make a great mother, Cassie. And you and Alex will have little geniuses, too, I'm sure."

"Don't start with that," Cassie glared playfully. "Alex is in Onondaga making history and I'm here, trying *not* to make history. And," she scooped little Robin into her arms, "trying to enjoy my baby cousins as much as possible before I leave, which could be any minute now."

"You're still sure you and Alex will vanish into thin air as soon as Kahnawakee's address to the Council is finished?"

"I'm hoping so." Cassie's tone grew wistful. "I love spending time with you, but every minute I'm here is a danger. You know that better than anyone. We have to keep history on course, or it might go the way it did that first time."

"I guess you're right. On the other hand," her eyes rebuked her gently, "by interfering with history, you saved my babies' lives."

"We don't know that for sure. John says Alex said there were rumors of danger. We don't know that means Fowler and Rubrier, although they were definitely evil enough to do something like that."

"But you won't even let John and me express our gratitude! It's so frustrating. And I'll bet it's even worse for poor Alex. How could you send him off to Onondaga when he was dying to be with you?"

"It all worked out," Cassie assured her airily. "I needed the time alone with Orimha, to thank him and to apologize for running away from him. And I needed to spend these last few weeks with you and John. Now our memories are firmly in place, and some day you can tell Philip and Robin about their Aunt Cassie and how much she loved them."

"And how stubborn she was," a voice added from the doorway. John Cutler dragged his splinted leg into the room, grinned proudly as always at the sight of his children being well tended, then stepped aside to allow a second man to pass into view. "Look who's come for a visit."

"Kahnawakee!" Shannon beamed from the rocking chair and gently unhooked Philip's hungry mouth from her nipple. "You finally get to see the babies!"

"According to John, they are superior in every way," the chief grinned. He took the male child into his hands and studied his features. "Very handsome. And the little girl?" He moved to Cassie's side and smiled. "She is named for my wife. It is a great honor." Shifting his gaze to Cassie, he added, "You are well, Cassandra?"

"Yes, Visionary. These weeks have flown by." She had to force herself not to ask for Alex. "How was the Council? Did all go well?"

"It was a great honor, and very educational. I felt the absence of my adviser, John, but Couteau was there and he was of great service. I'm grateful to you for insisting that he accompany me. His heart was here with you, but his fine mind was of great assistance to me."

"Are you hungry, Kahnawakee?" Shannon interrupted. "There's stew and bread. Cassie's been cooking up a storm."

"Because her father is a student of the weather?" the chief suggested impishly.

"That's lame," Shannon giggled. "Cassie, stop staring at him like he's some kind of saint. You're making him nervous."

"Actually, I enjoy being worshipped," Kahnawakee countered. "Perhaps Cassandra will spoon the stew into my mouth."

Cassie laughed sheepishly. She knew she was behaving irrationally, but as the importance of UNAP had been demonstrated to her again and again during her captivity, the importance of Kahnawakee himself had become so urgent. He was absolutely irreplaceable and vital. On the other hand, if he was going to tease her . . .

But the guest's expression had sobered slightly. "Couteau remained behind at the village, in spite of the fact he wanted to come here more than he wanted anything in this world. He stayed behind because you asked him to stay away from this cabin."

"You really shouldn't have come, either," Cassie

sighed. "Alex could disappear from this time at any moment. Aren't there any last-minute lessons you need to teach him or questions you need to ask him?"

"Now she's telling the Visionary himself how to be a visionary," John mocked. "This woman's nagging never ends, Kahnawakee. And with this leg of mine, I can't get away from her when it starts."

"I have come to take her back to the village," Kahnawakee smiled, "and so you will have some relief soon."

"I'm not going anywhere."

The chief frowned. "My little brother needs to speak to you. There is too much left unsaid, and it worries him."

"There'll be time for all that once we go home. For now, he needs to concentrate on his work with you."

"She says she won't get back together with him, even once they go home," Shannon blurted. "She's going to refuse to marry him and she's just stubborn enough to do it and wreck both their lives in the process."

"Thanks, Shannon," Cassie glared. "Kahnawakee, please don't repeat that to Alex. He needs to concentrate—"

"Which is the reason I have come for you," Kahnawakee shrugged. "On our long walk back from Onondaga I tried to converse with my little brother, but his thoughts drifted always toward you. When we arrived at the village, I tried to resume his lessons, but I could not hold his interest."

"Well," Cassie teased, "I guess it's time someone told you the truth, Kahnawakee. You're boring."

To her delight, he burst into the hearty laughter that John claimed was a "stress reliever" for him. "I preferred being worshipped to being jeered at," he

grinned when his laughter, and that of John and
Shannon, had subsided.

"Jeered?" Cassie smiled. "That's a great word. I
can tell you learned your English from big John
here." Then she added sincerely, "I know you mean
well, but I can't go with you. Alex would misunderstand. It would mislead him, and he'd expect to spend
time with me romantically, and that would distract
him even more from your lessons."

"He needs to see, with his own eyes, that you are
safe. Then he can concentrate. I will ensure that he
does not romance you."

"You will?" Her eyes narrowed. "Is this some kind
of trick? Honestly, Kahnawakee, try to be a little
more dignified, will you? You're making it hard for
me to worship you."

"Will you come with me if I guarantee Couteau will
not neglect his work? You can spend your time helping Kanasa. The corn needs to be husked, and she is
an old woman."

An old woman with five strong daughters to help
her, Cassie knew. Kahnawakee was playing matchmaker and it was sweet but pointless.

"If I return without you, Couteau will come here
himself," the chief warned. "He will lose much time
from his study, and I will not be nearby to restrain
him from courting you."

"That's John's specialty."

"Not any more, missy," Cutler chuckled. "Shannon and I have decided you're going to marry Alex,
and so a little time in the smithy together at night
won't do any real harm."

"Some head-of-the-family you turned out to be."
Cassie shook her head sadly. They were all being so
sweet, but so misguided. They just didn't understand,

and it was clear they all believed she would eventually weaken. On the other hand, they hadn't heard Fowler and Rubrier, and hadn't felt the future of the Susquehannocks slipping from destiny's hands because of bigotry and greed.

They knew she loved Alex. They simply didn't understand that she loved him so much, she had to let him go whether he wished it or not. If she did anything here in the seventeenth century to disturb history, Alex might never be born! And if she distracted him or diluted his effectiveness as a leader in the twentieth century, other innocent lives might be jeopardized. The risk was too great. The *love* was too great, and so she knew she could be strong.

"I'll go with you, Kahnawakee," she agreed quietly, "but you may wish I hadn't. While we walk to the village, I'm going to tell you the whole story— every hideous word uttered by the Euros who kidnapped me—and by the time we get to the longhouse, you may be more willing than you know to keep Alex from romancing me."

Kahnawakee nodded. "I wish to hear every detail. And I will keep my word to you. Couteau will study with me. His eyes may follow you, but he will keep his distance, as Orimha once did. Is that acceptable?"

"Yes."

"Fine. I will eat the stew, and then we will leave." He moved to the hearth and ladled the warm food into a crockery bowl.

Cassie turned to Shannon and murmured, "I'll miss you. I may not see you again . . ."

"I know." Shannon rose from her chair and embraced her cousin fondly. "But your place is with Alex, just as my place is with John."

"Shannon . . ."

"That's right, missy," John insisted, turning her toward himself for a hearty hug. "We'll miss you, but we'll know you're in good hands. You've been a blessing these last few weeks, helping with the little ones the way you have, but now it's time to get on with your own life, start your own family."

"You two are hopeless." Cassie smiled through her tears. "You deserve each other."

"And you deserve Alex. Don't punish yourself for some mistake you imagine you might one day make, missy. There's no sense in that, and there's too much at stake between you."

There's too much at stake, Cassie agreed silently. *That's why I can't afford to make any more of those mistakes.* She squared her shoulders proudly. *And I won't.*

She was unprepared for her reaction to the sight of the village, or for the reception she was given by the members of the Bear Clan, who swarmed around her, clamoring with welcome. The little ones competed for her arms, while Kanasa's daughters fussed over her, indicating in French and by expressive sign language that she had grown unacceptably skinny, a condition they were plainly going to remedy immediately, bringing her bowls of corn soup even before she had reached the longhouse or stowed her gear.

It was a homecoming and, to Cassie's shock, it was the most poignant of her lifetime. She had gone away so often—to boarding school and art clinics—and had always been glad to return to her parents' home or, later, to her own little A-frame, but this was somehow more intense, and comforting, perhaps because it was so unexpected, but also because she had been so supremely happy here, albeit for too short a time. The communal life-style, the cooperative craftswomanship, the glimpses of Alex in the distance . . .

And there he stood, once again, smiling the most gentle and loving of smiles, then he was striding toward her and the members of her extended family were eagerly making room for him by her side.

She wanted to keep him at arms' length but could see that it would be impossible. His eyes were shining with hope and determination, and her body was responding with a plaintive request that it be allowed to feel him, in a warm embrace, just one last time, and so she weakened and allowed him to gather her against his chest. "Cass. . . . You came."

"Oh, Alex," she sighed. "Don't misunderstand—"

"Shh, don't talk." He glanced behind her and grinned, "Thank you, my brother, for bringing her to me."

"She is not here as your woman," Kahnawakee proclaimed solemnly. "She is here as my guest. She has requested that you keep your distance from her, and I have given my word that you will honor that request."

"Huh?"

Cassie had been luxuriating in this one final heavenly embrace and wished for a moment that Kahnawakee would mind his own business. Then she remembered her resolution and withdrew from Alex reluctantly. "The Visionary's right, Alex. I didn't want to come because I didn't want to distract you from your time with him. Please respect that."

"Respect?" Alex grimaced slightly. "You know I respect you. Now," his tone grew stern, "tell me how you're doing. I've been going crazy wondering if you're still scared, or having nightmares, or blaming me—not that you shouldn't, but I swear, Cassie, I've learned my lesson. I want to hear everything about that ordeal, and I want to marry you."

"Kahnawakee!" Cassie wailed, overwhelmed by Alex's energy and determination. "You gave me your word."

"Couteau, walk with me now." Kahnawakee's tone left no room for argument. "Cassandra has shared every detail of her captivity with me on our walk from the cabin, and I will tell you all. You will be stunned, and you will understand why she has changed so greatly in response to it."

"Why?" Alex demanded. "What did those bastards do?"

"They talked, and their words frightened her."

"Words?" His jaw relaxed slightly. "This is all about words? Come on, Cassie," he cajoled desperately. "Tell me about it yourself. I've missed you."

"She has work to do with Kanasa, little brother. She will eat with us in our longhouse tonight, and you can see for yourself then that she is well."

"Eat with you?" Cassie blushed. "That wasn't part of the deal."

"Djisgaga will insist. If you wish to argue, you must argue with my wife."

"Clever, Kahnawakee," Cassie muttered under her breath. "You know she's the last person I can handle in an argument."

"Then it is decided? Fine. Couteau, you will walk with me now, while Cassandra works."

Alex seemed to read something in Kahnawakee's expression and he backed away quickly. "No problem. See you at dinner, Cassie. And Cassie?"

"Yes?"

"I love you." He turned before she could answer,

and as she watched him stride away, she began to suspect she had made a serious mistake. She had forgotten just how handsome and charming and persuasive this man could be, and she had definitely underestimated Kahnawakee. They were playing this as though it were a game, but she knew better—she knew it was a delicate situation of historical proportions—and so she would have to be the one to remain strong and to protect the vision from these misguided visionaries.

The men did not help with the harvest. That was the province of the women and young girls, with the children running and playing amid the high corn stalks all the while. Next would come the husking bees—the hadinowi yaki—and Cassie was learning that this time of hard work would also be a time of teasing and gossiping. Each female from her clan had made a point of informing her, through a variety of artful language strategies, that Couteau Noir was too attractive and strong and brave to be rebuffed. They teased her and scolded her and urged her to go to him, but she did not.

It was Alex who came to her, ostensibly to rescue her from an overloaded sack of corn that she was dragging from the fields toward the shade of the longhouse. The others had tried to warn her that she was being overly ambitious in her gathering and now she had no choice but to sheepishly accept his assistance. When he slung the heavy bag easily over one shoulder and grinned at her, she had to smile back, in admiration and gratitude, promising herself all the while that she wouldn't allow the temporary distraction to become anything more.

He was wearing his jeans and running shoes, with no shirt or vest to obscure her view of his bronzed chest and bulging arms. His always shaggy hair had grown even more luxurious and wild, tempting her fingertips as it had at that first meeting. Was it possible that that had taken place only two short months earlier? She had changed so much during that time, but some things would never change, and it seemed her physical reaction to his sexy hair and sexier smile were some of them.

And his voice! He was using the low, husky one, as they strolled side by side, and it was working too well, causing her heart to pound with memories and hope, despite the hopelessness of further flirting. He was telling her about the Council meeting, and while Kahnawakee had also given her a lengthy account of it, she had longed to see the experience through Alex's eyes. As she listened, she could picture him standing behind Kahnawakee, a bit to the right of him, and listening in silent wonder as UNAP came quietly into existence.

"It must have been the greatest moment of your life," she mused. "It's such a miracle you were allowed to see it."

"The greatest moments of my life are still ahead of us," he smiled. "Our wedding . . . our wedding *night* . . . the births of our children . . ." He deposited the heavy sack of corn near the growing stack beside the longhouse and motioned for Cassie to sit. "We need to talk."

"When we go home."

"Now," he countered firmly. "I'm not going to hit on you, Cass. I just want to help. Kahnawakee told me all about Fowler and Rubrier, and I can only imagine how shocking it was for you. It shattered your trust in human nature, didn't it?"

"It opened my eyes."

"Just don't let it blind you to the good side of things. The love, the trust, the creativity—all of that still exists, Cassie. Texture and color and passion didn't disappear from life, did they?"

"No," she admitted shyly. "I still want all those things out of life, but Alex . . . not with you. I'm sorry, but that's the way it is."

"I know. You don't want to jeopardize UNAP. That's how I used to feel about us—like we were perfect for each other, but we didn't dare dilute my effectiveness as a leader by selfishly indulging our attraction. Right?"

"And now you're going to say you've changed your mind," Cassie sighed. "Because we're here, in this beautiful, peaceful village, and the twentieth-century media are far away. And the Fowlers and the Rubriers are out of sight, out of mind. Except, for me, they'll always be lurking, and do you know why?"

"Tell me."

"Because there are thousands of them. Millions of them, I guess, by the time the twentieth century comes. They were *typical,* Alex. Not leaders, or aberrations, or exceptions to the rule. They were rank-and-file bigots, believing they were better than anyone whose appearance or culture differed from their own. Even Rubrier, who was half Indian himself, was obsessed with bringing this continent into line with traditional European thinking." Tears glistened in her eyes. "Three hundred years won't change any of that. Remember the headlines when Shannon disappeared? Remember the bigotry and fear? We can't afford to forget any of that."

"And now that you understand all of that so well, aren't you even more perfect for me?"

"This was never supposed to happen. You sent me away that day, and if I had just driven your car to the border like you asked, I honestly think we wouldn't have seen each other again, except for a brief meeting for you to tell me Shannon was alive and well."

"What about that? How can you say you were never supposed to come here? You saved Shannon's life!"

"Shannon's life isn't important."

"What?"

"Not anymore. She already changed history for the better, so her job was done."

Alex stared. "You're saying she's suddenly expendable?"

"To me, or to John, no. But in the big picture, yes. Shannon and I are expendable."

"I can't believe what I'm hearing," Alex whispered hoarsely. "You really think you're expendable? Don't you remember how Kahnawakee shaved his head and was willing to fight to the death to save you? Doesn't that tell you something about your worth?"

"It scares me to death," Cassie nodded. "We can never let anything like that happen again. Kahnawakee," her voice grew hushed, "has to survive until UNAP takes a firm hold. And you," she gripped his hands, "you have to make sure the vision survives its twentieth-century crises."

"I will. I promise."

A wave of relief washed over her and she released his hands. "Good. Don't take anything for granted, Alex. Don't trust anyone, and don't let your guard down."

"You'll be there to make sure I don't let my guard

down," he predicted calmly. "And as far as trusting people goes, you're dead wrong. Without trust, there could never be a UNAP. Without trust, we might as well all just give up our visions and our dreams. I'm not ready to give up, on UNAP or on you."

"You're just making this harder on both of us than it needs to be."

Kahnawakee stepped out of the shadows and chided, "I gave my word to Cassandra that you would keep your distance from her."

Alex shrugged. "I thought I could reason with her, but you were right. She's nuts. Irresistible, but nuts." His eyes began to twinkle, sweeping over her with libidinous interest. "See you at dinner, Cass." When he walked away, there was a spring to his step that warned her the upcoming dinner would be unmanageably provocative.

She blushed, then turned to glare at Kahnawakee. "Where were you? What about our deal?"

"He is as obsessed with courting you as you are with breaking his heart," the chief explained. "It is best if you stay inside the longhouse of my father's sisters, where Couteau will not be distracted by you. I have brought you a gift," he added, handing her a bundle wrapped in oiled skin. "You show such curiosity over our handiwork, and you are so talented . . ."

"What's this?" She removed the outer wrapping and shook free a handsome ceremonial belt. "Oh, Kahnawakee! It's absolutely breathtaking!"

"It is the work of my grandmother, although, as you see, she sadly left us before it had been finished."

"Quill and shell weaving." She peered into a leather pouch that had been wrapped up inside the belt and was delighted to see a hundred or so extra pieces of

shell in the same deep shade of purple as that used for
the beading. "I've seen a few examples of this, but I've
never been able to examine the work. Your grandmother was an amazing artist."

"I agree. Sadly, the younger women, including my
sisters, were not interested in learning from her. Glass
beads and silk threads had arrived, and this work
seemed laborious and dull."

"Dull? *Look* at it! Someone should finish it, Kahnawakee. Isn't there anyone who remembers?"

"Sadly, no."

"These two figures . . ." She traced her finger along
the purple shell outline of a man, over whose head an
eclipse was depicted. "This one is you, right?"

"That is correct."

"And this man, with the knife—is this supposed to
be your son?"

"My grandmother said it was my successor."

Cassie tore her eyes away from the artifact and met
his telling gaze. "You're saying it's Alex, right? Oh,
dear . . ." Her hands were suddenly trembling. "It's so
beautiful. Have you shown it to him?"

"A man should learn his destiny in his own time.
This might burden Couteau. It might trouble him."

"I guess you're right." She ran her palm over the
tight, even weave. "It's a crime this won't ever be
finished."

"Would you care to try? Kanasa tells me there is
magic in your fingers."

"Me?" She wanted to be humble, but the truth was
she also wanted this project, more desperately than
she had wanted anything in her life. "I can try. I won't
disturb what's done, and if I can't figure it out, it'll be
just as it is now. But if I can just understand how she
managed to keep it all so tight and even . . ." She was

musing aloud, forgetting her audience as she studied the shiny quills and perfectly shaped quahog shell beads, which had been ground flat on one side so as to stay even with the quills.

"You will finish it, then. It is decided."

"I'll try," she corrected. "Kanasa has a zillion quills, and I've seen how she flattens them between her teeth, so that isn't a problem. Now if I can only duplicate this pattern . . ." She had begun to walk toward the longhouse doorway, then turned to add firmly, "I won't be able to come to dinner tonight. This is going to drive me crazy until I get it figured out . . ." She shrugged, then gave him her most brilliant smile. "Thanks, Kahnawakee. I'm in heaven."

She spent hours hunched over her work until finally Kanasa coaxed her into eating a few bites of bread and soup. While the student ate, the older woman flattened quills for her with effortless skill. Together they ground pieces of purple shell into roughly the appropriate shape for the belt, then Cassie drilled the holes with a bone drill furnished by Kanasa's husband. It was painstaking work, and for the first dozen attempts, the result was more often than not a disaster, but Cassie had been challenged and she was determined to perfect the techniques.

Over the next two days she remained inside the longhouse for hours at a stretch, venturing outdoors only when the children's patience would snap and they would drag her, laughing and squinting, into the light. Most of the females had begun their corn-husking parties and they pleaded with Cassie to join them, but she was obsessed with her new project and would escape back inside the moment she was able.

Despite her intense concentration, she had not put
Alexander BlackKnife from her mind for even a moment. How could she, when his figure was there on the
belt, waiting for her fingers to complete his form and
seal his destiny. The more she studied the design the
more convinced she was that the second man had to
be Alex. His outline was much taller than that of
Kahnawakee, and the long rainbow that connected
them seemed to span centuries rather than one short
generation. With all due respect for Djisgaga's infant
son, Cassie knew in her heart it was the twentieth-
century Couteau Noir whom Kahnawakee's grandmother had envisioned as she worked.

Djisgaga herself seemed to agree when, during Cassie's third day of self-imposed exile, she strode into
the longhouse and sat herself on the edge of Cassie's
platform as though they were sisters rather than ri-
vals. "Pretty," she admitted, as she studied a handful
of newly polished beads.

"Thanks."

Then Djisgaga took the belt into her lap and examined it. "My husband," she pronounced, pointing to
the figure of Kahnawakee. Then she traced Alex's
outline and suggested, "Your husband?"

Cassie sighed. Where was all of this sweetness when
she needed it? "That's Alex," she smiled warily. "I'm
sorry I didn't come to dinner the other night, Djisgaga. I mean, *je regret non manger avec vous . . .*"

Djisgaga had covered her ears with her hands as
though Cassie's French were torturing her, then she
admitted, "Djisgaga will say English. Cassandra will
listen to Djisgaga."

Cassie bit back a retort, settling for taking the belt
away from the intruder and pretending to study it
intently. "Go on, then, Djisgaga. Let's hear it."

"You are safe. Djisgaga smiles."

Like I care? Cassie sniffed inwardly.

"Djisgaga is jealous."

Cassie's eyes widened. "Of me?"

The dark-haired woman scowled slightly and shook her head. At that moment, one of Kanasa's daughters whose English was passable entered the longhouse and Djisgaga commandeered her. After a hasty exchange, Kanasa's daughter explained, "Djisgaga is not jealous of *you*. She is jealous of the sisters of Kahnawakee. Kahnawakee sent her to you, to make you understand."

"Well, I'm confused. Tell Djisgaga I don't care if she likes me, or is jealous of me, or whatever. It's no big deal."

"Kahnawakee sent her to you. She must explain. You must understand."

"Fine. Why is she jealous of his sisters, and what does that have to do with me?"

Kanasa's daughter sighed. "When John Cutler wished marriage with Kahnawakee's sister, Kahnawakee refused. He said, no marriage with white men."

"I heard about all that."

"Kahnawakee allows Couteau Noir to marry with white woman. Djisgaga is jealous."

"Oh! You mean, it bothers her that he cared more about his sisters than about Alex? She's jealous on Alex's behalf?"

The two Susquehannocks conferred briefly, then Djisgaga nodded, while her interpreter explained with a sly smile, "Djisgaga has always been jealous of Kahnawakee's love for his sisters. She wants him to love her best, and to love their descendants best. But Kahnawakee loves his sisters, and their children, too much, and so she is jealous."

"And so this was never anything personal against me?" Cassie laughed. "I stepped right into the middle of a lover's quarrel. Tell Djisgaga I don't think she has anything to worry about. I've never seen a man quite as . . . blinded by love for his wife, shall we say . . . ? as Kahnawakee."

Djisgaga beamed at this, adding, "You marry Couteau. Djisgaga smiles." With one last admiring look at the pile of beads she was gone. Kanasa's daughter stayed for a moment, to gossip gleefully over Djisgaga's confession, then Cassie returned to her work, yearning just a bit to banish her principles and to yield to the romantic philosophy that seemed suddenly to permeate the village.

"The belt will be finished soon, Cassandra?"

"Oh!" She swept a blanket over her handiwork and jumped to her feet. "Shame on you, Kahnawakee. I told you, I want to surprise you."

"I am impatient," he admitted. "I wish to wear it, for the celebration tomorrow."

"Celebration? I guess I'm out of touch. What are we celebrating?"

"My village is saying farewell to you and Couteau. It will be a day of rejoicing despite the sadness. We will make it the finest farewell."

"Are we going somewhere?" She moistened her lips nervously. "Are you saying we're going home? How do you know? Are you and Alex done?"

"He and I could learn, one from the other, forever, but yes. I believe the time has come. He is restless to bring his new wisdom to his people."

"Is he? That's good." She forced a smile. "One more day? Is that all I have? The belt's almost done, but I've been neglecting everyone else. Kanasa and the kids . . . and I'd love to see Shannon one last time, but I guess, if it's time . . ." She straightened proudly. "I'm ready. Just a few more hours' work on the belt and it'll be all finished."

"And I will wear it."

"But you didn't want Alex to see it," she reminded him wistfully. "I think you were right about that. He doesn't need any more pressure."

"Then I will wear it when you have gone. It will be one way of remembering."

"I like that." She stepped closer to him and touched his arm. "It's been an honor."

"There will be time for that tomorrow," he protested. "Finish your work so that you can join the games. Shannon and John will arrive before noon," he added with a wink. "Did you suppose they would miss your farewell?"

"Oh! Is John's leg all better?"

"My men will assist him, although he will resist their help. I trust Shannon to see that he takes care and moves slowly."

"What an undertaking! John on crutches, and two babies to carry!"

"I have sent four strong men. The journey will be pleasant and, as soon as they arrive, the celebration will begin." His smile faded and a stern leader stood before her. "I expect you to join us. You will not be allowed to hide in the longhouse. It is a day for you and for Couteau, and you will allow us to give you a fine time."

"It sounds wonderful," she admitted shyly. "I

wouldn't miss it for the world. Have you told Alex it's time to leave?"

"Never have I seen a man more eager to begin his new life. When you see him, and the light that shines in his eyes, you will know the time has indeed come."

"That's wonderful," she repeated, but her voice had grown weak with the realization that the beginning of Alex's new life meant the end of something so precious and so unforgettable that her heart might never fully recover. She didn't dare allow them—Kahnawakee, or Shannon, or especially Alex—to read any of that in her expression during the "celebration." It sounded as though Alex had finally come to terms with his fate and she would never forgive herself if her clouded future cast a shadow, even momentarily, over the light Kahnawakee had seen shining in those incredible ebony eyes.

Chapter Twenty

A Susquehannock celebration proved to be unlike anything Cassie had ever experienced. By sheer intensity of participation alone it surpassed even the wildest party of her college days. Gambling was rampant, whether it was betting on the lacrosse match or wagering on the bowl game, in which a player would shake flat shells in a clay bowl, hoping they would all come to rest with their dark side up, which meant victory for all who had predicted such an outcome.

Cassie had attended many lacrosse matches, but never had she seen anything like the contest between the Wolf Clan and the Bear Clan. Every able-bodied man from those two longhouses participated in a rough-and-tumble free-for-all in which Alexander Couteau Noir reigned supreme as the most agile and skillful of players. Cassie and Shannon cheered until they were hoarse, while John grumbled and bemoaned the injury that was keeping him from "showing Alex a thing or two."

Twins were apparently rare among the Susquehannocks, and so the women literally lined up to view the Cutler babies, who cried lustily, unaccustomed to the many faces and the incessant noise. Shannon was radiant, and to Cassie's delight, had chosen to wear one of the daringly altered dresses she had left for her. The former model's figure had returned with a vengeance, and Cassie grinned at the look of frustrated lust that would pass across John's face each time he laid eyes on her anew.

Cassie herself was wearing a modest sunbleached deerskin dress brought by Shannon, who explained that it was her favorite garment in the world and she would be honored to see her cousin in it for this, their last visit together. In a similar vein, John had brought a shirt for Alex, explaining that his stepmother, an Ojibwa, had made it for his father, Jack, who had tragically died before he'd had a chance to wear it. It was a fabulous work of craftswomanship, from its heavy, fringed sleeves to its intricate beading, and Cassie had to restrain her hand from exploring it whenever Alex came within touching distance of her fingers.

He had never been sexier, she told herself again and again. While she attributed some of it to the light that indeed was shining in his eyes, there was also a roguish quality to his grin that seemed out of place at a farewell celebration. While she realized the philosophy of rejoicing rather than lamenting this occasion was a sound one, it almost seemed as though these Susquehannocks were taking it a bit too far. Was she the only one aching inside over the impending goodbye? Despite the good-natured antics surrounding her, she found herself struggling not to burst into tears on innumerable occasions.

She was losing Shannon, and John, and Kanasa, and Kahnawakee, all at once and forever. And she was losing Alex, although she would see him on occasion, if only on television or from a distance during some political rally. He had apparently abandoned his romantic designs on her and she was disappointed, just a little, despite the fact that she herself had insisted he do so. Was he simply respecting her wishes, or had he belatedly come to agree with her? Did he still want her? Did he know how much she still ached for him?

Then he grabbed her from behind and spun her around, eyeing her dress with lustful appreciation. "Thanks for rooting for me, Cass. The whole Bear Clan considers you a traitor, but I'm really grateful."

"You were terrific," she blushed, pulling free of him quickly. "Aren't you going to watch the Turtles play the Beavers?"

"That's why I'm here. To ask you to come and sit with me and watch the game. You can be my date." He chuckled in anticipation of her protest. "Just kidding, Cass. There's no more dating for you and me, right? So come and sit with me."

His cavalier attitude stung her, and she snapped, "I'm trying to spend time with the others. I'll never see them again after today. *You* may be having fun, but *I'm* distraught."

"Yeah?" He was completely unrepentant. "Lighten up, Cass. This party is in our honor. You don't want to depress everybody, do you?"

"No." She was regretting her petulant outburst and decided to follow Alex's example. "I'm ready to party. Let me get something to eat and I'll find you in a few minutes over by the game."

"I'll eat with you. I'm starved, and Kanasa said something about a special treat for us."

They sought out the old woman, who beamed at their request and quickly spread a blanket on the ground, urging them to sit. She disappeared for a few moments, then returned with a basket filled with delicacies. The *pièce de résistance* was two round loaves of cornbread which had been cooked in corn husks that were twisted together at the top, joining the breads together.

"This is so fancy," Cassie marvelled. "Like a double tamale. Ooh, there's little bits of cranberry inside."

"This bread is reserved for very special occasions," Alex informed her, munching contentedly.

Kahnawakee had been watching from a distance and now approached. "You are enjoying yourselves?"

"Mmm, try this!" Cassie insisted, holding out a piece of the bread. "It's sensational."

The chief laughed. "I have tried it, and I agree. It is the best of our many foods. Now, I have some words to say."

"Now who's depressing everyone?" Cassie quipped. "Tell him to lighten up, Alex."

"I want to hear this, Cass."

"Oh, sorry." *There you go again,* she told herself morosely. *Interfering with his relationship with his Visionary. Aren't you ever going to learn?* Aloud, she urged, "Go ahead, Kahnawakee. We all want to hear this."

"May I speak in my own language?" he requested cautiously. "These things are important and must be said with great care."

"Of course."

The Cutlers had joined the group, and as they seated themselves, John stretched his splinted leg carefully and offered, "I'll translate for you later, missy."

"Should we stand or something, Alex?" Cassie whispered, intimidated by the unexpected solemn overtones. Kahnawakee had accepted a fur cloak from one of his men and was adjusting it carefully around his shoulders. She realized this was the moment he probably would have wanted to wear the ceremonial belt, which was all finished and hidden under her platform. The temptation to run and retrieve it was strong—how would they all react? Would they be pleased with the results? Would their eyes fill with tears, as hers had, when they saw how intimately bound these two men were, both in nature and in purpose?

Then she glanced at Alex's face and knew the belt would be too much. As it was, he seemed almost transformed, and when he reached for her hand and pulled her to her feet, she allowed him to keep that hand in his own for moral support as Kahnawakee's rich voice began to address all who had gathered. Unable to understand the words, but enchanted by the tone, she found herself edging closer and closer to Alex, basking in the glow of his clear, complete happiness.

It's all been worth it, she sighed inwardly. *Even if my heart breaks, I'll never regret meeting him. He's my hero, my escort, my protector, and my friend, even if I can never let him know how deeply my feelings will always run.*

Then Kahnawakee had finished and the gathering dispersed. "Do you want me to tell you what he said, Cass?" Alex murmured.

"No thanks. It was perfect just like it was."

"I agree. This has been a perfect day." He was still holding her hand. "Would you like to go for a walk?"

She blinked back hot tears, all too aware of his meaning. "I can't, Alex. Forgive me, but I can't. I just need to let it go. Please?" She pulled her hand free, then used it to stroke his tensed jaw. "It looks like another game is starting. Why don't you go watch? I'll join you in a while."

"Soon the sun will be setting, and you'll be helping put the children to bed," he predicted softly. "Can I see you after that?"

"Of course. We have plans to make, I guess. About going to the burial ground."

"Right. I'll come and find you then."

"Okay." She turned away quickly, unwilling to allow him to see her tears. Then he was gone, and Shannon was embracing her lovingly.

"Poor Cassie. This was too much for you. I warned them . . ."

"*No!* I loved every minute of it. I'm just so tired." She wiped her eyes and tried to smile. "Where are the babies?"

"Sound asleep. John and I thought," she hesitated, then admitted, "we'd like to say goodbye to you and Alex now, and maybe go to bed ourselves. It's been a long day. But if you need some company . . ."

"Are you kidding? I've got dozens of things to do," Cassie insisted brightly. "Go to bed with John, but in that dress, don't expect to get any sleep."

"Watch that raw talk," John chuckled, taking her from his wife and hugging her fiercely. "Farewell, missy. If you and Alex want to slip away tomorrow without any more fuss, we'll understand. This has been quite a day for you both."

"Thanks, John. I think that's how Alex will want it, so you're right, I'd better start saying goodbye to people now." She embraced him heartily. "I love you, John Cutler. You've been a terrific cousin-in-law."

"And I love you, missy. We'll never forget you."

When he had stepped aside, the cousins embraced

one final time. "Take care of the babies. I'm so glad I met you."

"Give Phil my love," Shannon sobbed. "Tell him I'm happy. Tell him he's an uncle. And, Cassie? You and Alex—"

"Shh . . . don't, Shannon. Don't say another word, please?" The tears had returned and she needed to be alone. Shannon had John to comfort her, and John had Shannon. . . . "I love you, but I have to go . . ." She kissed her cousin's cheek and stumbled away.

Countless women and children obstructed her path, trying to console her, and she loved them all but rebuffed them gently, making her way back to her little platform. Even when Kahnawakee himself approached, she simply hugged him close, then pushed him away, insisting, "Not now, Kahnawakee. Tomorrow, before we leave, but not now." When he backed away respectfully, she flew to him, weeping against his chest and telling him she would always adore him, then she escaped to the longhouse and threw herself onto her bed, sobbing without restraint. It was all too much! She was never supposed to have come here, because women needed to be strong here, and she was weak, and lonely, and so madly and hopelessly in love with Alexander BlackKnife . . .

Except he's not Alexander BlackKnife, she reminded herself unhappily. *He's Couteau Noir. You have to let go before your heart really does burst.* As her crying subsided, she reached under the platform and found the belt. There he was—only a geometric outline of a warrior, of course, but above that warrior's head was a blazing sun, and on that warrior's thigh she had woven a scar, so that no one would ever dare to doubt that it was Alex. Stretching out on her platform with the belt clutched to her breast, she closed her bloodshot eyes for a few moments' rest.

The long days of painstaking weaving had combined with the emotional traumas of the celebration to exhaust her, and her short rest became a deep two-hour sleep. When she opened her eyes the longhouse was dark, with the late-night silence only occasionally broken by the sounds of the members of the Bear Clan settling down for the night. The children had apparently been asleep for quite some time, although none had bothered the diligent golden-haired weaver by scurrying into bed with her as they usually did. She was selfishly glad of it, knowing she would now toss and turn all night in anticipation of the next day's departure. She was even tempted to go for a walk, but she knew she couldn't bear to run into any loved ones, so she shrugged out of Shannon's lovely deerskin dress, exchanging it quickly for the oversized shirt she kept handy at the foot of her bed. Then she pulled her blanket back into place and tried to summon some trace of optimism over the upcoming return to her parents and friends. It would be nice, wouldn't it, eventually? More important, it would be safe. And it would be over. *Fini* . . . forever . . .

"Scoot over, Cassie," a husky voice urged from out of the darkness, and then a lean, hard, naked body joined her, snuggling against her with astonishing impertinence.

"Alexander BlackKnife!" she scolded under her breath. "Have you lost your mind? Go away."

"I thought we should finalize our plans for tomorrow. We're leaving at dawn, right?"

She couldn't see the expression on his face, but his

voice told her he was teasing, and she wondered how he could manage such brazen humor in the face of their imminent parting. "I'll meet you at dawn. *Outside,* near the entrance to the village. Now, go away before Kanasa or the kids realize you're here."

"Kanasa and the kids expect me to be here," he countered patiently, nibbling on her ear as he spoke. "For some strange reason, they think we're married."

She drew away, offended by the nonsensical suggestion. "Would you please stop teasing me?"

"It's your fault, Cassie. You ate the wedding bread, right in front of everyone."

The wedding bread? She was momentarily speechless, but visions of the two loaves, tied together and cooked as one, were confirming the fact that she had made a bizarre but ultimately meaningless mistake.

"And you wore Shannon's wedding dress," he reminded her. "And I wore John's wedding shirt. But of course, the big clue was the actual ceremony. That *was* you standing by my side, holding my hand and smiling, wasn't it?"

She loved him for this lunacy. "John and Shannon knew? And Kahnawakee was tricking me from the start?"

"I love you, but you're gullible," he confessed fondly. "In case you haven't put two and two together, this is our wedding night."

"Alex," she sighed, melting and resisting in one confusing moment, "you're just making this harder— you have to leave. In a twisted way, this is all very charming and flattering, but this is *not* our wedding night."

"Sure it is. Unfortunately," his tone was now infused with frustration, "you know how I feel about longhouse sex, so you're safe with me. I can't consum-

mate a marriage in front of an audience, but," he
nuzzled her hopefully, "I'd like to stay. It was just a
symbolic wedding, and this is just a symbolic wedding
night. It symbolizes our love. Maybe you won't marry
me, but," a hint of vulnerability now surfaced, "you
still love me, don't you, Cass?"

"Yes, Alex," she sighed, snuggling against him in
wistful surrender. "I adore you."

"So? Where's the harm in a little symbolic cuddling?"

"You can stay. It's crazy, but it's our last night,
and," she slid her arms around his neck and brushed
his lips with hers, "I'm weak."

"You're also warm, and soft, and you smell great.
You've taught me to use all my senses, Cass, but I
have to admit," his hand slipped between her thighs,
"my favorite is still touch."

"Texture," she confirmed in dazed delight. "It's my
life."

"So, Alexander Couteau Noir," she murmured
softly while she stroked the handsome face of her
husband as he slumbered by her side. "You tricked
me into wearing a wedding dress, eating wedding
bread, listening to some pseudo-wedding ceremony
. . . and now you've tricked me into consummating
our marriage. I give up. If you want me this much—if
you need me as much as I need you—then we really
have no choice. Maybe we never did. Maybe this love
of ours is a gift we don't even have the right to refuse." Kissing his cheek gently, she added, "I tried to
resist, but thank heaven you won me over. Let's hope
it's the first of many successful campaigns."

Too happy and invigorated to sleep, she pulled the

ceremonial belt from under the platform one last time. This would be the most important tangible reminder of their time in the village and she wanted it to be perfect. With a sheepish smile she remembered the huge "scar" of purple beads she had placed on the second figure's thigh.

"You had no business doing that," she sighed, ashamed of having taken such bold creative license. "And when Djisgaga sees it, she'll think it's an insult to her, since she's the one who did such a crummy job stitching that wound. Just fix it, Cassie. What would Kahnawakee's grandmother say?" Shaking her head in amusement, she grabbed her jeans and carried her project outside, hoping to avail herself of the moonlight. The belt had to be completed and perfect by the time she and Alex left for the burial ground at dawn.

It was relatively simple for a camouflage expert to rework the design, and she was soon putting the finishing touches, once again and for all time, on the handiwork, hoping to slip back into bed beside Alex before he had noticed she was missing. The night was cool and clear but as Cassie's skillful fingers came finally to rest, a hazy warmth enveloped her. It was all-too-familiar, and blessedly welcome, and she surrendered to it, knowing that it was also embracing Alex, transporting him back to the twentieth century to fulfill his amazing destiny with his new bride by his side.

Epilogue

"Wake up, sleepy head. We're home."

"Oh, Alex . . ." She stared up into her handsome husband's shining eyes. "Are you sure?"

He nodded and pulled her to her feet and into his arms in one strong motion. "This is the spot where Kanasa's longhouse once stood, I guess, but now it's gone back to being woods. My village is about five minutes from here, so I guess we'd better get our stories straight. After you kiss me and tell me you love me."

"I love you," she cooed, draping her arms around his neck. "My handsome, clever husband."

Their kiss was leisurely, as though they had all the time in the world—as though they had learned, as Cassie had always suspected, that time was a fiction, to be used as a tool rather than as a limit. Their love would never be bound by such fictions as time or place, nor would it be limited by the customs, or opinions, or interferences of others. This they vowed to one another, as husband and wife, through this gentle, endless kiss.

"We have to get our stories straight," Cassie reminded him finally, her voice weak with love. "Should we say we've been wandering for all this time? Or are you going to say you found Shannon?"

"Let's see how many days we've been gone first," he suggested, taking her hand and leading her toward the modern-day Susquehannock capital. "Shannon seems to think it'll just be two or three at the most."

"I'll just follow your lead, then. Or better yet, I'll just keep completely quiet and let you do all the talking."

"Right," he grinned, "like that's actually possible?"

She laughed ruefully. "I guess you're stuck with a talkative bride." They had reached the edge of the wooded area and Cassie peeked from behind a tree cautiously. "At least we're wearing our jeans. It looks like something's going on, Alex. There are cameras . . . do you recognize anybody in that crowd?"

"I recognize almost everybody, unfortunately. Apparently, something really big is going on. Let's hope," he grinned uneasily, "we're not it. Oh, man, look over *there*. That's my uncle, and the man next to him is the sachem for the Sierra Protectorate."

"And I see Philip Tremaine," Cassie murmured. "Why is *he* here? This doesn't look good, Alex, but . . ."

"I know. You can't wait to tell him Shannon's okay?" He shook his shaggy mane in frustrated amusement. "Let's go, then. You talk to Philip, *quietly,* while I deal with my uncle."

"Wait." She raised up on her tiptoes and kissed him, "For luck," and then they proceeded, hand in hand, into the village proper.

Leah Eagle was the first to catch sight of them, and she rushed to greet them. "Couteau! We were so worried! Where have you been?" She hugged him desperately, then pulled away and glared, "What were you thinking? You scared us to death, and . . ." her voice lowered to an ominous growl, "you've created a scandal that makes *her* cousin's disappearance look like nothing."

"I'll explain later," Alex grinned. "For now, what's going on? I'd like to think all these big guns are here because they're worried about me, but . . ."

"Don't flatter yourself, Couteau. You were simply the last straw. Proof positive that the Susquehannocks are a mismanaged bunch of bumblers."

"Leave him alone, Leah," Cassie warned sweetly. "There's a perfectly logical explanation for all of this."

"Fine, let's hear it!" she snapped.

"Yeah, Cass," Alex teased, "let's hear it."

Cassie blushed. "I forgot. You do the talking, I'll just stand by and be a nice, supportive wife." She glanced slyly toward Leah and was pleased by the look of horror on the woman's face at the announcement of their marriage.

"I don't understand," the dark-haired woman gasped. "Are you saying you eloped? You leave for two full days without a word, just for a honeymoon with this . . . this . . ."

"Two days? Is that all it was?" Alex slipped his arm around Cassie's waist. "Unbelievable."

"I know." She enjoyed the look of wonder in his eyes—he could be so innocent yet so strong—then she reminded him softly, "You need to speak to your uncle, and I have to . . . oh! Hi, Phil." The man's shocked expression touched her and she took his hands quickly, explaining, "I'm fine. Alex and I ran into some really strange circumstances . . ."

"Wait." Philip shook his head slowly. "Alex, you

explain. I can tell Cassie's about to confuse me even more. You've been together?"

"Right. And things couldn't be better, Phil. You don't have anything to worry about, anymore. I give you my word on that."

"So? You went there?" A dazed smile lit his face. "With her? And she's happy?"

Cassie's eyes filled with tears. "She's so happy, Phil, and she named her first son after you, and I promised I'd tell you all about it and I will, but for now, just know she's safe, and she loves you, and . . ."

"And it's a miracle." Philip hugged Cassie gratefully, then extended his hand to Alex. "I'll never be able to thank you. As soon as you're free, we'll talk. In the meantime," he glanced with concern toward the crowd that was now openly gawking in their direction, "you've got other problems, Alex. I wish you luck with them. I'll just get lost for the time being, okay? Cassie, do you want to come with me? This could get a little complicated."

"Alex and I are married, Phil," she smiled. "I'd love to ditch, but I'm stuck here, forever." She sent Alex a playful pout. "Right?"

"Right. If I'm in trouble, you're in trouble. And I think," his grin was now a little desperate, "we're in big trouble."

The chief, a well-built man with steely gray hair and warm ebony eyes, had apparently tired of waiting for his nephew and now strode to meet them, followed by the Sierra sachem and a trickle of other dignitaries. "Couteau," he scolded, but abandoned that tone immediately, reaching forward to grab both of Alex's hands and murmuring something in Susquehannock that was so clearly an endearment that Cassie thought her heart would melt with instant affection for the man.

"I'm fine, Uncle," Alex replied in English. "Before you say anything more, let me introduce my bride. Cassandra Stone BlackKnife. She doesn't speak our language yet, I'm afraid, but we'll have fun teaching it to her, I promise."

The old man shook his head. "You are full of surprises, nephew. This one, at least, is a lovely one. I am pleased to meet you, Cassandra, and we are all relieved to see that you are safe."

"It's nice to meet you," Cassie smiled. "I'm sorry I've been monopolizing Alex—"

"Cass," Alex warned patiently.

"Oh! Sorry. I'll be quiet, I promise."

The chief grinned ruefully. "You have chosen a demanding husband, Cassandra. Do you intend to allow him to do your talking for you?"

"Only today, and then I'm taking over," she smiled. When he laughed, he reminded her of Kahnawakee, although the physical resemblance was not strong. It was reassuring nonetheless and she smiled as sweetly as she could.

Then the chief's expression grew melancholy. "Six protectorates are withdrawing from UNAP today, Couteau. It is a dark day. If you had not returned to bring a small ray of light, I'm not sure what we would have done."

"Six?" Alex groaned. "Is it official yet? Will they listen to me for a few minutes, do you think?"

"What could you have to say?" the leader of the Sierra Protectorate interrupted harshly. "While we have waited for some last minute reason to stay faithful despite the futility of it, you have been romancing this Eura. Please excuse me," he added quickly, bow-ing in Cassie's direction, "but these are severe times for us all."

Cassie longed to sing Alex's praises, but contented herself with nodding slightly in acceptance of the apology. Alex stepped forward and suggested, "You say you have waited for a reason, and I have brought it. If you'll sit down with me, I swear I will give you renewed faith in our association, and we will continue for another three hundred years of peace and progress."

"You are confident," the sachem muttered. "I have watched you for years, did you know that? Your ambition was so obvious, I found it disquieting. Then you became Council Adviser and you worked harder, and with more dedication, than any man I have ever known. Reluctantly, I came to agree with those who believed you were the Couteau Noir on the ancient belt, but you have disappointed us all with your inept handling of this model-scandal, not to mention your ill-timed romance with this woman."

"Ill-timed?" Alex shrugged. "When you've heard what I have to say, you'll understand how well spent my time has been these last two days."

"The time for talking is over. I speak for my five brothers when I say it is time to put UNAP out of its misery."

"And I speak for Kahnawakee when I say it is time to give new life to UNAP."

Several dignitaries gasped, and even the Susquehannock chief's face darkened with annoyance. "That is too bold, Couteau. As my brother has said, we have all hoped you were the Couteau Noir who graces the belt, but that cannot be proven by brash words and blasphemy. It can be proven only by cour-

age and hard work, and you will be silent until you
have demonstrated those to my satisfaction."

"The belt?" Cassie blurted. "Do you mean, the
quill-and-shell belt with the rainbow?"

"Cass, don't," Alex groaned. "I'll find a way to
make them listen, someday soon. For now," his eyes
reproached the gathering, "there are men here too
eager to see UNAP disappear from this turtle's back.
You have said you have doubts about me. Well, I
have doubts about *you.* Where would you be today if
the Visionary had lacked faith in the vision? Do you
think he demanded proof of every element before he
went forward, to address the Council of the League of
Five Nations? Do you think he never doubted, never
wearied, never wondered if his time might not be
better spent in seeing to his own nation's narrow interests?"

Cassie's heart was swelling with pride and she could
see, from the look on the Susquehannock chief's face,
that he, too, was moved and perhaps humbled by this
address. Alex had his audience in the palm of his
hand, but she couldn't shake the feeling that the belt
was the key to ensuring his success.

"I want to hear him say it," the Sierra sachem
suggested quietly. "He believes he is Kahnawakee's
successor. That is clear from his every word. I want
him to admit it. He is no longer content to be Council
Adviser. Do you believe you are the one on the belt,
my son? Tell us what has made you believe it?"

"One day, I will lead you," Alex shrugged. "For
now, there is much I need to learn from you. How can
I learn it, if you withdraw from UNAP? And how can
you take such a step? You justify it on the ground of
technology, and convenience. They are powerful
lures, and we must accommodate them if we are to

survive. It will take hard work and courage, just as my uncle has so wisely observed. I am willing to work hard. I am determined to be brave. If that is the proof that I am the man on the ceremonial belt, so be it."

"Well . . ." The Sierra sachem shifted his weight uneasily. "I want to hear more. I'm not guaranteeing we'll stay, but I want to hear more."

"Great." Alex exhaled gratefully. "I have a lot more to tell you. Shall we adjourn to the meeting hall? I want to get my new bride settled, and then . . . in an hour? Uncle, is that acceptable?"

His uncle nodded. "I will walk with you, so that Cassandra can speak her mind."

"Pardon?" Cassie blushed.

They flanked her, the nephew and the uncle, and escorted her quickly toward the government apartments. "It was clear," the chief assured her teasingly, "that you were about to burst with some vital information while Couteau was making his amazing speech."

"It's true, Cass," Alex chuckled. "What's up?"

"Am I that obvious?" she sighed. "I just wanted to tell you about the belt. I wanted you to be able to tell them that I know, for a fact, that Alex is the second figure depicted."

"We know that," Alex reprimanded her gently, "but we can't expect anyone else to just take our word for it."

"No one has to take our word," she sniffed, "I can prove it. Where is it?"

"Do you mind a short detour, Uncle?" Alex sent the old man a knowing glance. "She won't let this rest until we've heard it."

"I never tire of seeing the work of the Time

Weaver," the chief smiled. "A detour to the office building is fine with me."

"The Time Weaver?" Alex frowned. "Who's that?"

"You have forgotten the legend?" the old chief murmured. "That is odd, Couteau. You have heard it so often. The grandmother of the Visionary began to weave the belt, but was called before she could finish the work. The Time Weaver came to the village, with magic in her fingers, and finished it."

They had reached the lobby and Alex strode to the case. "The belt was never finished," he was muttering under his breath, then he gasped and turned to his uncle. "I don't understand! The belt was never finished! Oh, no . . ." He stared into Cassie's laughing eyes. "Is that what you were doing, all those days and nights in the longhouse? Kahnawakee told me you were weaving, but I never guessed . . ." Turning back to the display, he murmured, "It's incredible, Cassie. Absolutely beautiful."

"Thanks."

The Susquehannock chief touched her shoulder. "Can this be so? It makes no sense."

"Things don't always make sense at the beginning," Cassie informed him gently, "but eventually, you find out that everything happens for a reason. I thought I wasn't supposed to be with Alex, these last 'two' days, but now I see that I went with him for a reason." Love and pride were welling up inside her as she turned to Alex. "Do you realize what this means? I was *always* supposed to go."

"Yeah." He pulled her close and whispered, "Great job, Cass. It doesn't really prove I'm him, of course, but we'll both know the truth, and that's all that's important."

"What do you mean?" she demanded, annoyed by

the possible insult. "Of course it proves you're him! For heaven's sake, Alex!" Turning to his uncle, she insisted, "You see it, don't you?"

"I want it to be him," he soothed, "and in my heart I know now that it is, but you must admit . . ." He gestured toward the figure. "It could be any of a thousand men. Black hair, well-built, with a black-hilted knife strapped to his thigh . . ."

"And with a scar as big as my fist right under that knife?" she countered swiftly. "Alex has the same scar."

"Scar?"

"Right under that knife. You can't see it, of course, but if you run your finger over it, you'll see it's raised." She sent Alex a playful smile. "I was too lazy to take out the beading, so I just camouflaged over it with a quill I had dyed black. Your scar is under there, any time you want to prove you're him."

"If this is so," the old uncle proclaimed, "the others must be told immediately. The belt will be examined, and I will step down, so that you can take your right-ful place."

"Hold on!" Alex laughed. "I'm only twenty-eight years old. I've got a new wife, and plans for a big family, and a lot to learn from you. I'd like to be your Council Adviser for a while longer, and," his tone was stern and directed toward his bride, "I'd like this information kept just among the three of us for a few years. Okay?"

Cassie grimaced. "I don't see the point . . ."

"I want to earn their respect through my efforts and contributions, not because of some sign."

"But, Couteau," his uncle mourned, "they should know. They would listen more intently, and they would see that this woman is the Time Weaver, and they would be amazed."

"We want to impress them with our skill, not our titles, right, Cass?"

"Well, basically, yes, but I'd like to have a little clout around here right away. There are some changes I'd like to make, and maybe as this Time Weaver, I could get them made more quickly."

"Changes?" the chief mused. "What kind of changes?"

"I think it's a shame we don't live in longhouses anymore," she insisted with as innocent a smile as she could manage. "I think the sense of community was so strong, and healthy, and maybe we should go back to that."

"Do you?" he frowned.

"She's flirting with me, Uncle," Alex explained with a lustful grin. "She knows how much I want to be alone with her. Very funny, Cass."

"You have been married less than three days," his uncle remembered with a sympathetic smile. "Perhaps I should inform the others that it will be two hours, rather than one, before you make your address?"

"No!" Cassie gasped, immediately contrite. "Nothing is more important than that address—oh! Alex, no!" She was shrieking with gleeful laughter as he whisked her, without further hesitation, to her new apartment, where she knew he intended to teach her, once and for all, that he could juggle his demands as Council Adviser and as lover without depriving her of any of life's pleasures along the way. It was a lesson she was willing to learn time after time after time.